THE

EYE FILES

A NOVEL

PETER WASSERMAN

For my children, Mimi, Jason, and Katie, and my grandson, Kiran. I love you all, and this book is for you.

SECTION I

SUMMER HEAT

CHAPTER 1

"WHY DO WE NEED to kidnap the President? Can't we just kill him? And why do we need to kill the girl?"

"Quiet," warned Jack Chauncey, their host, who spoke with a dismissive upper-class accent. "The walls could have ears. We'll talk about this after dinner where it's more private. And remember, no names." He tucked his long, white hair behind his ear as he picked up the fork he had dropped on his plate.

The participants resumed their meal within the large dining room, on a table of dark mahogany, set off by a centerpiece of deep red roses. Thick red curtains covered the windows, obscuring any last rays of daylight as well as any possible prying eyes from outdoors. The room was in keeping with the rest of the fourteen-bedroom mansion, where each room was fitted with exquisite antiques. It was fitting for a man of wealth and taste, and Jack Chauncey, President, and CEO of Decorp Technologies was that sort of man.

The house made visitors feel intimidated and small in comparison. In this case, however, his guests were also persons of great wealth, and they felt at home in an environment of opulence.

The temperature outdoors had cooled slightly from ninety-four degrees to just ninety degrees Fahrenheit, and the air was thick with humidity. It was a typical July day in Arlington, Virginia, a suburb of Washington, DC. Indoors, the air conditioning cooled the room to a very pleasant seventy-two degrees.

Closest to Jack at the table was Tim Braun of Raymore Industries. Short and thin, he sat quietly, mostly listening to his companions, and only speaking when they touched on his favorite subject, expensive cars. He himself drove a Bugatti Chiron Super Sport, valued at $3.3 million.

Next to him was Theresa Jones of Healthcare America, heavy-set, with bleached blond hair and slightly exposed dark roots. Her excessive make-up couldn't cover her hard features and a small smile that looked more like a smirk. Theresa's favorite topic of discussion was racehorses, as she had recently bought a new colt. Its lineage and high cost gave her hope that this one would be a champion, as none of her prior horses had won anything. Theresa, who cared about these horses as much as the people her company insured, sold the losers off to the highest bidders.

Furthest away from the other guests was Billy Joe Scranton of Stillwater Aerospace. Billy Joe was about six feet three and close to 300 pounds. His size was only matched by his deep, booming voice. He had opinions about everything, whether racehorses, cars, yachts, or servants, accentuating his thoughts with wild movements of his thick arms and hands. Aside from his size and arm flailing, the reason no one sat near him was his propensity to bark out his opinions while chewing, spattering the table with fine bits of meat.

Finally, after the dinner of cabernet filet mignon matched with a 2019 Louis Latour Chateau French burgundy, all staff members were sent home. The four diners reconvened to a small, windowless room lit by a single chandelier over a round, marble table. Already seated at the table was a man with shoulder-length dark hair, approximately six feet tall, with broad shoulders. He had a small scar over his left eye from a fight in his younger days. Behind a pair of thick-rimmed glasses, his eyes were dark brown. It was impossible to judge his real age, as he could be anywhere from thirty to fifty.

Leaning back in his chair with arms folded neatly on his lap, he sat quietly and impassively, without greeting or introducing himself to the recent arrivals. His eyes were fixed on each one as they took their seats, and they in turn, him. He had a slight grin on his face, but there was no warmth from his eyes. He did not seem intimidated by the house or the wealth of his companions and was seemingly comfortable in his surroundings.

All took seats, with Jack Chauncey sitting next to the man with shoulder-length hair. Beside Jack on the other side sat Billy Joe Scranton, with his arms crossed, resting on the table. Continuing around the table was Theresa Jones. Her forced wide smile, exposing sharp, gleaming white teeth, made the stranger think of a great white shark. Finally, next to the stranger on the other side sat Tim Braun, whose gaze wandered from guest to guest. He sat quietly, biting his lower lip.

The host rose and addressed his companions. "Thank-you all for coming. You know why you're here. If the President goes ahead with his directives, all of us here and our companies will be ruined. As I'm sure you've heard, he's planning on canceling Decorp's contract for the long-range missiles we've been working on worth over twenty billion dollars. I'm not telling you something that hasn't been reported in all the financial papers and blogs. We've already sunk so much in for fixed costs so that if it doesn't go through, we could be ruined. Already, I have lenders calling us and demanding extra security on their money."

Billy Joe slammed his fists onto the table. "You think you've got problems? How about all the helicopters the Navy was supposed to buy from us? That's been put on hold. The man's a menace. Knows nothing about national security."

Chauncey, still standing, looked over at Braun. "Tim, I understand your missile defense system is on the chopping block too."

Tim Braun shook his head solemnly in agreement. News about the potential cancellation had been on the front page of the day's *Wall Street Journal*.

"Might have to sell your Lamborghini," interjected Billy Joe in a derisive tone.

"It's a Bugatti," said Braun acidly, injecting his first glimmer of emotion.

"And Theresa, what are you going to do if half your clients decide to ditch your insurance plan for other options, especially if they're cheaper? Will Healthcare America survive?"

Jaws clenched, Theresa Jones did not answer. She just stared at Chauncey without answering.

"I know we've all spent a lot of money fighting his election, but it was money down the drain now that we lost. So, if we want to save our companies, and ourselves, we really have no choice. We've discussed this, and I believe we are all of the same mind in our approach."

"How do we know this is going to work? We could all land up in jail," demanded Billy Joe.

Jack continued without answering. "I'd like to introduce Phoenix here," and he pointed to the stranger on his right. "His references are excellent, and we have used him occasionally in the past for jobs that, shall we say, no one should ever know. I have already spoken to you all about him, and I believe we agree to utilize his services."

Theresa Jones sat quietly, biting her fingernails. Tim Braun stared at his feet, tapping softly on the floor.

Rising slowly, his frame leaning against the table, Billy Joe Scranton looked at Phoenix, and spoke to him almost in a shout.

"Again, I ask, how do we know it's going to work? We need to know your full plan in detail. We're all at risk here."

"Yes. We need to know your plan is foolproof. I can't even imagine what would happen to us if we were found out," said Theresa Jones, a slight bead of sweat forming at the top of her forehead.

Tim Braun said nothing, but the tapping of his feet, now quite loud, served to increase the rising tension in the room.

Phoenix sat forward in his chair and looked Scranton directly in the eye. When he spoke, it was in a clear, calm voice, with a slight accent that was difficult to place.

"I understand your apprehension. I can see why you are all anxious about this. It is a big step. But I can assure you, it can be done with virtually no risk to you. I stand by our plan one hundred percent. I have performed countless complex missions, and this mission certainly is that. But know this, I have never failed. I'm sure Mr. Chauncey has filled you in on my resume. As you know, I was responsible for the planning and assassination of Jovenel Moise, president of Haiti, in 2021. In 2016, we carried out the murder of British lawmaker Jo Cox and blamed it on a far-right supporter. Before that, in 2013, we took out two Tunisian left-wing leaders, Chokri Belaid and Mohammed Brahmi. My track record is flawless.

"As far as this mission, I understand Jack has given you the outline of what I am proposing. I can't presently divulge certain intricacies at this point but know that your adversary will be eliminated. The specific details will come later, and you will all be kept fully informed through your host here," pointing to Jack. "Know I have your interests in mind."

"Yes, I understand you're very good at what you do, but you can disappear if things fall apart, and we can't," said Tim Braun, now looking at his companions for reassurance.

"There is virtually no chance of anything getting back to you. I have multiple contingencies if things don't go perfectly to plan. Not to worry. Again, I can only point to the success of my previous jobs, including some for Mr. Chauncey. But this is up to the four of you. If you say no, I will leave quietly, with no ill will. You can all go back to your companies and watch them fail."

Chauncey nodded. "We will talk about it and get back to you."

"One more thing before we adjourn," interjected Billy Joe, still standing, looking directly at Phoenix. The price. Twenty million is too much.

"I know twenty million is a lot of money, but as I said before, it's a complex mission. The price is non-negotiable. Consider how much you'll lose if his policies go through. But again, it's up to you. One last thing, though. Once you have given me the green light, it's full steam ahead. There's no turning back on the mission, and no turning back on my money.

"As far as payment, I will give you account numbers and codes to be able to wire the money. It will be routed through various shell companies, almost impossible to trace."

"How about paying you in crypto?" suggested Jack Chauncey.

"It's become too risky lately, and the US government has gotten very good at tracking it. In fact, that's how they've been pursuing Hamas' financial backers. My way is safer.

"I require thirty percent as a down payment. The rest will be required at various points along the timeline, which will be arranged with Jack here. I will allow you to hold back ten percent until the very completion of the mission."

"Ten percent down payment, and ninety percent on completion," demanded Scranton.

"Not acceptable. Those are my terms. Non-negotiable. Take it or leave it."

Chauncey stood up and addressed Phoenix. "I think we need to have further discussion on this. Can we ask you to come back one week from today, and we'll give you our answer?"

"That's fine. I know it's expensive, but this mission requires much skill, planning and time. Killing the President of the United States is a tough, risky assignment, and I'm the only one who can accomplish it. I can guarantee its success. But the question remains, do you have the backbone to go through with this?"

With that, Phoenix left the room.

CHAPTER 2

A WEEK LATER, all four conspirators were seated at the small marble table when Phoenix arrived and took his seat. This time, one other member was present. He sat quietly, in the corner of the room, listening to the others.

As usual, Jack Chauncey started the meeting.

"It is a large sum of money, but we realize twenty million is nothing compared to how much we'll lose if the President gets his way."

Billy Joe interrupted. "I still have a question. Why don't we just kill him rather than kidnapping him first?"

"Two reasons. First, it's too risky to kill a sitting President. He's got too much security around him. It's much safer to do once he's out of the White House. Once we replace him and have our imposter resign, he can die in what will look like an accident rather than a murder. Second reason relates to an issue some of your friends here have. They can explain it to you later, if they haven't already," said Phoenix.

Now remembering an earlier discussion, Billy Joe nodded.

"Who's your imposter, and are people really going to believe he's the President?" asked Theresa Jones.

"I have the perfect person in mind. No family, and he won't be missed. It will take a lot of work over many months and some plastic surgery, but he'll be great. I've used imposters before, and I'm meticulous in the training.

"I believe this plan has the greatest chance of success and the least risk. So, I ask you all again, each one of you, are we going ahead with the plan to kidnap and execute the President of the United States, and are you prepared to pay me the money in the manner I have laid out?"

Phoenix looked at each in turn.

"Yes, kill the bastard," said Billy Joe Scranton, slamming his fist on the table.

"You know I'm for it," said Chauncey.

Theresa Jones sat quiet for a moment, biting her lower lip before answering, "Yes."

Tim Braun's feet were not tapping on the floor this time. Instead, it was now his fingers drumming on the table. He looked around the room, from one to the next, before answering quietly, "Yes."

The new member nodded his head and answered, "Yes, I agree. Also, I know someone we can use if needed. His name is Jonathan Brodsky, undersecretary at the CIA. He's looking to move up and is highly motivated by power and money."

"That could be very useful," replied Phoenix. "Thank you."

Jack stood up now and spoke for the group. "We agree with your terms. We will wire the six million deposit by tonight, twelve million according to timelines we've worked out, and the remaining two million upon the confirmation of the death of the President. Anything else, Phoenix?"

"One more thing," and it was the first time Phoenix smiled. "I need you all to see something. Please all gather around behind me."

He removed his glasses and pulled a small card out of the frame. From his jacket pocket, he took out a small box attached to a tiny screen. The five conspirators stood up and arranged themselves behind him, staring at the screen. After inserting the card in the box, Phoenix pressed a small button, turning the screen on. Immediately, it showed a clear video with equally sharp audio. All present could see themselves agreeing to kidnap and execute the President of the United States.

"What the hell?" shouted Billy Joe Scranton.

"Please take your seats, and I will explain everything," said Phoenix calmly.

No one moved. Finally, Jack Chauncey sat down, and the others followed suit.

"What the hell are you playing at?" shouted Billy Joe again, his face flushed with anger. Slamming both fists on the table, Jack Chauncey's wine glass crashed to the floor, spattering red wine on the host's fine linen pants.

Theresa Jones white teeth flashed. The great white shark looked like it had eaten something putrid.

Tim Braun just sat quietly, too shocked to tap his feet or his fingers, but the blood had drained from his face.

"How dare you!" shouted Jack Chauncey, wiping away the wine from his pants. Gone was his upper-class accent.

"Calm down, everyone," said Phoenix. "This recording is purely for insurance. I need to know I will be paid for my efforts. Once I get my money, you will get this SD card. Nothing to worry about, as I'm sure you'll keep your end of the bargain. You're all gentlemen here. And lady."

"We could take it from you now," said Billy Joe.

"You've got to be kidding me," said Phoenix, shaking his head. "There would be five elderly people discovered dead with broken necks here in this house. But let's not talk violence. If we work together, all will end up well for everyone. You will get a dead President of the United States, and I will get my money. But you do have a choice. If you pay me two million now, you get the card back, I go on my way, and the mission is canceled. Or we go ahead with it as planned."

"If we go ahead, how do we know you won't make copies of it even after we pay you and blackmail us with it?" asked Theresa Jones.

"Here's how it works. The Arlington Savings Bank is open late today. I will take this SD card and place it in a safe deposit box, where it will stay until the successful conclusion of the mission. Once the President has been eliminated, I will meet Mr. Chauncey outside the bank in his car. He will pay me the remainder, and I will give him the SD card."

"You could still make copies," pointed out Jack Chauncey. "You could do it on the way to the bank."

"If you wish, one of you could ride with me to the bank. Once I go in, I have set up a closed-circuit camera attached to my briefcase, so you will see me in real time open the safe deposit account and put the card in the box."

"What's to stop you from going back to the bank, opening up the safe deposit box and making copies."

"Good point. I anticipated that question, as you are all very smart people. Here is the answer."

Phoenix reached into another jacket pocket and pulled out a small box with a small antenna sticking up. Reaching again into his pocket, he pulled out what appeared to be a tiny speaker, and he handed it to Clancy.

"The box is a small radio transmitter. Once I put the SD card in this little box, if opened, you will hear the most god-awful deafening noise through your speaker. If I move the box more than one yard in any direction, again, it will go off. Here, I'll show you. I'd suggest you cover your ears."

Phoenix put the card in the box, and then opened it again. Even with their ears covered, the sound coming through the speaker was deafening. Quickly, he turned off the speaker and closed the box with the SD card still in it.

"Range is twenty miles. You're only four miles from the bank here. I'll do another test run at the bank so you can double-check that it works. Always carry the little speaker with you and you'll know your information is safe. If you plan to travel more than twenty miles away, give it to one of your staff. They will only know to alert you if it goes off, but I assure you it won't. Hopefully it gives you some peace of mind.

"As I said, I will hand you back the evidence at the same time you wire me the remainder of my fee once the deed has been completed. You can smash it, burn it, do whatever you want with it. Any questions?"

The five conspirators looked stunned. None said a word, not even Billy Joe Scranton. Phoenix got up and looked at his employers.

"Not to worry. We are all in this together, and I won't fail you. I will wait on the other side of the door, as I assume you have some things to discuss. You can decide which one of you wants to accompany me to the bank."

Once out of the room, the conspirators looked at each other.

Theresa Brown addressed Jack. "Do we still go ahead?"

Everyone turned to look at their host.

"Our objective is still the same. I don't like what he's just done to us, but we still hold onto our money until the President is dead and we get the evidence back.

Tim Braun spoke up. "I don't like Phoenix's methods, but I've got to hand it to him. He's smart. The taping, and the radio transmitter thing."

"He's an asshole, and I don't like him," said Billy Joe.

"You don't like him because he's smarter than you," replied Braun.

Scranton rose and took a step towards Braun, and Jack Chauncey jumped up between them.

"Easy Billy Joe. Easy. Please sit down everyone. Understandably, our tempers are a bit raised. The question is, what do we do now? I don't think there's much choice but to go forward."

Everyone nodded.

"I can take Phoenix to the bank if you're all okay with that. Who will hold the speaker to make sure it works?" he continued.

"I can do that," volunteered Theresa Jones, "My house is about ten miles away, so it should be in range if he's telling the truth.

"Everybody on board with that?"

All nodded again, and they headed out. Jack walked to his Rolls Royce in the four-car garage. It had been some time since he had driven the car himself. This was not the time to call for his chauffeur.

The others walked out through the wide double French doors, out to the four black limousines with tinted windows awaiting them. They moved quickly, whether to get away from the ninety-degree heat, or the situation they found themselves in.

Theresa Jones looked back at the mansion one last time before stepping into the back of her limousine. Slightly nauseous, she had second thoughts about the evening's decisions. But by now, it was too late to change the course of events.

CHAPTER 3

ZACHARIAH WEBSTER, MD, sat on the stool of his examining room next to Matilda Patterson, who sat in his examining chair. The room was nondescript, and the chair and stool looked like they had seen better days. The medical equipment all looked slightly tired, but functional. In fact, the entire office, including the chairs in the waiting room, all looked second-hand, which they were.

The diplomas on the wall, however, revealed a doctor with excellent training. Pictures on the walls of the waiting room showed no specific personality, as if taken from a hotel lobby. One was of two boats, one yellow, and one red, floating in an unspecified harbor. Another was a city scene of what appeared to be Boston.

In contrast to the generic pictures and magazines, there were two small photos on the wall. One showed a young man crossing the finish line first, accompanied by a certificate declaring him the number one high school track athlete in New Hampshire. The second photo showed the same man, now slightly older, with his arms around two small children.

In addition to the standard doctors' office magazines of *People*, *Women's Day*, and *Field and Stream* were additions of Dr. Webster's choosing, *Runners World, Popular Mechanics, and Scientific American*. He had been a physics major in college and still enjoyed performing hands-on projects in his spare time.

No one called him Zachariah, as Zach thought it much too biblical. He was an ophthalmologist, but most people just referred to him as an eye doctor. Handsome in a kind of nerdish way, about six feet tall and thin, with moderately long, brown hair, he wore wire-rimmed glasses and had an easy smile. Zach was thirty-six years of age, but there was already a bit of gray in his dark locks and a few wrinkles on his forehead. Trying to get back into shape, he had restarted running regularly, near his apartment in Washington, DC.

The same could not be said for Matilda. She was eighty-five years old, considerably wrinkled, and quite heavy. She also had a patch covering one of her eyes, her good eye. Matilda had not seen out of her other eye in many years, after a retinal detachment and unsuccessful surgery. She had been led into the examining room by her husband of six months, whom she had met just one year prior. The eye with the patch, her good eye, had not seen well for the past five years due to a progressing cataract. Understandably, Matilda had been reluctant to have surgery on her one good eye, due to the risk of losing full sight in both eyes.

Dr. Webster had finally convinced her to have the cataract removed in that eye, pointing out that she had already lost sight in it because of the cataract. She had finally allowed him to perform the necessary surgery the prior day. Since she could not see out of her bad eye, she felt her way onto the examining chair after initially being guided to it by her husband. He returned to sit in a chair across from her, ten feet away.

Everything had gone well with the cataract operation, and it was now time to remove the patch. As Dr. Webster removed it, he jumped back due to an ear-splitting scream from his patient.

"That's what you look like!" shouted Matilda Patterson, staring at her new husband.

Then, turning to Dr. Webster, she said, "Put the cataract back!"

Zach Webster laughed, but he was not quite sure if it was a joke or not, until Matilda laughed, got up from her seat, and hugged her husband.

Finally, when the exam was over and multiple thank-yous were delivered to Dr. Webster, Matilda left the room holding hands with her husband.

"That's why I do this," thought Zach Webster. "That, and it pays the bills."

Paying the bills was important, as Dr. Webster had relatively few patients. He had only been back in Washington, DC, in solo practice, for less than a year. Bills were piling up, as prior to moving to DC, he had not worked for just over a year. Zach had been fired by the senior members of his ophthalmology group in New Hampshire two years prior for coming to work drunk and smelling of alcohol, on a day he was to operate.

It was 3:00 pm, and Matilda was his last patient. Time to go home and take his dog Ripley out for a run. It was still hot and sticky in DC, but he and Ripley had to make the best of it.

CHAPTER 4

LOOKING OUT OF THE WINDOW of his small study next to the Oval Office, President Francis Peterman took a break from his briefing sheet. He shook his head in disgust. His bright red hair, a bit thinned on top, had become gray at the temples, a sign of his advancing years. President Peterman cut an imposing figure, six feet tall with broad shoulders, although his waistline had grown several inches. "Pressures of the office and not enough exercise," he told himself when at times he saw himself in the mirror. "Not bad for a sixty-six-year-old."

"Why can't there ever be any good news to read?" he mused, getting back to the briefing sheet. It was another hot, sticky June day in the capital. The oppressive weather matched the mood of the brief, which described the buildup of North Korea's nuclear weapon arsenal.

Peterman's dark mood was broken up by two voices laughing loudly in the hall. The President knew instantly who was responsible. The first was his grandson, Jefferson, and the second voice was that of Ray, his most trusted secret service agent.

Ray Lincoln had been with Francis Peterman starting on the first day of his presidency, and the two men had formed an easy bond. They came from very different backgrounds, but both respected and valued each other. President Peterman felt comfortable with Ray and appreciated his loyalty, and Ray, honored to be treated as a valuable confidant and protector, thought the world of his President.

Ray's appearance could have made him a poster boy for the Secret Service. He was six two and dark skinned, with a thickly muscled torso beneath his white shirt. His face looked like it could have been carved from stone, with sharp features. His appearance, however, hid a genial personality.

"Mr. President, your daughter and grandson are here to see you," said Ray still laughing, as he knocked on the door.

"Definitely let them in."

In bounded Jefferson, an eight-year-old bundle of red hair and energy, along with his mother, Sarah. Jefferson, or Jeff as everyone but his mother called him, had insisted his hair grow long. Presently, it was down to his shoulders. "He will let us know when he wants to get his hair cut, and it won't be done before that time," Sarah had declared fiercely when her dad had asked. President Francis Peterman was known as a tough negotiator, never backing down from a fight, but the one person he knew not to challenge was his daughter Sarah, so he accepted it with a smile. She was just like her mother, Katherine, who had also stood up to him, just as powerfully as any politician from either side of the political spectrum. Sadly, Katherine had passed away a few years prior in a fire, along with the President's only other child, William.

Sarah was tall and slender, with long, brown hair, pulled back behind her head. Unlike her father and her son, she had missed out on the flaming red hair. A passerby might describe her as very pretty, but not to the degree of being overly beautiful. She had a determined look about her, softened with a winning smile.

Jeff had already jumped up on his grandfather's lap and begun drawing on the brief with one of his pens, before his mother grabbed him and pulled the pen away.

"That's probably the only thing this paper's good for!" said the

President.

"I just stopped by to say goodbye. Our car is leaving in a few minutes to take us to the airport to head back," said Sarah.

"Why do you need to leave so soon?"

"Yeah, why do we have to go, Mom? Can't we stay a little longer?" asked Jefferson.

"I have patients scheduled for tomorrow, so I need to get back tonight." Sarah was a family doctor who worked at a clinic in Chula Vista, just south of downtown San Diego.

"How about just one more day? Please?" pleaded Jefferson.

"I told you; I have to get back."

Jefferson gave his mother an angry stare.

"Listen to your mother, Jeff, but here's something for you to eat on the plane," as the President pulled out a big KitKat Bar from the drawer in his desk. Jeff's eyes grew wide, and his smile was even wider.

"Thanks Grandpa."

Sarah grabbed the bar and put it back on the desk. "Dad, how do you expect him to sleep on the plane with a sugar high?"

All the President could do was chuckle and say, "Good luck. Have a safe trip! Love you."

"Bye Dad. Love you too. We've got to go now, Jefferson. We've got a plane to catch."

"Bye, Grandpa."

Jeff jumped off his lap, gave his grandfather a quick hug, and slyly grabbed the candy bar, putting it in his pocket without his mother noticing. The President did, and he gave his grandson a quick wink. Jefferson responded with a smile and a wave.

CHAPTER 5

JACK CHAUNCEY parked his car across the street from the Arlington Savings Bank. He already regretted taking the Rolls. It was much too conspicuous. It would likely be noticed, and that was the last thing Jack wanted.

After dropping his passenger off near the bank, he decided to move his car to the next street over. Parking as far as he could from any others, he turned on a small screen, the receiving end of a CCTV camera Phoenix had placed on the briefcase he carried into the bank. To avoid being seen by passersby, Chauncey placed a large sunscreen over the inside of the windshield. Fortunately, all the other windows were tinted. He now felt comfortable watching Phoenix as he entered the bank, although he looked nothing like his former self. Chauncey had seen him change his appearance in the car, so it was not a surprise.

Phoenix was now an older gentleman of perhaps eighty-five years of age with a cane and a slight limp. His normal clean-shaven face sported a grizzled gray beard. He wore an old black suit with a white shirt and a bow tie that had a scent of mothballs. Chauncey could see a bank employee meet him in the lobby and lead him to an office with the nameplate *William Grayson* on the door. He noticed Phoenix looking up to spot the CCTV cameras on the ceiling. This man was a pro, he thought.

After a few minutes, Phoenix was led into a room with safe deposit boxes. The bank employee left, and Phoenix moved the camera around to show that no one else was present. He took the box with the SD card, opened it, and then quickly closed it again. After placing the box into safe deposit box number 307, and then locking it, Chauncey watched him leave the room and make his way out of the bank.

The phone in the Rolls rang immediately. It was Theresa Jones.

"The damn speaker went off and I couldn't figure out how to turn it off. I thought it would break my eardrums, so I stuck it in my make-up drawer. It's still loud. Okay, it just went off. Did everything go okay at the bank?"

"Fine. I guess it did what he said it would. He's leaving the bank now. He can find his own way home. I'm certainly not waiting for him."

Jack Chauncey hung up the phone, put his car in gear, and drove off quickly. Everything was going according to plan, but he was still nervous. Phoenix was smart, maybe too smart. Had they made the right decision hiring him in the first place for this mission? It had been his idea. There was no turning back now.

Checking his bank account on his laptop, Phoenix could see the six-million-dollar deposit. He had his insurance SD card safely tucked away in a safe deposit box. He also had one other thing the conspirators didn't know about. The SD card viewer he had used to show the Arlington conspirators had one other function; it was also a recorder. Using a thumb drive, Phoenix produced an additional copy. It would later be placed in a safety deposit box at the Congressional National Bank in Georgetown.

Phoenix had another appointment in less than half an hour. He'd hail a cab and be there in plenty of time.

Standing near the Jefferson Memorial in Washington, DC, Phoenix could see him coming from fifty yards away. Approaching him was Kwan, and he worked for the North Korean government. He joined him, and they walked around the Tidal Basin together.

"A pity we are not here in April. The cherry trees are magnificent when in bloom," said Kwan.

"I could care less. Skip the pleasantries."

"I can see you've got a one-track mind."

"You agree on the price I set?"

"It's very high, but we agree, provided you've got those industrialist pigs to go along."

"They've agreed."

"Very well. And they don't know about me?"

"Of course not."

"Then we will pay once the deed has been done."

"Negative. Once the job has been completed, I risk that you might withhold payment. I require forty percent prior to commencement, an additional fifty percent on the death of the girl and prior to final completion of the task. I'll let you hold back the remaining ten percent until the successful conclusion. Those are my terms. Take it or leave it. I have plenty of other job offers, so decide now."

They continued to walk silently around the basin until they returned to their starting point, at which point Kwan finally gave his answer.

"You leave me no choice. We will conduct business on your terms. I still think you are asking a lot."

Phoenix took his time answering, and looked Kwan straight in the eye. "Killing the President of the United States is very high-risk job, involving much planning and skilled execution. I'm the only one who can pull it off."

CHAPTER 6

PHOENIX RECEIVED phone calls from Jack Chauncey almost every other day looking for updates. He had given his employer a burner phone with which to communicate, something he now regretted, as he had little progress to discuss.

Although he had told the Arlington group he had the perfect candidate already arranged, it was not until he had six million dollars deposited in his bank account that Phoenix started looking to find the right candidate. He was not going to waste time and money if the plan was not to move forward. Once he recruited the imposter and started his training, he could then fill them in on the details.

He was looking for a man who needed to have some resemblance to the President. It didn't need to be exact, as plastic surgery could fill in what was needed. There had to be some similarity in voice intonation, but then again, voice lessons would be provided. He would need some intelligence but be willing to follow orders. Most of all, he had to be someone with nothing to lose, and someone who would not be missed by friends or family.

Phoenix would look for him on the streets of Washington, DC, for one of the five thousand homeless, destitute citizens living outdoors in the nation's capital. Picking the right man for the job was crucial, so he would have to do this mission personally, spending time on the streets talking to the outcasts of society.

It took him about three weeks to narrow the choice down to twenty potential candidates, who, with enough plastic surgery could pass for the President. He then did background checks on the men. On some, there was no information at all, so they were eliminated. Some had substance abuse issues, and they were also eliminated. That left seven potential candidates. Unfortunately, none of the seven had been ex-cons, as that could have been perfect.

He settled on James Staples, a former Special Forces soldier who slept in a cardboard box barely three blocks from Phoenix's plush, DC hotel suite. Physically, he resembled Francis Peterman, his voice was close, and he appeared intelligent. He had been a former Special Forces soldier, so knew how to follow orders. He had a violent streak, but that was okay; Phoenix had one too. In addition, he had no known living relatives and few friends.

First, he would need to convince him to take the job. Promised money to follow him back to a safe house in Virginia, Staples was initially reluctant, unsure of the stranger's motives. It was not until shown the money, and then getting a more substantial offer, that the former soldier agreed. Once there, Phoenix began providing him with limited details.

"I'm looking for just the right person to impersonate a very important man. You have a similar build, height, and eye color, along with some other matching physical characteristics."

"What's in it for me?" asked Staples.

"Half a million dollars."

"I like the sound of that."

"And you'll be one of the most powerful men alive."

"I really like the sound of that."

"You'll need plastic surgery, voice lessons, and you'll need to study our subject over the next few months."

"No problem. I'm a fast learner, and a good impersonator. I used to do impressions for my buddies in Special Forces."

"I know that. Aside from your physical attributes, that's one of the reasons I picked you for this important mission. This is the deal. Once you commit, you must see it through. No backing out, even after I tell you who you need to impersonate."

"I'm in. I don't care who the subject is."

"Also, do you have some friends from your days in the military who would be in for a quick influx of cash? They would need to be reliable and discreet, and willing to take risks."

"What's in it for me?"

"I'll give you another hundred thousand for each name that works out."

"Sounds good."

"You'll be in charge of recruiting them and relaying their orders from me."

"I can do that."

"One other thing. In reading your file, I know you have a history of violence. Now that's okay; I can show a little violence myself. But in this job, you've got to keep it under control and follow orders. Do you understand?"

"Sir, yes Sir!" said Staples, and he rose to attention and saluted Phoenix.

It wasn't the answer or the salute that unnerved Phoenix. It was the sly grin on the man's face. For a moment, he hesitated. Was this some-one he could trust with such an important mission? By now, though, it was getting late to look for someone else. Besides, this man was otherwise perfect for the job. He would just have to make clear the penalties for disobedience.

Now that he had the imposter, there were still some additional roles to fill. Staples would give him the names of some of his past military colleagues who were down on their luck. If they checked out okay, he would get Staples to hire them.

He had men for other jobs that would need doing. He still needed a nurse. Through a doctor he had used in the past, he came up with a name, a nurse in need of money who worked at the Washington Hospital Center, named June Temple.

Phoenix found her at work one day.

"Are you June Temple?" he asked pleasantly.

"Yes. Which patient are you here for? Friend or family?"

"Neither, but I think I have an offer that will make you very happy."

June looked at him with a furrowed brow. "What do you mean?"

"I understand you have a sister, Mary Ann, and she's dying of cancer."

"That's none of your business. How did you know that?" she asked angrily.

"I hear things. I apologize if I upset you. But I can help."

"How can you help?"

"I know she's had all types of the best treatment, surgery, radiation, and chemo, but the tumor is still progressing and is now in her liver and her bones. I also know you've been looking into an experimental treatment in Mexico that's shown some good results, but it's very expensive."

"Again, how did you hear about that?" she demanded, glaring at him.

"From some of your coworkers, but that's not important. What's important is that I can help."

"How so?" she asked in a gentler tone.

"I'll pay you $20,000 for one day's work. Any additional day will be reimbursed at the same rate. One condition. You can't tell anyone, you can't ask any questions, and once you agree, you can't back out."

"What would I have to do?"

"Remember, no questions. Are you in or out?"

"I can't agree to something without knowing what it is, so I have to say no."

"Okay, but if you change your mind, here is my phone number."

He handed her a card and walked away.

At the end of her shift, June arrived back at her apartment building in Silver Spring, Maryland, just over the border from Washington, DC.

She lived here with Mary Ann, in a small two-bedroom apartment walk-up on the third floor. The white paint on the exterior of the building was peeling off, revealing a dull gray undercoating. The interior hallways were dark with faded carpeting, and the walls looked like they hadn't been painted in the past twenty years. Inside their apartment, though, all was bright and cheery. The furniture was old, but everything was clean and in good condition.

June walked in to see Mary Ann lying asleep on her bed. Her normal athletic body was now extremely thin, her face gaunt and pale, and she was breathing slowly in a raspy wheeze. The room had a sickly, disinfectant smell.

It was too much for June to bear. She walked back to the kitchen, tears running down her face. If there was any hope at all, she had to do everything she could. She pulled out the stranger's card and dialed. Mary Ann would never know how she got the money.

SECTION II

WINTER CHILL

Months passed, and it was now winter. A defense funding bill bearing the President's wishes was being debated in the House and Senate chambers and would likely pass. It was time to put the plan in motion.

CHAPTER 7

IT WAS ANOTHER SLOW DAY in the office. Business had picked up in the fall, but as it was now almost Christmas time, people were more reluctant to head out to have their eyes examined. Most of Dr. Webster's patients were elderly and afraid of falling on ice.

He was reviewing some old charts when interrupted.

"Dr. Webster, you have a phone call. It's from a Dr. Brannigan from Walter Reed Army Hospital," came Veronica Klein's voice over the intercom. "Do you want to take the call?"

Veronica was Dr. Webster's receptionist, his only employee.

"Sure. He's an old colleague of mine." Andy Brannigan had been an ophthalmology resident with Zach Webster in DC and had stayed to take a job at Walter Reed Hospital. Veronica connected the call.

"Hi Andy. What's up?"

"Zach, I heard you're back in DC. Can't stay away, huh?"

"It's the only way I could see my kids. You know Samantha and I broke up, and she's got custody."

"Yeah. Sorry to hear about everything that went down."

After an embarrassing pause in the conversation, Zach broke the silence. "Well, that's old news. Here for a fresh start."

"You'll have no trouble. You're the best," Andy responded quickly.

"Only problem is there's an ophthalmologist pretty much on every block here."

"How about working for us at Walter Reed? I'm sure we could use you."

"No thanks. I don't think the military, even as a doc, would work for me. Plus, I've got some baggage your friends in personnel probably wouldn't approve of."

"Actually, what I'm calling about is getting some old records from you."

"Sure. What do you need? Have they signed a consent?"

"Not your typical patient, and yes, they've signed a consent, which I'll forward to you. I remember you told me once he was your patient a while back. It's President Francis Peterman," said Andy.

"Wow. I do have some of those old records somewhere. I'll look for them. How do I get them to you?"

President Francis Peterman had been his patient back in Concord, New Hampshire during Zach's first year in practice, when Peterman was still a congressman. The Petermans were neighbors and friends of his parents, and their daughter, Sarah, had been one of his friends in high school. One evening, Congressman Peterman got a metal fragment in his eye while chipping off some rust on a car. He called Zach, who came in that night to see him and removed the metal sliver. He had then followed him as a patient during his time in New Hampshire.

"We have a special, encrypted online service you can use. You'll get his signed consent as soon as we get off the phone."

"No problem," said Zach. "I'll get it out to you as soon as I can."

"One other thing. I need it right away. Sorry for the rush, but his exam's in two days, on Saturday. And let's set up a time to play tennis."

"No problem. I'll get them out immediately. You're working Saturday?"

"Hey, when duty calls. When they say jump, I jump. And what about tennis? I remember you were pretty good on the courts behind the hospital."

"Tennis sounds great. I could use some extra exercise, but it's getting cold."

"Don't be a wimp. Wear some sweats."

"Fine. When?"

"How about this Saturday evening, after I've seen your star patient. Lydia and the kids are away this weekend, so it works for me."

"Sure. What time?"

"How about 7 pm on the courts behind my building at Walter Reed. It's lit up for night play."

"Sure. I'll be there. See you then," said Zach, hanging up the phone.

A strong waft of perfume told Zach that Veronica was entering his exam room. It wasn't a bad smell, quite floral, but a bit too much. It was not the same high-class perfume he had come to know when he was married to Samantha. Everything about Samantha was high-class, and expensive.

Veronica had short, dark hair and long, red-painted fingernails. He had always marveled at how she could type so quickly with nails that long. She looked flustered. "I have a consent for records for President Francis Peterman, and it's signed by him!"

"Yes, I know about it. He was a patient in my old practice in New Hampshire. I'll find those records, and then, could you digitize them? They need to go out tonight. There's a special encrypted link to send them over to Walter Reed." He left the exam room and rummaged through the back hallway.

"Here it is. Let me know if you have any problems with it."

Veronica shook her head. The chart was on paper, not digitized.

"It's going to take me a lot of time to enter it all into the computer. You know it could get busy here with patients, and I must leave on time today."

Zach looked about the waiting room, where no patients were waiting to be seen.

"Just do your best, Veronica. Thanks."

With a frown, Veronica went back to her desk and started entering the information. Maybe she would go outside for a smoke first. She had once tried to do her cigarette break in the back kitchen area, but Zach had smelled the smoke and given her an ultimatum. It was the only time he had ever reprimanded her.

CHAPTER 8

"I'M SICK OF LENTIL soup and this damn veggie wrap," said President Francis Peterman to his intercom.

"How about your damn cholesterol and blood pressure?" came the response from his administrative assistant, Rose Goodwin, who was sitting at her desk in the next room.

"Okay. I know. You're right. It's just been a busy day."

"It's only going to get busier."

Peterman frowned while fiddling with papers on his desk. "Damn those Iranians. They're building up troops along the Iraqi border. Could start another war."

"You're in a right pleasant mood today, aren't you!" said Rose. "I'll be right in."

In strode Rose Goodwin, President Peterman's administrative assistant, without knocking. Her short stature was in sharp contrast to the power she yielded. Everyone knew you didn't cross Rose Goodwin if you didn't want a dressing-down. She had worked for the President for many years, starting when he was a junior congressman from New Hampshire.

"Could you please knock before entering?" asked the President.

"I'm too busy to waste the time."

"I could be changing my clothes."

"It would just give me a good show."

Resigned, the President shook his head and went back to his brief. He knew he was fighting a losing battle. Aside from being a fabulous assistant, she was also a good, loyal friend, and a great protector of his privacy.

Peterman let out a sigh.

"What's that for?" asked Rose.

"Both for the brief I'm reading about Iran, but also about my lunch."

"Can't help you on the Iran business, and are you still complaining about your lunch?"

"I know, but couldn't we do a not so healthy option some days? How about a burger occasionally?"

"I thought you wanted to lose a few pounds, and then there's your blood pressure and your cholesterol. Remember you have a medical check-up on Saturday."

"Okay, okay. I'll keep eating like a rabbit," he said resignedly.

Rose shook her head. "What to do with you!"

She proceeded, looking down at her notepad. "Here is your schedule for the rest of today. You have a call with the President of Mexico regarding your new immigration policy at 2:30. Secretary of Defense James Abel is at 2:45 about the defense bill. Next is Secretary of State Lisa Atkinson, who wants to discuss immigration, followed by Health and Human Services Secretary Hannah Tish, who wants to talk to you about your health care initiatives. Then, we've got House Majority Leader Randal Gray at 3:30, and he would like to beat your brains in, and have you dismembered about all those issues, and who knows what else. You have a break until 5:30, at which time you'll be meeting with the Undersecretary of the CIA and a General Gomez who have worked on strategies for dealing with the new Iranian threats. But first, Vice

President Richardson would like to talk with you for a few minutes about a couple of things.

"Also, I need to leave early to pick up my grandson from school, if that's okay with you. My daughter just texted me from one of her work associates' phones. Her phone's dead. You know how these young people spend so much time on their phones. Anyway, she's in a meeting and can't get out in time, so she wants me to pick him up."

Peterman sighed again. "What an afternoon. Of course, you can take off early, but can you take 'Richy' with you? I've already got a headache thinking about all the others this afternoon, and then to top it off with him."

Vice President Arnold Richardson was not President Peterman's first, second, third, or fourth choice to share his ticket. It had been a tense, nasty primary fight, that the President had won against Richardson, his top challenger. Political expediency and the chance to pick up the swing state of Georgia, where Richardson was governor, had been the reason his advisors had pushed the Georgia governor down Peterman's throat. Vice President Richardson had beady eyes, a narrow face, and a distinct chin, reminding the President of a large rodent. He was still nauseous when he thought about agreeing to pick Richardson, almost two years later.

Rose smiled, then remarked, "Mr. President, is that anyway to talk about your VP? Not very respectful."

"You're right. It is what it is. I'll behave. Have fun with your grandson."

He went back to his briefing sheet but was interrupted by the incoming call from the President of Mexico, thirty minutes earlier than scheduled. The two men discussed Francis Peterman's new immigration policy initiatives, which were still in Congress. It involved allowing some limited legal immigration, but also money and initiatives for private businesses to open south of the border to encourage development and create jobs. It was a multi-pronged, complex approach, and the bill ran a full 242 pages.

Republicans hated the idea of even limited border immigration, and Democrats, especially union Democrats, hated the idea of American jobs moving south of the border. Mexicans, including their president, were also somewhat wary of the United States sticking its hands into Mexican affairs. The call with the President of Mexico started a bit tense, but by the end of the thirty-minute call, the tone had loosened up, and both presidents shared a few laughs. President Francis Peterman could turn on the charm when he wanted, and he was very good at it.

Looking at her watch and concerned about traffic, Rose Goodwin collected her winter coat and umbrella. *What a dark, dismal day*, she said to herself as she left.

The call with the Mexican president over, in walked Vice President Arnold Richardson. "Hello, Mr. President."

"Good to see you, Arnold," but Peterman's tone was not as jovial as before on the phone.

"I need to talk to you about health care, and what you're planning on doing."

"OK. Shoot."

"You're making a big mistake. Taking health care out of the hands of the insurers will ruin our top-notch health care system, not to mention the enemies you'll make. They have big bucks, and they'll fight you not just on this, but really fight you when you come up for re-election. They have good memories, and they'll use everything they can against you."

"First of all, I'm not taking health care away from the insurers. I'm just giving the people other options. That's the platform I ran on, and that's what I plan on delivering." Francis Peterman was still trying to keep his tone light.

"You're taking a big political risk. I also need to talk to you about your defense bill. It's supposed to hit your desk within the next few days. There are a lot of very important people who are going to be really upset. Taking money from companies like Decorp, Raymore, and others will make some big enemies."

"The world is changing, Arnold. We're not preparing for World War II anymore. The next war will be fought with technology and cyber warfare. We need to prepare for incidents that occur throughout the globe, like what's happening in Iran right now. China and Russia are trying to hack the shit out of us. That's what we need to prepare for, not the standard war machines of Decorp and the like. And remember, as I promised you long ago, I was able to get that little sweetener put in the bill for you, big money for that tech company in your district. I know they were big contributors to your campaign."

"Thank-you for that. And you know you can always count on me to support you."

"Thank-you, Arnold," said the President, indicating the meeting was over by turning to the paperwork on his desk.

With that, Vice President Richardson walked out of the office.

The next meetings with Secretary of Defense Abel, Secretary of State Atkinson, and Secretary of Health and Human Services Tish all followed on schedule. Each had some disagreements with his proposals, but all agreed to back him in the end.

Finally, House Majority Leader Randal Gray marched in. President Peterman didn't get up but indicated a chair on the other side of his desk. Majority Leader Gray was from the opposition, and one of the President's least favorite people. He had the appearance of a boxer who had lost too many fights, with a large, flat face and a pugnacious nose, and was known to "get in your face" when he disagreed with you. Randal Gray, quite simply, was a bully.

"What can I do for you Randal?" asked Peterman, with a smile on his face.

"I think you know. You're in for a fight. Your health care policies, your immigration policies, and this defense bill; we'll fight you on all of those. You'll never get anything accomplished."

Peterman backed up his chair to avoid getting hit by the spittle coming from Gray's angry mouth. Still maintaining his smile, he looked the Majority Leader in the eyes. "You know, I got elected by the largest majority in the past fifty years. Go ahead and fight me. I look forward to it. Not only will I win, but you're going to look bad in losing. Doubt your party will keep you as their leader in the House."

Randal Gray's face turned bright red, and he scowled. Without so much as a word, he got up from his chair and headed out. On his way out, Peterman shouted, "Have a good rest of the day!"

CHAPTER 9

SAMANTHA WAS WORKING late. She had to come up with a new identity for some idiot informant who got himself found out at the Russian embassy in India. His life depended on how quickly she could get him out of India and placed somewhere else under a new name.

She was dreading the next call she had to make, and it wasn't to the informant. It was to her ex-husband, Dr. Zachariah Webster. He had called the other day, asking when he could see their two children, Emma and Liam, for Christmas.

"Louise, I need to make a personal call, so would you mind if we go over the identity details in a few minutes?" she said to her assistant, who was sitting across from her desk. "It's to my ex."

"Is he still on the booze? Oh, I'm sorry. None of my business."

"Quite all right. It's not a secret. Now he wants to come over to see the children for Christmas."

"So, he doesn't have partial custody?"

"No way. The kids are better off without him. Can you believe it? He came to the courthouse drunk. Do you know what he called me? A whore, in front of the judge."

"That must have been awful."

"It was, but the good part was when he called the judge a loser and claimed he was being paid off. That did it, and the judge gave full custody to me."

"Sounds like a real loser. Good you divorced him."

Samantha sighed. "Well, it was mutual. We were both young and did stupid things. He was a good guy, and I really loved him once.

"We met in my last year at Georgetown Law, before I started working for the CIA, and he was in his ophthalmology residency at the Washington National Eye Center. I was proud of him, an eye surgeon and all. Swept me off my feet. I even moved up to New Hampshire when he got a job there. But then he started drinking after his mother died. I tried to make it work, but I couldn't."

"I didn't know you lived in New Hampshire. Were you working for the CIA then?"

"Yes, I worked remote, and made regular trips back to Langley every month. Didn't help me move up within the CIA, though."

"Sounds like you sacrificed a lot for him."

"I did, but those early days were good days, and I don't regret that. And I have Emma and Liam as a result, and that's what keeps me going."

"Well, it's good that he's not involved with the children now. Sorry you have to deal with that. I'll let you be. I'll get my stuff and work on the new identity in the office across the hall."

Louise walked off, and Samantha dialed the number she knew all too well.

"Hi, Zach."

"Hi, Samantha. How are you?"

Just hearing Zach's voice brought back the anger she had temporarily shelved. A hard edge returned to her voice.

"I'm fine. I'm returning your call from the other day."

"Yeah. I wanted to know when would be a good time to come over for Christmas. I have presents for the kids."

"Are you still sober?"

"Of course," said Zach. "Been sober for a year. You know that."

"Just want to make sure. Hard to picture you without a glass in your hand."

"How about you? Any new affairs recently?"

No one spoke for about the next ten seconds, until Zach finally broke the tension.

"I'm sorry. I shouldn't have said that."

"You've said a lot worse."

"I know, and I'm sorry."

Again, silence.

Finally, Samantha spoke in a lighter tone. "We've both done and said terrible things to each other. But the past is the past, and hopefully we've both moved on. I'm glad you're staying sober.

"Problem is we're going to be away for Christmas week at Auntie Sophia's house in New York. Kids are off school, and I've got the week off. You'll need to drop the presents off before that. We've got a flight out of Reagan Airport at 5 on Monday. We're busy on the weekend, but you could come over early on Monday."

"That's fine. I'm taking the week off myself. Thanks, Sam. See you then."

Zach wasn't sure why he was taking the week off. Certainly, there was no one he was going to spend the week with. Maybe it was force of habit. If anything, it was going to be downright depressing.

CHAPTER 10

"CAN'T YOU DRIVE FASTER? We'll be late for our appointment with the President?" demanded Jonathan Brodsky, Undersecretary of the CIA.

"What do you want me to do? The traffic is backed up here on the G.W. Parkway."

"Look for an alternate route, idiot."

Under normal circumstances, the driver, a man of short temper, would have stopped the car, flung open the door to the back seat, and beaten the crap out of someone who called him an idiot. But these were not normal circumstances. Instead, he switched on the GPS of his phone and let Google Maps find him a less-trafficked route to the White House.

Arriving at Pennsylvania Avenue, the large limousine with five passengers passed through the first checkpoint with ease. However, at the next guardhouse, the agent demanded to check the IDs of all the cars' occupants. Brodsky protested loudly.

"We don't have time for this. You have my ID. I'm Undersecretary of the CIA. This here is General Gomez, and the others are our assistants. We have an urgent meeting with the President. If we're late, you're getting fired. Check your logs. You'll see we have authorization."

"Yes, Sir. I see it. Go right ahead."

Gomez and Brodsky were dropped off near the entrance to the White House, where a uniformed officer helped General Gomez into his wheelchair. The limousine then drove out to wait on Pennsylvania Avenue.

Once inside, they first needed to pass through the metal detector.

"You will need to get out of that wheelchair, Sir, to pass through," said the officer standing by the detector.

"If he could get out of the wheelchair and walk through it, he wouldn't need a wheelchair," said Brodsky, angrily. "I'm Undersecretary Jonathan Brodsky, and we have an urgent meeting with the President."

"Sir, if you had let me continue, I was going to say that if he can't get out of the wheelchair, I can just wand and search him."

"Go ahead, then, wand me," said Gomez, throwing up his hands with a short laugh.

Once through, as soon as they were past the guards, Brodsky quickly pulled apart one end of a hollow tube on the wheelchair frame, grabbed something hidden in it, and placed it in his pocket. He reinserted the tube just in time, as they were soon met by Agent Lincoln, who walked them down the hallway to meet with the President.

Inside his office, Francis Peterman was back reading the brief he had looked at earlier. He wondered to himself why he spent so much time and money campaigning for a job that gave him ulcers. In fact, he could use some antacid right about now. Rather than dealing with another Iranian crisis, he would much rather have been joining his daughter and grandson in San Diego for Christmas.

Peterman stopped reading for a moment, took a drink from his coffee mug, sighed, and then went back to the brief.

There was a sharp knock on the door. The President rose, surveying his new guests.

In walked Jonathan Brodsky, Undersecretary of the CIA, accompanied by Agent Lincoln. The President had met with Brodsky a few times and had always found him slightly dull. Brodsky talked in a monotone, and at times, people sitting right next to him at meetings would later forget he was even there.

However, his companion, the general, sitting upright in his wheelchair, stood out. His dark eyes, behind thick spectacles and a long, black beard, made him look like he came right out of a Russian novel. He was dressed in a sharp, well-pressed army uniform with a blanket over his long legs.

"May I introduce General Gomez, Mr. President. He is our lead on the Iranian mess," remarked Brodsky.

"Nice to meet you," said the President. "Are you the one who wrote this crap?" holding up the brief he had been reading earlier. "And Ray, you can leave us now."

Ray left the room, smiling. He loved President Peterman's bluntness and lack of formality.

"Uh, no, no. That was someone else. He's gone," said Gomez. "I have something here I'd like you to see, Mr. President," indicating a folder sitting on his lap. "I think you'll appreciate this more," he added, putting the folder onto the desk.

As the President reached down to pick up the folder, Undersecretary Brodsky slowly walked around behind the desk, as if to read the folder from the President's perspective. Fumbling in his pocket, he finally found what he was searching for. He pulled it out. It was a syringe, and he plunged it into the President's neck.

President Peterman immediately went rigid and would have fallen out of his chair if he had not been held up by Brodsky and an amazingly quick General Gomez, who somehow did not need his wheelchair anymore.

"Pancuronium, a derivative of curare. Fast acting and reversible. Mixed with a strong sedative. We still need him alive, at least for the time being," said Brodsky quietly, sweat beading up on his forehead.

Gomez smiled, and then quickly started his transformation. Off came the spectacles, the beard, and the dark wig under his beret. Out came the colored contact lenses, revealing striking, blue eyes. Finally, the uniform was discarded. Brodsky by that time had most of President Peterman's clothes off. Gomez put on the President's clothes, and Brodsky dressed the President in military attire. Dark contact lenses were placed over Peterman's blue eyes, and the wig and spectacles were applied. Gomez removed glue from his pocket and used it to apply the beard on the President's face.

"Amazing," said Brodsky, looking over at the former General Gomez, as a drop of sweat fell off his brow into the President's coffee mug.

He was staring at a man, six feet tall, broad shouldered, with red hair and bits of gray at the temples, penetrating blue eyes, and a face revealing a broad, smirking smile.

CHAPTER 11

PEOPLE THINK POLITICS can be rough. Ray knew differently. He knew what a rough life really looked like, growing up on the mean streets of Washington, DC. His father was killed in a drive-by shooting when he was five, and he became the only child of a single mom who made rent money by cleaning houses. Ray's physical attributes made him attractive to the local gangs in the neighborhood, but his mom kept him in line and away from what she called "the bad elements." She made him work hard in school, only allowing the sports he loved, basketball and football, once he maintained a B+ average.

He worked his way out of the neighborhood to become a police officer, never forgetting the death of his dad to random violence and vowing to keep others away from harm if he could. Watching her son graduate from the police academy to becoming an officer in the Washington, DC police was the proudest moment of his mother's life. One year later, though, his mother suffered a massive stroke and died within three days.

Ray was now alone. He worked through his depression by focusing on his job, becoming a rising star in the police force. A few years later, when he heard of an opening in the Secret Service, he was ready for a new challenge. Here again, he moved up to eventually be a protector for the President of the United States, and President Peterman's favorite Secret Service agent.

Ray had been inside all day and felt the need for a break. He was an outdoor type, and he found waiting around by the President's office all day a bit tiresome. He much preferred action and movement, and there was to be none of that today. After finding another agent to relieve him, he decided to check out the grounds surrounding the White House, to get some exercise.

As he walked toward Pennsylvania Avenue, he heard a loud crash followed by the sound of a car speeding away, but he was unable to see anything. His job was to protect the President, but anything happening near the grounds of the White House was also within his scope. Running towards Pennsylvania Avenue, he noticed a black limousine pulled over by the curb. Wondering if they had seen anything, he walked over to question the occupants. Getting closer, he could see a pretty woman in a nursing uniform standing by the door. That made it even more enticing, having recently broken up with his girlfriend of six months.

"Hi, I'm Ray Lincoln, Secret Service. Can I ask you some questions? What's your name?"

The nurse appeared anxious. "June, June Temple."

"I'm sorry to make you nervous, June. I'm here to find out about that noise in the street. Did you see anything? It sounds like there might have been a car accident."

Two men stepped out of the black car. The driver was a short, round man with a big, round head. In fact, to Ray, he looked like two bowling balls, with a fat, round head sitting on top of a thick, short neck, which was in turn sitting on top of a massive, round belly. Next to him was another man, of average height and weight, with a snake tattoo covering most of his right arm. The bowling-ball man turned to Ray and said, "Mister, we didn't see anything."

Ray then focused again on June. She was quite pretty. "June, did you see anything?"

"No," she said in a nervous voice, looking over her shoulder at the driver.

Ray then pulled out a card with his name and phone number and gave it to June. Then realizing it was obvious what his real intention was, he handed it out also to the two men. "Call me if you think of anything," he said with a smile and wink to June. She took the card and put it in her pocket quickly. Reluctantly, the two men did the same. Ray then walked back to the White House to retake his post.

Rose Goodwin made the trip to Fairfax, Virginia in thirty minutes, to arrive at Dale Country Day School at 3:30 pm. She parked her big, black Cadillac in the back parking lot and walked quickly over to the school building. She did not notice the tall, thin man with just one arm. If she had, she might have ignored him as being one of the other parents who had come to pick up their children.

Marty Green, however, had no children at the Dale Country Day School or anywhere else for that matter. He was there for something else, a mission given to him by Phoenix.

Marty had been in the explosive ordnance disposal unit in the army, where he came to lose most of his left arm disarming a road-side bomb in Afghanistan. He was then discharged with a measly pension and a "good luck in the future" handshake to his one good arm. His later career as Phoenix's right-hand man made him realize that he was better at making bombs than disarming them.

Immediately after Rose entered the building, Marty walked slowly to her car, looking out for any cameras along the way that could show his face. Convinced he had seen none, he placed something under the car's chassis. He then moved quickly away, got back in his car, and sped off.

Rose marched quickly to her seven-year-old grandson Kiran's classroom, admiring the artwork on the walls and the big sign that said, "Happy Holidays!" She was looking forward to his big grin as he jumped into her arms. Instead, when she arrived at the classroom, Mrs. Jones, her grandson's teacher, had a puzzled expression on her face.

"Kiran left with your daughter twenty minutes ago," she said.

"But she texted me that she was in a meeting she couldn't get out of, and I was to pick him up," Rose responded, annoyed.

"Maybe she was able to leave her meeting. All I know is she was here and left with him."

Rose left the room and went back to her Cadillac in an angry mood. "What a waste of my time," she thought. "I've got so much to do and I'm stuck driving back and forth to Virginia for no reason. Why wouldn't Lisa let me know I didn't need to come out?"

This was her last thought, as after pressing "start," her car exploded in a fireball at the Dale Country Day School parking lot. Rose Goodwin would never be able to ask her daughter anything ever again.

CHAPTER 12

BRODSKY AND GOMEZ placed Francis Peterman's body onto the wheelchair and covered up his legs with the blanket.

"Goodbye General Gomez," laughed the former Gomez, as Brodsky started wheeling the President to the door.

"Quiet," hushed Brodsky as they got to the door.

"Relax, Johnny-boy. It's all good," said the man now dressed as the President.

Brodsky turned around and pointed at his companion. "Behave! Do what you're told!"

"At your service, Sir," he said with a mock salute.

Brodsky started opening the door to leave, with one hand on Peterman's wheelchair. From the other side, Ray Lincoln pushed the door open wider.

"Can I help you push the wheelchair, Sir?" he asked.

"No!"

Ray looked at Brodsky, who realized he was a bit too sharp in his response. As they began walking down the hallway, Brodsky recovered.

"That's quite all right, Agent. I can do it myself. I could use a little extra exercise. I do need to move along, though. The General is very tired and needs to get to bed. He's getting on in years and has a bit of a bug."

Ray looked down at the General. His eyes were closed.

"He doesn't look well. Maybe we should get the doctor."

Ray pulled out his phone and started dialing.

"No. He just needs a rest. Thank-you for your help, Agent. What's your name?"

"Agent Ray Lincoln, Sir."

"Thank-you for your help, Agent Ray Lincoln. We're fine from here. You can leave us now."

"Yes, Sir."

As they walked away, Jonathan Brodsky noticed the odd stare he was getting from the President's agent.

Only a little further to go, and he'd be home-free. No one stopped him by the metal detector or by the exit door. They were more concerned with who was getting in than who was getting out. Finally, they were outside, on their way to Pennsylvania Avenue, where the black limousine was waiting. Once there, the driver and his companion lifted President Peterman onto the back seat. The nurse still stood outside the car, looking from one to another.

Brodsky stared at her. "What are you waiting for? Get in and do what you were told to do."

Biting her lower lip, she obeyed, following the President into the back seat.

The car headed off, out of DC, and Brodsky walked off in the opposite direction. He could breathe freely again.

Staples, the former General Gomez, was now alone, and he thought about his situation. Brodsky, always so nervous. He had met plenty of those types in the Army. They always sounded so high and mighty, but when it was time for action, they would shrink back into their little holes. That wasn't him. Jim Staples didn't let anything scare him.

He had never put much stock in politics. His feeling was that most politicians were crooks, and he didn't want much to do with them. In fact, prior to the recent training he received, he had no idea who the members of the cabinet were, or even who the vice president was. Jim Staples now knew all their names and faces.

He sat reflecting on the turn of events that put him in the White House, sitting at the President's desk. *Not bad for a guy kicked out of Special Forces. What did they know? Too violent; sociopath; racist, they called me. My 'superiors', those bastards. I'll make them pay.*

Staples had a rough few years after being dishonorably discharged, multiple jobs with multiple bosses who thought they could tell him what to do. Sometimes he just quit. Other times he left after inflicting violence. But always, he left. Eventually, no one would hire him, and he became one of the homeless on the streets of Washington, DC.

Now here he was, President of the United States, sitting in the Oval Office. He, James Staples, was now in charge of the most powerful country in the world.

Putting his feet up on the desk, he hit the intercom button and announced to no one in particular, since Rose was now gone, "I am not to be disturbed. I'm meditating, and then I will head to my private chambers."

Ray Lincoln, who had returned, looked up with a puzzled expression on his face. *Meditate? I've never seen him do that before. Maybe Sarah is getting him to do it. Probably do him good*, he thought, smiling.

CHAPTER 13

THE BLACK LIMOUSINE continued its trip southwest toward coal country in West Virginia. The two men upfront were laughing and joking, while in the back, next to the unconscious man, sat nurse June Temple, trembling. The man's costume had partially fallen off, and she knew who it was. She had no idea the patient she had been hired to treat was the President of the United States, but it was too late to back out. She had no choice.

She took the loaded syringe, and with a shaky hand, injected it into his arm. The President gave a jerk, and then fell still again. The man in the front passenger seat turned around.

"What's going on?"

"He'll be fine. I've given him a dose of pyridostigmine, an antidote to pancuronium," she responded, her voice cracking. She could hear the two men in front laughing at her nervousness.

The car headed towards the border with West Virginia. As the President began to stir, a black cloth bag was placed over his head, and his wrists were tied together with thick rope.

"Where am I?" he asked in a soft, muffled voice. He was cold, exhausted, and nauseous. His mouth was dry, and his throat hurt.

"Keep quiet, or we'll have to silence you permanently," exclaimed the man with the snake tattoo.

It had been smooth sailing on the interstate, and they had made good time. It was just outside of Lewisburg that they saw the flashing lights of a police car behind them.

"What do I do," yelled the driver to his companion. "Should I try to outrun him?"

"Don't be more of an idiot than you already are. Pull off. You, nurse, put him down on the floor and put the blanket on top of him. And you, Mr. President, if you make a sound, I'll kill both the cop and you, so be quiet."

The driver pulled off on the side of the road and stopped. The nurse did as she was told. The President lay motionless on the floor.

The cop stepped out of his car and walked over. The driver opened his window.

"Yes, officer?"

The cop looked at him suspiciously. The view of the back seat was hindered by the tinted windows.

"Do you know how fast you were driving?"

"Umm, no Sir."

"You were going 85. The speed limit here is 70. License and registration, please."

The driver hunted for the car registration, which he found in the glove compartment. Reluctantly, he handed it over, which listed his name as Joey Petrone.

The cop went back to his car, while Joey practiced deep breathing exercises to stay calm. June's face had lost all color.

Finally, the cop walked back to the car, where he handed Joey back his license, registration, and a speeding ticket.

"Don't drive so fast, next time," he said.

"Okay, officer." Joey rolled up the window and proceeded, continuing to take slow, deep breaths.

"You did good. I thought you were going to pee in your pants, you were so scared," said the man with the tattoo, laughing at his companion.

"You watch your mouth, or I'm going to shut it for you," responded Joey.

"In your dreams. You wouldn't last a minute. Just do what you've been hired to do, drive."

Joey glared at him but didn't say anything more.

Eventually they came to the town of Fayetteville, West Virginia. Heading down a very bumpy, narrow, gravel road for another half hour, they finally arrived at a small clearing. There was a large brown structure heading up the hill on one side, leading to railroad tracks on the other side. A sign in the parking lot read, *Nuttallburg Coal Mining Tipple.* Other than the occupants of the black limousine, not a soul was in sight.

A narrow, winding path led up the hill. The driver and his companion grabbed the hooded, drowsy President under each arm and frog-marched him up the path. June followed behind. Sweating profusely, the party arrived at a ramshackle building.

An ancient elevator took them slowly down below the surface of the mine. Hearing a loud creak from the elevator, Joey flinched, causing his companion to laugh and shake his head in disbelief.

"You are such a loser."

"Hey, I just don't like elevators. Okay, Barty?" said Joey.

Once outside the elevator, the air felt heavy and damp, with a strong smell of coal. The tunnels were narrow, and Joey, a big man, felt as if they might close in on him.

The tunnel widened, revealing a small, steel-enclosed cell, furnished with an old musty cot with two blankets, a chair, and a small writing desk, lit by a single incandescent bulb hanging from the ceiling. Peterman was led in, and the bag was removed from his head.

Head spinning, the combination of medicines and the fetid air made him feel as if he needed to throw up. He looked around warily at his captors through the locked door.

"Where am I? I'm the President of the United States. Let me out," he shouted.

There was no response. Joey left immediately to head back to the surface. Even the creaky elevator was better than staying down below. Barty Strang, the man with the snake tattoo, sat down in a chair outside the cell, dressed in his camo uniform, with an automatic weapon by his side. June took the President's blood pressure and pulse with quivering hands.

"He's okay," she said softly to Barty.

"Then get your stuff and get the hell out of here."

June left the cell, and Barty closed the door behind her as she made her way to the elevator.

The President called out again. "Why am I here? Open the door and let me out. I'm the President."

Barty looked up from the magazine he was reading. "Oh, shut up. I know who the fuck you are and you're not getting out."

"I can pay you whatever you're getting paid for this and make sure you don't go to jail."

Strang laughed. "Like I trust you. All politicians are liars, and I don't fancy going back to jail myself. I don't need your money. I'm getting paid well for just keeping you here, and the people who hired me wouldn't be too pleased if I let you out. So, you're staying put where you are."

"Please, I'm telling the truth."

"Enough. Be quiet. Anymore and I'll come in there and shut you up."

Barty went back to reading his magazine. The President sat down at the desk and placed his head in his hands. His nausea had been replaced by fear and rage.

Joey found it a lot easier going down than up. He waited for the nurse in the car, tapping his fingers on the steering wheel with nervous energy. He couldn't wait to get out of this god-forsaken place. Eventually, June came down the path and joined him.

"What took so long?" asked Joey, annoyed.

"I had to make sure the President was stable before I left," she replied, still trembling.

"Okay, let's go," grumbled Joey as he started the car.

They drove in silence, under the speed limit, to avoid being stopped. Even so, Joey constantly checked his rearview mirror for any sign of police cars.

Near the outskirts of Charleston, West Virginia, not only did Joey see a police car in his mirror, but now they could hear its loud siren as it approached their car.

"Oh, shit!" said Joey, grabbing the steering wheel tightly. He looked at the glove compartment, thinking about the gun that was hiding there.

June was too scared to say or do anything.

The police car passed them and continued, siren still blaring. Finally, Joey loosened his tight grip on the wheel and took a breath. They continued to a warehouse on the other side of Charleston, where they left the car and arranged for an Uber to take them to the airport. Once there, June took a rental car back to Washington, DC.

Joey had a plane ticket waiting for him, and he gladly took his seat in first class. He was now finally able to relax and enjoy the perks of his job.

"Look at me, Joey Petrone, flying first class," he thought. "Who would have believed it!"

He ordered one drink, then another. *Hey, it's free. Why not?*

Ordering yet another drink, Joey's courage had returned. *All told, it's not a bad way to make $20,000,* he thought.

Back in his coal mine cell, President Peterman took in his surroundings. *Why am I here? Who are these people? Are they agents of some foreign government looking to get secrets out of me? If so, they won't get anything from me, try as they might. Someone will rescue me. My secret service agents will know I'm missing, and they'll move heaven and earth to find me.* He just had to be tough and survive until they did.

CHAPTER 14

CHIEF OF STAFF Robert Benton had little tolerance for people who got in his way. This morning, as he drove to work with his foot on the gas pedal, he was even more intolerant. Anyone who slowed him down was a jerk; anyone who got in his way was an asshole. It was all he could do to stop himself from giving the finger to other drivers. It wouldn't look good for the President's closest advisor to be involved in a road rage incident.

Bob Benton was not in a good mood. His wife had just given him a hard time after telling her that he had to miss his daughter's dance recital on the day before Christmas. He didn't want to miss it, but he had to work. The President had a huge agenda that would need congressional approval, and it was his job to push for it. It would need cajoling and even some good, old-fashioned threats to make it happen. Chief of Staff Benton was the man to do it. Sandy Benton was not happy, and she made her husband know it.

Benton turned on the radio to his favorite radio station, WAMU, the NPR station in Washington, DC to try to calm his nerves prior to arriving at the White House. Almost instantly, news came about Rose Goodwin's death. He now drove even faster. The President would need him.

Upon arriving at his office, he was surprised to see another coat already on the brass coat rack by the door. He looked over at the desk, and someone was sitting in his chair. Undersecretary Brodsky was sitting there with a big smile on his face. Brodsky handed him a note. It read simply, "Chief of Staff Benton, you have been replaced as my Chief of Staff. Former Undersecretary of the CIA Jonathan Brodsky will be taking your place. Thank-you for all you have done. Wishing you the best, Francis Peterman."

It was not possible, thought Benton. He reread the letter three times, with raised eyebrows and an open mouth. Finally, he slammed it back down on the desk.

He had always been loyal to the President. He had worked with him through multiple campaigns and been with him through thick and thin. There had been no sign that he was unhappy with his performance.

"What the hell is going on? And on the day after Rose dies? I don't believe it."

"Call him yourself," answered Brodsky.

"I will," and he picked up the phone to call President Peterman's private line.

Jim Staples picked up the phone. "Yes, I'm sorry Bob. I just feel with everything coming up that Jon Brodsky is the man for the job. Good luck to you in your next career." With that, he hung up the phone.

Robert Benton grabbed his coat and marched quickly out of the White House to his car. He didn't know what he was going to do next, but at least he knew he would now be able to go to his daughter's dance recital on Christmas Eve. He wasn't sure if his wife would be upset or happy that he had lost his job.

Brodsky's next guest was James Allen, Director of the Secret Service. He had been summoned by a phone call from the President to meet with Brodsky for an early appointment. They had met a few times in the past, and Allen did not hold Brodsky in very high regard.

"Director, in my new role as Chief of Staff for President Peterman, it is my job to let you know that he wants a shake-up in the secret service personnel guarding him. He wants them to be rotated to different positions, and he wants it done immediately," said Brodsky.

"I don't understand. What's his reasoning? Does this have anything to do with Rose's death? Does he think the Secret Service was lax or had any hand in it?" asked Allen, frowning.

"I don't know. It is not for me or you to question his decisions. He wants it done immediately. Also, there's a new agent, named Walter McCoy, that he wants guarding his daughter, Sarah. McCoy's on the plane now to San Diego. Here is a copy of the President's orders," said Brodsky.

"So, who is this new guy, McCoy? I don't know him."

"He comes from my old department, CIA. He's the best."

"I want to meet him before he guards the President's daughter."

"Too late. As I said, he's already on the plane. You can meet him later."

"I don't like it. I want to talk to the President."

"He's busy. You have your orders."

Allen looked at the orders again from the President. "Okay, I'll get it done this morning," he said with a sigh, and left the room.

Brodsky picked up his phone and dialed Staples.

"Get in here. I've written a press release about Rose Goodwin's death. You need to read it over in case anyone asks you about it."

"You don't order me about like I'm some dog. I'm the President of the United States."

Brodsky listened in amazement. Not only did this imposter not show any nervousness in his assignment, but he really thought he was now President.

"You're not the President, idiot. You're an actor."

"Careful boy how you talk to me. I'd hate to have to teach you a lesson. But let's be friends. I'll give you a free pass on this one. Be right in."

"One other thing. You have a medical exam tomorrow."

"What? They'll know I'm not the real President." For the first time, Staples' voice showed some anxiety.

"Not to worry. I've got a different doctor to examine you, not the President's regular doctor, who mysteriously woke up this morning with a very nasty stomach bug. Since his replacement has never examined the President before, you'll be fine. For the right fee, he's going to say you're in perfect health, and keep it at that. Peterman just has some high blood pressure and elevated cholesterol. Otherwise, he's healthy."

"My blood pressure's fuckin' fine," said Staples, his voice rising.

"That's okay. Peterman takes blood pressure and cholesterol medications to keep it all normal, so the doc won't know the difference."

He's also got an eye exam the same day, but we'll get that fixed too. Not to worry."

"My eyes are perfect," said the impostor.

"Good. Just behave, and you'll be fine."

Ray Lincoln arrived for his shift in the White House at 10 am, surprised to see the Director of the Secret Service waiting for him.

"Sir, what brings you here?" he asked.

"Ray, the President has requested a rotation of the secret service personnel guarding him, effective immediately," said Director Allen.

"I don't understand, Sir. Why?"

"I can't answer that. All I know is that it comes directly from the President. Effective immediately, you are now protecting the Vice President. There's a new staff coming in to guard POTUS."

Ray stood stone-faced. Inside, he was seething. He liked and respected President Peterman, and he thought the feeling was mutual.

"Why would he do this to me?" he thought.

"Yes, sir. Where am I to be stationed?" he finally responded.

"To the Vice President's residence, on the grounds of the US Naval Observatory."

"When do I start?"

"Immediately. Get your things together and head out there now."

Ray picked up his coat, the few articles he routinely kept in his locker, and proceeded to leave the White House. On the way, he met up with his best friend in the service, Frank Baldwin.

Frank was a good agent, one of the best. The two of them would sometimes hit the DC bars together after work, and Frank was the first one to reach out to him after his girlfriend, Cynthia, left. Once, another agent referred to the two of them as "White Chocolate," as Frank was as white as Ray was black. Neither Frank nor Ray took it kindly, and they let him know in dramatic fashion. No one called them "White Chocolate" after that.

"I've been transferred to the VP's residence, Frank."

"You're shitting me. I don't believe it. Peterman would never get rid of you."

"I just heard. I don't know why. I thought we got along great."

"I know. You're his favorite."

"Was. I guess not anymore."

"But to send you to the VP's residence." Frank lowered his voice. "That guy's a complete asshole. He treats people like shit."

"I know. How about you? Have you been reassigned?"

"Sorry, man. I hate to tell you. They put me on POTUS detail now."

"Hey, that's okay. I'm not mad at you. He's a good guy. You'll like him."

"Hope so, but I'm sorry for you. So, what are you going to do?"

"I do what they tell me to do. I'm on my way there now."

"Sorry, man. But we'll still go out, right?"

"Of course."

"Will do. See ya."

With a nod of his head and a slight wave, Ray was off. On his way to the Vice President's residence, anger turned to confusion. It just didn't make sense. He surely would have known if the President was unhappy with his performance. Finally, confusion gave way to suspicion. He would need to put that away for now. He was always one to follow orders.

CHAPTER 15

JIM STAPLES SLEPT LATE, got dressed, and sent a message to the kitchen to send his breakfast up to his bedroom in the White House. He looked out the window, which was streaked with rain. The sun was completely covered by thick gray clouds, and little rain droplets were forming, slowly dripping down over the window ledge. It brought him back to the days when he was homeless, living on the streets. That was then, but now, here he was, the most powerful man on earth.

The bedroom was large and well-decorated, but not as opulent as he had expected. The bed, however, was very comfortable, and he had slept well. Getting dressed, the President's clothes fit rather well, although slightly loose around the middle. "Nothing a few good meals won't fix," he mused.

Breakfast, however, was a major disappointment: orange juice, a bran muffin, raisin bran cereal with a few strawberries mixed in, skim milk for the cereal, and black coffee. All in all, a pretty lousy breakfast. He had eaten it the prior morning, but enough was enough. "I can't believe he eats this shit!" he thought with disgust.

"I'm the President, and I can get what I want," he said out loud to no one in particular.

Staples picked up the phone and called down to the kitchen. "Bring me a western omelet, some hash browns, bacon, and some sugar for my coffee. How about a couple glazed donuts to top it off?"

"Sir," said a hesitant voice from the kitchen staff, "Are you sure that's good for your diet? And we don't have any glazed donuts."

"I'm taking the day off from my diet. What kind of donuts do you have?"

"No donuts. We didn't think you liked donuts. We do have a few chocolate croissants left over from when your grandson was visiting."

"A couple chocolate croissants will be fine, and don't forget the rest of my breakfast."

"Yes, sir. I'll have them up to you in a jiffy."

"Fine."

About fifteen minutes later, there was a knock on the door, and a man in a well-pressed uniform presented a tray with the omelet, bacon, potatoes, and croissants, along with sugar for the coffee. Leaving it on a small table, he left quickly. The smell of bacon was overwhelmingly enticing.

"Finally, something decent to eat," thought Staples as he started his breakfast. "I think I like being President."

There was another knock on the door. "Damn," he said to himself. "Who's interfering with my breakfast?

"Who is it?" he shouted, with a touch of anger.

"It's me, Jonathan Brodsky, your Chief of Staff."

"Come on in. Do you want some breakfast?" Brodsky walked in. He was already dressed in his pressed suit, with a white shirt and starched collar. When he saw the President's breakfast, a scowl appeared on his face.

"What the hell do you think you're doing?" asked Brodsky angrily. "You're not supposed to be acting differently than Peterman, and here you are, sleeping late and eating crap for breakfast. The President always gets up at 7 am and has a healthy breakfast. And you've got to leave for your medical exam over at Walter Reed in about an hour."

"I'll do whatever the hell I please. They can wait for me if I'm late. Did you read the sign by the door? It says, 'President's Bedroom,' and don't you remember, I'm the President."

Brodsky sat quietly for a minute, not quite sure what to say. Finally, he responded, "I'll tell them you feel you need a day off from your usual diet, but please remember everything we taught you about the President's habits and act accordingly. Everything is proceeding to plan, but we need time to roll it all out. And please get dressed so you can be taken over to Walter Reed for your medical exam."

"I understand," said Staples quietly. "I'll do what I'm told," but in his head, a new sense of power was raging. "So, what's the plan?"

"All in good time. When the time is right, we'll let you know. Until then, just stick to the script."

"I have a right to know what's going on."

"You don't need to know more. Do your job. Anything comes up, you refer them to me. Got it?"

"Yes, sir," said Staples with a mock salute to his Chief of Staff.

Brodsky walked out of the room, now even more mistrustful of the imposter. Staples should be on his guard to act like the man he was pretending to be. He should even be slightly nervous, for if found out, the consequences would be severe. But Staples was not nervous at all. The man was really a true psychopath.

He was not sure he had made the right decision hiring Jim Staples for the job, but then he remembered it was Phoenix who hired him. So, it wasn't Brodsky's fault if something went wrong, but that wouldn't be much of a consolation if things backfired.

Jim Staples, on the other hand, felt a surge of power. After finishing his breakfast, he put his feet up on the table and thought to himself, *I can do whatever I damn well want. I know they want me to pretend for a while, and then they'll toss me back when they don't need me anymore. I may want to stay President, and they can't stop me. I could blow their whole operation.* Then he remembered Phoenix, and he wasn't so sure anymore. Phoenix was not one to be messed with.

CHAPTER 16

ZACH'S APARTMENT was one of the only ones available at the time he was looking for a rental, and it came at a good price. It was located on the fourth floor of a large building, overlooking Connecticut Avenue near Cleveland Park in Washington, DC. It was a view Zach rarely saw, as he made it a point to never look down through his windows.

Zach had a fear of heights ever since the age of nine. On vacation with his cousin's family, they had all climbed to the top of Cadillac Mountain at Acadia National Park. Looking at the view near the edge, his cousin, as a joke, gave him a slight push. Surprised, he lost his balance, but was saved from a possible fall by his father. Zach never forgot that incident, and neither did his cousin, who was severely punished.

His apartment was small, with one bedroom, a tiny kitchen, and a living room/dining room combination. The dining room consisted of a small folding table with only one chair. It was a big change from the house in New Hampshire he had shared with Samantha and their young children, but he was fine with it. After all, he didn't go out much and never invited anyone back to his apartment.

It was a gloomy, rainy Saturday, scuttling Zach's hopes to take Ripley on a run through the Rock Creek Park. First came Ripley's breakfast, and then a short walk, marred by a broken umbrella. By the time they returned to the apartment, Zach was drenched, as was Ripley. Zach dried him off with a towel.

"Poor timing, Rip. We should have waited a little longer to go out."

Ripley, tail wagging, appeared totally unconcerned.

After changing out of his wet clothes, it was finally time for breakfast. This morning's meal was a smoothie containing yogurt, kale, blueberries, and strawberries. It was all part of his new healthy lifestyle that he had started one year ago. Gone were the donuts, muffins, and cinnamon rolls smothered with frosting. They had been tossed out with the vodka, gin, and tequila.

He sat down to enjoy his breakfast while Ripley drooled expectantly by his feet.

"Sorry, Rip. This is my breakfast. You've had yours."

Ripley just looked up mournfully with a look of, "Please, just a little bit?"

Zach ignored him and opened his phone to check the news feed.

"Oh my God, Ripley, Rose Goodwin is dead."

Zach read on:

> Rose Goodwin, age 62, perished in a car fire at Dale Country Day School in Fairfax, Virginia. She was administrative assistant to President Francis Peterman, and had worked for him for many years, starting when he was a congressman from New Hampshire. The cause of the fire is unknown. Witnesses claim to have heard an explosion prior to the fire, but this has not been confirmed. The Fairfax police have not given out any further information as they say it is part of an ongoing investigation. President Peterman has been reported to be devastated by the news and will be preparing a statement.

Zach's phone rang. Upon seeing the phone number, he picked it up after taking a deep breath.

"Hi Dad. How are you?"

"Do you really want to know? If you did, how come you haven't called in forever?"

"Phone calls go both ways, Dad. You could have called me."

"I'm calling you now."

"So how are you?"

"I've been better. Did you hear, Rose Goodwin died."

"Just saw the news article. Awful."

"She was good people. I always liked her, though I didn't know her well. Tough lady. Met her at Francis' house a few times."

"Yeah. Met her a few times myself. Sounds very suspicious."

"I'm sure Francis is taking it hard. She was always there in the background, making sure he came out looking like roses. Are you going to the funeral?"

"I didn't really know her that well. She had a daughter a few years ahead of me in school, but again, I didn't know her all that well either. Also, I don't know when the funeral is."

"You should go. Maybe Sarah will be there, as she's Francis' daughter, and maybe she was friends with Rose's."

"Let it go, Dad. I know you thought I should have asked Sarah out in high school, but that was a long time ago."

"Just saying..."

"Bye, Dad."

Zach hung up. It was the most he had spoken with his father in months. Robert Webster had been so proud of his son, and so let down when things went terribly wrong. Zach carried the guilt of their estrangement like a tourniquet around his neck.

He spent the next half hour wrapping his children's Christmas presents. For Liam, age 9, a Washington Commanders football fan, he had a signed jersey by Walter Brown, Washington's star running back, who happened to be one of Zach's patients. For Emma, age 7, he had an American Girl Doll, Kit Kittredge, along with several books that described Kit's life. Em loved American Girl Dolls, and already had several.

With nothing else to do once the presents were wrapped, Zach spent the rest of the day watching college football games on television, including USC vs. UCLA. He really didn't care who won, not being from California. He enjoyed going to football games at Dartmouth, but maybe that was because of all the beer he and his friends smuggled into the game.

At five o'clock, Andy Brannigan called.

"Hi Andy, are you calling to confirm tennis for tonight? Are the courts dry?"

"Yes, they're dry, but that's not why I'm calling. I thought you were going to send over those records I needed."

"We did. Didn't you get them?"

"Nope. I had to go in blind, and that's not a pun. But everything was fine. Could you bring over the records tonight when we meet for tennis?"

"That's weird. I thought Veronica was going to send them over. Sorry. I'll stop over at my office before coming over this evening. I'll bring it to your office."

"Thanks. Examining the President was a bit stressful. I didn't want to screw up. See you at seven. Prepare to get the crap knocked out of you on the court."

"Don't think I ever lost to you when we were residents, so I doubt it."

"I've developed a killer serve, so watch out."

"I'm shaking, with laughter. See you soon."

Zach was puzzled. He was sure that Veronica had sent the records. Taking a chance she hadn't gone out early for a Saturday night date, he called her, and fortunately, she was home.

"Veronica, you sent out the records on President Peterman, didn't you?"

"Of course. I had to type them all up by hand. Then I sent them over the classified, encrypted email account. It was a lot of work and I don't get paid for overtime."

Zach's first thought was that he had never seen Veronica work one minute past 5 pm. In fact, by 4:30, her car was usually gone from the parking lot.

"Funny. They say they didn't get any of the records."

"Don't know what to say. I sent them. Gotta go. Have a date. Bye."

Zach hung up puzzled, but at least he could bring Andy another copy. He left at six, first stopping at his office to make a copy of the chart Veronica had digitized. He made it to Walter Reed Hospital a little before seven, where he handed Andy the President's old records before trouncing him in tennis.

CHAPTER 17

JOEY PETRONE SAT in the bar at the Mayflower Hotel. There were flowers everywhere, mostly in red, green, and gold for Christmas. Madonna's version of "Santa Baby" was playing in the background. There was a festive flower display sitting in the window, and the Christmas tree by the door was adorned with garlands and twinkling little lights.

Here he was, Joey Petrone, in a classy bar, and now much more relaxed. No one had followed him, and he felt home free. He had even stopped watching the entrance to the bar for any sign of danger.

He ordered the most expensive whiskey he could think of; Chivas Regal. Having seen an ad for it on TV, it sounded like something an important guy would drink. Usually, his whiskey choice was whatever was cheapest. But now, he was a rich man with money in his pocket and a room in an expensive hotel in downtown DC.

He deserved it, he thought. Fired from his job at the warehouse for beating up the little shit who stole his sandwich. How was he to know that the little shit was the boss's son? Then, his wife leaving him for Joe Businessman; he never did know his name but that's what he called him. Joe Businessman would get his comeuppance one of these days.

Yesterday was his first big paycheck, although he had gotten some smaller jobs working as a small-time hood for some local crime bosses in his hometown of Newark, New Jersey. It was there that he got paid to beat up a guy. It was a warning to some guy who owed protection money. He knew he might eventually be asked to make a real hit, but it didn't bother him one bit. *We all gotta go at some point, so what's the big deal,* he told himself.

Joey looked at his watch. It was now 8 pm, and he was told he would receive his next instructions in his hotel room at 8:15. He had been warned not to be late, and although he wasn't the sharpest, he knew it was not good to let Phoenix wait. Joey tossed back the remainder of his drink and headed up to receive instructions.

Once inside his room, he found a manila envelope that had been slid underneath the door. Opening it, he saw a photo, detailed instructions, the next payment of $10,000, and the promise of an additional payment of $20,000 once this new mission had been completed. There was also a plane ticket, this time to San Diego, California.

Phoenix sat in his hotel suite at the Waldorf Astoria in downtown DC, less than ten minutes by car to the White House. Distance didn't really matter. There was no way he would want to be connected to anyone or anything going on there. He too noticed the rain coming down, but he couldn't care less. Weather didn't bother him, nor did politics or religious beliefs. There was no right or wrong as far as he was concerned. There was just money, and he was looking forward to the bounteous purse which was soon to rain down on him for this job.

Phoenix grew up in Lebanon. The only child of parents who were killed during the war with Israel, he learned to survive on the streets by his own wits. By the age of twelve, he had formed his own gang that demanded protection money from downtown merchants. By eighteen, he graduated to running guns to various terrorist organizations. In his early twenties, tiring of the gangs and terrorists, he realized he could do much better on his own. His only political belief centered on who would pay him the most money. In fact, his most recent job was a hit for the Israelis in Iran.

He had been completely honest with the Arlington conspirators; he had pulled those assassinations and more, throughout the world, and had never been caught. He was wanted by police in over ten different countries for crimes including theft, murder, and political assassination under multiple names. All were aliases, linked to mythical creatures: Sphynx, Chimera, Griffin, and Dragon. Phoenix was his favorite. He saw himself as the mythical Phoenix bird; powerful, and able to regenerate from the ashes of each job.

He was a hired gun, and an expensive one at that. It was an inaccurate term for Phoenix, as he rarely pulled the trigger himself these days, though not because he couldn't do the job. He was well trained and experienced.

He preferred finding low life's to do the deeds for him; men who lived alone, needed money, and above all, lacked a conscience. Intelligence didn't matter, as he would do the thinking for them. He preferred them to be a bit dim upstairs. Joey Petrone fit the bill perfectly. He was starting to feel less sure about James Staples, but he knew he would take care of him at the right moment. Both Staples and Petrone would be eliminated when not needed anymore.

The nurse, June, was another loose end, but she would be dealt with at some point. She might be needed temporarily to keep the President healthy enough to stay alive until the right time for his death.

This was to be a complex, high-risk job. For the plan to work perfectly, the President would be kidnapped and replaced by a look-alike stooge. So far, so good. Next, the President's daughter, Sarah, would need to be eliminated, and then the President himself would die.

He had made it sound so simple to the Arlington conspirators, but in fact it was a highly complex and difficult mission to carry out. Phoenix was confident that it could be done successfully. He was being paid a huge sum of money for this job, and he would make it work.

CHAPTER 18

SUNDAY WAS A BEAUTIFUL DAY in DC, 43 degrees and not a cloud in the sky. Zach and Ripley were out on a run when his phone rang. As he had no interest in listening to another sales pitch for an extended warranty or some other come-on, he let it go to voicemail. His phone rang a few more times during the New England Patriots vs. Kansas City Chiefs football game, but again, he let them go to voicemail. It wasn't until the end of the game that he pulled out his phone to check them out. They were all from his friend, Andy Brannigan. On each successive message, Andy seemed more stressed, pleading for his friend to call him back.

Zach dialed immediately.

"Sorry, Andy. I just got your messages. What's up? If it's about working at Walter Reed, I'm not interested, and they wouldn't want me anyway."

"No. It's about Francis Peterman's chart you brought me yesterday."

"What about?"

"Your chart must have been wrong. Could another patient's chart have gotten mixed in with his?"

"What do you mean?"

"Look. I did a complete eye exam on Peterman. Everything was perfect. I even did a visual field exam which was normal. On your chart, it reads that he had a small retinal artery blockage, and because of that, he had the loss of part of his side vision in the left eye. There was no block-age of his retinal artery that I noticed, and I did a very thorough retinal exam. It's possible I could have missed it as I didn't know to look for it at the time, but that doesn't explain the normal visual field. If he had the permanent blockage of the retinal artery as you describe, there is no way his side vision could have gone back to normal."

"That doesn't make sense. I remember distinctly. I remember the night he called me in, when he complained of suddenly losing part of his sight in the left eye. I followed him for months after that, and the blockage in his artery remained constant, as did the loss of his periph-eral vision on the left. There is no way it could have improved. There must be something wrong with your visual field machine, and I don't know why you wouldn't have seen the retinal blockage."

"What a mess. I'll need to get in touch with the White House tomorrow and try to get him back for a repeat exam. I could get fired for this," sighed Andy.

"Don't know what to tell you, buddy. Hope it works out okay. Why don't you send me a copy of what you found, and I'll see if it makes sense at all with what I remember."

"This is all classified stuff. I don't think I'm supposed to. But I really need help here, so I will. I'll email it to your office. Delete it after you examine it."

"Got it. I'll compare it and see what I come up with, but I do know that my chart is correct."

"I better stay here for a while and figure this thing out. I need to know what to say if you can't come up with anything" he said anxiously.

Zach put down the phone, troubled. Rose Goodwin's death, and now this. It just didn't make sense. Andy was a good doctor and wouldn't have missed such a relatively simple finding on examination, especially for the President of the United States.

In a small cubicle inside a darkly lit room at CIA Headquarters, a young technician put down his headphones and called his superior.

"Sir," the technician said. "There was a call placed from Dr. Andy Brannigan to a Zachariah Webster regarding his examination of President Peterman. I was told to inform you of any calls going in or out from Dr. Brannigan's phone."

"Do you have a recording of the wiretap?" replied his superior.

"Of course, sir. Do you want me to play it for you?"

"No, but the orders are for you to send it directly to Jonathan Brodsky, who is now Chief of Staff to the President. Do you know how to get it to him?"

"Yes, sir. It's here in the directions I received. I'm to do it if you say to send it."

"Go ahead. Good work."

Phoenix's phone rang, and he could see the caller was Jonathan Brodsky.

"Brodsky, I told you to call me directly only in a true emergency. So, it better be important."

"Believe me, I wouldn't be calling you if it wasn't of the utmost importance. We've got a problem that you need to fix, and quickly." Brodsky sounded on edge.

"What's the matter this time? The imposter giving you a hard time?"

"He's a pain in the ass, and I don't trust him, but that's not why I called. It's that eye doctor who examined him. Turns out there was an old chart that shows his eyes are different. The doc who sent him the chart lives in DC, and they discussed it on the phone."

"Damn. Get me both docs information and addresses. I'll take care of it. Now go and make sure Staples behaves. He's your responsibility."

He hung up before Brodsky could complain in more detail about the imposter.

Phoenix would deal with the eye doctors in a few minutes, as he had unfinished business with Kwan to take care of first.

Dialing his number, Kwan answered on the first ring.

"Ahh, Mr. Phoenix. Good day to you. And what does the Phoenix bird want?"

"Skip the pleasantries. You know what I want. I have yet to receive my most recent installment."

"Twenty million is such a large number. Let's talk about that."

"No. A deal's a deal. You agreed, and there is no going back. If you don't follow through, I'll be certain to make sure you and your country are seen to be responsible for what happens. I'm sure your government will love that. They'll hang you out to dry."

"Just joking, Phoenix. Of course, you'll get your money. The next installment will be transferred within the hour."

"Good. I'll be watching for it."

Twenty minutes later, Phoenix checked his bank account. He was a few million dollars richer, but he still didn't trust Kwan.

His next call was to Marty Green.

"Marty, I have a job for you. In fact, several jobs."

CHAPTER 19

JOEY PETRONE LEFT his luggage in the storeroom at the Mayflower Hotel, took a cab to the airport, and then boarded a flight to San Diego. He made sure to take with him the packet that had been delivered the previous evening, containing several pictures and directions.

It was a long flight, which gave him a chance to watch "The Godfather," and "The Godfather 2." He saw himself as Clemenza, one of Vito Corleone's most trusted lieutenants.

Joey landed in San Diego and took a quick 15-minute cab ride to his hotel, the Hyatt Regency, near Seaport Village. Everything in the lobby was decorated in green and red for Christmas, and a large Christmas tree stood in the center, adorned with lights and large, glass ornaments. Instead of being green, it was frosted with what looked like snow. It was so incongruous with the outdoor surroundings of palm trees and exotic flowers that it made Joey laugh. Then he saw the wrapped packages under the tree, and he thought of his childhood, and the presents that stopped by the age of nine. That's when his mom left, leaving his alcoholic father alone with three young boys. As he was the oldest, he turned to petty crime early to help feed the family.

Turning away from the tree, he checked in and went to his room. Looking out his window, he could see the skyline of San Diego. It certainly wasn't the skyline of New York or other big cities on the east coast, but on the other hand, there was no snow on the ground and the temperature was a pleasant seventy degrees.

It was still early enough for him to case out the area he would need to know for the following day. He called for an Uber, which took him to a block in Chula Vista, south of downtown San Diego. Much of Chula Vista was scenic and pleasant, but this was a particularly uninspiring block. There was a liquor store on one corner, a pawn shop next to it, and a boarded-up pizza joint just down the street. An unpleasant stench of urine seemed to emanate right up from the pavement. Looking closer, he could see a man dressed in rags curled-up in the doorway of the deserted pizza restaurant. Across the street was a rather small building with a sign reading, *Pleasant Street Medical Clinic*. Joey laughed out loud.

He had seen bad areas before, and "Pleasant Street" was one of them. He tried coming up with alternate names, with "Shit-Hole Medical Clinic" his favorite. On the other hand, this block was just the right spot for his mission.

He crossed the street to enter the medical building. There was no guard outside or inside the small lobby, which had just a few chairs adjacent to the elevator entrance. A sign in the lobby listed the different departments and their respective floors in the building. Joey sat on one of the chairs and waited. Things were quiet. He then headed up to the third floor, looked quickly around at the waiting room, and then took the elevator back down.

Perfect, he thought, as he ordered an Uber to take him back to the hotel. He had already been kicked out of the bar at his hotel, but found another in the adjacent Seaport Village shopping area, where he satisfied his new taste for expensive whiskey.

After stumbling back to his hotel, he found another package waiting for him in his room, a 32-caliber gun, along with one round of ammunition.

Walter McCoy had arrived on Friday into San Diego International Airport and then Ubered to the San Diego Hilton. He was to start his secret service job, guarding the President's daughter on Monday, so he had the next few days to himself.

Walter spent the weekend hanging out by the pool and checking out women in bikinis walking by. He made sure they caught a glimpse of his six pack abs as each came by, but so far, no takers. Perhaps it was his untanned skin, he thought, and he resolved to get himself some bronzing lotion when he had the chance. It couldn't have been his pickup lines of "Hey babe, what's happening?" or "Hey babe, I'm here for you," that made him unsuccessful, he believed. Self-reflection was not his strength.

On Sunday evening, Walter received a phone call from Phoenix. His instructions were simple: just act like the secret service agent he's supposed to be. Stop the perpetrator, but only after the perp had performed his mission. It was to be a simple shot to the head. He was just to add some additional items to the man's pockets. It was going to be simple, and there was easy money to be made for doing his job.

Jim Staples sat at his desk in the office adjoining the Oval Office. Some of his initial excitement had worn off. Here he was, the acting President of the United States, just sitting around doing nothing. He had played a couple of games of solitaire but was now bored with it. He then made a game of trash bin basketball using rolled-up papers he found on the desk. The fact that some of the papers he used had the word "classified" on them made no difference to him. They worked equally well as papers with nothing written on them.

Jonathan Brodsky walked in, not bothering to knock.

"Shouldn't you knock before entering the President's office, Mr. Brodsky?" said Staples with a smile on his face.

Brodsky gave him an angry stare.

"Tomorrow is supposed to be your last cabinet meeting of the year, but as I've explained to the Secretaries, you've called it off to allow everyone to leave town early, to be able to spend more time with their families. They all seemed appreciative."

"I was looking forward to it. It would have given me something to do. All I'm doing is sitting around doing nothing."

"Watch TV in your chambers. You've got cable and every streaming service imaginable there," said Brodsky curtly, and walked away.

CHAPTER 20

IT WAS ANOTHER gray day in the nation's capital. Ripley's walk was again cut short due to light, freezing rain. They walked only a few blocks beyond the apartment building before turning back, just enough for Ripley to do what he needed.

Zach noticed a tall, thin man dressed in a black raincoat near the entrance to the apartment building, holding a black umbrella in his right hand. Either his left arm was missing, or it was inside his coat. As Zach approached the door of the building, he had the distinct impression the man was studying him.

Breakfast was dampened when Zach thought about the day. Yes, he would be able to see his children, but it would be only for thirty minutes or so. Samantha was not one to give him much family time, as she felt uncomfortable being anywhere near him. He understood; he was uncomfortable around her also. Afterwards, he would head back to his apartment where maybe he'd watch some old, lousy Christmas movie. He had all week to wallow in pity. What had he been thinking when he decided to take Christmas week off? He had hoped that Samantha would let him take the kids to the zoo or some other outings during their Christmas school vacation, but it was not going to happen. Time to call.

"Hi Samantha. What time would be good to stop over?"

"You can come over at eleven with your presents. Sorry you can't stay long; we've got to get ready to leave for the airport."

Zach noticed the hard edge in her voice. How much time did they really need to get ready to fly out of Reagan Airport in DC at 5 p.m.? Were they going to arrive at the airport four or five hours ahead of time? He held back those thoughts.

"That's fine, Samantha. I'll be there then."

After a quick cup of coffee, it was time to go. Zach grabbed the presents and Ripley before heading down to the basement, where his Honda Civic was parked. Samantha got the BMW in the settlement, but Zach was just as happy with his post-divorce used car with eighty-thousand miles.

Driving to Samantha's house in Bethesda, Maryland took only about twenty minutes, as there was little traffic. He noticed a gray SUV behind him as he was driving north on Connecticut Avenue. It turned with him on Bradley Boulevard and then again on Wisconsin Avenue. He stopped in front of Samantha's house, and he saw the gray car pass by and continue.

"I've been watching too many movies," thought Zach.

The freezing rain had stopped, and the sun was trying to break through.

"Maybe it's a sign, Rip, that the day is going to get better. Things are going to work out. You'll see."

Zach rang the bell, and was almost knocked over by Liam and Emma, who both grabbed him at the waist in a big three-way hug.

"Daddy!"

Samantha was not part of the hug. She stood about six feet away with a forced smile on her face.

"Come in, Zach. Merry Christmas."

"Merry Christmas, Samantha."

He looked at her. Petite, thin, with long, dark hair, she was just as he remembered. He knew her apparent happiness to see him was an act for the children, but at least he knew his kids' excitement was real. Noticing Ripley, Em bent down to pet him.

"Mommy, can we get a dog too?" begged Emma.

"I'll think about it," replied Samantha.

Zach knew Samantha would never buy a dog. The fact she was letting Ripley in the house caused her anxiety. A part of him was secretly pleased to be providing her with a bit of discomfort. He knew Samantha was excessively neat and hated the mess a dog would cause, but he held his tongue.

Once inside, Zach looked around and saw Christmas decorations everywhere. Tinsel was spread around the house, on the banisters, chairs, bookcases, and even on the Christmas elf figurine in the hallway. It must be driving Samantha crazy, he thought with amusement.

The tree was beautiful, adorned with red, green, and blue lights. The smell of Christmas baking brought back old memories of Christmas, before things fell apart. At first it was a happy thought, but almost immediately it brought on a feeling of sadness as he realized what he was missing.

"What did you get us, Daddy?" asked Emma.

"Can't you wait a bit?" asked Samantha.

"That's OK," said Zach, pasting a smile on his face as he reached into his bag and pulled out the presents. Liam ripped off the wrapping of his present.

"Wow, wow, wow." Liam was speechless.

"He's a patient of mine, and he signed it for you," said Zach. "See, it says here, 'For Liam, from Walt Brown.'"

"He's my favorite player," his voice returning. "Thanks, Daddy."

Emma took longer opening her present.

"I love it, Daddy. Now I have three American Girl Dolls," she said, holding it and the accompanying books up for all to see. "Can we read one of them now?"

Zach looked over at Samantha, who gave him a quick nod.

"Sure."

Zach spent the rest of his allotted time reading the story of Kit Kittredge to Emma. After a while, a look from his ex-wife told him it was time to go.

"Your mom can finish the rest of the story. I've got to go."

"No, you can't go yet. I want you to finish the book." Em crossed her arms and stared at her parents.

"That's right Dad, you only just got here," said Liam, pleading.

"Kids, your dad has to go. Give him a hug and say goodbye. And you need to get ready for our trip."

Zach fashioned a false smile to his face, realizing if he wanted to spend more time with his children in the future, he better go along with Samantha's edict.

"Yeah, I've got to go. Sorry I can't stay. Have a fun time with your aunt. Love you both. See you soon," and he gave both kids huge hugs.

Samantha escorted Zach and Ripley out the door.

"I will let you get together with them soon. They do miss you."

"Not as much as I miss them," said Zach, as he and Ripley got into the Civic and drove off.

It was about two miles later, while on Wisconsin Avenue, that Zach looked in his rear-view mirror and noticed what appeared to be the same gray SUV behind him.

"It's got to be my over-active imagination," thought Zach, but he speeded up anyway. So did the SUV behind him. Zach then slowed down, hoping the gray car would pass. It did not.

Zach was now seriously alarmed. He turned off Wisconsin Avenue onto Bradley Boulevard. So did the gray SUV. Worry turned to panic. Instead of staying on Bradley to Connecticut Avenue, where he lived, he made a few quick turns. The SUV stayed a few cars behind him.

Stopping at a red light, the SUV was now directly behind him. Through the rear-view mirror, he could see a man quickly get out and approach his car. He recognized him as the tall, thin man with one arm that he had seen near his building.

Now, directly to the side of his window, Zach saw the man raise his arm. Something metal and shiny was in his hand. Zach's foot hit the accelerator, and the car shot through the intersection with the light still red. He narrowly missed hitting a bus driving through from a cross street and a white corvette coming from the opposite direction.

The thin man returned to his car quickly, but his way was blocked by the bus and corvette. By the time his car was able to pass through, Zach was long gone.

Marty Green, the driver of the gray SUV, picked up the phone and called his boss.

"Phoenix, he got away."

"Where were you?"

"Near Connecticut avenue in DC."

"You could have been seen. I expect better."

"I know where he lives, and I put a tracker on his car when he went inside the house."

"Don't approach him inside his apartment building. Too obvious; you might get caught. Keep your distance until he's in a secluded spot."

"Okay. I'll wait."

Zach drove as fast as he could back to his apartment. His knuckles were white and his fingers almost numb from the grip he had on the steering wheel. Finally reaching the underground parking lot of his building, he grabbed Ripley by the leash and ran to the elevator. Upon arriving at his apartment, his shaky hands dropped his keys twice while trying to unlock the door. Once open, he hurried inside and quickly locked the door with a dead-bolt.

Zach dropped down onto his living room chair. He could feel the cold sweat on his forehead, and his heart was beating so fast and hard that it sounded as if a machine gun was firing in his chest.

He sat quietly for a few minutes, waiting for his pulse to slow while trying to figure out what to do next. Finally calmer, he knew he should call the police.

"Sargent Canto here, what can I do for you?"

"I'd like to report a man threatening me with a gun."

"Why was he threatening you?"

"I have no idea. I was driving. He followed me, got out of his car, came around by the driver's side window, and raised his arm to shoot me."

"Did you cut him off or something?"

"No."

"Did you see a gun?"

"I can't say for sure, but I think it was. It was dark and shiny, but I didn't stick around long enough to be certain it was a gun."

"What did he look like?"

"He was tall and thin, with wavy dark hair. And he had only one arm."

At that, there was silence on the line. Finally, Canto spoke.

"Are you sure it wasn't your imagination? Have you been watching old episodes of 'The Fugitive?'"

"It was not my imagination. He was going to shoot me."

"It was probably road rage. There are a lot of kooks out there," responded Canto, now wondering what scraps from dinner would be left for him at home, when he would finally be off duty.

"It was clearly not road rage. He was following me, and then he got out of his car and was going to shoot me if I didn't get away quick enough."

"OK," said Canto, dismissively. "Come down to the station and file a report."

"He knows where I live. I've seen him before hanging out in front of the building. He's probably waiting for me to leave, and he could shoot me in the garage or on my way. I'm not leaving my apartment today."

"Suit yourself. If you still want to file a report, come down here when you're ready."

Canto hung up.

Zach was incredulous. "They don't believe me, Rip. What should I do?"

He got up and checked the door and window locks. All were set. His eyes then turned to the cabinet where he used to keep his booze, his solace from the perils of real life. He had not opened it for a year, after having thrown out any remaining bottles. Could he have missed one?

Walking to the cabinet, he wasn't sure if he wanted it to be empty or not. Part of him, the part that was trying to rehabilitate his life, wanted it to be empty. The scared shitless part longed for just a taste.

The cabinet was empty.

He turned on the TV and watched *It's a Wonderful Life* with Jimmy Stewart on TNT. He tried to concentrate on the movie, but it was almost impossible. His head kept replaying the one-armed man slowly raising his gun.

By the time the movie had ended, the excitement and terror of the day had given way to exhaustion, and it was time for sleep. He checked the door and window locks again. For good measure, he pushed his sofa against the door. It took almost two hours lying awake in bed before he was able to fall asleep.

CHAPTER 21

JIM STAPLES was still bored. He could only spend so much time watching television. Occasionally, he would get up and go for walks out on the grounds, accompanied by secret service agents. He felt as if he was under house arrest, spending almost all his time in his chambers.

His only regular visitor was Brodsky, and he was not much fun. The topic of their talks was almost always "lay low, stay out of sight."

At least tonight held promise, as there was to be a huge boxing match. Jay Lewis was to fight Trevor Brown for the title of "Middle-Weight Champion of the World" at 8 pm, and Staples was looking forward to it on pay per view. Brodsky had arranged for the fight to be shown on the TV in the president's bedroom. At least he was good for something, thought Staples.

At 7:45, Staples turned on the TV and sat down in a comfortable chair. Something was missing. He needed a beer, or perhaps a few beers, to watch the fight. He picked up the phone and dialed the kitchen.

"Bring me up a few beers," he demanded.

"What brand do you want, Sir?"

"Bring me a six of Budweiser."

"Sorry, sir, but we don't have any Budweiser."

"Well, what do you have?"

"We have Corona Light and Heineken, and we also have some imported German Beers: Wurzburger Hofbrau and Erdinger Kristall. The German beers are left over from the banquet we had for the German Chancellor."

"What American beers do we have?"

"Uh, none."

"I want good old American Budweiser, not any of that foreign stuff. If you don't have any, go to the store and get me some, and I want it now," he said forcefully.

"Yes, sir. I will send someone to get it right now, and we'll bring it up to you."

"Be quick about it," he said, as he put the receiver down.

The fight started, there was no beer yet, and Staples was becoming annoyed. A few minutes later, there was a knock on the door.

"Come in."

A young man entered, out of breath from running, with a Budweiser beer in his right hand and a glass in his left.

"Here, Sir," he said, about to pour the beer into the glass.

"Stop. Just give me the bottle. And where are the rest?" asked Staples.

"The rest, Sir?"

"The rest of the six pack."

"Oh, I thought you just wanted the one, but I can go back to the kitchen and bring the others."

"You do that," and the man hurried out of the room.

A few minutes later, he was back with the remaining five bottles, which he left on a small table beside the President.

Staples settled in to watch the rest of the fight, finally happy to have beer by his side. Being President of the United States was alright.

CHAPTER 22

PRESIDENT PETERMAN sat alone in his cell. He had to get out. Why was he here? What was happening in his absence? So far, no one had come to rescue him. Would they ever? What could he do?

Maybe he could talk his way out. He would wait for the weakest link, perhaps the young guard with sandy hair. Out of all of them, he seemed the least belligerent. Finally, it was his turn to guard the prisoner.

"Can I talk to you?" asked President Peterman, standing by the bars of his cell.

"What about?" asked the guard.

"We're both stuck here. Might as well talk to pass the time. What's your name?"

"None of your business."

"Okay, you don't have to tell me. My name's Francis."

"Eugene."

"Do people call you Eugene or Gene?"

"Neither. They call me Al."

"What does Al have to do with Eugene?"

"It doesn't. Alan is my middle name. Eugene is my dad's name so I'm a junior. Everybody's always called me by my middle name, so it doesn't get confused."

"Al, how much are they paying you to keep me here?"

"I shouldn't be talking to you," and he turned his back to the President.

"Just having a friendly conversation. I can tell you're not like the rest of the guards here."

"I'm not talking to you."

"How would you like to make four times the amount they're paying you to get me out of here? Full presidential pardon to go with it."

The young man now turned around to face his captor.

"Even if I went for it, there's no way I could get you out of here alive. We'd both be dead within minutes. But," he said, after a few moments of contemplation, "if we all got paid, that could work."

"Fine. We'll pay all you guys."

"I'll get the guy in charge."

"You do that."

When Al returned five minutes later, Peterman was discouraged to see that the guard's superior was the man with the snake tattoo. He was the worst of the bunch.

"What does he want?" asked Barty.

"He says he'll give us four times the amount we're being paid to let him go, and full presidential pardons."

Barty laughed. "You're an idiot, Eugene."

"Don't call me that. My name's Alan."

"I'll call you whatever the fuck I like. As for this piece of shit, he's lying. We'd never get the money. We'd get a cell or a quiet execution, and that's if the people who hired us don't get to us first."

"But Barty..."

Barty's fist hit Alan in the jaw, knocking him backwards.

"Don't talk to him. If you do, you'll get worse, and you know I'll do it. As for you," he turned to Peterman, "you keep your mouth shut or I'll shut it for you. I already told you we can't be bought." Barty spit, landing on the President's shoe, and then walked away.

The young guard sat back down on his chair, not looking at Peterman. The President sat back down at his table. He realized Alan was right. Even if he was able to convince him, there was no way they could get out alive. Snake tattoo guy would never go for it.

CHAPTER 23

IT HAD BEEN a tough night. Even through his closed windows, noise on the street below woke him at 2 and 4:30 am. Both times, Zach got up out of bed to check the door. The sofa was still in place, and for good measure, he rechecked all his windows, which remained locked.

When awakened again around 6 am, he decided to just get up. He clicked on the TV to hear the news anchor discussing Rose Goodwin's death.

"Forensics have revealed the remnants of a supposed incendiary device from the wreckage. We are told that the FBI is investigating, and of course, President Peterman is keeping a close watch on the situation, as she worked for him over many years. According to the President, the family has requested the funeral service to be performed as soon as possible. We have just been told that it is scheduled for the day after tomorrow.

"In other news, a prominent Army Eye Surgeon was killed last night in a hit and run accident outside Walter Reed Hospital. A police source has told this station that a gray SUV was captured on video at the time of the accident, but the license plate numbers were hidden from view. Anyone having information, please contact the police."

A picture of his friend, Andy Brannigan, flashed on the screen.

Zach fell into his chair. All thoughts of breakfast were extinguished. Something terrible was clearly going on. Andy Brannigan dead and he himself almost shot in a car chase. Rose Goodwin dead. Was this all somehow related to the President's eye exam not matching up with his old records? It was the only thing that made sense.

Zach's eyes again fell upon the liquor cabinet. There was nothing in there. He could run down to the neighborhood liquor store and buy a bottle, but no, that wouldn't solve anything. He was not going to succumb.

He needed Peterman's eye chart. What to do with it once he had it, he had no idea. First step, go to his office and retrieve it.

Zach looked through the peephole in his door and could see no one in the hallway. Quickly he made his way to the elevator, down to the basement, and to his car. There was no sign of the man with one arm.

He drove to his office, constantly checking the rear-view mirror for a gray SUV. Seeing nothing alarming, he pulled into the parking lot of his building.

Marty Green did not need to follow Zach to his office. The GPS tracker he had placed on Zach's car told him exactly the right location. While driving, he called Phoenix.

"Looks like he's heading to his office."

"If he's smart, he's looking for Peterman's old eye chart. Did you find the other copy in Brannigan's office?" asked Phoenix.

"Yeah. I burned it."

"Good. Now, for the original in Webster's office, let him find it before you kill him. That way, we get rid of the chart and the doctor all at once. Just do it quietly."

"Should I somehow erase Doctor Brannigan's email with his own findings from Webster's computer?"

"You don't need to. That's the exam we're going with. Plus, it's out there in cyberspace so it would be almost impossible to erase. Once we get rid of Peterman's old eye records, we're okay."

"Gotcha. Will do."

Marty arrived at the office parking lot about five minutes after Zach arrived and attached the silencer to his gun, which he placed in his jacket pocket.

CHAPTER 24

ZACH'S OFFICE WAS on the third floor of a four-story office building. The first and second floors included a pharmacy, a home title company, an attorney's office, and a dental office. He shared his floor with a physical therapy practice and a computer repair company. Walking up the stairs, he could tell all the offices were closed. After all, it was Christmas Eve. All was quiet, until he reached his floor. Coming from up above, he could hear people singing. He remembered part of the fourth floor was rented out as an event space. It seemed odd that people were partying on Christmas Eve rather than at home with their families, but as Zach thought about it, not everyone had a family to share the holiday with, including himself.

The stairways were lit, but the hallways were dark, illuminated only by a slight bit of daylight peeking through the windows. Upon arriving at his office, all was completely dark, and Zach felt his way to the reception area.

Veronica's reception desk was about twenty feet from the front door, with the waiting room between them. A glass partition rose above the desk, with a wall to either side, and an open entrance to the reception area located on the left side.

Zach slowly made his way to the reception entrance and turned on the master light switch, illuminating the entire office. Turning on her computer, he found the email from Andy Brannigan.

He began his search for Francis Peterman's old chart at Veronica's desk. No luck. Next stop was the back closet, thinking she might have refiled it. Again, no sign of it. He looked on his desk. Maybe she had put it back there. Still no. Swearing loudly, he went back to Veronica's desk and opened all the drawers. Finally, in the last cabinet, there it was.

With a sigh of relief, Zach grabbed Peterman's old records. He then went back to his desk and turned on the computer, where he printed Andy's email and accompanying attachment detailing Peterman's recent exam. After combining the pages with his own chart, he heard a door slowly opening. His heart rate immediately quickened.

He didn't wait to see who was opening the door, instead hitting the master light switch. All went dark. He crouched low, hiding under the desk, trying not to make a sound.

Marty turned on his flashlight and swung it slowly, side to side, gun still in his pocket. He shined the light through the glass partition, seeing only the back wall of the reception area. Standing in its entrance, he directed the flashlight around towards Veronica's desk, but Zach was too well-hidden to be seen. To the left of the reception area was the corridor that led to the rest of the office. Marty pointed his flashlight in that direction but saw no one.

Down the corridor were three examination rooms, built by the previous tenant, all with separate entrances to the hallway. Each room also had a door halfway along on the side, allowing entrance from one room to the next. As Zach was not busy enough to need them all, he had turned the last one into a small kitchen.

Marty proceeded down the hallway, shining his flashlight unsuccessfully into all the rooms. Zach could have used this time to make his way through the waiting room to the door, but he was too frozen with fear. By the time his nerve returned, his pursuer had returned to the waiting area.

"I know you're here, Doc," said Marty, looking around for the light switch. "All I want is that chart, President Peterman's chart, and I'll leave you alone."

Zach had seen too many movies to believe him. He remained silent, still hidden.

"I'm going to search this place up and down, Doc, and I'll find you. Be a good boy and show yourself. No harm will come to you if you come out."

Marty walked into the front office, next to Veronica's desk, only a few feet from Zach. Realizing he was about to be discovered, Zach jumped up and hit the master light switch, totally illuminating the area with bright fluorescent lights. The sudden brightness temporarily blinded Marty, and Zach took his chance to run.

Instead of running to the front door, he ran down the examination corridor, with his sights on a back entrance leading to the ground floor.

Marty regained his sight in time to pull out his gun and direct a shot just missing Zach's shoulder, striking the back door. Zach knew a second shot might not miss, and he quickly ducked into the first exam room on his right.

Immediately, he remembered that the exam room did not have a lock. Why would it? Frantic, he pushed the heavy exam chair against the door, blocking the way.

Marty pushed against the door. Slowly it opened just a crack, then a little more. Zach could now see his face, and he recognized it as the man from the car chase.

Knowing he had almost no time left, he raced through the door between the exam rooms to the second room, where again he barricaded the side door and the hallway door with heavy medical equipment.

Marty had seen enough to know Zach had escaped into the second room, and he was now at the side door, trying to push it open. Again,

Zach knew he had limited time. If only he had his phone, but he had left it in his car.

Then he remembered; there were locks on the doors to the kitchen. Veronica complained that the cleaners who came at night might have stolen some food she left in the refrigerator, so he put locks on the doors to placate her. Many evenings, though, he forgot to lock them. Hopefully, this would be one of those times.

Zach tried the side door to the kitchen, and it opened, while Marty was still trying to make his way into the second exam room. Zach locked both doors, but he knew it wouldn't last forever. If only he had his phone, he could call for help.

Frantic, he opened all the drawers in the kitchen cabinet, looking for something, anything. Then he spotted it. Matches. They must have been Veronica's, the time he caught her smoking in here.

Quickly, he tried to light a match. It went out. He tried another. Same thing. A third lasted longer, but not much. Hands shaking, he lit a fourth. This one remained lit. Standing on a chair, he held it directly under a smoke detector. A loud, piercing alarm followed, sounding throughout the building.

Marty didn't know what to do. Having broken into the second exam room, he was working on breaking down the door to the kitchen when the alarm went off. It would take some time before any firefighters would reach the building, so he'd probably have time to finish his job before they'd arrive. It would be best, though, to turn off the lights.

Marty went back up the hallway to the reception area to find the main light switch, when there was pounding on the door. Deciding he better answer it rather than risking an early firefighter breaking their way in, he opened the door.

It was none other than Santa Claus, or at least several people in Santa Claus costumes.

"Yes, can I help you?" said Marty.

"There's a fire alarm. Ruined our Santa Claus party upstairs. I saw your lights on. You must get out," said a large, slightly intoxicated Kris Kringle, slurring his words, his hat askew on his head.

"Oh, it's probably just a false alarm."

"False or not, you can't take the chance. We've got to evacuate until the firemen arrive and tell us it's safe to go back," said another who appeared more sober.

"No. I'm fine here. You better go, though."

The first Santa put his big arm around Marty's shoulder. "You've got to come. Santa doesn't leave anyone behind."

Marty had no choice. To brandish his gun or resist in some manner would create a scene, something his boss would not tolerate. He allowed himself to be pulled out with the other Santas, and he found himself on the street.

Zach, having heard the commotion, opened the door from the kitchen. He was about to run out through the back door, when he suddenly stopped, turned back to Veronica's desk, and grabbed Peterman's chart. He then fled down the hallway to the back door. Once out, he saw what looked like fifty people dressed as Santa standing in the parking lot.

As he raced to his car, he spotted the one-armed man. Marty Green saw him, but there was nothing he could do in front of so many witnesses.

Zach sped back to his apartment, where he locked the doors and double-checked the windows again. Pacing around the room, he pondered his next step. He would try the police again.

As before, it was Sergeant Canto who answered the phone.

"Sargeant Canto, it's me, Dr. Zach Webster, the guy who called you yesterday."

"Oh, you again. What is it this time? The one-armed guy again?"

"Yes, he tried to kill me again today. He shot at me but missed."

"Where did it happen?"

"In my office. I was there to retrieve a chart he wanted."

"Why did he want the chart? Was it his?"

"No, it was President Peterman's. I think there's some conspiracy going on, all related to the President's eye exam. Doctor Andy Brannigan was killed, and now they're after me. I'm only safe because a bunch of Santas came to my rescue."

There was a prolonged silence on the line before Canto spoke.

"Look, buddy. I don't know how much you've been drinking or what drugs you're on. Why are you wasting my time? I'm stuck here when I should be home with my wife and kids on Christmas Eve, and I've got the duty again tomorrow on Christmas. Instead of eating a turkey dinner, you're feeding me this bullshit about a conspiracy involving the President and being rescued by Santa. Sober up, and if you want to make more out of it, come by the station tomorrow and fill out an incident report."

With that, Canto hung up. Zach sat down, unsure what to do. He read through Francis Peterman's old records again. There was no way Andy could have missed those findings.

It was clear to Zach now that he was on his own. The police were not going to help, at least not until he himself was a victim. Again, he looked at the cabinet that used to hold his booze, longingly. Even if there was anything left, which there wasn't, this was no time for getting drunk, and he was not going to look for a liquor store open on Christmas Eve. He needed a plan. The only thing he could come up with was Rose Goodwin's funeral.

CHAPTER 25

THE ALARM on his phone buzzed incessantly until Joey finally turned it off. He still felt hungover from the previous evening's binge, but he knew he had no choice other than to start the day. After splashing some water on his face, he got dressed in the ragged, distressed-looking clothes that had arrived with the Sunday evening package.

Forgetting he looked like one of the homeless living on the street outside the hotel, he took the elevator down to the Starbucks in the lobby. The barista looked him up and down, but then reluctantly made him a large cappuccino. Adding a large muffin to his order, he then returned to his room to eat breakfast.

After finishing the muffin in less than a minute, he reviewed his directions.

"Subject will be brought to the medical clinic at 8:30 am, where a secret service agent will escort her up to her office. The agent will wait in the reception area during patient hours, as she does not let him into the exam rooms. You have an appointment at 9:30 under the name of Harry Beltone for a new cough and sore throat. Your gun has a silencer attached. With all the noise from the other rooms, no one will hear the gunshot. Leave quickly, through the waiting room, and take the stairs down to the first floor. Don't worry about the secret service agent as he works for us. There will be a car by the back door of the lobby that will take you to the airport, where you have a 1:30 pm flight from San Diego back to DC. Once there, go straight back to the Mayflower Hotel and await further instructions.

Sarah and Jefferson lived in a small, nondescript house, in an area accurately called North Park, being just north of Balboa Park in San Diego. Nothing about it indicated that the President's daughter lived there, other than the occasional secret service agent standing in front. To Sarah, it was the best place to live in downtown San Diego, close to restaurants and shops, but still a real neighborhood where you knew your neighbor. It was the rare person who knew she was the President's daughter. She was just Doctor Sarah to everyone.

May was the prettiest month of the year in North Park, as the Jacaranda trees lining the streets began to bloom with bright, purple flowers. Today, the trees were barren. The temperature was only forty-six degrees, the sky was cloudy, and there was a chance of rain later in the day.

Sarah had to get her son, Jefferson, dressed, fed, and ready for a drop-off at her friend's house. The Secret Service was to pick her up at 7:45 am sharp in front of her house, to take her to work. Even though it was Christmas Eve, she still had patients to see.

An agent was already stationed in front of the house, waiting. The whole Secret Service thing was a real nuisance, but she understood its necessity.

Jefferson was in a really challenging mood, dawdling and complaining about everything.

"Mom, I don't want to go to Aunt Jessica's house today. I want to stay with you."

"I'm sorry, Jefferson, but mommy has patients to see. I thought you liked spending time with Aunt Jessica."

"I like her, but I want you to stay home and be with me."

"Like I said, I can't today, honey. But tomorrow is Christmas, and I'll be with you all day. But you need to get ready to go, so please get dressed."

"How about Dad? Is he coming home? Is he going to be here for Christmas?"

Sarah bent down to talk to her son at eye level. "Remember, he doesn't live here anymore. And I don't think he's coming for Christmas. I'm sorry."

Jefferson ran back down the hallway to his room and slammed the door shut.

"Jefferson, please open the door."

The door remained shut.

"Jefferson, I know you're upset. We'll talk about this more tonight, but you need to get dressed now. Please move along. I can't be late."

Sarah walked back to the kitchen and took a long, slow sip from her coffee. Holding back tears, she slammed her cup down on the table. How could Morgan, her ex, have done this to Jefferson? It was one thing to leave her, but another to abandon their son.

She cleaned up the spilled coffee and looked at her watch. At that moment, Jeff returned, fully dressed.

They finished breakfast quickly, Jefferson with Fruit Loops, as she had temporarily given up trying to get him to eat healthier varieties, while she downed a bowl of Special K.

The car came right on time at 7:45 am, and the driver, a new agent called Walter, got out and stood beside it, waiting for them to come out of the house.

Sarah had just met Walter the day before. She preferred her former agent, who had been with her for almost a year. She was not given any explanation as to why he had been withdrawn.

This new guy seemed a bit full of himself. Sarah could see him admiring himself in the side view mirror while showing off his muscles to passing women out front.

Once in the car, Walter dropped off Jefferson first. He then drove Sarah to her medical office on Pleasant Street in Chula Vista, parked the car out back, and together, they took the elevator to her floor. He took a seat in the waiting room, appearing to read his phone, while Sarah continued to the clinical area.

She went about her business, seeing a variety of patients that morning. Mrs. Eggleston had a rash. Mr. Gonzalez was constipated. Eduardo Diego had diarrhea. It was all basic stuff, and she longed for something more dramatic.

Joey Petrone walked up to the reception desk at 9:20 am and was told to sit down and wait. Finally, at 9:40, he was escorted to an exam room by a nurse, who asked him a few questions about his health and medications. She saw the notes about recovering drug addiction but didn't feel it was her job to ask about his rehabilitation. "That's for the doctor to do," she reasoned.

The nurse left the room, leaving Joey to go over the instructions in his head, which didn't take long. He looked around the sterile room. White cabinets with a sink, some gauze pads on the counter, tissues in a tissue box. It was all very white and sterile.

Finally, at 9:50 am, Sarah Peterman knocked on the door, entered, and smiled at Joey. "Hi, Mr. Beltone. I'm Dr. Peterman. What can I do for you today?"

CHAPTER 26

JOEY DIDN'T SAY a thing. Instead, he pulled out the gun from his coat pocket and pointed it at Sarah's chest. Instead of shooting her right off, he hesitated. It was just enough time to allow Sarah to grab the metal tissue box and bring it down on Joey's gun, knocking both items to the floor with a loud bang.

Sarah screamed, "Help," and Joey, confused, ran out of the exam room. By that time, Walter McCoy, who was now by the door to the clinical area, stood blocking Joey's escape route through the waiting room. In the confusion, he forgot he had been told that the Secret Service agent was on Phoenix's payroll.

So instead, Joey ran through the back hallway and down a set of rear stairs. Walter McCoy followed, but he was too late to intercept Joey and thus unable to perform his given task. Bursting through the first-floor lobby, Joey ran to the back door, looking for the waiting car. The only transport he could see was a kid's bike near the door, so he grabbed it and started riding off through a back alley behind the building.

Walter ran down the stairs, but there was no sign of Joey. For a big man, Joey could move quickly. Walter thought for a moment and dropped the things he was to put in Joey's pocket down the stairs: a few pills and some old needles. He then proceeded to run back upstairs, where he called in the attempt on Sarah's life to his superiors at the Secret Service. Following that, he made a second call, this one to Phoenix.

Sarah was shaken. Nothing like this had ever happened to her. Yes, she had lived in cities where violent crimes were committed. She had seen them reported on TV and the newsfeed on her phone but had never seen one up-close. Certainly, she had never been the victim of one.

Sarah spent the next half hour in the small break room, where her coworkers made her a cup of tea. Her hands were shaking so badly the tea spilled out of her mug as she brought it to her lips, staining her white coat.

After about ten minutes, her hands stopped trembling, and she was able to regain her composure.

"Thank-you for the tea," she said, and smiled to the anxious staff huddled around her, to show she was alright.

"Are you okay?" asked her nurse, who was still pale as porcelain.

"Of course I'm not okay. I spilled tea on my white coat, and I'll need to get it cleaned."

The nurse's anxious look slowly returned to a smile, and she shook her head. "You're one tough lady, Sarah."

"Wish I was. Okay. I guess my break has ended and I need to get back to the patients."

The office administrator looked at her quizzically. "I would think you'd want to go home after something like that. I'm sure the other doctors would cover for you."

"No. I can do it. It'll keep me busy. Otherwise, I'll just keep playing it back in my head.

"Okay. Who's my next patient?"

"I don't believe how calm you are."

"Maybe on the outside. Inside I'm still shaking."

CHAPTER 27

HANDS WHITE FROM gripping the handlebars, Joey rode the kids' bike between buildings in Chula Vista, all three hundred pounds of him. Down an alley, the bike finally gave way, and Joey landed awkwardly in the mud. Picking himself up, he started running, though in no specific direction.

Finding another bike, this time an adult one, he stopped running and took time to catch his breath. His heart was beating what seemed like a million times a minute. He knew he wouldn't be able to hail a cab or summon an Uber, as he'd be caught for sure. Pulling out his phone, he found a bike path that would take him to the airport. His breath a little easier now and his heart beating slower, he mounted the bike and headed off for the airport. He knew he had to make his flight and await further instructions. Phoenix would know what to do.

Muddy, tired, and sweating profusely, Joey made his way to Harbor Drive, adjacent to the airport. It had started to rain, he was drenched, and it was hard to see where the sweat stopped and the rainwater began on Joey's oversized body. Ditching the bike, he walked quickly to the airport, at least as quickly as a 300-pound, exhausted, soaking-wet man could. It was already 12:30 pm. Once inside the terminal, dripping wet, he realized he had no idea which airline he was supposed to take. Fortunately, he did not see any police.

Joey was not able to contact Phoenix, as communication always went one-way, from Phoenix to him. Finally, as he had taken an American Airlines flight to San Diego, he walked up to the AA check-in desk and asked if they had a 1:30 pm flight to DC. After being told they did not, he asked them to look for other airlines that might have that flight. He was then informed that there were no 1:30 pm flights to DC on any of the airlines. The earliest was a 2:00 flight changing in Chicago, arriving late at night at Reagan National Airport in DC. Pulling out a wad of cash from his pocket, Joey paid for the ticket and waited nervously for his plane to take off. Other passengers in the waiting area gave Joey plenty of space. His appearance and temperament were enough to ward off even the least observant, and fortunately, no police arrived.

Joey arrived late, around 1:00 am. He was exhausted, hungry, and scared. Unable to sleep on the plane, he was worried about Phoenix's response. What would he do, knowing that Joey had messed-up?

He took an Uber back to the Mayflower Hotel. Lights in the lobby were dimmed, and there was no one in sight. He rang a small bell on the counter of the check-in desk, and a tired-looking young man emerged.

"I'm Joey Petrone. There's supposed to be a room reserved for me."

The clerk looked at him with surprise. Between his ragged clothes and his unkempt appearance, he did not look like the typical Mayflower Hotel guest. Turning his attention back to his computer, he spent the next few minutes pulling up multiple screens. Finally, with a yawn, he looked up.

"We have no reservation for you here. We do have some rooms available, though, so I could set you up."

This was not what Joey wanted to hear. Even to someone not mentally gifted like Joey, it was clear that Phoenix had not expected him to return. A chill ran through his body, and he just stood there quietly, without speaking, trying to figure out what to do.

"Sir, would you like me to get you a room?" asked the clerk, who was now looking at Joey suspiciously.

In that second, Joey realized that the last place he should spend the night was the Mayflower Hotel. He needed time to think. Phoenix did not tolerate mistakes.

"No, I think I'll be staying somewhere else."

Joey left the hotel lobby, passing by a mirror near the door. Seeing his appearance and realizing he had a suitcase in the storeroom with better clothes, he came right back in. The clerk reluctantly found it for him before heading back to his office for another nap.

Joey went back outside and was hoping to arrange for an Uber at this late hour, but fortunately, a cab arrived right next to him, dropping off another late arrival.

"I need you to take me to another hotel, somewhere away from here," Joey muttered to the cabbie.

"Which one?"

"Uhm, somewhere out of DC."

"Would you like to be a little more specific? It's late and I need to get home. It's Christmas."

"Uhm, I don't know."

"Okay, pal. How about I take you to Crystal City, Virginia? It's right over the DC line and there's lots of hotels. I live nearby so I can go right home after I drop you off."

"Okay, sure. Any of those hotels, but we need to go now."

"Do you have money for the ride?"

"What do you think?" said Joey, flashing a wad of bills.

Joey got into the back seat, and the cab took off. They arrived at the

Marriott Hotel in Crystal City, where Joey reserved a room and went straight to bed. He'd figure out what to do in the morning. It had been a long day.

CHAPTER 28

"IT'S CHRISTMAS, wake up!" shouted Jefferson, jumping on her bed.

Sleepily, Sarah got up, put on her robe, and walked slowly down the steps to the living room, where the wrapped presents were waiting.

"Hurry up," shouted Jefferson.

"Keep your shirt on, I'm still half-asleep," replied Sarah, with a loud yawn.

They made their way to the large tree, which was twinkling with little white lights. The room was decked out with handmade paper garlands of angels, from one wall to the other. Jefferson turned on the singing, dancing, five-foot blow-up Santa Claus in the corner. It started belting out, "Have a holly, jolly, Christmas."

"Please turn that thing off. It's way too early," moaned Sarah, and Jefferson turned it off.

"I just need a cup of coffee before we get started," said Sarah, as she headed into the kitchen. A few minutes later, she was now more awake, with a smile fixed upon her face.

Sarah was still very distressed about the events of the prior day. She had done her best to keep her emotions in check at home, not wanting to show fear in front of Jefferson. Still, it was a battle. The police had wanted to interview her again about the attempt on her life, but

Sarah put them off. She agreed to meet with them the following day. Christmas belonged to Jefferson.

Sarah started handing Jefferson his presents, which were stacked neatly under the tree. Perhaps there were too many presents, Sarah thought guiltily, but he seemed to enjoy them all. She then went back to the kitchen to prepare his favorite breakfast, pancakes with chocolate chips, while Jefferson played with his new toys in the living room.

Along with the pancakes, Sarah placed a glass of milk on the table and added one more touch, a 6-inch-tall chocolate Santa Claus. Jefferson's eyes lit up on approaching the table, and he headed first for the chocolate Santa. On any other day, chocolate for breakfast would not be allowed, but she wanted to make this day special. This was Jefferson's first Christmas without his dad being present.

She had already told her son that his dad was not going to be home for Christmas, but she knew it would still be on Jefferson's mind. That asshole could at least have left a present for him.

Thinking back, she thought they had a good marriage. Yes, she sometimes worked long hours at the Clinic, but she thought Morgan understood. She believed him when he said he had to work late at the office. She didn't know that Morgan's administrative assistant "worked" those long evenings with him.

She might someday forgive Morgan for betraying her trust, but she would never forgive him for betraying their son. Sarah was not a violent person, but if there was anyone she could kill, it was Morgan.

Fortunately, Jefferson did not bring up his father's absence or the lack of any presents from him. He was too busy playing with all his new toys on Christmas Day.

Sarah wondered why her father had not called her after the attempt on her life. Now it was Christmas morning, and still no call. He always called on Christmas if he couldn't be there in person, even if he was busy. She knew he must be busy with his duties as President, but still it was unusual.

Sarah decided to call him. She dialed his private cell phone number, but there was no answer. She left a message to call, but he never did.

CHAPTER 29

ALREADY ANXIOUS by the attack on her life, Sarah was worried when, on awakening, Jefferson was not already up. He was usually awake by 7:00, and here it was 8:00. She walked quietly into his room so as not to wake him, and she was relieved to see him still peacefully asleep. He had been up late the evening before, probably from all the chocolate.

She then went downstairs to pour herself a cup of coffee and read the newspaper. On the front page of the San Diego Union-Tribune, staring straight at her, was a half-page picture of herself. It was accompanied by an article describing her near-death experience at the clinic.

The article described her attacker as a drug addict, who was looking for more drugs. To Sarah, this just didn't make sense. She had taken care of drug addicts in the past, and no one had acted anything like this before. In fact, he had never even demanded any drugs from her. Because of her status as the President's daughter, she was sure the article would be picked up by newspapers throughout the country. She was convinced that her father, alarmed at seeing this, would certainly call her. But still, nothing.

In addition, she saw with horror, an article on the death of her father's administrative assistant, Rose Goodwin, in a car fire. She had always liked Rose. Yes, she could be abrupt, but she had a good sense of humor and was incredibly loyal to her father. Maybe that was why her father had not been in touch.

Sarah took the newspaper and hid it in her sewing basket. Jefferson was not to know anything about the attack.

She had arranged to meet with the police at 1:00 pm to go over the details of the attack. A blond, petite 15-year-old girl, Jasmine Marone, came over to the house at 12:30 to babysit. Jasmine lived across the street and was frequently called upon to babysit. Sarah liked her because she was outgoing and perky. Jefferson liked her because she let him do anything he wanted, which included watching TV shows his mother would never allow. Not taking any chances since the attack, Sarah had arranged for an additional secret service agent to be stationed outside the house while she went to the police station.

Once Sarah left, Jefferson took the TV remote and found old episodes of "Teenage Mutant Turtles" to watch. Jasmine spent most of her time on the phone.

Sarah was accompanied by Secret Service Agent McCoy. On arrival, they were quickly ushered into the police chief's office. After the initial greetings, the chief got right to it.

"It certainly looks like a typical drug addict interaction. You're not the first physician to be accosted in the hunt for narcotics. You were very brave."

"I really don't think it was for drugs. He never even asked for them," remarked Sarah.

"No. It must have been drug related. The guy was listed as a drug addict in your chart, and we found some of his paraphernalia on the stairs: syringes, pills, you name it," replied the chief.

"I agree with the police, Sarah. He was a druggie, and you're lucky you escaped," said McCoy.

Sarah shook her head. "I've had many patients with drug problems, and this is not how they've acted."

"I have no reason to think it's anything more than a drug-related incident," repeated the police chief.

After another hour of fruitless questioning, Sarah was finally allowed to leave. Agent McCoy asked if he should stay at the house, but she told him he could leave and that she was fine.

Sarah checked her cell phone for the umpteenth time for a message from her father, but there was nothing. She tried again to reach him on his phone, but there was no answer. Her next call was to Robert Benton, her father's Chief of Staff, who she had known for many years.

On the fourth ring, Bob Benton picked up the phone.

"Hi Bob, it's Sarah Peterman. I've been trying to reach my dad, but he hasn't picked up. Could you give him a message to call me as soon as he can?"

There was silence on the line for about five seconds.

"Bob, are you there? It's me, Sarah."

"Yes, Sarah. Sorry. How are you? I read about your altercation in the paper this morning. You were very brave."

"It was just instinct, and I got lucky. How's my dad?"

"I don't really know," replied Bob Benton. "He's replaced me as Chief of Staff, so I don't have access to him."

"I can't believe that," said Sarah. "He's always held you in such high regard."

"I didn't believe it either, but it is what it is."

"I heard about Rose."

"Yeah, terrible. Her car caught fire and exploded, with her in it. She's gone."

"I'm so sorry."

"Yeah, it's been a terrible week. If you want to reach your father, I understand he has a new administrative assistant, named Judy. I don't know her last name, but I do have her phone number, so I'll text it to you. His new Chief of Staff is a guy named Brodsky, who came over from the CIA. I don't know anything about him. I didn't know your father knew him either, but he must have, if he made him his new Chief of Staff."

"I'm sorry you lost your job, Bob. I'll talk to my dad about it when I can get through to him."

"Thanks, Sarah. Good to talk to you." Bob Benton hung up.

Sarah stood there for a minute with the phone in her hand, not sure what to do next. Then, the text from Bob Benton came through with the new administrative assistant's phone number. Sarah dialed the number and was relieved when a pleasant voice on the phone responded, "Judy Mairston, Office of the President."

"Hi. I'm Sarah Peterman. My dad is the President. Is he there so I can talk to him?"

"I'm not allowed to bother the President with phone calls unless I can be certain of your true identity."

"I understand that, but could you please give him a message to call his daughter?"

"I'll give him the message," and she hung up.

CHAPTER 30

ZACH WAS ABLE to find the location of Rose Goodwin's funeral online. It was to be at 9:00 am at the Rock Creek Cemetery in DC. He wasn't sure why he was going or what his plan would be, but somehow, he knew he should go. If the President was there, maybe he could get a message to him. After all, Francis Peterman and his father had been good friends, and he had seen the President professionally. Zach needed to clear up the eye exam mystery, and most of all, he needed help and didn't know where to turn.

How to get there? It was too far to walk. The cemetery was about an hour away. His car, parked in the basement, might be watched, so that was out too. He came up with another option, his bike. If he could take it down the back stairs to the rear door, perhaps it would go unnoticed.

Zach gave Ripley a quick pet and apology and headed out without incident. Constantly looking over his shoulder for a pursuer, he made it to the cemetery in twenty-two minutes.

Zach had been to funerals before. His mother's was a small affair with only immediate family and a limited number of friends. Rose Goodwin's funeral was a large event, with speakers broadcasting the service to the crowd, who were kept behind ropes, far from the actual service. Keeping them away from the ropes was a large contingent of police, and behind them were men in suits, with wires hanging down from their earpieces.

Zach reasoned that the men in suits were secret service, and that the small group clustered around a distant cemetery plot were family and VIPs, and presumably, the President.

Zach made his way around the cemetery grounds, often turning around to look over his shoulder, until he was at the far edge of the roped area. No police were there, so he crossed beneath the rope. Almost immediately, he was stopped by a large man in a suit.

"Can I help you?"

"Are you Secret Service?"

The man nodded, "Yes."

"Would it be possible to get a message to the President?"

"Sorry, no."

"He and my dad are friends, and I was his eye doctor."

"I'm happy for you. The answer is still no."

"But this is important. I think there's something going on involving the President. He could be in danger, and someone is after me, too."

"Go to the police."

"I tried, but they don't believe me. I don't know what else to do. I wrote out a letter explaining everything I know. Could you give it to him?"

"I don't have immediate access to the President. Used to, but not anymore. But if you have something, I'll see if I can send it along to someone who does."

"Here. Please get it to him as soon as you can. My life's in danger."

The Secret Service agent looked at Zach, studying his face. He believed himself to be a pretty good judge of character, and what he saw in Zach was someone who looked and sounded believable.

"Okay. Give it to me, and I'll see what I can do. If you're telling the truth and you find out something more, call me. Here's my card."

The card simply read, *Ray Lincoln, Secret Service*, and listed his phone number below.

Realizing there was nothing more he could do, Zach moved back. He would have liked to stay for the entire service, but anxious about possibly being followed, he found his bike and headed back.

Ray read the letter, but it didn't make a whole lot of sense to him. The President's eye exam was different. So what? Then there was all this stuff about the doctor who did his exam killed in a hit and run accident. That does happen. DC is a big city, and not necessarily a safe city. As for the writer of the letter being chased and hunted down by a one-armed assailant, who knew if it was real or just an overactive imagination?

It was concerning enough that he passed it on to Director Allen, who walked it back to the President. Staples was standing near the casket, next to Rose Goodwin's daughter, and flanked on the other side by Jonathan Brodsky.

"Mr. President, I have a letter here by a guy who says he was your eye doctor back in New Hampshire. His name's Zachariah Webster."

Before Allen could give it to the President, Brodsky grabbed the note.

With Staples reading over his shoulder, Brodsky forced a laugh. "The writings of a crazy person," and he ripped it up.

Director Allen looked at him quizzically. "Shouldn't we at least follow-up on this?"

"I'll take care of it. Go back to protecting the President. Keep these crazies away."

Standing next to him, the President nodded in agreement.

Allen backed off, but he was not happy. He had already dealt with his agents complaining they had to work overtime, and now here he was being undermined by this Chief of Staff asshole. It should be his job to investigate, but what could he do? He would do what he was told.

Back in the White House after the funeral, Chief of Staff Brodsky dialed the number he was to call in an emergency. Phoenix answered.

"What is it Brodsky?"

"That damn eye doctor, Webster. He's got eye records that could louse things up for us."

"I know that."

"He was here at the funeral trying to get a message to the President about it. He could cause trouble if his information falls in the wrong hands."

"He's become more trouble than I expected, but I'll deal with it."

"I want something done about it immediately."

"Who the fuck do you think you are, Brodsky, giving me orders? Remember, you work for me, not the other way around. Got it?"

Jonathan Brodsky was not about to challenge Phoenix.

"Sorry. But I think something should be done about it sooner rather than later."

"I told you. I'll deal with it."

After hanging up, he immediately called Marty Green.

"Marty, where are you on tracking that idiot, Joey Petrone?"

"Don't have him yet, but I will."

"As soon as you do, let me know. If the cops get him, it could really screw things up. Work on that, but also get the records from the doc. Break into his apartment if you need to."

"Do you still want him dealt with? The doc, I mean."

"What do you think?"

"Got it. He won't be hard to find. I've got a tracker on his car if he tries to run."

"No fuckups again, understand?"

"Understood."

CHAPTER 31

"HELLO," said a sleepy voice.

"Hi, Dad. It's me, Zach."

"Of course it is. Don't you think I recognize your voice? And it's 6 am," he said grumpily.

Zach knew well enough to avoid an argument.

"Dad, can I stay with you for a little while?"

There was a brief silence on the phone before Robert Webster responded in a much friendlier voice. "Of course, you can stay with me as long as you like. But you're not on the booze again, are you?"

Zach took his time answering. "No, Dad. I'm sober, but I'm in trouble and I need to get out of DC as soon as I can."

"Did you break the law or something?"

"No. I haven't done anything wrong. I'll tell you when I see you."

"Okay. Come anytime, but do you remember how to get to the house? You haven't been here in a long time."

Of course, Zach knew where to go. He had grown up there and his parents had never moved. He stifled a sarcastic retort.

"Thanks, Dad. See you soon," and hung up.

The next question was how to get the car from the garage. The one-armed guy could be waiting there to attack him. He could try to get the super from the building to get it for him, but that could put him in danger. Finally, he came up with another idea.

Searching in his closet, he pulled out a large container with clothes. Why he still had it, he didn't know. They were his mother's final things from when she was in the hospital. He had taken it from his father's house to bring to Goodwill, but he never had the heart to part with them. It was still a connection to her.

He reached into the container and pulled out a wig, the wig she had used to cover up her loss of hair after chemo. He then pulled out a pink dressing gown and robe, along with fuzzy, blue slippers. After applying the wig and dressing himself in his mother's attire, he packed a small suitcase with his own clothes.

Zach turned to Ripley, who was looking at him curiously. Ripley knew a suitcase meant a trip somewhere.

"Don't worry, Rip. I'm taking you. We're going to Grandpa's. You'll like him; he likes dogs. The guy who's looking for me might recognize you, so once I get the car, I'll come back for you. Okay? I'll put your leash on now."

Ripley wagged his tail. Zach took it as a sign that he understood, but then again, Ripley wagged his tail over almost anything Zach said to him.

Zach took the elevator down to the basement car park. Fortunately, it was early enough that no one joined him in the elevator.

Zach wrapped the robe tight around him and pulled the collar up to cover the lower half of his face. Looking all around, he saw no sign of the one-armed man, and quickly he made his way to the car.

Zach started the engine, used his remote to open the garage, and made his way to the back door of the building. Again, he saw no one. Running up the stairs, he unlocked his door and grabbed Ripley by the leash. They were almost out the door before he realized there was something else he should take. Turning back, he grabbed Francis Peterman's old eye records, and then headed back downstairs to the car.

The roads were clear, and there was no sign of the gray SUV. It took them nine and a half hours to drive to Zach's father's house in Hopkinton, New Hampshire, stopping only briefly for gas, coffee, and bathroom breaks. The weather held, and it was an easy drive aside from fatigue, relieved through the multiple cups of coffee.

Arriving at the family house, Zach turned into the driveway where he used to play basketball. The hoop was still there, but the net was totally gone. Snow covered up the lawn that his father took so much pride in maintaining. The house looked just the same as he remembered, blue aluminum siding with white trim around the windows.

Zach's first thought as he approached the door was whether to ring the doorbell or just go in. It had been a long time, and he wasn't sure how his dad would respond. Would there even be anything to talk about? Taking a deep breath, Zach opened the door, not knowing what to expect.

Just inside the door was his father, who met him with a huge bear hug, tears streaming down his face. Zach's own eyes became misty, and they both quickly wiped away the tears as they broke apart.

Ripley came between them and jumped up on Robert. Looking concerned, Zach yelled at Ripley to get down.

"Don't worry about it, son. Remember, we had dogs for years while you were growing up. What's his name?"

"Ripley."

"Well, hi Ripley. Let's get you something to eat."

"I've got dog food in the car, Dad."

"Oh, he looks hungry. I'll make him a burger."

Zach had no desire to start his home-coming by arguing with his dad over Ripley's food, although he was a firm believer in not feeding dogs "people-food."

"How about you? Do you want a burger?"

"Sounds good. What can I do to help?"

"Just relax and put your things in your old room. That's where you'll be staying."

"OK." Zach went back to the car and grabbed his suitcase, along with Ripley's gear and dog food. Coming back into the house, he walked up the steps in the front hallway to his old room.

It looked just the same as he remembered. Even the sports posters he had put up in high school were still there, looking down at him. Trophies from his running competitions were perched on top of the dresser. There was a picture of him breaking through the tape first, cheered on by both his mom and dad.

"Burgers ready," came the call from downstairs.

"On my way." Zach headed back down to the combined living, dining, and TV room. Maybe there was a little more dust on top of the furniture, but otherwise things were just the same as the last time he had been there. A few of his trophies had made their way downstairs to sit on top of the old TV.

The room was devoid of anything to denote the holiday. There was no Christmas tree, no lights, and no Christmas cards hung up on the mantel. This would not have been the case if his mother was still alive. She loved all holidays and decorated to the hilt. Her favorite was Halloween, and the house would be draped in spiderwebs, talking skulls would greet trick or treaters at the door, and scary music would be blaring through the windows. She loved seeing the kids smile.

Dinner was served, and Ripley was the first to finish his burger. He then lay under the table, hoping for crumbs. When Robert quietly dropped part of his meal off the table for Ripley, Zach pretended not to notice.

After finishing, Robert Webster looked at his son, and finally asked, "OK, so what's going on?"

"I really don't know, Dad. First, I took Ripley out one day, and there was this guy standing by the door watching me. Then, there was this gray car that followed me to Samantha's house and followed me when I drove back. Then..."

"You went to Samantha's house?" his dad broke in. "Are you back together?"

"No, not even close. I just went there to drop off presents to Liam and Em. Can I continue?"

"Sure, but how are my grandchildren? I haven't seen them since you two broke up."

"I'll tell you all about them, but first, can I continue?"

"OK, go ahead."

"So, I stopped at a red light, and this guy gets out of the car, a gray SUV, and he looks like he's about to shoot me."

"Did he have a gun in his hand?"

"I think so, but I didn't wait around to check. I went through the red light and lost him."

"What did you do then?"

"Drove back to my apartment building."

"You live in an apartment? I thought you lived in a house."

"Dad, please, let me continue, and yes, I live in an apartment in DC."

"OK, keep going. Don't let me stop you."

Zach took a deep breath and continued. "So, I get to the garage which is down below the apartments, and Ripley and I run out and take the elevator to my apartment, where I called the police."

"So, what did they say?"

"I'm not sure they believed me, especially after I told the cop that the guy who was going to shoot me only had one arm."

"Like the TV show, 'The Fugitive'?"

"Yes, like 'The Fugitive.'"

"I liked that show. The movie was good too. Harrison Ford is a great actor, though I liked him in 'Star Wars' better."

"Can I continue with my story?"

"Of course. Who's stopping you?"

"You! You never change. You always must have the last word, never listening to what I have to say. I don't know why I came back here. Maybe I should just go."

Silence fell between them, as father and son just looked at each other and then looked away.

Finally, Zach broke the silence. "Sorry, Dad. I guess I'm just really upset about what happened. Thank you for inviting me to stay."

"I'm sorry too. I should have just let you tell me what happened. It's just that it's been so long. I've really missed you and want to be included in your life. Go ahead and tell me what happened next. I won't interrupt."

"Okay. The police said I should come down to the station to give a report. For all I knew, the one-armed guy could have been waiting for me to show myself, to put a bullet in me on my way to the police station. He knows where I live."

"Why do you think he's after you? Do you have any angry patients? I know Samantha works for the CIA. Could you have gotten her so angry that she put a hit on you?"

Zach laughed for the first time in what seemed like ages.

"No. It's not like that. Let me continue."

Robert nodded, and Zach resumed.

"I think it has something to do with Francis' eye exam. Do you remember Andy Brannigan? He was in my ophthalmology residency program."

"Yeah. Nice kid, good family."

"I just played tennis with him a couple days ago. On his way out of work at Walter Reed Hospital he was killed in a hit and run."

"I'm sorry. I liked him."

"He had just examined President Peterman, and he found some things that didn't agree with my exam from a few years ago."

"You examined Francis?"

"Yeah, years ago when I was working in New Hampshire, and he was still a congressman. My exam showed he lost vision in one of his eyes, and Andy's exam showed his vision was back to normal."

"Well, maybe it got better."

"That sort of problem doesn't get better, Dad. He lost part of his side vision, and that doesn't really improve over time."

"So, that is strange."

"What's even stranger, and much scarier, is when I tried to go back to my office to get the records, the one-armed guy followed me there and tried to get the chart. I was able to get away, and I still have the chart. I'm not sure what's going on, but it obviously has something to do with those old records. I went to Rose Goodwin's funeral, and I gave a letter to one of the Secret Service agents to give to the President. Hopefully it gets to him, and this gets resolved."

"If I know Francis, he'll figure it out, and everything will be fine."

"I hope so. In the meantime, can I stay here to figure out my next steps? I need to have a plan in case he doesn't."

"Of course. Stay as long as you'd like. But there's something else you need to see."

Robert grabbed a newspaper and handed it to Zach.

"Read this. It's about Sarah Peterman. I know the two of you were an item in high school."

"I wouldn't say we were an item. We were friends. I liked her, but she was too popular, and I was kind of a nerd."

Zach picked up the paper, and there on the front page was a picture of Sarah Peterman below a headline reading, "President's Daughter Escapes Drug Addict Shooting." Zach read on:

"On Tuesday, Christmas Eve, Sarah Peterman, physician, and daughter of President Peterman, was attacked by a drug addict at her medical clinic. He brandished a gun and was fought off by the quick reactions of Dr. Peterman. She was not hurt, and the suspect made off after being pursued by secret service agents attached to Dr. Peterman."

The article continued to describe the attacker's appearance, and that he was thought to still be in the San Diego area. There was also a gritty picture, taken by a security camera, to go with the description. It added a warning to readers not to approach him if recognized. Instead, they should call the police, as he could be extremely dangerous.

Zach bit his lip and rubbed the back of his neck. He sat silent for a minute before speaking.

"Wow, Dad. I don't know what to make of that. I don't know why it would have anything to do with what's going on with me, but who knows?"

A silence fell over the room again. Finally, Robert got up. "I need to stretch my legs. I'm going to walk down to the market up near Maple and get a newspaper. Do you want to come?"

"No, I think Ripley and I are just going to rest here while you're out," said Zach.

As soon as he lay down on the couch, Zach fell fast asleep. Suddenly, he was awakened by the agitated voice of his father.

"Wake up, Zach!"

He immediately sat upright and rubbed his eyes. Robert Webster's face looked ashen.

"What's up, Dad."

"It's him. There's a gray SUV parked two doors down with some guy inside."

CHAPTER 32

JOEY PETRONE woke up sweaty, in his modest hotel room at the Crystal City Marriott at 9:00 am. Normally, the first thing on his mind at this time of day was what to eat for breakfast. Today was different. He wasn't hungry. Just slightly nauseous.

Joey lay in bed, awake, trying to decide what to do next. The fact that there was no car waiting for him at the Clinic, there was no plane ticket arranged for him to fly back to DC, and there was no reservation at the Mayflower Hotel, meant only one thing. He was not expected to survive.

After about half an hour, still unable to come up with a plan, he got up out of bed, dressed, and went for a short walk outdoors, to clear his brain and consider his options.

He had no way to contact Phoenix, even if he wanted to. As Phoenix didn't know where he was staying, he could go back to the Mayflower, rent a room, and wait for his boss to get in touch with him. He disregarded this option quickly, as it was likely to end with a bullet in his brain. He could use the $20,000 he had already been paid to disappear, but where would he go, and what would he do once the money ran out? In this second option, he would also likely end up with a bullet in his brain, but at least it wouldn't happen as quickly. At minimum, it would give him some time to come up with other ideas.

But where to, he wondered. Joey had heard of people hiding out in South America, but he didn't want to go someplace where they didn't speak his language, as Joey had enough trouble with English. He thought about an island somewhere far away, but he didn't know which one or how to get there. Joey had never left the country, and it all seemed too confusing.

At that moment, he heard an airplane over his head and looked up. A small plane pulled a sign advertising the MGM National Harbor Resort and Casino, just over the DC line, in Maryland.

A lightbulb went off in Joey's head. "What better place to hang out while figuring out what to do than a casino?" He could eat, drink, and gamble, and at least enjoy himself. It wasn't far to get to.

Now that he had something resembling a plan, he could finally feed his growling stomach. Time for food.

Joey went downstairs for breakfast, where he enjoyed a hearty meal of eggs, sausage, potatoes, pancakes, bacon, and coffee. He then called an Uber and made his way to the MGM hotel.

President Francis Peterman sat ruminating by the little table he used as a desk within the cell. There was little to do, so he used the time to write his memoirs on the paper the guards provided.

He had no idea how long since he had been kidnapped and placed in that stinking cell. It seemed like forever. He was starting to lose hope that he would be rescued.

Still, no one had tried to extract information from him, not by coercion or torture. What did they want from him?

Every four hours, there was a change in the guard sitting across from his cell. This morning, it was Barty Strang, the same man with the snake tattoo, who had been in the car with him when he arrived.

Barty looked in at the cell and smiled. "Here, I'll give you something interesting to read."

He handed his newspaper through the bars to the President. The first thing Peterman saw was the date of the newspaper, December 27th. He had been here a week.

Snapping his head back in shock at what he saw on the front page, he was greeted by a picture of his daughter, Sarah, along with the story of the attempted shooting. Peterman read the story thoroughly, both proud of his daughter and angry that it happened.

"Does this have anything to do with me?" he demanded.

Barty laughed. "What do you think?"

Peterman's face was red with fury, matching the color of his thinning hair. "Leave my daughter out of it. What the hell is going on?"

"I don't really know much, but my guess is your daughter won't be so lucky next time," taunted Barty.

Peterman threw his leftover dinner dish at the bars in anger. "Damn you. You tell them to leave her alone, or I'll make sure you all rot in jail the rest of your miserable lives."

"Temper, temper. If you break your dishes, you won't get food."

The President sat back down at his desk. Another angry outburst would not fix anything. If no help was coming, he had to work out an escape. All thoughts regarding his own safety were extinguished. Sarah was in danger, and he had to get to her.

An early conception of a plan came to him, but it would require a weapon.

CHAPTER 33

ROBERT WEBSTER spent the night sitting by the front door with a shotgun at his side, and with a look of excitement in his eyes. Zach, too exhausted to argue, allowed himself to be shooed back to his old room to sleep.

Upon awakening, he came downstairs to find his father fast asleep, still sitting in a chair by the door, and the shotgun by his feet. Looking out the window, the car was gone.

"Dad, wake up. The car is gone. It's okay."

Robert Webster awakened with a startle.

"I'm sure it was a gray SUV, Zach, and there definitely was a guy sitting in the driver's seat."

"I believe you, Dad, but he's not there now. Maybe it was just some guy who was lost or needed a break from driving."

"We should call the police."

"What good would that do? The car's not even here now. Go get some sleep."

"Guess you're right."

Yawning, Robert trotted off to his bedroom. Zach rechecked all the window and door locks.

By mid-afternoon, the gray SUV returned, parked about two blocks away. They could see there was someone in the driver's seat, but it was too far away to identify the occupant.

Robert Webster's earlier excitement returned, and he grabbed his coat from the closet.

"I have an idea. I'll go to his car window and ask if he's lost and needs directions. Then, I'll be able to see if he's got one arm."

"No, Dad. It's too dangerous. Let me check it out."

"He knows what you look like, so it has to be me." With that, his father was out the door before Zach could stop him.

Robert returned ten minutes later, with a gleam in his eyes, and grabbed the shotgun by the door.

"It's him. He's got just one arm. He's going to regret he was even born!"

"Dad, put that thing away. When was the last time you shot anything with that gun?"

"Can't remember, but I was a good shot in the Army."

"Dad, that was forty years ago! I don't want to get you mixed up in this, whatever this is. I need to think."

"We could call the police."

"What am I going to tell them? There's a car parked two blocks away with a one-armed guy, and he's trying to kill me? I've tried that one before, and they don't believe me."

"Okay, then we'll deal with the guy by ourselves."

"Look, I'm not getting you involved. I shouldn't have come here in the first place. I'll work this out on my own."

"I can handle myself."

Zach put his arm on his father's shoulder and spoke to him in a quiet, gentle voice. "Dad, I love you, and I can't bear the thought of you getting hurt because of me. I need to get out of here and go where he can't find me, until I come up with a plan.

"Here's what we do. I'll slip out the back door, go through the

Henderson's back yard, and head over to Pleasant Street. Then, you get your car from the garage and meet me there. And one last thing, could you take care of Ripley for me? It's going to be difficult hiding out with a dog."

"Sure. Ripley and I get along great."

"Drive past him slowly, so he sees that you're the only one in the car. Make it look like you're just out for a nice Sunday drive."

"Zach, it's Friday."

"I know. Just a figure of speech," said Zach.

"Sure. I'm a great actor."

"Don't try to do too much; just drive slowly and don't look anxious."

"No problem," said Robert, the excitement returning to his eyes. "Where are we going after I pick you up?"

"I'm not sure yet. I'll work that out as we're driving."

The scenario worked perfectly. Zach headed out the back door, and Robert got in his car, drove slowly down the street, passed the gray car, and eventually doubled back to pick up his son on Pleasant Street.

"How did it go?" asked Zach. "Did he see you leave?"

"Yeah, no problem, but I still think you should have left him to me and my shotgun! Okay, where to?"

"Drop me at the Enterprise Car Rental on Manchester Street in Concord. I'll rent a car and find a place to stay, probably somewhere outside the area."

"How about the Comfort Inn in Manchester? Aunt Edith stayed there at your cousin's funeral. It was nice."

"Sounds good. I don't really care much, if it's got a bed to sleep on. I just need to use it as a base to figure out what to do next."

"Okay, fine. I can drive there later with some food for you, and to make sure you're alright."

"No, Dad. In case he follows you, I don't want you to lead him there."

"Okay, but keep in touch. I need to know you're safe."

"I will, thanks," he said, closing the car door behind him at the rental agency.

It was late, and the staff at Enterprise was about to close for the evening. They had one car left, a blue Chevy sedan. Zach took it and drove twenty minutes to the Comfort Inn in Manchester, where he checked in for the night.

Marty knew he had been spotted by Robert Webster the previous evening, and had therefore pulled his car out of sight, keeping a watch on the tracker still attached to Zach's car. It was now time to get closer, to make sure Zach didn't make a run for it with Peterman's eye chart. Parked behind a tree, he thought he could keep a watch out for Zach while not being spotted himself.

When Robert Webster knocked on his window, he knew he hadn't done the job well enough. The fool thought he was being clever, trying to identify him to his son while asking if he needed directions. He thought briefly about finishing off the father before going to the house and finding the son, but it would be messy, and Phoenix didn't like messes.

Marty assumed, as he had been spotted, that Zach would try to leave without being seen. When Robert Webster drove away from the house, smiling and waving, he felt certain Zach would be hiding underneath the seats, or meeting his father elsewhere, to be driven to a new location.

From a distance, he watched Zach get into his father's car and drive to the car rental agency. He then followed him to the Comfort Inn.

It was late, and Marty was tired. He would deal with Dr. Webster tomorrow. He would return tonight to his room at the Centennial Inn, a four-star hotel in downtown Concord. As he was also still searching for Joey Petrone, he needed to check in with his contacts in DC.

CHAPTER 34

THE ONLY TRUE weapon President Francis Peterman could see was the automatic weapon in the hands of his guard, sitting about six feet away. There was no way he could get that. The only other possibility was a coal shovel leaning against the wall across from his cell, about four feet across the dirt floor. That would be his target.

Feigning fatigue, he went back to bed, underneath the flimsy blanket. Slowly, he removed the sheet underneath him, being careful to keep it well hidden. By twisting and making small knots along the way, he was able to make it into the shape of a rope. Still, to grab the handle of the shovel, he would need some hook to attach to this homemade rope.

An answer came to him with his lunch. It was a microwaved TV dinner of turkey, mashed potatoes, and peas, with a glob of greasy brown gravy on top. There was no knife to cut the turkey, but at least they gave him a fork.

If he could keep the fork, bend it, and tie it onto his rope, that could be a hook. Before the guard could retrieve the empty tray, he would need to hide the fork.

The door to his cell opened, and the guard walked cautiously in, holding his weapon in front of him with one hand and grabbing the tray with the other. It was the guy with the snake tattoo, Barty Strang. He had almost walked out when he turned around and looked at Peterman.

"Where's the fork I gave you?'

"Don't know what you mean."

"The fork. I let you borrow mine. I need it back so I can eat."

"I don't know."

The guard pushed the President to the ground and pointed the gun at him.

"Give it to me now, or I'll finish you here. If you think you can use that fork to hurt me, you're a bigger fool than I thought. I want it now!"

President Peterman reached in his pocket, pulled out the fork, and threw it to his captor. The guard grabbed the fork, and with his other hand, smashed the butt of his rifle against Peterman's head, who crashed down in a heap.

The President didn't awaken until later that day, head aching. He checked his forehead. There was a lump the size of a golf ball, some dried blood, but apart from that, his head seemed okay other than feeling a little groggy. He could still move all his extremities.

The younger guard, Al, brought Peterman his dinner. He put the tray down gently on the President's small table. It was the same type of turkey dinner he had been served at lunch, but this time, there were no utensils. He would have to use his fingers, and so the fork idea was now out of the question.

At least they gave him a beer to drink with his meal. Not being a beer drinker, Peterman looked at it with distaste, but he needed something to wash down the turkey.

The guard came in to remove his tray while the President continued to sip his beer. It was better than he expected. Not great, but not terrible. He would rather have had a glass of wine, but at least it was something to do. A thought came to him, and he called out to the guard, "Can I save the rest of this beer for later?"

"Sure, why not," said the guard as he locked the cell door.

Quietly, Peterman finished his beer and put the empty can under his blanket. When he would later lie down to sleep, he could then crush the can into the shape of a hook.

CHAPTER 35

HE COULD HEAR Al snoring. He slept a lot while on duty.

This was his chance. Quietly, from under his blanket, Francis Peterman removed the rope formed from his sheet. It was time to tie the beer can residing at the end of his bed onto the rope. Gradually, using his left foot, he slid the can up towards his hand. Already crushed into the shape of a hook, it caught onto the side of the bedframe and fell to the dirt floor with a soft thud.

The prisoner held his breath. His captor's snoring had stopped. Had the guard heard the noise and awakened?

To Peterman's relief, snoring resumed. He took a deep breath and removed the laces from his shoes. He used them to tie the beer can hook on to the end of the rope.

Now came the difficult part. He would need to use the hook on the end of the rope to grab the handle of the shovel. He would then have to drag it across the ground, pull it in through the bars, and do all of this without the guard waking up.

Had the President been a rodeo performer who had experience throwing a lasso, it might have helped. Five times, he threw the rope, and each time it fell to the floor without grabbing anything. The dirt floor muffled the sound of the beer can, and he could hear the guard still snoring. Finally, on his sixth attempt, the hook grabbed the handle, and the shovel fell onto the floor with a crash.

Quickly, Peterman pulled the rope back and hid it under his blanket. The guard, now awake, grabbed his gun, and looked around. Seeing no one in the hallway, he looked inside the cell. Standing next to the table, now partly overturned, was the President.

"What was that?" asked the guard.

"I guess I got up a little too quickly from my chair, and somehow, I knocked over the table. Sorry."

"Just don't do it again."

The guard went back to his chair. Peterman could see the end of the shovel only a few feet away from the bars to his cell. It was still too far out of his reach. He prayed the guard would fall asleep again before another came by and noticed the shovel, now on the floor.

About an hour later, Peterman's prayer was answered. Snoring resumed. He grabbed the rope, and with the hooked end, he was easily able to pull the shovel to him and through the bars.

He hid the shovel under the blanket and returned the laces to his shoes. Escape would have to wait.

A short time later, Peterman heard a commotion outside his cell. Snake-tattoo guy had returned and was yelling at the guard who had just awakened.

"What the hell. Were you asleep on duty?"

"No, of course not."

"Then how come you were snoring?"

"Don't know what you're talking about."

"You could be shot for that."

"Look, Barty. We're not in the Army anymore. Everything's okay. He's still in his cell. No harm done."

"Okay. I'm here to relieve you. Just don't fuck up again, or there'll be consequences."

Barty sat down, replacing the other guard, who walked down the hallway and out of sight.

About an hour later, the President heard a rattling of his cell bars.

"Hey, Mr. President, I've got your breakfast. In case you've stolen another fork, please don't stick me with it," said Barty Strang, laughing, as he made to unlock the cell door.

Quickly, Peterman grabbed the shovel and placed it behind his back. As Strang was in the process of tossing the tray onto the table, he struck.

With a powerful, swift blow, he landed the shovel blade to the side of Strang's head. Down he went, laying still on the ground within the cell.

The President grabbed the automatic weapon, locked Barty in the cell, and proceeded down the hallway. He had no idea where it headed, but somehow, it must lead out. He needed to escape, not just for himself, but for his country. Most of all, he needed to get out for Sarah.

Peterman arrived at the elevator shaft and pressed the button. He could smell fresh air coming from up above. Down came the elevator, and the President jumped in. As it rose, Francis Peterman felt a thrill of excitement. He felt young and vital. He was going to escape his captors through his own resourcefulness and bravery.

The elevator door opened, and before he could raise his own weapon, Francis Peterman was instantly hit with a rifle barrel in his gut, doubling him up. Looking up, he could now see the rifle pointed at his head. It was Al, the youngest guard.

He picked up the President's gun and tossed it aside, and then brought the President back down by the elevator. Smiling, he pulled the unconscious Barty Strang out of the cell as he locked Peterman back in. He wasn't sure which was better, recapturing the President, or having something to lord over Barty Strang for his mistakes.

CHAPTER 36

SITTING ALONE in his room at the Comfort Inn, Zach needed to make some calls. His first was to his one and only employee, Veronica. Fortunately, he had her cell phone number listed as a contact.

"Hello, Veronica. It's Dr. Webster. Sorry to call you at home."

"Hi Dr. Webster. You know it's only 8:30," she said in a sleepy voice.

"Sorry if I woke you, but I need you to clear my schedule for next week."

"Do you want me to do it right now?"

"Sometime this weekend. You should be able to download my patient schedule to your home computer, and it will have their contact information. My patients need to know in advance that their appointments are moved. I don't want them coming in and finding out I'm not there."

"That's a lot of patients to call and reschedule. It will take up most of my weekend."

Zach knew there would not be many patients to reschedule, but he was in no mood to argue.

"I know it's an imposition, but you can take Monday and Tuesday off, and have all the calls go to the answering service. Call Rob Reed and ask him if he'll cover emergencies for me until I get back. I'm sure he will. I've done the same for him."

Veronica answered with a sigh, "Okay, I'll take care of it."

"Thanks, Veronica. I'll be in touch."

Zach's next call was to his father. He waited until it was 9 am. By then, his dad would be awake. But before calling, he planned what to say, and what not to say. He needed to sound calm, or his dad would be at the Comfort Inn in a flash, shotgun by his side. Aside from his dad either shooting himself or Zach by mistake, he might also unknowingly bring the assailant right to the Comfort Inn. Zach also knew he had to keep his father informed, as he would be very worried if Zach didn't make contact.

He dialed and tried to keep his tone of voice calm.

"Hi, Dad. How's everything going? How's Ripley treating you?"

"I've been worried as hell, not knowing what's going on."

"I'm doing okay, still trying to figure out what to do," said Zach.

"You should try calling the police again. This time you can call the New Hampshire police. They'll listen to you. You're a New Hampshire boy."

Zach didn't think growing up in New Hampshire would be of much use in talking to the police, but trying them again was not a bad idea. He didn't have any better ones.

"Maybe I will. How's Ripley doing?"

"He's great. He can stay with me anytime. He lets me sleep late. In fact, he's still asleep now. We watch the same TV shows and like the same foods."

Zach couldn't remember the last time Ripley let him sleep late. As for watching the same TV shows, Zach wondered if his father had consulted Ripley as to what shows to watch. One thing he knew; it was going to be a tough job to get Ripley back on dog food when he returned.

"Thanks for taking care of him, and thanks for everything." With that, Zach hung up.

He then sat at the small desk and looked at the eye records again. Nothing made sense. This whole mess must somehow relate to these records. The only thing he knew was that his old records didn't match Andy Brannigan's examination of the President, and that someone was willing to kill him for it. His friend had already succumbed, dead from a hit and run.

What he didn't know was who those people were that wanted the records, and most importantly, why? Every answer seemed more implausible than the last. Could he have made a mistake on Francis Peterman's eye exam years ago? Unlikely, and why would someone want to kill him for it? Could the administration at Walter Reed be so upset about a mistake their doctor made, that they would try to hush it up? Ridiculous. Could Peterman's eye findings have changed over the years? Physically impossible. Could the President somehow have faked the eye exam to show himself being completely healthy, and now the Administration was trying to hush it up? That wouldn't be the Francis Peterman he knew. Could there be someone else pretending to be President Peterman? Ludicrous.

None of the potential explanations made sense.

Maybe his dad was right, and not knowing what else to do, he called the Manchester, New Hampshire police.

"Hi, I'm Dr. Zach Webster, and I'd like to report a crime." With that, Zach reported his altercation in DC and that his assailant turned up outside his father's house in Hopkinton. He purposefully omitted both the information about the confusing eye exam and his assailant having just one arm, as they might make his story less believable.

Finally, after a few moments of silence, the policeman responded.

"Did you call the local police?"

"No, I was too interested in escaping to stop and call them. Does that mean I need to call them instead of you? I'm staying at a hotel in Manchester now."

"No, that's okay. We can handle it. Have there been any threats against you since you've been in Manchester?" asked the cop.

"No, but I'm not sure what to do next or where to go."

"Where are you staying now?"

"I'm at the Comfort Inn, Room 311."

"Stay right there. We're a little busy, but we can get someone out to you in about two hours."

"Okay, thanks," said Zach, hanging up. He felt better now that it sounded like someone believed him and would help him return to normal life.

Zach wasn't sure what to do while waiting for the police to arrive. He briefly considered calling the secret service agent who gave him his card, but it all seemed so implausible that he would not be believed. If he found out any additional information, then it might be worth a call.

Zach wandered around the room a few times, stopped to sit on the edge of the bed, got up, and then repeated the process. He knew he should probably stay in the room, but he was going stir-crazy. He made coffee, but that just made him feel more jittery. Finally, he turned on the TV in his room and watched reruns of NCIS, which made him feel even worse. There were murders and odd plot twists, which reminded him very much of his present situation.

Unable to take it anymore, Zach turned off the TV and brought over a chair to the window. Here he could survey the parking lot, watching for a police car to arrive. Instead, he spotted a different car pull into the parking lot, a car he knew well, a gray SUV. Fear flew through Zach's body like a lightning bolt. His heart started pounding, and he suddenly felt like he might pass out. Realizing this was no time for panic, he closed his eyes, took a few slow, deep breaths, and immediately started feeling somewhat better. He didn't see Marty place a tracking device under his blue Chevy car.

He needed a plan. If his assailant knew his hotel, he might also know his room number. Staying in the room was not an option. He opened his door and looked down the hallway, but there were no closets or empty rooms to hide in. He could try escaping by the stairs or the elevator, but then his pursuer might be coming up at the same time. Where could he go so that he wouldn't be seen?

Zach looked around the room. He could try hiding under the bed. No, there was not enough room. He could try hiding in the shower, but certainly, the one-armed guy would look in there. Finally, he noticed an air duct over his head.

Standing on the desk, he was able to slide the vent covering the duct off to one side. The duct was small, but Zach was thin, and he was just able to wriggle himself in and replace the vent when he heard a knock on the door. He knew it was not going to be the police.

Trying to breathe as softly as he could, he heard a scraping of metal on the outside of his door, which then opened quietly. Looking through the openings in the vent, he saw the same one-armed man walking around the edge of the bed. Zach took his phone out of his shirt pocket and, putting his phone on silent mode, snapped his assailant's picture. Perhaps someone would be able to identify him.

Marty Green walked into the bathroom, and Zach could hear the shower curtain opening. Zach attempted to put his cell phone back in his pocket, but it fell out of his hands, and with a soft thud, it landed on top of the metal grate. Quickly, Zach grabbed the phone and scrunched himself further down the duct, away from the grate.

Having heard a noise, his assailant rushed back into the room and looked about. He could see no one, so he began to search through all of Zach's belongings, emptying the contents of the suitcase onto the desk.

Inside the duct was hot, and Zach was covered in sweat. Dripping down from his forehead onto the grated floor of the duct, it collected into a small droplet. Unable to stop it, it dropped in a tiny splash onto the desk.

Marty looked up, but Zach had already inched silently further from the grate. Convinced it was just condensation from the duct, Marty renewed his search. The eye records were not there, as Zach had left them in his car.

Finally, appearing annoyed at not finding what he had been searching for, the one-armed man left, and Zach could hear his footsteps walking down the hallway.

CHAPTER 37

ZACH WAITED ABOUT ten minutes before he shimmied his way out of the duct. Without taking the time to pack up any of his belongings, he grabbed his car keys, wallet, and phone, and left the room. He quickly headed down the hallway to the stairway, hoping that his attacker would have taken the elevator and would be long gone.

Down at the lobby level, Zach walked out of the stairway and almost right into the back of his assailant. He hadn't left. Not sure what to do, he hugged the wall and headed toward a sign that said, "Swimming Pool and Exercise Area." Using the key card in his wallet, Zach quietly opened the door to the swimming pool and looked in.

No one else was in there. It seemed as good a place to hide as any, and it would be unlikely the assailant would look for him there. Zach quietly slipped in and tried to find a place to hide, but realized too late he had made a bad choice. The room was completely empty, with nothing more than a few reclining chairs. It was also totally visible through the glass entrance door, and he could easily be spotted. Now that he was already in the pool area, leaving it to walk back to the lobby would almost guarantee being discovered.

The only place to hide would be in the pool or hot tub, but there was a problem. He had no bathing suit, or anything else to wear other than what he was wearing. Either strip down to his shorts or go in wearing all his clothes. No one else was there, and making a hasty retreat with sopping wet clothes didn't sound too appealing.

Zach pulled off all his clothes, down to his briefs, and put them in a small pile in the corner of the room. Quietly, he eased himself into the water, spending most of his time underwater as not to be seen. Realizing his briefs were colorful and likely could be seen through the door, he stripped them off.

All was well, until a family with three children opened the door and proceeded to make their way to the edge of the pool. All three kids jumped in, laughing, and jostling each other.

Zach grabbed two flotation devices and placed them in front and back of where his shorts had been. He added a pool noodle between his legs. It was not enough.

Almost immediately, the youngest child stared at Zach, and shouted, "Mommy, there's a guy in here with no clothes on!"

The ruckus from his parents at that announcement could have awakened the dead. Their shouting, "Get out of here, you pervert!" most likely would have been heard in the lobby.

Zach jumped out, dropping the pool floats and noodles, and grabbed his clothes. In case the man with one arm was still around, there was no time to put them on. He ran out of the pool area, through the lobby, and to his car. Without looking around to see if the assailant was still there, he started up the car and drove quickly out of the parking lot. By the time Marty saw the naked man drive his car out of the parking lot, it was too late.

It was the middle of winter, and here he was, sopping wet, completely nude. Just like Ripley when he was damp, Zach shook his hair to try to remove the water. Unlike Ripley, however, the maneuver was not very successful, and water continued to drip down his neck. Blowing hot air on his hands didn't help to warm them. Fortunately, the heat came on quickly, and he began drying off. Pulling into a Walmart parking lot, he parked away from the other cars, and proceeded to dress himself in the car. With that accomplished, he proceeded into Walmart to get more clothes, other essentials, and a coat.

Everything flew round in Zach's head. Rose Goodwin dead. Andy Brannigan dead. Sarah, the President's daughter, attacked. Some one-armed guy trying to kill him and steal the President's old eye chart. The President's new eye exam different from his old exam. They must all be linked. But still, he didn't know what to do about it. At least he had a picture of his assailant, but who could he trust to show it to?

And how had the man found him? Did he have connections with the police? That would have been a good plot on NCIS. But that's a TV show, and this is real life, Zach reasoned.

Still, the thought stayed with him, and the idea of trying to contact the police again moved further from his mind.

Marty walked back to his car. He wasn't worried about finding the doc, knowing he had placed a tracker on his car. He had another job that needed doing, locating Joey Petrone, and he would deal with Zach later.

CHAPTER 38

"IT'S SATURDAY, MOM. You said you were going to take me to the zoo."

"I'm sorry, Jefferson, but I have clinic this morning. I forgot."

"But it's Saturday. You shouldn't have to work, and you promised."

"I said I was sorry. We'll go another time. Soon, I promise."

"Another promise. How do I know you'll keep this one?"

"Jefferson, I don't have time for this. And I didn't promise we would go today. I just said soon."

"No. You said you would take me on Saturday."

"Enough. Eat your cereal. We have to go. It's getting late."

Jefferson knew he had lost, and he glared at his mother while eating his breakfast.

Sarah looked down at her breakfast omelet as she ate. She couldn't remember if she had promised Jefferson to go to the zoo on Saturday, and guilt started rising in her throat. Was she screwing up this single mom thing?

"Jefferson, I only have to work until noon. How about if I take you out for ice cream when I get back, if you can get ready soon?"

Jefferson's head nodded slowly, and the slightest smile began on his lips.

Great, thought Sarah. Now I'm into bribery.

"You'll be staying with Aunt Jessica this morning."

Jefferson now smiled more broadly. "Okay!"

Jessica was not really his aunt, but Sarah's best friend from college, and she lived about twenty minutes away in Coronado. He loved spending time with Aunt Jessica, mostly because she let him do whatever he wanted and eat whatever junk food he could find in the house.

Walter McCoy, the Secret Service agent, had arrived to take Sarah to work. In fact, he had arrived much earlier in the morning, prior to anyone in the household waking up. He pointed to his watch to indicate the time as Sarah and Jeff finished breakfast.

"Okay, Jefferson. Brush your teeth and get whatever toys you want to take to Jessica's house, and be ready to leave in five minutes. We're already late."

"Okay, Mom."

Jefferson jumped off his chair and headed to his room.

"Excuse me, Dr. Peterman." said Agent McCoy, "Would you like me to take Jeff to your friend's house? I know you're running late. If you're okay with driving yourself to work, I could meet you at work after dropping him off."

Sarah was surprised. This was certainly not protocol, but the thought of getting behind the wheel again sounded wonderful. Plus, she'd still be late to work, but not by as much.

"That would be great, Agent McCoy. I'll be out in ten minutes."

Sarah combed her hair, put on a bit of makeup, and proceeded out of the house with Jefferson.

"Mom, I want to go with you."

"I'm sorry, but I don't have time. This nice agent will take you to Jessica's house.

Jefferson again gave his mother an angry stare as he reluctantly headed over to McCoy's car.

"Remember, I'll take you out for ice cream later!"

Great, bribery again, as she frowned to herself as she sat down in the driver's seat of her car.

Jefferson and McCoy drove off, and Sarah left for her office in Chula Vista. She took Landis Street to the 805, heading south. Knowing she was running late, Sarah sped up. The car in front of her slowed down, and she applied the brakes. There was no response, even after slamming her foot hard on the brake pedal. She pushed the pedal all the way down to the floor, and still, no response. Swerving at the last minute into the adjoining lane, she missed the car in front of her, but continued picking up speed as she headed downhill.

She could see the traffic backing up ahead of her. Cars were fully stopped. Heading into the breakdown lane at almost 80 mph, she hit the guard rail, bounced off, side-swiped the car on her left, broke through the guard rail, and came to rest on an embankment on the right side of the highway. Airbags opened, cushioning Sarah, who by this time was unconscious.

By the time the ambulance arrived, Sarah was conscious, but foggy. She was brought to the hospital, battered and bruised. The emergency room staff first took blood samples, looking for alcohol or drugs, and treated her as if she was on some illicit substance. Their demeanor changed markedly when they found out she was not only a physician, but the daughter of the President of the United States. After running multiple tests, they found no major injuries, and she was released from the hospital. Sarah called Jessica and was relieved to find that Jefferson was there and safe. She had a bad feeling about Agent McCoy.

Jessica and Jefferson picked her up from the hospital about half an hour later. Sarah put on a brave face for Jefferson, but her bruises and cuts gave her away.

"Are you okay, Mom?"

"I'm fine. Just a little traffic accident. A little problem with the brakes."

"Are you sure you're okay?"

"Of course. Now let's get you that ice cream."

CHAPTER 39

NONE OF THIS made sense, thought Sarah, sitting out on Jessica's porch with her glass of wine. She couldn't get in touch with her father. Someone had tried to kill her in her office. The police thought it was a druggie, but Sarah was unconvinced. Yesterday her brakes had failed, and she almost died. She didn't know what it all meant, but she knew enough to realize her life was in danger. It also meant that those closest to her might be at risk also. There was no way she could risk endangering Jessica, with whom she was staying, or especially, Jefferson. Thank God he was not in the car with her.

That meant she couldn't be with them until she was able to reach her father and figure things out. She needed to stay somewhere else. Jessica and Jefferson should also find another location.

Sarah walked back to the kitchen, where Jessica was treating Jeff to home-made chocolate chip cookies. She couldn't show fear in front of her son, so she gave a fake smile.

"Jess, you're giving Jefferson chocolate chip cookies before dinner? I reserve cookies for dessert."

"Well, you might, but I think cookies go well at any time of day. What do you think, Jeff?"

Jefferson nodded vigorously. Through a mouth filled with cookie pieces, all he could get out was, "Uhh, huh."

"I don't have any children, so who else am I going to spoil?"

"I think you've had enough, Jefferson. And Jess, can I talk to you for a minute outside?"

"Sure."

"The cookies are really good, Mom," interjected Jeff. "Do you want one?"

"No thanks, but you stay here. You can eat another cookie."

On their way out, Sarah could see Jefferson grab two. That was the last of her concerns now.

Once they were out of earshot, she turned to her friend.

"Jess, I'm going to ask a big favor. I'm really worried about things right now. First, the attack at my office, and next the brakes in my car failing. I think someone could be out to get me. I don't trust the secret service agent attached to me, and I can't get in touch with my dad. I can't put you or Jefferson at risk. I need to slip away while I figure out what to do. Can I leave Jefferson with you for a few days?"

"Of course you can. I love having Jeff around."

"I have another request. I don't think it's wise for you and Jefferson to stay here either. Is there somewhere you two can go?"

"Yeah. My sister lives on the other side of the island, near dog-beach. We can probably stay with her."

"Make sure you leave here without being seen. I don't trust the secret service agents right now."

"Okay. I'll call her up now. I'm sure she'll say yes. And I'll be sneaky leaving here, like I was at school smuggling vodka in under my shirt. Looked like I had three boobs."

Sarah forced a smile. In a different situation, she would have laughed out loud at the memory.

"Don't worry about us. But I'm worried about you. Is there anything I can do?" asked Jessica.

"No. I need to deal with this by myself. I'll leave tomorrow. I'm sure the secret service agent will be looking for me. If he shows up here before you go to your sisters', just tell him I've gone away for a few days, but you don't know where."

"No problem. You know I'd do anything for you and Jeff. Just be safe."

"Thanks so much. I'll check in every day. You're the best."

The next morning, after phoning her office to reschedule patients, Sarah found her son playing with Legos in the living room.

"Jefferson, I have to go away for a few days. You'll be here with Aunt Jessica. I've told her not to spoil you while I'm gone, so if she gives you chocolate chip cookies for breakfast, you can say 'No, Aunt Jess, please only give me healthy food.'"

Jefferson laughed, but then his smile turned into a frown.

"Mommy, why do you have to go?"

"There's something I have to do."

"What is it? I can go with you."

"No, I'm sorry. You can't."

Jefferson's head now inclined downward, as he gazed at his feet.

"Is it about your accident?" he asked quietly, "or is it about the guy who pointed a gun at you at your office?"

"You know about that?"

Jefferson nodded.

"Everything's okay. Don't worry. I just need to do some things. I'll call you every day. Be good. Love you," and she gave Jefferson a big hug.

Jefferson returned the hug. He didn't see the tears on her face as she turned away. Saying goodbye to Jessica, Sarah grabbed her things and headed out. Once outside, she summoned an Uber, and had the driver take her to the first hotel she could think of, the Hotel Del Coronado.

Sarah had been to the Hotel Del Coronado once before, for a conference. She remembered it to be a glorious old hotel, updated with modern amenities, and with a beautiful view of the Pacific Ocean. Dropped off at the entrance, she walked up the steps to the majestic, wood-paneled lobby.

She made her way to the reception desk. On the off chance someone might recognize her, she wore a big, floppy hat and sunglasses. She didn't have to worry. The lobby was packed with tourists admiring the artificial tree in the center of the room, parents were chasing after their children, and guests were busy looking for their luggage. The desk clerk seemed harried by the long line of people checking in. Everyone was too consumed with their own needs to wonder whose face was under that hat.

"Our lowest price room for a week starts at $3500. We have a few more deluxe rooms if you wish to spend more," said the clerk.

Sarah's head jerked back in surprise at the cost. "Are you sure that's the price for a week rather than a month?"

"That's our special weekly rate, madam. We don't have many rooms left."

"Wow. Okay, I'll take it," said Sarah, reluctantly.

"One king bed or two queens?"

"Doesn't matter, whichever is cheaper."

"Both are the same price, madam. The view is nicer in the room with two queens."

"That's fine. I'll take the two queens."

"Good choice. Can I see your credit card for payment and incidentals?"

"Here you go," said Sarah, handing the clerk Jessica's credit card."

"Ms. Abelson, do you need a bellman to take up your luggage?"

It took Sarah a moment to remember that Jessica's last name was Abelson.

"I don't have much. I can do it myself," she said, quickly recovering.

Sarah took the wrought-iron elevator up to the fourth floor, walked down the long hallway, and found her room down at the end. The clerk was right, she had a fantastic view of the wide beach and blue ocean. Her room was decorated with a bright wallpaper, and fresh flowers sat in a vase by the bed. If she hadn't been concerned about someone trying to kill her, or worried about her father and Jefferson, it might have been a very pleasant vacation. Instead, she just sat down on the edge of her bed and bit her fingernails, something she hadn't done since she was six years old.

CHAPTER 40

JIM STAPLES WOKE UP to another lousy breakfast of orange juice, a bran muffin, raisin bran cereal, and black coffee. He was not in a good mood. Brodsky had picked this moment to arrive.

"I can't stand it. I start the day with a crappy breakfast. Who eats like this?" complained Staples.

"The President eats like this, and you need to do the same."

"And now there's nothing to do. I need to do something."

"We all need to do what we're told. You need to stay out of the way."

Staples glared at Brodsky; his face screwed up in a scowl. "I'm the President, damn it. I need to act like it; not just hang out in my chambers. People will start to wonder."

"You need to stay here. Don't screw up."

Staples rose, fists now clenched. "Sitting around doing nothing and eating crap for breakfast makes me angry. I feel like hitting something."

Brodsky instinctively moved his chair back quickly, away from the imposter. "Okay, okay. I'll give you something to do. Go somewhere people will see you writing a speech."

Staples smiled and sat down. He liked this idea.

More relaxed now, seeing the imposter less confrontational, Brodsky continued, "Go to your office and write." He knew he would never give Staples the opportunity to deliver the speech.

"All right. How do I get there?"

"Follow me. I'll take you there."

Staples followed Brodsky outside to the Oval Office, and then to his private office nearby. He announced loudly to the nearby staff, "The President must not be disturbed. He is writing an important speech."

Brodsky left, and Staples sat down to write. He had never written or given a speech before, and he was quite excited to write this one. He thought of all the things that had gone wrong for him and where the country should be headed.

Writing quickly, he was surprised at how the words flowed from brain to pen. He should be the President of the United States; he would fix what was wrong, starting with the military. After approximately thirty minutes, he put his pen down and smiled. He had just written a manifesto. Yes, there would be changes, and Staples would make them happen. He was no longer Jim Staples. He was now President of the United States.

Staples picked up the phone and called in his new secretary. She came right in.

"Remind me of your name," he asked.

Surprised, she responded, "Judy Mairston, Sir."

"Okay, Judy Mairston, this is what I want you to do. I want you to call the reporters of all the TV stations and newspapers, and anybody else you can think of. Tell them I'm going to give a speech."

"Do you mean you want to hold a press conference?" she asked timidly.

"Yeah, sure."

"When do you want to do it?"

"How about in an hour."

"That's awfully soon. I don't think they can all get here that quick."

"Okay, two hours. Now move and get it going."

At once, Judy left the office to start arranging the press conference.

As she left, she turned around to look one more time at the President. Something just didn't seem right. Granted, she had never actually worked directly for the President. Rose did that, but Judy had been around enough to hear the President talk to his staff. Was it his voice, or his mannerisms that somehow were a bit off?

Judy put it down to her imagination and started notifying the press of the upcoming address. It must be something important for such short notice.

Brodsky returned to the buzz of activity. "What's going on?" he asked.

"The President has called a press conference in two hours."

Jonathan Brodsky's face first showed shock, then anger. He hurried into the President's personal office, where Staples was sitting happily, smiling in anticipation of the speech he was about to give.

"What the hell do you think you're doing?" asked Brodsky angrily.

"I'm giving a speech to the American people, as President."

"First of all, you're not the real President of the United States, you idiot. No one authorized you to give a speech. Second, a press conference is where they'll ask you questions about whatever they want, not just an opportunity for you to give a speech. Third, if you go up there and it's clear you're not the real President, we'll be dead men. The people behind this will make sure we never have a chance to open our mouths to say anything more to anybody. Do you get it?"

Staples didn't respond.

Interpreting silence as acceptance, Brodsky continued. "Now let me get out there and see if I can stop this thing."

It was too late. The press had already been notified, and they were on their way.

There was a knock on the door, and Vice President Richardson strode in.

"Mr. President. I understand you are about to give a speech to the American people. What are you going to be discussing? I'd like to be kept in the loop."

Staples looked at him and smiled.

"Oh, it's just a little bit of this, and a little bit of that."

"Would you care to be a little bit clearer as to the topics?"

"You'll find out when I give the speech."

Brodsky hurried back in. "Mr. Vice President, would you mind leaving us? We've got some important work to do."

Vice President Richardson left in a huff.

Brodsky now turned to Staples. "Let me see your speech."

Staples handed over his remarks. Brodsky's eyes widened with every page he read. His only response was, "Holy shit!" which he repeated three times.

After reading it all, he glared at Staples. "You can't say this. You can't say we need to execute the generals because they're all ass-kissing pieces of shit. You can't say that blacks are getting promotions over whites, and that they're no damn good and need to be kicked out of the military. You can't say we need to invade China so we can run the world our way. You can't say any of the crap you've written. You'd be signing our death warrants."

Staples again just looked at him and didn't respond.

Brodsky took Staples' speech, ripped it in half, then in half again, and threw it in the trash basket. Next, he called the President's speech writer, Bill Duffy. "I need a speech for President Peterman to give to the press, and I need it in half an hour."

"What did you say? Half an hour? I need at least an hour," said Duffy. "And what's the speech about?"

"You've got half an hour. Just boilerplate stuff. Just dig out some stuff he's talked about before. Just leave out anything about the military or health care."

"What do you want me to write about?"

"I don't care. Just do it fast."

"Okay. I'll write something."

Half an hour later, Bill Duffy came running into Brodsky's office. Drops of sweat dripped off his forehead, onto the paper he was holding. He handed it to Brodsky.

"Get it on the teleprompter, Duffy."

"Don't you want to read it? It's basic stuff. Just how we're all Americans, and we need to work together. Crap like that."

"No time to read it. Get it on the teleprompter now. He's about to go on."

Jim Staples entered the Brady Press Briefing Room in the White House with Jonathan Brodsky by his side. Clicks from the many cameras in the room announced their arrival.

As the reporters were taking their seats, Brodsky whispered to Staples, "Just read the teleprompter, and everything will be fine. After your speech, don't take questions. Say you've got important business to attend to."

Staples nodded, and Brodsky walked off to talk to the television cameraman who was filming the press conference for all the TV stations.

"The President is not feeling well and doesn't want close-ups on his face today, as he thinks he is not looking his best. So please, shoot him from a slight distance. Thank-you."

The cameraman nodded and Brodsky walked away.

The imposter's initial panic was replaced by excitement. He was no longer James Staples, labeled as a sociopath and a discarded soldier living on the streets. He was now President of the United States. All these people were waiting for his words of wisdom, and he would deliver. A broad smile grew on his face.

The teleprompter started rolling.

CHAPTER 41

"MY FELLOW AMERICANS, I've come to talk to you about what's important to our country," he repeated.

He stopped and turned away from the teleprompter. He was not going to read some junk they wrote for him. He was going to speak his mind. After thinking about it for about five seconds, he began.

"Ladies and gentlemen of the press, and all you Americans out there watching, I want to talk to you about something that's been on my mind. I want to talk to you about beer, my drink of choice."

Faces in the audience that had been lowered to type on their laptops and write on their notepads, now looked up in surprise at the President. The CNN reporter in the first row dropped her notepad onto the floor. The television cameras clearly picked up a man's voice in the back saying, "What the hell?"

"I asked for a beer a few nights ago while watching the Lewis/Brown fight. Do you know what they tried to give me? They wanted to give me a Corona Light. That's piss water."

From behind the wings of the stage, Jonathan Brodsky's face turned red in a mixture of anger and fear. "This idiot is going to ruin everything," he murmured to himself, but he felt powerless to stop the press conference.

Staples continued. "When I said no to that, they tried to give me German beer. What's up with that? We whooped their asses in the second world war. Now they think their beer is better than ours? Fat chance. Give me a Budweiser, or a Miller or Coors, any day. And don't give me any of that craft beer crap. Some of that tastes like dirty feet. From now on, the only beer served in the White House will be good old American beer."

Members of the press stood silent, not believing what they were hearing. Brodsky was about to burst.

Staples continued, "Now I have a plan. I'm going to give every red-blooded American a case of American beer, for free." You'll get your choice; Bud, Coors, or Miller, or some other American beer as long as it's not a craft beer. If you want a light beer, that's okay, as long as I don't have to drink it."

Now, the press corps was eager to jump in. Most raised their hands with questions on their minds. Brodsky was signaling to Staples to end the conference, using a slicing motion to the neck with his hand. Staples ignored him; he was enjoying being President.

"Yes, you over there with the blue shirt and yellow tie, what's your question?" as he pointed to a tall man in the front row.

"Mr. President, I'd like to ask you about your health insurance initiative. How do you think the insurance companies are going to respond?"

"I'm not here today to talk about that, or anything else other than beer."

"How about you, with the red dress in the second row? You're cute." He pointed to a young woman with blond hair pulled back in a tight bun.

Shocked to be addressed in this manner by the President of the United States, with a flushed red face, the young reporter took a minute to compose herself before asking her question.

"Mr. President, what about the French response to your plans for reducing troop deployment in Europe?"

Staples sighed. "I'm only here today to talk about beer, but since you brought France up, I guess I can talk about wine too."

Backstage, Brodsky found the circuit breakers and cut power to the room. Suddenly, the lights went out. He walked quickly up to the presidential podium and made an announcement. "Ladies and gentlemen, we've lost power. Sorry, but the briefing is over for today."

Bewildered, the press filed out slowly, most grumbling to themselves about being summoned to a press conference at the last moment focused only on beer. Others decided to take the President's advice and found the closest tavern to the White House.

Jim Staples walked back to his office, quite proud of his speech. Jonathan Brodsky joined him there, mouth clenched in anger.

"How stupid can you get, or are you just totally nuts?" he snapped at him, trying to keep his voice calm.

Staples' face changed from a smile to fury in an instant.

"Nobody tells me I'm stupid, or that I'm crazy. The doc at the VA said something like that. He called me a crazy sociopath, and I put him in the hospital. Say anything more and you'll regret it."

Brodsky's face went white, and he just stood there, looking at the man who was now President of the United States.

A grin came back on Staples' face. "Just kidding, Johnny-boy. I wouldn't hurt you," and he walked out the door.

CHAPTER 42

THE ATMOSPHERE in the White House on Monday morning could best be described as chaos, due to the President's speech the day before. The President's advisers, cabinet members, and just about every member of the White House Press Corp wanted to speak to him.

Back in Chevy Chase, Robert Benton was puzzled by Peterman's sudden interest in beer. He had never been a "beer guy." Perhaps Jonathan Brodsky had suggested it to better connect to average Americans. It was a strange speech by the man he knew so well. Hopefully it would backfire on the Chief of Staff.

Jonathan Brodsky had trouble falling asleep the night after the speech. It didn't help that he was awakened at 5 am by a phone call from one of the conspirators.

"What the hell is going on? What are you thinking, letting that asshole give a speech that I can't even believe? If we're found out, we all go down, and we go down bad," the man shouted as soon as Brodsky picked up the phone.

His voice was so loud, it awakened Jonathan Brodsky's wife, who was lying next to her husband.

"What is it dear? Who's talking so loudly? It woke me up."

"Go back to sleep. It's a work call. I'll take it downstairs."

Grabbing a robe and slippers, Brodsky headed downstairs before answering. "I couldn't stop him. He called the press conference without my knowledge. I gave him a speech to read, and he went off on his own. Remember, I didn't pick him, Phoenix did."

"Say that to Phoenix and you'll end up in the Potomac River. You might still end up there if you can't control him and things go bad."

"I'll keep a tighter rein on him. You won't hear a peep from him."

"Better not. I'm getting pressure from the others. They're getting nervous. Hope you have good life insurance."

"I've got it under control." With that, the line went dead. He knew he had another phone call he had to make.

Shaking, Brodsky reluctantly dialed Phoenix. He had to redial four times, as his trembling fingers mistakenly hit the wrong keys.

"Phoenix, this is Jonathan Brodsky."

"I know who the fuck you are. Why are you calling me and waking me up? I am only to be called in a real emergency. Is this a real emergency?"

"It's about the speech yesterday."

"I know about it, you idiot. All of Washington's talking about it. It's gone viral on social media. If you can't control him, I'll put someone else in there who can. But I'll be nice about it; I'll send flowers to your funeral. Now do your job."

With that, Phoenix hung up. Brodsky knew it would be pointless to try to go back to sleep. He boiled some water for tea, but his shaking hands caused the kettle to miss the teacup, and water spilled on the floor, splashing onto his foot. In pain, he screamed, waking up his wife for the second time that morning.

As she yelled at him from upstairs, he wondered how he had ever gotten himself mixed up in this. Nothing to do now but carry on.

CHAPTER 43

IT WAS COLD in the Walmart parking lot, where he spent the night, but he had a warm coat and some blankets from the store.

Zach's first decision of the day was where to go next. He didn't look forward to another night in a parking lot. He also didn't like the idea of jumping from hotel to hotel. Finally, he called his father.

"Are you okay, Zach? Did you call the police?"

"The same guy returned. He found me at the hotel, but I was able to escape."

"You need to call the police."

"They may be in on it. It was after I called the police that he showed up."

"What are you going to do now?"

"I was thinking about our fishing cabin in Maine. Can I stay there for a little while?"

"Sure, but it's not insulated. There's a wood stove and plenty of wood, so I guess you could use it. I can meet you up there. Key's under the mat."

"Thanks, Dad, but I don't want you involved. Plus, he might be watching you and you'd bring him right here."

"Okay but call me and let me know you're safe."

"Thanks, Dad."

The drive to the cabin took about an hour and a half. On the way, he listened to a replay of the President's speech on the radio. It didn't make sense. He remembered his father offering Francis Peterman a beer at his house, and him refusing, saying he was not a big beer drinker.

Upon reaching the cabin, he had to park on the road and walk in, as snow and ice had made the long driveway impassable.

It was just as Zach remembered it. A couple of fishing poles were lined up on the far side of the house. One of them used to be his. Just behind the house was an old fishing boat, which sat on top of the small jetty jutting out over the bay leading to the ocean. The boat had seen better days, as small holes had developed in the hull. Some were below water level, and a few were above.

The inside of the cabin was very simple. There were two wood-paneled rooms, a bedroom and one room for everything else.

The temperature outdoors was twenty degrees, and inside the cabin felt just the same. Once Zach got the wood stove fired up, it finally became warm enough for him to take off his new down coat and gloves. He pulled the mattress off the bed and laid it beside the wood stove, where it was warm enough to allow him to sleep.

It took him a while to fall asleep; his mind was racing. First, he needed a warning if someone was sneaking up on him at the cabin. Second, whatever happened with the letter he gave to that secret service agent at the funeral? He would try to follow-up. Did he still have the agent's card?

Early the next morning, Zach drove to the Home Depot in Portland, Maine. There, he bought some Tear-Aid tape, a package of clothespins, screws, wire, and a wireless doorbell transmitter and doorbell.

Back at the cabin, after watching a YouTube video, he fashioned a tripwire alarm. He placed the tripwire low, between two trees, on the only path from the road to the cabin. In a backpack that he found in the closet, he put in an extra set of clothes, other necessities, and Francis Peterman's old eye chart. He sat it next to the back door, along with his coat, just in case.

The next order of business was to find the agent's card. If it had been in his clothes, there would have been no hope, as he had left them all at the Comfort Inn in Manchester. Fortunately, he found Ray Lincoln's card in his wallet, and he called him on his cell phone.

"Hello, is this Ray Lincoln?"

"Yes, who's calling?"

"My name is Dr. Zachariah Webster. I'm the guy who gave you the letter to give to the President at Rose Goodwin's funeral."

"Okay. I remember you. Why are you calling?"

"I'm still being hunted by the same guy, and I really think it has something to do with the President. Did you give him my letter?"

"I believe he got it."

"So, what did he say?"

"I wasn't there, and even if I was, I wouldn't be able to tell you."

"You've got to believe me. Something's wrong. And, when I was driving yesterday, I heard the President's press conference. I remember you said you used to have direct access to the President. Did that sound like him, talking about beer?"

Ray was quiet for a minute before answering, "No."

"And the attack on his daughter, Sarah. We were friends in high school. And I read she was almost killed in an automobile accident. Can't you see? It's all connected."

"I'm not sure what you want me to do about it? Why don't you call the police?"

"Like I told you. They don't believe me, and the last time I tried to call them, the same one-armed guy showed up at my hotel. I don't know if they're in on it too."

"This all sounds crazy."

"I know it does. Is there a way I could talk to Sarah Peterman? As I said, we were friends once, but I don't have her phone number anymore. Would you be able to find it for me?"

"No way."

"Look. I know you think I'm nuts, but I'm not. Please."

"How about this? If I can find her number, I call her, and if she wants, she'll call you back. I have your number."

Click.

Ray sat down at his chair by the door of Vice President Richardson's office, deciding what to do. He could at least call Peterman's daughter, Sarah, as he did have her number, having asked her out on a date not long ago. He had heard about the attack at her office and the auto accident, he wanted to make sure she was okay anyway.

Startled by the loud ringtone of her phone, Sarah quickly picked it up. Could it finally be her father? Could something have happened to Jefferson?

Instead, it was a voice she recognized, but didn't know well.

"Is this Sarah?"

"Yes. Who's this?"

"Ray, Ray Lincoln. Remember me? Your Dad's bodyguard, or at least I was."

"Of course, Ray. What do you mean 'was'? Is he okay?"

"As far as I know. I've been put on a different detail. I'm with the VP now."

"I've been trying to call him, and he hasn't called back. I'm really worried."

"That's strange. I know anytime you've called he's always broken away from anything he's doing to call you back."

"And did you see that beer press conference? Dad would never do something like that."

"Yeah, that's not like him, but let's talk about you for a minute. Are you okay after that attack at your office by the guy looking for drugs?"

"Yeah, I'm okay, but I don't think it had anything to do with drugs. Doesn't make sense. I'm more shook up about my brakes giving out on the highway."

"I heard about your accident."

"It was no accident. My brakes totally failed. My foot was down to the floor and there was no response."

"Where was your secret service agent?"

"He was driving Jefferson to school, and I drove myself."

"That's not protocol. What's his name?"

"McCoy."

"I don't know any McCoy. I need to do a check on him. Something's not right. Also, I got a call from a guy who says he knows you and wants to get in touch with you. It's something about your father's eye exam being different from old exams. His name is Dr. Zachariah Webster, and he's in DC."

"Yeah. I know him from high school. If it has anything to do with my father, I want to talk to him."

"Fine. I'll text you his number. Stay safe. I don't like what's going on. I'll check into some things, and I'll be back in touch."

"Thanks."

Sarah got the phone number and was about to call, but then realized it might be too late to call the east coast. She didn't know Zach was wide awake, listening intently to the receiver of his tripwire alarm, in case an intruder was about to make a night visit.

CHAPTER 44

ZACH SLEPT IN HIS CLOTHES, in case he had to make a quick exit. He had already jumped out of bed once that night to the sound of his tripwire alarm going off. Turning on the porch lights, he could see a moose pulling down small branches from the willow tree in the front lawn. Sleep was even more difficult to come by after that, so he was awake when he heard the tripwire alarm sound for the second time. The sun had just risen, so he was able to see out front without turning on the lights. This time, there was no moose or any other animal.

He had to make a quick decision. It could just be a false alarm again, possibly an animal that fled before it could be spotted out the window, or it could be an assailant, lurking behind a tree. He couldn't take the chance.

Grabbing his coat and backpack, Zach raced out the back door of the cabin. If it really was someone out to get him, his only route would be by water. Quickly, he pushed the small boat behind the house out into the water. Now he could hear someone in the cabin, so escape was necessary, and it had to be fast. He had put gas in the engine the previous evening, but he cursed himself for not testing it. Hopefully the boat was sea-worthy.

Zach pulled the cord to start the motor, but it sputtered. He tried once more, and again it sputtered. Each time he pulled the cord, he could feel his heart pound faster. By the third time he pulled the cord, the same one-armed man was coming through the back door, gun in hand.

Third time was the charm, and the motor caught. Zach gunned the little outboard motor, and the boat pulled away from the jetty. As he headed out into the bay, a gunshot landed just to the right of him. Zach turned the boat to the left, and another shot landed in front of him. Another appeared to fly just over his head.

There was no time to waste. Zach turned the boat towards the ocean. Hopefully the holes he had patched with Tear-Aid tape would hold. If they didn't, and the boat sank, he would surely die of hypothermia.

The ocean was rough, the air temperature freezing, and saltwater waves splashed over the edge of the little fishing boat. Staying as close to the rocky shore as possible, he headed north. One of the tape patches on the side of the boat started to peel off, and trying as he might, he could not get it to stick any better. Icy cold water started collecting on the bottom of the boat, freezing Zach's feet. Using an old rusty coffee can, he began bailing, reaching an equilibrium with the amount coming in.

In the distance, he saw what appeared to be a marina, and he headed straight for it. By now, water was collecting faster than he could bail, and the boat was sinking deeper into the ocean. By the time he reached a slip, the little boat was half-filled with water.

Grabbing his backpack, Zach jumped out of the boat. He didn't even have time to tie up the boat before it sank in the cold water.

Shivering, he looked up to see a man running toward him.

"What the hell are you doing out in weather like this?"

Zach was so cold he couldn't even answer. The man grabbed him by the arm and brought him into his car, where he turned up the heat, grabbed a blanket in the back, and threw it over him. Finally, Zach warmed up enough to speak.

"I had to get away from someone."

"Was it your wife?"

Not wanting to go into the whole story, Zach just nodded.

"Sometimes I feel the same way. But really, you've got to have some sense in weather like this. Where should I drop you?" he asked.

Zach didn't know what to say. He had no idea himself.

"Where are you headed?"

"Going to the mall in Portland. Gotta buy my wife a birthday present. Not a bad idea for you either to get your wife a little something. Makes them less angry."

"Sure. Drop me off at the mall. Thanks so much."

Once at the mall, Zach bought some new clothes and shoes, and tossed away the damp ones he was still wearing. He checked his backpack, and although many of his packed clothes were wet, the plastic bag covering his phone and the President's file had kept them both dry.

Examining his phone, he saw a missed call from a number he didn't recognize. There was no voicemail. Unsure if he should respond, he finally dialed the number.

Recognizing the number she called earlier in the day, Sarah answered.

"Hello, is this Zach?"

"Who is this?"

"Sarah, Sarah Peterman."

"You must have been given the message to call me by that agent."

"Yes, Ray told me you wanted to talk to me. It's been a long time, Zach."

"It sure has."

"Ray said you're in some sort of trouble, and you think it has something to do with my dad."

"It's a really long story, Sarah, but I think someone's trying to kill me, and yes, I think it has something to do with your dad."

Zach gave Sarah an abridged version of the events he endured over the past week, including her father's eye exam, and Andy Brannigan's subsequent death. She remained quiet.

"Sarah, are you still there?"

"Yes," she said. "I'm trying to process it all. I've had some trying times myself, but mostly, I'm worried about my father. I can't reach him."

"I have his old eye files, and the new exam from Andy Brannigan showing a difference that's not possible. And I've heard about the attack at your office and your car accident.

"Yeah, with the last name of Peterman, it's hard to go unnoticed."

Sarah thought for a few moments, and then spoke. "We seem to be in this together. It does seem like it's all related to my dad. I'm not sure what to do. The people I know in DC who are close to my dad are either dead or removed from their positions. Maybe I should just go to DC and demand to speak to him."

"I'm not sure if that's wise. They've already made multiple attempts on both your life and mine."

"I guess you're right."

"I'm not sure what to do either. I've tried the police, but either they think I'm crazy or they're somehow involved."

Sarah took her time before speaking again.

"How would you feel about coming out here, and we can try to work it out together."

"Where's here?"

"San Diego, California. Can't tell you more on the phone. What do you think?"

"Frankly, I don't know where else to go."

"When could you get here?"

"Tomorrow?"

"Text me your flight information. I'll send it to my friend Jessica, and she'll pick you up at the airport and bring you to my hotel."

"Thanks," said Zach, writing down the number. "See you later."

"Bye," said Sarah, hoping she had done the right thing. It had been many years since she had seen Zach, but he had always seemed like a good guy.

CHAPTER 45

WHILE SITTING in the limousine on that fateful day, June still did not know the job she had accepted, until the President was loaded into the car. By that time, it was too late to do anything other than the job at hand. She knew she had made a terrible mistake.

Now, a week later, she was becoming increasingly anxious. If found out, she would surely go to jail for many years. Racking her brain to figure out a solution, none presented itself. She knew if she went to the police, either they would say she was crazy, or they would put her in jail. If the people who paid her the $20,000 knew she was cooperating with the authorities, they would likely put her in that cell with the President, or worse.

Finally, she envisioned a plan of action. It would necessitate borrowing some items from the hospital.

June worked on the fourth floor, but that didn't stop her from accessing other areas. She took the elevator down to the basement, where the operating rooms were located. She told herself to look confident, as if she was supposed to be there.

June had escorted patients to the operating rooms before, so she was familiar with the layout. She knew pre-op, post-op, the anesthesia office, and the location of the anesthesia medication closet. The door to the cabinet was locked, but June knew where the key resided.

When no one was looking, June grabbed the key and opened the closet. She removed a few bottles of midazolam and ketamine and put them in a pocket of her coat. Quickly, she shut the closet door. Upon turning the corner, she came face to face with a severe-looking nurse anesthetist.

"Who are you?" she asked in a demanding tone of voice.

"June, June Temple."

"And June, what are you doing down here?"

"I, uh, I'm supposed to pick up a patient in post-op and bring them upstairs."

"Well, this is anesthesia, not post-op."

"I'm sorry. I got lost. I'll find my way out."

The anesthetist glanced at her suspiciously, but then walked off into her office. June took a breath and let it out slowly. Her pulse was racing. She had come so close to being discovered.

Later that day, after work, she stopped at the supermarket, and then the liquor store, before returning home. In addition to the supplies she needed, she obtained the ingredients to Mary Ann's favorite meal, chicken penne pasta.

The next step was getting Mary Ann out of the kitchen.

"Mary Ann, I'm making a special dinner for you that I don't want you to see until it's done, so please keep out of the kitchen for a while. Watch TV."

"I can help," said Mary Ann.

"No, I want it to be a surprise."

"Okay, I'll wait in the living room."

June made cupcakes, mixing the drugs into the batter. She then poured the remainder of the medications into the bottle of whiskey. To keep herself calm, she tried humming the theme song from *Gilligan's Island* to herself. She knew all the words, it being her favorite old television show, but she kept losing her place from constantly checking to make sure Mary Ann didn't enter.

All was going according to plan, until her sister walked in unexpectedly.

"You made me cupcakes? Great, I'll have dessert before dinner."

"Mary Ann, no! I need those for work. Please don't take that," June shouted.

Mary Ann backed away.

"How about just one," she asked timidly.

"I'm sorry. I need every cupcake for work. Eat something else."

"Okay. I thought you were making me a special meal. I won't eat your precious cupcakes. Really...," and Mary Ann stomped out of the kitchen.

CHAPTER 46

JIM STAPLES NOW had all his movements inside the White House curtailed by Jonathan Brodsky. He was allowed to be in his quarters, or his office, but nowhere else. He was told not to speak to anyone, including his administrative assistant, without the Chief of Staff by his side. The conspirators were now increasingly nervous that Staples would blow everything, and they would all land in jail. Brodsky felt their wrath.

The fact that the speech on Monday evening had raised the President's favorability ratings did not make the Arlington conspirators any happier; far from it. Staples himself discovered it was well received by the American public.

Staples' boredom was replaced by a new sense of power. Sitting in his chambers, he considered his options on how he could use this new power. As he was no longer allowed to write or give speeches to the citizens of the United States, he needed a new way to reach them. Finally, it came to him, "X", formerly known as "Twitter."

First, he had to decide what to say. It had to be short and sweet. He thought about beer again but decided he had covered the topic enough in his speech. No, this was going to be about other problems the country faced. He came up with two tweets, which he placed, one after the other.

The first one read: "Foreigners are taking our jobs. If you can't speak English, go away, and go back to where you came!"

The second one read: "Go to hell, western Europe. Without us, you'd all be speaking German!"

Within minutes, the White House switchboard was overloaded with phone calls from all over the nation. Now, foreign leaders were asking to speak with the President.

Jonathan Brodsky received calls from every one of the Arlington conspirators. Each berated him for allowing the posts. Billy Joe Scranton threatened to come down to the White House and "ring his neck." Through tight lips, Brodsky tried to remain calm and reassuring.

His answer was the same to all of them. "I'll handle it."

Immediately, he put out a statement. "The President's X feed has been hacked. Obviously, he does not feel this way. We're looking at who could have been responsible. We can't rule anyone out. No further comment until we get to the bottom of it."

Anger having abated slightly after putting out the statement, Brodsky felt he could now breathe easier, that was, until he received his next call. This one was from Phoenix.

"What the hell do you think you're doing? Why does he have a phone?"

"He was the one you picked. I'm babysitting a mad man."

"If you can't control him, then you won't be babysitting him for long. You won't be doing much of anything from the bottom of the Potomac River."

"I'll take his phone. It will all be okay. I'll keep him quiet. You'll see."

"It better be," and the phone went dead.

Phone still by his ear, Jonathan Brodsky took a few calming breaths and closed his eyes. He rubbed his sweaty forehead with his other hand

and put the phone back in his pocket. He had to make it work. He had to keep that asshole sitting in the Oval Office from ruining everything, or he would pay for it with his life.

Phoenix next turned his attention to other matters, calling Marty.

"Where are we on locating that idiot, Joey Petrone?"

"I'm still looking for him. Not to worry. I've got a tap on his phone, so I'll find him at some point and know if he talks to anyone."

"Okay. Keep me informed, and locate the doc."

"Will do."

CHAPTER 47

JUNE TURNED ON the kitchen tap, so that Mary Ann would not hear her, and dialed her supervisor at the Washington Hospital Center. She rehearsed what she was going to say numerous times until she felt she could say it without her voice quivering. Her supervisor was not in yet, which made it that much easier.

"Hi Suzanne, it's June Temple. I'm not feeling well, probably a bad cold, so I'm not able to go to work today. Sorry about the late notice, but it just hit me in the night. Bye."

She then went to Mary Ann's room to say good-bye, but Mary Ann was asleep. June looked at her sister, and quietly whispered, "Good-bye, Mary Ann. I love you."

She then turned around, walked to the kitchen, and grabbed the bag filled with various items from the refrigerator. About to head out the door, she changed her mind and turned back to the kitchen. Finding a pen and paper, she wrote out a note for Mary Ann. Fishing in her coat pocket, she pulled out a card, which she placed together with the note in an envelope on the table. Deciding she didn't want Mary Ann to see the envelope that day, she picked it up and went back to her bedroom. There, she placed it under her pillow. It would be her back-up plan if things didn't work out.

It was an exceptionally cold day, and she pulled the collar of her coat tight around her neck. Whether from cold or fear, she could feel herself shivering. She told herself there was no turning back.

June slipped on the ice that had formed in the night but caught her balance before she fell. The ice had also glazed her windshield, and she spent the next five minutes scraping it off. Aside from a few cars parked on the street, there were no other cars in sight.

June got on and started the car. Despite the frigid temperatures, her car started just fine. *A good omen*, she thought.

She had only a vague idea of where she was to go. Her first trip to the coal mine was a journey she had tried to forget, sitting in the back seat of a limousine with a semi-conscious President of the United States. The trip this time was to be in a ten-year-old, broken-down, Kia sedan, hopefully to rescue him. If she rescued him, how could they send her to jail?

She knew the destination was the Nuttallburg Coal Mining Tipple, only because she happened to see a sign at the foot of the hill where they had stopped the limousine. June had googled Nuttallburg and found it to be part of the New River Gorge National Park. Trembling, she entered it on Google maps and discovered the trip would take about five and a quarter hours. After a few deep breaths, she grabbed the steering wheel firmly with both hands and headed off.

To calm herself down, she put on her playlist, mostly oldies from before she was born. She loved Motown, Elvis Presley, and the Beatles, songs her parents played on their stereo when she was little. It didn't work. Constantly looking in her rear-view mirror, she imagined the police stopping her, or even worse, the guy who hired her.

Eventually, June made it to West Virginia, and then to the Canyon Rim Visitor Center at New River Gorge. With a shaky voice, she asked for directions to the mine.

"Ma'am, are you okay? You seem upset," asked the national park ranger.

"I'm fine. I just have a little problem with my voice, that's all."

"Okay. Here's a map. Just follow this red line. It will take you where you want to go, but the road's rough. Hope you have four-wheel drive."

"I'll be alright. Thanks."

June's car was anything but a four-wheel drive. It was a Kia, but at least it was front-wheel drive.

June began the drive to the mine. It was a slow trek, with huge potholes, rocks, and ice, making for a very bumpy journey. With white knuckles, she hung tight to the steering wheel, and eventually, the little car made it all the way to a small parking area. She recognized this lot from the previous trip. Not a soul was in sight.

June stayed in her car for a few minutes, gathering her courage. She could feel her heart racing, as she steadied her breathing. Slowly, she opened her door.

I can do this. I know I can. I just have to stay calm, she repeated to herself three times.

She picked up her backpack, stuffed with the coffee-filled thermos, cupcakes, and the whiskey flask. She then locked the car and made her way across the parking lot. In front of her was the Nuttallburg Coal Tipple, which she remembered well from that fateful day. It was a long, brown structure, heading down from the top of the hill.

Taking time to gather her courage, she read the sign describing the history of the tipple, long abandoned. In its heyday, it housed a conveyor belt bringing coal down from the mine on top, to be loaded onto train cars on tracks beneath the end of the tipple. Next to the railroad tracks was the swiftly moving New River, with its many rapids. Presently, the tipple was in poor repair, with missing and rotted floorboards.

The trail up the hill was hard to find, as a recent light snow had made everything appear different. Eventually she discovered some landmarks that seemed familiar, and she headed up what she believed was the path. Trudging up the mountain with her backpack on was a difficult climb, made worse by the nurses' shoes she was wearing. The path was icy, and she had to take care to avoid falling.

About halfway up, she heard what sounded like crunching leaves behind her. Fearing the worst, June turned around too quickly, losing her balance on the ice. She stumbled, causing her backpack to fall noisily to the ground, scattering its contents behind her. Looking wildly about, she could see no one, only a rabbit hopping through the snow. She quickly refilled her backpack with the items that had fallen out and sat for a few moments on the path to compose herself. Eventually her heart rate returned to normal, and she resumed her trek.

I can do this.

Arriving at the mine, she immediately came upon a guard dressed in camo clothing, sitting, head in his hands, looking almost asleep. Seeing June, he jumped up, a large automatic rifle in his arms pointed at her.

June's heart rate started racing again; she could almost hear it pounding.

"Hi. I'm June, the nurse. I'm here to check on the prisoner," she said in a quivering voice.

The guard looked wary. "Did Staples send you?"

"I've been directed here to make sure he's still okay," she said, avoiding answering his question.

"I'll take you down there," said the guard, and he lowered his rifle slightly.

Together, they made their way to the elevator and took it down to the next level. When the elevator door opened, the first thing June saw was an automatic rifle being pointed at her, held by another guard. He was wearing the same camo clothing.

"Who are you, and what are you doing here?" he demanded.

"I'm here to check the prisoner."

The second guard looked dubious, but slowly lowered his rifle. "Follow me," he said.

June followed, first left, then right, then right again, until they came to the entrance to the cell. Here was the man with the snake tattoo that she recognized from her first trip to Nuttallburg.

"Why are you here?" asked Strang.

"I'm here to check on the prisoner," she said. Her nervousness had abated, and she felt slightly more confident.

"It's okay," Barty Strang said to the other guards. "She's one of us."

"Hey. I figured you guys were bored and cold hanging out here," said June. "I brought you some whiskey and cupcakes. I realize they don't go all that well together, but I had leftover cupcakes from my nephew's birthday party, and I thought you might want some whiskey to keep out the cold. Only take them if you want them."

The cupcakes were devoured almost immediately. The whiskey took a little bit longer, but within a few minutes, the guards had consumed everything.

"Can I see the prisoner now?" asked June.

"By all means," said Barty, who unlocked the cell door and ushered June in with a wave of his hand.

The whiskey had its effect. None of the guards saw June slip a piece of thick tape over the latch before the door closed.

President Peterman was sleeping on the cot in his cell. June awakened him with a gentle nudge. He awoke with a start.

"What's going on?" he cried out.

"Quiet," she whispered. "I'm here to help you. My name is June. I've got some coffee for you. Drink this," and she held out a mug of hot coffee from her thermos.

President Peterman drank quickly, using the heat from the coffee mug to warm his hands. He looked at her quizzically, but she put her finger to her lips to indicate he should remain quiet. Looking at her watch, she saw that it had been approximately half an hour since the guards had started on their cupcakes and whiskey. Beyond the cell, she could see Barty asleep. There was no view of the other two guards, but she hoped they shared a similar fate.

She opened the cell door quietly and indicated for the President to follow her. The tape had done its job, and the latch stayed open.

President Peterman slowly got to his feet and haltingly followed June out of the cell. Walking down the hall, she spotted the two remaining guards asleep on the floor. The elevator door was still open. By pushing the "up" button, it rose, clanking loudly, to the surface of the mine, where no guards were now stationed.

Walking out, Francis Peterman could feel fresh air again, and immediately he felt better. Weak though, through inactivity, June had to hold him steady on the downhill trek to the car. They walked down slowly, so as not to slip.

Finally, they made it down the hill to the parking lot. Upon reaching the car, June helped the President on to the back seat.

Her heart was still racing, but they had made it this far. They just needed to get back on the main road, and then they'd be safe. She had saved the President, and maybe she would get a medal.

Her temporary feeling of relief did not last long. Before she even turned the key to start the car, she heard a smash from the passenger side window. Looking over, she could see an automatic rifle pointing at her head. June had not counted on a guard in the parking lot, as he had not been there on arrival.

"Both of you, out of the car," demanded the guard. With his rifle, he pointed the way for them to walk, uphill on the path. June helped the fatigued President up the path, stumbling a bit herself. They finally made it to the top, where one of the formerly drugged guards met them and escorted the President back to his cell.

The last thing Francis Peterman heard before being thrust into the elevator was the sound of an automatic rifle.

CHAPTER 48

JOEY PETRONE was having the time of his life. He was eating and drinking to his heart's content, and he was even up a few bucks in the casino, where he spent most of his time. He continued to lose at craps and roulette, but he had a big payoff on one slot machine that made up for the losses and then some. So overall, things were good, except for one major issue. Joey knew that each day could be his last, and he constantly found himself looking over his shoulder.

Finally, today, Joey had an inspiration. He remembered the day he was to drive the unconscious President to Nuttallburg, and the secret service agent who had spoken to him while he was waiting. The agent had given him a card. Where was it? Did he still have it? Joey searched through his clothes, finally finding some he used that day, and he came up with the card. He held it up in front of him, thinking.

If he was to confess to kidnapping the President and help get him released, perhaps he might get a reduced sentence. At least it would be better than a bullet in the head. He could try to negotiate his fate by slowly giving out information. Joey nodded his head as if agreeing with himself. Yes, this was the answer.

He dialed the number. There was no answer, so he left a voicemail.

"Mr. Lincoln, I got your card. I'm calling you to tell you about a plot regarding President Peterman, and I want to negotiate. Call me back at this number and I'll tell you more."

Ray was working out in the gym. His shift at the Vice President's residence was not supposed to start until 2 pm. The first task was thirty minutes on the treadmill, running full blast. Next was a full weight workout. He could feel the tension within him ease as his muscles burned from the effort. His Air pods were playing Beyonce when the call came in from Joey Petrone. Looking at the number on his phone, he saw it was from an "unknown caller."

Probably someone wanting me to buy an extended warranty or something, he thought, and he let the call go to voicemail. *If it's important, they'll leave a message.*

It wasn't until around 1:30 in the afternoon on his way to the Vice President's residence that he heard Joey's message. Putting it together with Sarah's situation and the call he had received from that doctor, it certainly appeared something unusual was happening.

Ray immediately called back the number, and Joey answered.

"Is this Ray Lincoln?"

"Yes, what's your name?"

"That's not important. But if you want to find out about the plot against the President, meet me at the Lincoln Memorial tomorrow at 7 am. Come alone. I'll recognize you."

The phone went dead. Ray stood there for a moment, deciding what to do. About to call it in to his superiors, he had second thoughts. They might not believe him. He would check it out first and call it in if there was anything to it.

Joey felt very pleased with himself. He was going to spoon out the information slowly. Maybe he would even be seen as a hero. To celebrate, he went back to the casino and ordered a few more drinks.

CHAPTER 49

ZACH'S PLANE LANDED right on time, at 3:15 pm. He had been told to meet Sarah's friend at the airport, but he had no idea how he was to recognize her, or she him. He imagined walking around the airport for hours, asking all passers-by if they were Sarah's friend, Jessica.

Fortunately, after passing through the secure area, he saw a well-dressed, petite woman with a cardboard sign which read, "Z. Webster."

"Are you Jessica?"

"That's me!" she said spritely. "Can you show me your ID?"

"Sure," and Zach pulled out the license from his wallet. "Can I see yours?"

They compared each other's licenses.

Both satisfied, they continued through the throng of passengers heading for the exit to finally arrive at Jessica's car.

Neither spoke for the first ten minutes of the trip. Zach could see her holding tight to the steering wheel with white knuckles.

Finally, Jessica spoke in a quiet voice. "I'm here to deliver you to Sarah. I was told not to ask you any questions. I feel like I'm in the middle of some TV mystery. She doesn't want me to know too much. But I hope she's okay. Tell her to let me know if there's anything more I can do."

"I will."

Not knowing what else to say, the rest of the trip passed in silence. Fifteen minutes later, they were at the entrance to the hotel.

"She's on the fourth floor, Room 402."

"Thank-you so much," said Zach, and Jessica drove away.

Zach proceeded to the entrance hall, and then into the lobby to take the old-fashioned elevator up to the fourth floor. He walked down the corridor to Room 402, and hesitantly knocked on the door.

"Who is it?"

"Zach."

The door slowly opened. He recognized Sarah right away. She was as pretty as ever.

Both stood silently in the doorway for a few moments, indecisive of how the greeting should go. Sarah made the first move.

"Hi, Zach," and she gave him a brief hug.

"Hi, Sarah. You haven't changed," he said, feeling awkward, not sure if he should hug her back.

"I don't know about that," she said, smiling slightly.

"I guess we've both changed a little."

Sarah ushered him inside, shutting the door behind them.

"Why don't you sit down. There's a chair over in the corner. Would you like a glass of water?"

"Sure. It's been a long day. In fact, it's been a long week. I guess we've both had better weeks."

After a few minutes of light conversation, Zach got right to business.

"Okay, Sarah. Let's go over each other's weeks to see if we can make some sense out of it all."

"Sounds good. You start." Zach proceeded to retell his story, this time in more detail, starting from the time he was asked by Andy Brannigan to send over her father's eye chart.

"I didn't know you saw my dad as a patient. He did tell me that you had become an ophthalmologist."

"And he told me that you had become a family doctor in California, and that he was really proud of you."

Zach got up and paced around the room as he continued his story.

"So, as I might have told you on the phone, Andy Brannigan got killed in a hit and run shortly after telling me that the eye exam he did on your dad didn't match up with my old chart. Then this one-armed guy follows me and tries to shoot me in my car, before coming after me in my office when I tried to retrieve the old chart."

"Did you call the police?"

"Yes, but they didn't believe me. The guy made two more attempts to get me, once in a hotel and once in my dad's old fishing camp in Maine. I've been lucky to escape both times, but eventually I won't be so lucky."

"Did you try the police again? They've got to believe you after all these attempts."

"I tried, but the one-armed guy showed up at one of the hotels right after I called the police, so I don't know if I can trust them. Maybe I'm just getting paranoid, but I don't know who to trust right now."

"I understand. I'm not sure who to trust either. It was no addict looking for drugs who pointed a gun at me in my examining room, and I doubt it was a mechanical failure of my brakes that almost killed me. Rose Goodwin's car explosion was no accident, and my dad's most trusted advisor, Bob Benton, has been fired. I can't get a hold of my dad, and I'm worried. What if something's happened to him, and what if they come after Jefferson?"

"Who's Jefferson?"

"My son. He's eight years old."

"Didn't know you had a kid. I've got two, Emma, age 7, and Liam, age 9."

"That's nice," said Sarah, with a slight smile. "Anyway, we need to figure out what to do so we can get back to them."

He nodded, not ready to reveal that he did not have custody of his children.

They both sat quietly for a few minutes, letting everything sink in.

"Okay, I should go downstairs and get a room," said Zach.

"I'll go with you. I can tell you it's expensive."

"I guessed that."

They took the elevator down to reception, where Zach encountered the same clerk Sarah had worked with on her registration.

The clerk looked Zach up and down.

"I'm sorry, but we don't have any rooms available," she said brusquely.

"Anything at all, even a broom closet?"

"I'm sorry, Sir. I have nothing at all."

Looking past Zach to the woman in line behind him, the clerk announced, "Next, please."

Zach moved out of the way, uncertain what to do next. Sarah had been listening and came over to him.

"You can stay in my room. No problem. I have two beds. I only need one, and you can take the other."

"Are you sure?"

"I trust you, Zach. You were always a good guy. And anyway, since we're both targets, why make it tougher on the people trying to do us in? This way, they only need to clean one room if we're both shot."

Zach smiled for the first time in a while. Sarah still had her sense of humor, even if it was gallows humor. That was one of the things he had really liked about her in high school.

"I haven't eaten in ages," said Zach. "I need to get some dinner. Would you like to join me?"

"Sure. Good idea."

They proceeded downstairs and allowed their tension to dissolve by discussing old friends from high school, making a point not to discuss their predicament. Both needed to decompress, and they found meaningful company in each other.

After dinner, they went outside to stroll around the gardens. The sky was dark, and they could see the moon glimmering over the ocean.

The tranquility of the evening suddenly disappeared, as the sound of what appeared to be loud gunfire rang in their ears. Looking up above them, the dark sky had dissolved, revealing brilliant displays of gold, silver, and red, shot off from a barge in the ocean. Their ordeal had made them forget it was New Years Eve.

They sat down on the grass and silently watched until the grand finale was completely over.

Turning to Zach, Sarah finally spoke. "I just have one question. A serious one. How come you never asked me out in high school?"

"What?"

"How come you never asked me out in high school? We did a couple things along with some other friends, and I thought you liked me."

"Here we are, on the run from people who want to kill us, wrapped up in something we don't understand, and you're asking about high school?"

"Why not? We need to talk about something else."

Zach looked down at his feet. He was back in high school again. "Okay. I didn't think I stood a chance. You were so popular. You'd be going out with the star football player or some other popular kid, and I was a nerd."

"Well, that's where you were wrong."

After a moment of silence, Zach looked up at Sarah. "Guess I missed my chance."

"Yeah, you did. But that was a long time ago."

Zach nodded in agreement. He thought back to high school, and how things might have worked out differently if he had the courage back then to ask Sarah out on a date. Finally, with nothing left to talk about, they returned to the hotel.

Just as they reached their room, Sarah's phone rang.

"Hello."

"This is Ray. I know it's late. Just wanted to fill you in. I heard from an unknown source about your father. He wouldn't tell me more over the phone, but I did set up a meeting with him for tomorrow morning at seven by the Lincoln Memorial. I'm to come alone, and he said he'd recognize me. It may just be a prank, but with everything else going on, I'm taking it seriously, so I'll be there. I'll call you back after I talk with him. That's if he shows up."

"Thanks, Ray."

"Bye."

Sarah turned back to Zach after hanging up the phone.

"Did you hear the speech he gave about beer? I saw it on TV, and that's not my dad."

"I know, and unless he's changed, I don't think he really likes beer."

"That's right. He much prefers wine. He would never go on TV and start talking about beer. Even though the camera angle didn't do a close-up, which is strange, I really don't think it was him."

"I know this sounds crazy, but do you think someone could have taken your dad's place and is pretending to be him? That could explain a lot."

"It's pretty far-fetched, but it would explain things: why he hasn't called me back, the speech about beer, the attempts on our lives because we could expose it."

"I don't know how else to explain it. Maybe we're missing something. I think I need some sleep. Let's talk about it in the morning."

"I need to call Jefferson before I go to sleep. Just want to make sure he's okay, even if he's asleep already. Do you want to call your kids?"

Zach paused before answering. "They're with their mother. I should call my dad. I'm sure he's worried. And thanks for letting me stay here."

After making their calls, both went to bed, but neither fell asleep quickly nor slept well.

CHAPTER 50

RAY WAS NOT due to work at the Vice-President's residence until noon, so he had plenty of time. He left for the Lincoln Memorial early, as he wanted to get there before the crowds, to look about freely. After first walking about the circumference of the property, he made his way up the steps to the statue of Lincoln himself. It was a chilly day under blue skies, and the wind whistled through the pillars of the Memorial. There was an absence of tourists, likely due to the early hour and cold temperatures. The only people he could spot were the sanitation workers emptying trash receptacles.

Ray paused for a moment to look up at Mr. Lincoln. He took the time to read the Gettysburg Address and the Second Inaugural Address, on opposite sides of the statue. He then proceeded to walk around the back of the memorial, looking for any potentially looming risks. Not seeing any, Ray sipped at the coffee he purchased on his way, leaning against one of the pillars.

Ray checked his watch. It was now 7:15, fifteen minutes beyond the time they were to meet. He would wait until 7:30.

Finally, at about 7:20, Ray spotted a large man slowly making his way up the steps. He was laboring from the effort, and as he got closer, Ray recognized him. He was one of the men he saw near the black limousine, parked outside the White House, almost two weeks ago.

"Bowling-ball man," Ray thought to himself.

Instantly, Ray made another possible identification. Grainy as the picture in the paper had been, this could have been the guy who had tried to kill Sarah Peterman.

Huffing and puffing, Joey made his way up the last of the steps and approached Ray.

"You're Ray Lincoln, right?" asked Joey.

"That's right. And you are?"

"Joey."

"What's your full name?'

"You don't need to know."

"Okay. Tell me what you got, Joey." Ray escorted him to a quiet area, near the top of the stairs.

"Okay, but I need to know I'll be getting protection. If I tell you, I'm a marked man. I'm probably a marked man now, anyway. And I need clemency. I don't want to go to jail."

"I can't promise anything. If your information is important, and you need protection, I'll do what I can. I can't promise anything about clemency. That's not up to me. I can't make any deals. So, tell me what you've come to say, or just get lost. I'm freezing up here," said Ray, blowing on his hands to keep them warm.

Joey stood there, not quite sure what to do. Finally, he said, "There's been a plot regarding the President."

"You've already told me that."

"Okay. Here's what's happened. The President's been kidnapped, and he's been replaced by another guy who's been told what to do and how to act," said Joey, for the first time, looking Ray straight in the eyes. "We did it on December 19, the day you saw us outside the White House in the black limousine."

"That's crazy."

"I know, but it's true. I was forced to drive the President away."

"Where is the President now?"

"I need to speak to someone about clemency before I say anything more."

"Who's behind it?"

"I'm not saying anymore until I get clemency," repeated Joey.

"Why did you try to kill Sarah Peterman?"

Being identified as Sarah's would-be assassin was not what Joey expected, and it took him a minute to recover.

"It was the mission I was given. I don't know why."

"Who gave you this mission?"

Before he could answer, Ray heard what sounded like a car backfire. It was the sound of a gunshot, and immediately, he could see Joey fall backwards. Ray reached forward to grab him, but too late. He slipped out of his hands, but as he fell, he uttered one word, "Phoenix," before crashing down the steps of the Lincoln Memorial, one at a time.

The few tourists who had finally arrived at the monument on that cold, windy morning screamed as Joey, the human bowling-ball, rolled by.

Ray charged down the steps two at a time. By the time he reached the bottom of the stairs, Joey was now lying on his stomach. He turned him over and could see the red stain on his chest, and he was unable to feel a pulse.

The few tourists who witnessed the scene scattered, not knowing if a random gunman would continue to shoot at others nearby.

Ray quickly dialed 911, reaching an emergency operator. "We need an ambulance here at the foot of the Lincoln Memorial. A man has been shot."

He then raced back up the stairs and looked about, trying to spot where the gunshot came from, but it was too late. There was no sign of anyone with a gun.

Ray was left with a dilemma. He could stay and tell the police what he knew, but they might not believe him, and it would surely anger his superiors in the secret service since he didn't come to them first. He could report what he knew to Director Allen, but it was possible he could be involved. After all, wasn't it Director Allen who had him reassigned? He decided at that moment to leave the scene.

Phoenix packed up his rifle. He was an excellent marksman, self-trained. No one had seen him climb up the tree with his "guitar case," and no one had seen him climb down.

"I hate doing this shit myself," he thought to himself, as he headed back to his hotel suite.

CHAPTER 51

"**HELLO.** Who is this?" asked Sarah.

"It's Ray, and I've got news."

"What is it?" Excited, Sarah put the phone on speaker.

"It's crazy. I don't believe it myself," said Ray.

"Start at the beginning. Did you meet him?"

"Yes, I met him at the Lincoln Memorial. He was the same guy who tried to kill you at your office."

Sarah shuddered.

"He told me he was part of a plot to kidnap your father, and now there's some other guy who looks like your dad and is pretending to be him. He told me he wouldn't say anymore until he got protection and clemency."

"Then what did you say?" asked Sarah.

"Couldn't say much more because then he was shot dead."

After a long pause, Zach spoke. "Did he say where the President is being held?"

"No. He just said one word after he was shot. 'Phoenix.' Does that mean anything to either of you?"

"No," said Sarah.

"So, do you think he's being held in Phoenix, Arizona?" asked Zach.

"No idea."

"We need to find him, and we need to find him now." demanded Sarah. "Who can we trust?"

"I really don't know. If I go to my superiors, they'll think I'm nuts. I just got back home, and I need to think it over some more. And Sarah, you need to be careful. Until we know more, I think both of you should disappear. I don't know how, but you need to find a way."

"I don't want to hide out. I need to find my dad, and I need to keep Jefferson safe."

"The fact that they put him in another car rather than your car where the brakes failed means that whoever is behind this doesn't want him hurt. But where is he now?"

"He's with my best friend in San Diego."

"The secret service will be looking for him, as they are for you. Until we know who to trust, he should be hidden also, and away from you. It will be too easy for them to find Jeff if he's with your best friend."

"She's taken him to another location."

"Don't tell me over the phone, just on the chance we're being overheard."

"Maybe I should go to DC and demand to see my dad."

"I don't think that's the right thing to do now. You could be making things worse. We don't know what we're up against."

"I feel like I need to do something."

"The best thing you can do is to stay safe and hidden until we work out a plan. That's the best way to help your dad and keep Jefferson safe. Gotta go now. We'll talk later. Bye."

Neither Zach nor Sarah spoke for the next few minutes, trying to put the pieces together. Sarah spoke first.

"I don't like this. I need to find out what's happened."

"I understand. But we can't help him if we're dead.

"My ex-wife works at the CIA. I think she works with informants, giving them false identities. At least she used to. Maybe she'd help us hide out until we can figure out a plan."

"You don't sound too excited about calling her."

"Not excited at all."

Sarah looked at him inquisitively. "So, your divorce didn't go well? I didn't even know you were married."

"Long story. I'll tell you about it later. First, I need to think about what to say to Samantha to get her help."

"Will she believe you?"

"I don't know. I've never told her a full-on lie that would sound anything like this, even when I was drunk, so maybe."

"Can you trust her?"

"I think so. I can't imagine her having a part in any of this."

"Okay. Call her."

"I'm not sure what to say."

"Just start at the beginning and tell her what's happened to you, and what's happened to me. Tell her about Ray's phone calls, but don't give his name, just in case."

Zach picked up the phone, reluctantly. "Okay, here goes." This time he did not put the phone on speaker.

"Hi, Sam. It's Zach. I need your help."

Zach proceeded over the next half hour to fill Samantha in on the events over the past two weeks. He then mentioned Sarah's details and the phone call he had just received from an agent in the Secret Service. There was silence on the other end of the phone until Samantha finally spoke. Her response was not what Zach expected.

"Were you seeing Sarah while we were married?"

"Are you crazy?" Zach snapped, his voice raised. "Here I am telling you about how I was almost killed, and the President of the United States has been kidnapped, and you're asking me if I had an affair with Sarah while we were married? The answer is no, I did not see Sarah while we were married. In fact, I've never gone out with Sarah. We were just friends in high school for a while. I haven't even seen her since high school until yesterday. If you remember correctly, it was you who had the affair."

"Well, you were no peach either."

"Let's leave it. Neither of us would win any awards for our behavior. I need your help. Our kids need a dad who's still alive."

"And maybe one who's not a drunk?"

After a pause, Samantha continued. "Sorry, that was uncalled for. Let me think about it and call you back in an hour."

"Thanks, Sam. Bye."

"That was interesting," said Sarah.

"We didn't have the best marriage. The first few years were good, but then it went downhill."

"Do you want to tell me about it? We've got an hour to wait, and nothing else to do."

"Sure. Why not."

He proceeded to discuss Samantha's affair, his alcoholism, his road to recovery, and his hope to be allowed to spend more time with his children. He realized he had never told anyone the whole story before.

Sarah didn't say much. She just sat listening quietly until Zach mentioned his children, when tears welled up in her eyes. She grabbed a tissue and wiped the tears away quickly.

"I'm sorry, Sarah. I didn't mean to burden you with my problems," he said, seeing her reaction.

"No. I'm sorry. Thank you for sharing such a personal story. The tears are my own problem."

"Would you like to tell me about it?"

"Okay. Why not? So, I met Morgan in college, but then we broke up. I found out he was seeing someone else. That should have been a sign to me, but it wasn't. Eventually, he moved to San Francisco, where I was doing my residency, and we started going out again. We got married at the end of my residency, moved to San Diego where I joined my clinic, and he started working for a big financial firm. We had a son, Jefferson, almost immediately.

I had to work occasional long hours, but I thought Morgan understood. He also started working late, though not on the nights I worked late, so that at least one of us was home early enough for Jefferson. Everything was going great, or so I thought.

Then one evening, after we put Jefferson to bed, he pours me a glass of red wine and tells me he's leaving. He's fallen in love with his assistant at the firm, and they're moving to San Francisco together. I didn't know what to say. Neither did he, after I threw the wine in his face. So, he packed up his clothes and walked out. That was February of last year, and I haven't seen him since."

"I'm really sorry," said Zach.

"But the worst part of it is he not only abandoned me, but he also abandoned Jefferson. Jefferson adored his father. On his birthday, he waited around the house all day expecting his father to arrive. I offered to take him to the zoo. I offered to take him out for junk food, which I normally never do. Still, he refused to leave the house, waiting for his father to arrive. The son-of-a-bitch never showed up. In the mail the next day was a birthday card from him with a twenty-dollar bill attached. Not even a present; a twenty-dollar bill. We haven't heard from him since."

"That's terrible. I don't understand why he'd do that. I know my kids are the most important thing to me."

"The only thing that brings me some relief is that I think I ruined his fancy leather jacket, the one he loved so much, with the red wine."

Zach looked at her, his mouth in a half-smile.

"So, tell me, Zach, how did you find out about Samantha cheating?"

"I thought we had a good marriage too, but things started to unravel. It was already a tough time for me. My mom had recently died, and to tell the truth, I wasn't handling it well. We had some friends at the FBI, back in DC, Darcy, and Tony, that Samantha had met through work. We double-dated with them often, back when we were living in Washington.

"One day, not long after my mother died, Darcy called me and asked if we could do a Zoom call. Sure, I said. I thought it was just to see how I was doing and pay their respects to my mom. I got on, and both she and Tony were there, I guess for mutual support. So, they laid it on me, and it wasn't about my mom.

"They were doing a joint project with the CIA, and Darcy mentioned to the agent that she had a friend, Samantha, in the CIA. Did she know her?

"The CIA agent said 'yes, and you must know about her affair with her boss. It's been going on for months, and she doesn't try to hide it. Everyone in the department knows about it.'

"Darcy told me she almost fell out of her chair on hearing the news, and then the agent apologized and said she shouldn't have said anything, but she thought Darcy would have already known. It took Darcy and Tony some time to work up the nerve to tell me about it, but they finally decided they had to. From there, everything fell apart. The rest you know."

"But you've gotten over it?" asked Sarah.

"Kind of. You never really fully get over it, but you forgive," said Zach. "Someday, you will too."

"I hope so. That sat in silence briefly before Zach's phone rang. It was Samantha.

"Zach, I believe you. I realize we've had our issues, but you've never lied to me, and you don't sound like you're back on the booze. I have no idea what's going on, but it sounds like you and Sarah are in real danger. We just don't know from whom.

"So, this is my idea. As you know, my parents live in Paris now, since they've retired. You can stay with them. I've called them, and they're happy to do it.

"The tricky thing is getting you out of the country unnoticed, especially as you've got the President's daughter with you. Word is that the secret service is looking for her. I've got to get you false passports. There's a guy not too far from you, in Los Angeles, that we've worked with who can do it for you quickly. His name is Louis Angelo, and his address is 354 Grovemont Street in LA. He's expecting you both later today."

"Thank-you so much, Samantha," said Zach.

"Good luck," and she hung up.

CHAPTER 52

"JEFFERSON, stay in the car, please."

He ran out anyway, to give his mother a hug, disobeying her orders.

"He's so happy to see you," said Jessica. She had brought Jeff with her to pick up Sarah and Zach from the hotel.

Sarah grabbed her son in a warm embrace. "I've missed you," she said with a big smile.

"Are we going home now, Mommy?'

Smile fading, Sarah changed the topic of conversation. "Jefferson, this is Dr. Webster. He's a friend of mine."

"Hi Jefferson. You can call me Zach. Everyone does."

"Okay. Mommy calls me Jefferson. Everyone else calls me Jeff."

"So, I'll call you Jeff and you call me Zach. Okay?"

Jeff nodded.

They drove to Los Angeles, to the address on Grovement Street given to them by Samantha. Sitting beside Jefferson in the back seat, she gave her son another hug.

"I'm sorry, Jefferson, but I still need to stay away for a while. Jessica will be taking care of you for a few days until I'm back."

"How about Daddy. Could he be with me while you're gone?"

"I don't think so. Not this time."

"Jeff, I'm off on sabbatical from work, so I've got lots of time to do really fun things," said Jessica. "You'll see."

"And I'll be home as soon as I can. I promise."

With a frown on his face, Jefferson nodded, "Okay."

Sarah gave him a smile as she and Zach left the car, which drove away with Jefferson waving good-bye from the back seat. He didn't see his mother crying as she walked with Zach up the path to 354 Grovemont Street.

By the time they knocked on the door of the small, blue house, Sarah had composed herself and was no longer in tears. A man who looked about sixty, with long, gray hair pulled back in a ponytail, greeted them with a smile.

"You must be the two young people Samantha told me about. Come in. Come in."

Hesitantly, they stepped inside the front foyer. From there, they could see most of the house. It was nothing like they expected. From floor to ceiling, everywhere they looked, the house was completely decorated in Star Wars paraphernalia. Life-size cutouts of Luke Skywalker, Han Solo, and Princess Leia decorated the walls. Full size models of Yoda, C-3PO, and R2-D2 took up most of the available space in the small living room.

"Welcome to Planet Tatooine. I'm Louis."

"Wow. You must really like 'Star Wars'," said Zach, gazing about.

"How did you guess?" asked Louis with a smile. "But just the original three episodes. The subsequent ones were trash."

"I agree with you," said Zach. "Jar Jar Binks had the most annoying voice."

At this point, Sarah interrupted. "Mr. Angelo – Louis – we need your help to get out of the country. Our names are…"

This time, Louis spoke. "I don't want to know your names. Come with me. Lots to do. Lots to do," he said in his best Yoda impression, motioning for them to follow him down the basement steps.

The basement looked nothing like the living areas of the house. In one corner sat a screen surrounded by photography lighting. In another corner was a table with multiple-colored bottles adjacent to the sink. Next to that was a barber chair and haircutting tools. Finally, there was a large desk with computer screens and printers.

Louis was now all business. "My job is to change your appearance and give you new identities. First, the hair. I think that's all you two need. First, we cut, then we color. What color do you prefer, young lady? Blond, light brown, red?"

"How about blond?" answered Sarah.

"Blond it is, but first, must I do some trimming. Yes, must I." he said in his Yoda voice.

At this, Sarah looked nervous, but Louis laughed.

"I used to be a hairdresser. Not to worry."

Sarah had her hair trimmed on the sides and back, and he gave her bangs for the front. Next came the coloring, and only after he had washed it out was she given a mirror to look at herself. He then added some dark-tinted, large-framed glasses.

"I like it!" she exclaimed, "but it doesn't look anything like me!"

"That's the point," he said. "Next up, you, young man. Come sit in my chair, and what color do you want?"

"I guess I'll go blond also," replied Zach.

"Another blond," said Louis. "Okay."

Zach had most of his hair trimmed off, and what remained was dyed blond. For an added touch, Louis added some Harry Potter style glasses.

"Can't say I like it much, but it certainly doesn't look like me," said Zach.

Louis brought them both over to the photography corner and took their pictures.

"Next, we will give you new identities and passports. You are a married couple, Robert and Lynn Frederic. Give me a few minutes to get your passports together. And here are your wedding rings."

Zach and Sarah sat quietly while Louis worked. They looked at each other as they slipped the wedding rings on their fingers.

"Feels weird to be wearing one again," said Zach, rotating the ring on his finger.

Sarah nodded.

After less than ten minutes, Louis approached them again.

"Here are your passports, and here is a thousand dollars of cash."

"We can't accept your money."

"Don't be silly. You can't use your credit cards, and you'll need money. And, anyway, it's not my money. It's from the CIA. Standard procedure.

"Also, I have you on the 9:00 flight tonight from LA to Paris. Here are your tickets, Mr. and Mrs. Frederic. I'll walk you out."

"Thank-you so much, Mr. Angelo. What do we owe you?"

"It's all been paid. And my name is not really Louis or Angelo. You don't know me, okay? There's a cab waiting for you two blocks south from here to take you to the airport. Have a good flight."

With that, he ushered them out of the house.

"Amazing," said Sarah, looking over at Zach. "Your Samantha is really something."

"I guess that's a good way of describing her," he replied, as they walked down to the waiting cab.

CHAPTER 53

SAMANTHA was not sure what to do with the information she received from Zach. She had gone over and over it in her head. It was crazy. Chances are Zach had things confused, but it did seem like his life was in danger. Why, she didn't know. Finally, she had an idea and picked up the phone.

"Hi. How are you? It's Samantha."

"I'm great," said the male voice on the other end of the line. "What's up?"

"It's been a long time since we spoke."

"Yes, it has. It's been a long time since we did other things, too. I miss those old days when you would come on your monthly visits to DC."

"That's not why I'm calling."

"But you do miss me, don't you? Just say the word, and I can arrange for a fun rendezvous. You name the place, and I'll be there. It will be like the old days. Even better, now that you're in DC full time."

"I'm done with that. It ruined my marriage, and I'm not going down that road again. I was young and stupid, and you were my boss. I was calling to try to get your help but forget it."

"Okay. Sorry. What do you need help with?"

"It's my ex, Zach. He's in trouble. He told me some crazy story about the President of the United States being kidnapped and people trying to kill him. I'm not sure what to do about it."

"Where is he now?"

"I'm flying him to Paris to stay with my parents. He tells me he has Sarah Peterman, the President's daughter with him, and she's also in danger. Is this crazy, or what?"

"Sounds crazy to me. Does he have any psychiatric problems?"

"Not really, but he was an alcoholic for a couple of years."

"Sounds like he's on a bender, now."

"He didn't sound that way. He sounds really scared."

"Okay, I'll check it out. Until you hear from me, let's keep this between us. People might think you've gone off the deep end, which could affect your job. I'll investigate it and call you back when I know more."

"Thanks."

"No problem, Sam."

Jonathan Brodsky put his phone down. He now knew where Zach Webster and Sarah Peterman were hiding.

His next call was to Phoenix, and then Phoenix called Marty Green.

"Marty, update on the status of the doctor."

"Sorry, Phoenix. I lost him. He abandoned his car at the airport in Maine."

"I know where he's going. Get on the next flight to Paris."

"Yes, boss."

CHAPTER 54

NEITHER SARAH NOR ZACH looked like themselves on arriving from the non-stop, red-eye Delta flight that touched down in Paris at 4 pm. Aside from their new hairstyles and glasses, both were bleary-eyed from lack of sleep. Their clothes were rumpled from failed attempts to sleep in their economy seats. First class would have made them much too noticeable.

They were met at baggage claim by Samantha's parents, Marie and Pierre Rochambeau. Pierre had a small sign he was holding that read "Mr. and Mrs. Frederic."

The sign was not necessary. Even though it had been a few years, Zach remembered them distinctly. Samantha's exceptional looks came from her mother, Marie, who even though now in her 60's looked like the cover model of a magazine. Pierre was also striking. He was tall and thin with jet black hair and a pencil mustache. There was not a hint of gray in his hair, which Zach assumed had been accomplished through the aid of a dye bottle.

Zach was very nervous seeing the Rochambeaus again. They knew all the details of his past marriage and breakup with their daughter. They were also aware of his alcoholism and what he had called Samantha that day in court. He was quite surprised they would have anything to do with him now.

"Hello, Marie and Pierre. It's me, Zach," he said on reaching them and holding out his hand.

Marie jumped back in astonishment as she gazed at the couple. "Mon Dieu. Is it really you Zach? You look so different. I don't remember you with blond hair."

"The hair and everything are due to your daughter," said Zach.

"If it was really Samantha's doing, your hair would be gray," said Pierre with a hearty laugh.

Instantly, Pierre's laugh had a calming effect on Zach. He remembered now that they spoke perfect English. Quietly, he introduced Sarah, but only by her first name.

"We know who you are, young lady," said Pierre loudly.

"Not so loud, Pierre. Remember what this is all about. They are undercover," said Marie.

"Ah yes. I forgot," said Pierre.

Once their luggage arrived, Samantha's parents drove them to their house, just outside the city limits. Arriving via a long, tree-lined driveway, the house was just as grand as Zach remembered, with tall stone pillars leading to a magnificent, oak entryway. The house was immense, especially for two retired people. Each room was furnished elegantly, and everything about it spoke of wealth and success.

"You two probably would like to get some sleep. You both look exhausted," said Marie.

"That would be great," said Sarah. "Where should we go?"

"You can take the room down the end of the hall on the second floor. Pierre, show them to their room. It's got a comfortable king bed."

"Uh, Mrs. Rochambeau, we're not really a couple. Is it possible to stay in a room with two beds?" asked Sarah.

"I see you are not French," said Pierre, again accompanied by his loud laugh.

"Ignore him," said Marie, giving Pierre an angry stare. "I understand completely. Pierre, show them to the room on the other end of the hall that has two beds."

Zach had little to say during this conversation, but he longed for a few hours of sleep. Upon reaching their beds, both Sarah and Zach fell asleep immediately, still dressed in the same clothes they wore on the plane. They were awakened a few hours later by Marie knocking on the door.

"Dinner will be ready soon. Why don't you two wash-up and then come downstairs. There are fresh towels in the bathroom down the hall. Come down when you are ready. We are eating in the kitchen."

They both roused quickly from sleep, and after showering and changing their clothes, they headed downstairs. Upon arriving in the kitchen, Zach cleared his throat and spoke.

"Pierre and Marie, I need to say something. First, I want to thank you so much for helping us and putting us up in your beautiful house."

With a quivering voice, he continued. "Most of all, I want to apologize for my past behavior. I was an idiot. I drank, I lost my job, and I treated people close to me terribly. I was not a good father to your grandchildren. I said terrible things to your daughter, things I know I shouldn't have said. I'm so sorry. Please forgive me."

The room went silent again. Finally, Pierre Rochambeau spoke.

"We are aware of everything that happened. We know that your mother's passing hit you hard, and we know about Samantha's role in all of this. She was not completely blameless. It was, how do you say, a bad situation all around."

Marie added, "We forgive you, as we forgave our daughter. We liked you from the moment we met you, Zach. We're sorry that you and Samantha are not together anymore, but we're glad you're doing better."

"Enough of this talk. Let us enjoy our meal. Oh, and I have an email I just received from Samantha," said Pierre.

After putting on his glasses, he read from his phone, "Go to the Champagne Bar at the top level of the Eiffel Tower tomorrow at 1 pm. You will meet a CIA contact there. The investigation has proceeded, and the contact will have further information about what the CIA has learned. They will instruct you what to do to stay safe. Tickets will be waiting for you at the ticket booth by the South Pillar. Good luck. Samantha."

"I'm so glad Samantha's helping," said Sarah. "Hopefully, they can get to the bottom of it, and we can return home soon."

Zach said nothing but looked down at his dinner plate.

"Thanks again for your hospitality," Sarah added.

Heading up to their bedroom, Sarah turned to look at Zach.

"What's the problem? I thought you'd be happy things are moving along."

"It's the height. I don't do well with heights. Never have. I don't know why Samantha picked this location. She should have known better. Maybe it's her way of sticking it to me."

"Just don't look down," said Sarah.

"Easy for you to say."

Sarah fell asleep quickly, but Zach lay in bed awake for more than an hour, before eventually nodding off to sleep.

CHAPTER 55

RAY HAD a pleasant, one-bedroom apartment overlooking a park, where later in the day he would be able to see the neighborhood kids playing ball. The bedroom was messy, with dirty clothes scattered like a rug on the floor. Cynthia, his former live-in girlfriend, always kept things neat, but as they had broken up, it was now up to Ray to keep things tidy. Housekeeping chores were not high on Ray's list of priorities.

The kitchen was not much better, with last night's dishes still on the table and unwashed pots sitting in the sink. The living room was furnished with a large, leather couch and a reclining chair in front of a 65-inch TV. An empty beer bottle sat on the coffee table by the couch. The focus of the living room was a picture on the wall of President Peterman, signed with the inscription, "To my friend, Ray, who keeps me safe."

He got out of bed and walked to the kitchen, where he made a big pot of coffee. Taking it into the living room, he made a point of not looking at Francis Peterman's portrait. He was failing him, his president. Now that his one lead was dead, he wasn't sure where to go next.

The DC police had labeled Joey Petrone's shooting a random act by persons unknown. There had been a shooting on the DC mall the prior week, and they believed they were related.

He had to do something. It was time to take chances, even if there was risk involved. In his phone contacts, he had Director Allen's private cell phone number, to be used only in an emergency. After staring at his phone for more than thirty seconds, finger held over the number, he finally dialed.

"Director, this is Ray Lincoln. There's something of utmost importance I need to discuss with you," he said, holding his voice steady.

"Okay, what is it?"

"I'd rather do it in person, Sir."

"Ray, it's Saturday morning. My kid has a soccer game in an hour. Can it wait?" said the Director in an exasperated tone.

"I'm sorry, Sir. It can't wait."

James Allen looked at his watch before responding. "Okay. I'll come over after the game. I can meet you in my office at 2 pm."

"Thank-you. I'll be there," said Ray.

"It better be important."

"Yes, Sir, it is."

Traffic in DC was unusually busy for a Saturday afternoon. Fortunately, Ray had left extra time to get to the Secret Service headquarters at 950 H Street, and he was able to find a parking spot on the street just outside the building. He took the stairs two at a time and arrived at the Director's office at exactly 2 pm.

The door was locked, and finally around 2:15, James Allen arrived. The director was not in a good mood. His kid had been demoted to reserve goalie and only played a few minutes once the starting goalie became injured. Then, he gave up the winning goal. To top it off, he was now missing the Washington Wizards basketball game on TV.

James Allen's office was larger than he imagined, with a dark mahogany floor that creaked when walked on, and an inlaid cherry desk about eight feet in length. Pictures of presidents lined the wall, the largest being President Peterman's, which hung immediately behind his desk. Unlike Ray's portrait of the President, it bore no inscription. Allen walked in and immediately sat behind his desk. He motioned for Ray to sit on a leather couch facing the desk.

"Sorry to keep you waiting, Ray. The game went a little long."

"No problem, Sir. Thank-you for coming in on Saturday to meet with me."

"Okay, Ray, shoot. What's up?" he said impatiently.

"Sir, I have reason to believe the President has been kidnapped and an impostor has taken over in the White House."

James Allen stayed silent for a moment, staring at Ray intently. Finally, he spoke. "Ray, I have seen the President and spoken with him since then. He hasn't been kidnapped."

"But it's not him. I've spoken with the President's daughter, and he hasn't returned her calls."

"I don't know why the President hasn't returned his daughter's calls. Maybe they had a fight."

"I spoke with a guy who says he was part of the plot, and then he was shot before he said anymore."

"What?"

"This guy called me and said to meet him at the Lincoln Memorial, and that he was part of the plot to kidnap the President. I met him there yesterday, but before he could tell me much more, he was shot dead."

"You did this on your own, without authorization?"

Ray hesitated before speaking, "Yes, Sir, I did."

"Have you no understanding of procedures and protocols?"

"I realize I was in error."

"You realize it now?" James Allen's voice rose. "What other evidence do you have to support such an outlandish claim?"

"None, but..."

"Look, Ray. I don't know what your deal is here. I would get laughed at if I went to the President with this. You get me here on a Saturday to hand me this crap? I've got better things to do," said Allen, now standing up.

"But Sir. Let me explain further."

"No, you've said enough. You've seriously broken protocol, enough to know we can't trust you. Give me your badge and your gun. You're suspended upon further review."

"Sir, listen to me, please."

"No. I'm wasting my Saturday here. Gun and badge, now."

Ray flung his badge and gun onto the desk and stomped out. Director Allen sat back down at his desk. Despite what he had said to Ray, he did have some misgivings.

CHAPTER 56

"THE PRESIDENT is not to be disturbed. He has a bad cold, and will be staying in his chambers," said Jonathan Brodsky to the President's administrative assistant, Judy Mairston.

"Yes, Sir."

"And if any emergencies arise, contact me before involving the President."

"Of course, Sir."

Brodsky had to keep a closer watch on Staples. He removed all the phones from the President's rooms and planned to sleep on the sofa in his office rather than going home for the night.

Staples was itching to do something, anything. He had to get out. He would figure out a way to have some fun.

Brodsky's phone rang. It was his wife, Rita.

"Jon, I know you're busy, but when are you coming home?"

"I'm sorry, Rita, but I'm too busy to leave right now."

"You need to come home. Remember we have theater tickets to see *Les Misérables* with the Newmans. I've been waiting months to see it."

"I can't. I'm too busy. Go by yourself with the Newmans. They're your friends."

"I will not. You're going with me, and that's that. You tell the President you must leave for a couple hours. That's not very much. I've put up with a lot from you, and now I want something in return. So, if you ever want to eat a hot meal again, or anything else from me, I need you to do this."

"Okay, I'll leave in a few minutes," he said, sighing dejectedly.

Jim Staples was watching a nature show documenting the lions of Tanzania when Jonathan Brodsky walked in. He felt like a caged animal himself, not allowed to do anything other than staying in his room. A man could only watch so much television. Granted, he could get any channel and any streaming service he wanted, but this was not how it was supposed to be.

"I have to leave for a few hours," said Brodsky. "You need to stay here."

"I know. You've told me a hundred times. But I'm the President, dammit."

"And as I've told you a hundred times also, you're not the real President. If you screw this up, our lives are not worth anything. Do you understand?"

Staples nodded in agreement, and Brodsky marched out.

Slowly, a grin came onto Staples' face. Yes, he understood, but that didn't mean he was going to follow his keeper's warnings. He was finally going to have some fun.

What should it be, he thought. *Another speech? No, too much work. What to do, what to do?*

Finally, the answer came to him while watching an old western movie.

I've got it. Time to go squirrel hunting. He had seen several squirrels on the lawn of the White House through the windows.

He looked around for a phone, but it had been removed. He tried the door to his bedroom, and it was unlocked. Staples went through it, walked outside, and took a big breath of fresh air. He walked back in and found himself in the Oval Office, where a phone was now readily available, and he called his administrative assistant.

"How are you feeling, Mr. President?" asked Judy.

"Much better, thank-you. I need your help on something."

"Yes, Mr. President. What can I do for you?"

"I need a gun," said Staples.

"I'm sorry, I must have misheard you. What was it you needed? You need some gum?"

"No, I need a gun. G, U, N, gun. Make it a shotgun."

"Are you sure, Mr. President? Is this for some photos or something?"

"Sure. I need a shotgun, and I need it within the hour."

"Okay, Mr. President. We don't have any shotguns here, but I'll send someone out immediately to get one for you."

"Sounds good. Just have them bring it to my bedroom."

Confused, Judy Mairston agreed, and sent out an aide to fetch a shotgun immediately.

An hour later, an aide knocked on the door of the presidential bedroom. Staples answered and opened the door.

"Here it is, Sir," said the aide, as he handed Staples the weapon.

"Good job, kid," said Staples. "Wait a minute, there's no ammunition. Where's the ammo?"

"I didn't know you wanted ammunition. I was just told to get the gun."

"Go back and get me some #6 lead shot. And I want it within a half hour." With that, Staples closed the door.

Half an hour later, literally dripping with sweat, the aide reappeared with #6 lead shot."

"Good job. What's your name, kid?"

"Jamie O'Reilly."

"Well, Jamie O'Reilly, I'll put you in for a commendation."

"Thank-you, Sir," said O'Reilly, backing out the door, although he didn't know what a commendation from the President meant. He was glad to get it, in any event. He had just taken the job recently. Maybe a Presidential commendation would help him get into grad school.

Staples loaded the ammunition into his gun and proceeded out to the White House lawn.

"Where are those darn squirrels, when you actually want them?" Eventually, he saw one, aimed his gun, and fired. It was a direct hit.

"Yes," he cried, as he ran over to his prey. At that moment, secret service agents from every direction came running, guns out.

Staples held up his arms, as if to say, "Don't shoot." Seeing the President and no other assailants, the agents lowered their weapons.

Agent Frank Baldwin came running over, and asked, "What's going on, here?"

"Just a little squirrel hunting, nothing more."

He stared at Staples with a look of shock, as did the other secret service agents. Nothing like this had ever happened before, nor had they ever seen the President even holding a gun. All was quiet for a few moments.

Finally, Staples spoke. "Someone bring this animal to the chef and tell him to make me some squirrel stew."

The agents disbanded and went back to their posts, shaking their heads in disbelief. Frank couldn't wait to tell this story to his friend Ray.

The President walked back to his bedroom. That evening, he had stew for dinner.

"What the hell is going on there?" said the angry voice on the other end of the phone. It was Jack Chauncey, who no longer spoke with the upper crust accent. "Can't you control him?"

"It's not so easy. I'd like to see you try," replied an aggravated Jonathan Brodsky.

"I'd do a damn better job than you. He's out there shooting off guns. If that gets out, all hell's going to break loose. The press would have a field day. I can imagine their reports now: 'Replacing easter egg hunts on the White House lawn, President Peterman is starting a new tradition of squirrel hunts.' You're supposed to be watching him every minute."

"Don't worry. I've got it under control. Everyone has been sworn to secrecy. If anyone says they heard a gunshot, we'll say it was a car backfire. And how did you find out?"

"I've got my sources. You can't let him do these idiotic things. I'm getting pressure from the others, and they're starting to panic."

"I can't appear to be doing my job and babysitting him every second," said Jonathan Brodsky, tired of being yelled at. "What more can I do? I've already moved my office just next to his bedroom. I keep my door open in case I hear if the asshole gets out. I'm even sleeping in my office on the couch, and my back hurts like hell."

"I don't know. Just keep him out of trouble."

"I'll try."

About two miles away in the Hart Senate Office Building, Senator Randal Gray was finishing his catered dinner of Pork Tenderloin with Rosemary Baby Potatoes, when his aide notified him that he had a call from the CEO of Healthcare USA.

"I'll take it in my private office," he said to his aide, and he closed the door to avoid being overheard.

"Yes, Stephen. How are you? I want to thank you for your wonderful donation to my campaign. I've always been impressed with your generosity and your commitment to the health needs of our country," said the Majority Leader.

"Enough flattery, Randal. I want to know where you are on your promise."

"Not to worry, Stephen. It's well taken care of."

"It better be. Money dries up if promises aren't kept."

"Don't worry. You'll be happy with the result."

CHAPTER 57

SATURDAY IN PARIS started rainy and cold. Sarah grabbed the umbrella by the door as they left the house. Huddled together under the umbrella, they found their way to the Paris Metro. They took it to Passy Station, where they exited.

Out onto the Paris streets, it was clear the weather had changed. The sun was shining, and instantly Zach felt better and more in control of his anxiety. He was going to conquer his fear of heights today. He didn't have a choice, he had to.

They walked along the Boulevard Delessert to the Avenue des Nations Unies and then crossed the Seine at the Pont d'Iena. From there, they could see the Eiffel Tower standing straight in front of them. As they approached, Zach could feel the old dread coming back.

Arriving early, they bought an English guide to the Tower. Although nervous herself, to keep Zach calm, Sarah read parts of the pamphlet out loud. "Okay, Zach. Fun facts: *Gustave Eiffel, architect of the Eiffel Tower, included a private apartment for himself at the top, where he hosted famous guests such as Thomas Edison.* Interesting. Don't think I would want to live there myself.

"Let's see what else. *Hitler ordered the Eiffel Tower to be destroyed, but fortunately, the order was never carried out.*

"Okay, this is interesting. *Underneath the South Pillar of the Eiffel*

Tower lies a relic of World War I, a secret military bunker. It goes on to say they used the bunker as a radio station, and that the Eiffel Tower was used to receive and send radio waves during the war, and that it was a key to victory in Europe. It was also used by the Resistance in World War II."

Zach listened to a degree, but mostly his mind was fixated on the height of the Eiffel Tower. He told himself that he didn't have a choice. He had to go up.

"Okay, let's go," said Zach, and they walked up to the ticket booth, where tickets were waiting for them.

Fortunately, the ticket agent spoke English. "Madame and Monsieur, this first ticket takes you up to the second floor. It will stop at the first floor, but do not get out there. Stay on until you reach the second floor. You get out there, and then the second ticket is for the next elevator that takes you up to the summit. From there you can access the Champagne Bar. Have fun."

Zach's face already showed that fun was not on tap for the day, but onward they went. It was the weekend, so there was already a queue. Finally, they reached the entrance to the elevator, where an attendant packed them in tight.

Being one of the first to enter the elevator, Zach and Sarah were pushed to the back of the lift, adjacent to the large glass windows. Looking out, Zach knew he would need to move away from the window, so as not to be terrified once the elevator left the ground. Together they squeezed into the middle of the car.

The lift started moving, and now it was Sarah's turn to feel severe anxiety. She had never been claustrophobic before, but in that elevator, surrounded by the many warm bodies pressed against her, she felt a new sensation of severe panic. She could feel her pulse racing, her whole body sweating, and a feeling that she might faint.

As the elevator stopped at the first floor, she rushed to get out, pushing people out of her way. Zach, confused by her sudden escape from the lift, was able to follow her out just before the doors closed.

Out on the first floor, Sarah closed her eyes and took deep breaths, steadying herself on the railings. Zach stayed close but made sure not to look out over the railings. Finally, after about five minutes, Sarah felt well enough to open her eyes and speak.

"Great pair we are. I fall to pieces in an elevator, and you can't look down."

"Are you claustrophobic? I didn't know," said Zach, concerned.

"I never was before. It felt so weird, like I was going to be crushed by all those bodies. It was like I had no air to breathe, and I thought I was going to pass out. I'm just starting to feel back to normal now."

"That's kind of how I feel with heights. It doesn't make any sense. I feel like I'm going to fall, and then I start to feel faint. It's called acrophobia."

"I guess we're equal now. An acrophobic and a claustrophobic in Paris, trying to survive assassins, while trying to figure out how to help my dad. Wow, what a team," she said, shaking her head.

Zach smiled back weakly. "We do the best we can. So, how do we get to the top to meet with the CIA?"

"I can tell you one thing. There's no way in hell I'm getting back on that elevator," said Sarah.

"Well, we can walk up to the second-floor landing from here. It says here there are 347 steps to the second floor," read Zach.

"Can you do it?" asked Sarah.

"I think so, if I don't look down."

"Okay, let's go."

They started climbing, and occasionally, Zach inadvertently would let his gaze point downward. He would stop, take some deep breaths while closing his eyes, and then proceed onward. It was tough going. Sarah, now more understanding after her own moments with irrational panic, was able to appreciate Zach's difficulties. More than once, she would steady him, while giving him a slight squeeze, to show she understood.

Finally, they were almost at the second-floor landing. Looking up through the windows, they could see the lobby, where tourists exited the elevator. They also saw two men waiting adjacent to the elevator doors. Zach stopped abruptly, causing Sarah to bump into him, and she dropped her umbrella. It crashed down multiple metal steps, making a huge clamor. People from the second-floor landing looked down, including the two men standing by the elevator doors. Zach and Marty Green made eye contact.

"I know one of those guys. He's the one-armed man, the guy who's been trying to kill me. We've gotta get out of here," said Zach.

"What?" asked Sarah, surprised.

"That's the guy who's been trying to kill me. We need to get out now."

"Where to?"

Just then, the elevator doors opened on the second floor. Marty stayed on the landing. They couldn't tell if his companion entered the elevator, or simply stood behind him.

"We've got to go down, I guess, but I'm not sure I can do it," said Zach.

"Just look at the step in front of you," pleaded Sarah, and they raced down.

About halfway between the second and first floors, Sarah stopped abruptly.

"Stop, Zach. One of those guys from the landing is coming up the steps from below. We need to go back up."

They began another uphill climb, trying to get to the second floor, but now, they could see Marty on the stairs in front of them. With a smug smile, waving a gun in his hand, he beckoned them to him. It was clear that he was going to keep them prisoner on the stairs until his associate arrived.

Assuming them no threat, he was too relaxed for his own good. Seeing her chance, Sarah, with all her force, brought her leg up and gave him a massive kick to the groin. Zach grabbed the gun and threw it from the stairs to the ground below. Running past him, they raced up. They reached the second-floor landing, where upon looking down, they could see the two men heading up the stairs toward them.

They had two choices.

They could wait for one of the elevators or try walking back down the stairs. Neither was a good option.

Quickly, they decided on a third option. Jumping over the barriers written in French saying "Defense d'entrer," they started racing up a second set of stairs, heading to the top level of the Eiffel Tower.

Beyond the physical exertion of climbing almost one thousand steps was the condition of the stairs, which were old, narrow, and rickety. It was only knowing that likely death was behind them that kept them going.

At several locations, Zach couldn't help but look down, where he would feel faint and almost lose his balance. With Sarah's help, he was able to grab hold of the railings. Each time, after taking a few deep breaths, he was able to continue moving upward.

Marty Green and his associate, seeing Zach and Sarah on the stairs, jumped the same barrier and headed upward. They were slower, but still relentless in their climb.

About halfway up, Sarah and Zach heard first one clang, then another, and then another. Sarah looked down, and she could see the one-armed man's partner pointing and then firing his gun.

"Don't look down, Zach. Just keep going," she shouted.

They picked up their pace. Three quarters of the way up, they stopped to catch their breaths, too exhausted to keep going. They could see their assailants much further down on the stairs, moving very slowly.

"What are we going to do, Zach?"

"There's supposed to be a CIA guy meeting us in the Champagne Bar at the top. Hopefully they can help us."

"What if there isn't? What if this was all a set-up?"

"I can't believe Samantha would set me up to be murdered."

"Okay. We need to keep going. Hopefully someone's there."

Zach didn't say anything more, but now doubt crept into his mind. They kept moving. Leg muscles exhausted from exertion, every step was like Mt. Everest. Still, they kept going.

Finally, reaching the top, they climbed over the barrier onto the top deck of the Tower. After resting for a moment, they raced around the top deck until they saw the sign for the Champagne Bar. Zach looked down at his watch.

"He should be here. It's 1:10."

"How do you know it's a 'he'? asked Sarah. "Why not a 'she'?"

"Good point. I don't care, if whoever it is can get us out safely."

"How do we recognize the agent?"

"No idea."

Fortunately, there were few patrons in the Champagne Bar when they arrived. No one looked up at them. Quickly, they ran around the tables, and again, no one approached them.

"We're on our own," said Sarah, speaking rapidly.

"I can't believe Samantha set me up," Zach said miserably.

"We can't worry about that now. We've got to figure out how we can get out of here," said Sarah. "Those guys will be here any moment."

"Isn't it obvious? We need to take the elevators down."

"I can't do that. I'll pass out. Don't you remember how I was on that short elevator ride up to the first floor?"

"So, we take the stairs down, once we see the one-armed guy and his friend up here. We race them down."

"I doubt you can do that, going down all those steps. I had to hold you up a few times, and that was going up. What happens when you're looking down those stairs? You'll pass out and fall to your death. Plus, how do we know they don't have people on the ground waiting for us?"

"I have an idea," said Zach.

He walked over to the bar and quickly ordered champagne and caviar. Sarah looked at him incredulously.

"Your idea is to drink champagne and feast on caviar until they find us?" she said, staring at him.

"No, the champagne and caviar are for you."

Guiding Sarah out with one arm and carrying the champagne and caviar with the other, they made their way out onto the observation deck.

"Here," he said, to Sarah, "drink a little of the champagne, and let it drool down your chin."

She looked at him with suspicion.

"Hurry up! We don't have much time."

She drank a sip of champagne and let it drip down her chin.

"Now, forgive me," said Zach.

He dumped some of the caviar in the champagne glass, and then he tossed the mixture all over the front of Sarah's shirt. She jumped backward.

"What the hell are you doing?"

"Quiet. You're sick. You've been throwing up. That will give you some space on the elevator. No one's going to want to get close to you. Let's go.

Still looking at him incredulously, she let Zach guide her to the elevator that would take them down to the second floor. Looking behind them, there was still no sign of the two assailants.

As the elevator door opened, Zach announced, "Please make way. My wife has been sick. I need to get her down as quickly as possible. I don't think it's catching, but I can't be sure."

Most of the passengers backed away. Only a few brave souls came on, cramming themselves by the windows as far away from the couple as they could. Zach and Sarah stayed in the center of the car, away from the windows for Zach, and far away from people for Sarah. The few other occupants stayed as far as they could from Sarah, making sure not to look at her, and upon arriving at the second floor, they all rushed out quickly. Following them out, Sarah was slightly shaken, but otherwise okay.

"Do you think you can do the next elevator, Sarah?"

"I think so, as long as we can keep people away from me."

"I don't think it will be a problem."

They walked over to the next down elevator, and again, Zach made his speech.

"Please let us go through. I've got a sick wife. She keeps throwing up."

This time, no one accompanied them on the elevator to the ground floor.

The elevator door opened, and they made their way out to the fresh air. They were happy to be back on the ground.

"Zach, you're a genius," said Sarah, with new respect in her voice.

"Sorry about your shirt."

"Hey. It can be washed. No problem. It does feel gross though."

"Let's get out of here."

Sarah looked up, and gasped. About fifty feet away, she saw a man staring at her, one she recognized well.

"Hey, Sarah, I'm here to help you," shouted the man.

It was secret service agent Walter McCoy.

CHAPTER 58

"**RUN,**" yelled Sarah. Looking back, they could see Marty Green and his associate running out of the elevator and joining McCoy.

They ran until they found a door near the south pillar of the Eiffel Tower. They raced through it, then down well-worn steps to a subterranean level. The sound of running feet and shouting behind them kept them moving swiftly. They didn't stop to observe the old black and white photos of French military personnel, together with ancient radio equipment, adorning the walls.

Ahead of them were two doors on the left and an additional tunnel on the right.

"In here," said Sarah, pointing to the door that had a sign reading *INTERDIT*, thinking it less likely their pursuers would choose it. Fortunately, the door was not locked.

"Shut the door," whispered Zach, once they were inside. It closed with a loud creak, and the room was pitched into total darkness.

They moved to either side of the door, hugging the wall. As they did so, Zach brushed against something hard with his back. He felt for it and realized it was a bolt lock. Quietly he pushed the bolt into its anchor, locking the door.

Soon, they heard racing feet and voices again. The footsteps headed down the right hallway and back again. They could hear the other door being opened, and the room behind it examined.

Finally, one of their pursuers tried to open their door, but the bolt kept it in place.

"Someone's going to see us if we stay here," said a voice.

"We can wait outside. Eventually, wherever they are, they will need to come out."

The voices stopped, and they could hear feet walking away. It was another ten minutes before either felt safe to talk.

"We can't stay here forever," said Zach.

"Remember what I read earlier, about the military bunker? If it was used by the Resistance, there must be another way out of here," replied Sarah.

Zach turned on his phone light and looked around the room. There was no way out other than from the door they entered. Hesitantly, Zach slid the bolt lock back and opened the door just a crack. Their assailants were nowhere to be seen, likely waiting just outside the bunker.

Proceeding to the next door, they looked inside, and again saw no other way out. The only other option was the tunnel to the right, which they followed. As they turned the corner, the tunnel became pitch black, and they had to turn on their phone lights to see the way. The floor turned to dirt, and they passed by old pieces of military and radio hardware. Eventually, they came to another door, which was padlocked with a rusty chain.

Zach walked back and picked up an old metal pipe lying on the ground. He returned to the lock and chain and proceeded to hammer them with the pipe. Eventually, the chain broke, and they were able to pry the door open.

As they continued through the tunnel, the air became thick with humidity, and a rancid smell filled their nostrils. Trying to preserve their phone batteries, they turned off their lights and walked slowly, feeling the walls around them to guide their path.

Sarah screamed, and Zach turned on his light.

"Something rubbed against my ankle."

Looking around, Zach pointed his light at a rat, running away.

"Eww. I'm keeping my light on from now on. You can keep yours off to preserve the battery, and we can just follow mine."

"Agreed."

Eventually, Sarah's phone died, so Zach turned his light on for a while, and then turned it off.

"Why did you do that?" asked Sarah.

"We need to preserve some power. We don't know how far this tunnel goes, or even if it goes anywhere at all. We might need to turn around, or we might need it for something we encounter later."

They went back to walking in darkness, guided only by feeling the wall next to them.

They continued to walk through the dark, narrow tunnel. More rats ran by their legs, and they could hear the crunch of what likely were old rodent bones beneath their feet.

Eventually, they came to another door, and this one was not locked. Once through, Zach turned on his light, and they could see the tunnel leading to stairs heading upward.

After proceeding up the stairs, they came to a hatch, which upon opening, thrust them into bright daylight. Once their eyes had recovered, they now could see that they were in a large courtyard, surrounded by multiple, tall buildings. In the distance was the Eiffel Tower.

After walking a short distance, they heard a commanding voice coming from behind them. "Que fais-tu ici?"

They turned around to see a uniformed soldier pointing his rifle at them.

"Where are we?" asked Sarah.

"Qui êtes-vous?" asked the soldier.

"Nous sommes américains, et nous sommes perdus," responded Zach, slowly.

"Ahh, you're Americans, and you are lost," said the soldier with a smile, lowering his rifle. I could tell you were Americans by the shoes you wear. Boots, I think you call them."

"That's what they say in England. In America, we call them running shoes or sneakers. How come you spoke to us in French if you knew we were from the US?"

"I wanted to see if you knew French. What brings you here? And what is the matter with your shirt, Madam?"

"My friend here was sick, but she's feeling better now. We wandered in here by mistake. You speak excellent english. Where are we, though?" said Zach.

"Thank-you. My mother is English, and my father is French, so I speak both languages poorly," he said, laughing. "You are at the Ecole Militaire. In America, you would call it the Military Academy. It's been here since 1750. Where are you trying to go?"

"The Metro."

"All right. Walk through that alley there, then turn left and walk down the street about 100 meters, and you will see it."

"Thank-you so much," said Zach, and they proceeded to hurriedly walk out of the complex.

Zach stopped abruptly, and Sarah walked into him.

"Why are you stopping?" she asked.

"Where the hell are we going? I'm not sure who to trust at this point. Do we go back to Samantha's parents? How do we know they weren't making up the text telling us to meet at the Eiffel Tower? And I don't think we can trust Samantha either, as she was the one who presumably set up this meeting, that is, if her parents weren't the ones responsible. Should we just find a hotel instead? We need to take some time to really think out what to do next."

"I agree," said Sarah. I don't think it's safe to go back to Sarah's parents. Let's just find a hotel nearby and regroup. But I do need to buy a new shirt. This one's disgusting."

"There's a hotel right here, the Hotel La Bourdonnais Paris. We can get you a new shirt after we check in, if they have room."

They walked in through an elegant lobby, decorated with red poinsettias, to the reception desk, where a young man dressed in a sharp business suit looked them over suspiciously.

"Do you speak english?" asked Sarah. "We're Americans."

"Mais oui, Madam, I speak a little English." He spoke with a slight frown, as they were quite disheveled and had no luggage.

"You know this is an expensive hotel, Madame et Monsieur. The room rate is approximately $300 per night in American dollars."

"That's okay," said Zach.

"All right. One bed or two?"

They looked at each other briefly, and Zach answered, "two please."

"Name?"

They hesitated again, and finally Zach answered, "Reilly, Mr. and Mrs. Reilly."

The reception clerk looked them over again briefly. Now with a smile, he gave them keys for the room.

"Is there a clothing store within walking distance where I can buy a new shirt?"

"Oui, madam. Go out the door you came in and go left two blocks, and there are many stores."

"Merci."

Stopping at the first store they could find, Sarah quickly picked out a few shirts, some underwear, and socks. The few other customers in the shop gave them a wide berth due to their appearance.

An hour later, they were back in the room. They sat down on separate beds, facing each other. She leaned in, bridging the gap between them.

"Zach, that was so smart to dump the champagne and caviar on my chest to get us out of that mess. But I'm also pissed at you. This was a $100 shirt, and now it's ruined."

"I'm sorry. I'll ..."

Sarah rose from her bed and sat next to him. Not letting him continue, she grabbed his outstretched hand and looked at him as she had not looked at him before. Still staring into his eyes, she brought him to her. They both stood up, and Sarah gently glided his hand onto her shirt.

Zach looked surprised, but then met her eyes with a smile. His lips met hers, and they embraced passionately. His hands found her chest, and he felt her hard breasts under the dank shirt.

"Don't know what to do here," said Zach.

Sarah looked surprised.

"With your shirt, I mean."

With that, he brought his mouth to her shirt and started licking it.

"Yum, champagne and caviar. Now I get to the best part," he added.

Sarah smiled. Zach unbuttoned her shirt, exposing her damp bra. He reached behind and undid the hooks. Soon, he was licking her exposed breasts. He made his way back to her lips, which still tasted of champagne.

They tumbled together onto Sarah's bed. They made love slowly, lovingly. Finally, after they both had climaxed, they lay on top of the bed, looking at each other.

"I haven't felt this way in a really long time," said Zach.

"I haven't either, not since Morgan left," and then she was suddenly quiet.

"I'm sorry," he said.

"You don't need to be sorry. You're something special, Zach."

"So are you, Sarah."

"I guess we just need one bed."

"One bed it is, from now on."

After a short nap, they woke up refreshed. After dressing, they sat down on the bed together.

"We can't stay here for too many days. It's expensive" said Sarah, "and I can't stay hiding out in Paris forever. I need to get back to Jefferson, and I need to find my dad, if ..."

She trailed off her last sentence. Zach knew what she was thinking but couldn't get herself to say, *if he's still alive.*

"First thing is we need to let Samantha's parents know we're not coming back, in case they weren't part of the plot, and they're expecting us," said Zach.

"Agreed, but our phones are both dead."

They called down to the front desk, and two phone chargers were brought up to the room. Zach was about to dial the Rochambeaus, when Sarah stopped him.

"If they know our phone number, we can be traced," she said.

"You're right and we can't use a hotel phone either as they could trace that also. I'll go downstairs to the lobby and see if I can borrow the receptionist's phone to make a call."

Looking more presentable, the clerk at reception greeted Zach in a much friendlier fashion and agreed to lend him his phone without asking questions.

Zach dialed the Rochambeau's number and spoke to their answering machine. He left a message thanking them for their hospitality and explained that they wouldn't be coming back.

On returning to the room, Zach could see a change in Sarah's demeanor. She was sitting upright, chin set, and she spoke to him with a look of determination.

"I'm not hiding out anymore. I need to find my dad. I need to end this nightmare. Hiding's not working anyway. They always seem to find us. I'm going back to DC, going back to the White House, and I'm going to demand to see my father. You can do what you want. Stay here or come with me. Your choice."

Zach thought for a moment before speaking. "You're right, and I'm coming with you. How much cash do you have left? I'm getting low."

"Me too. We can use our credit cards to get cash on the way to the airport. Since we're leaving Paris to fly to DC, and they know we're in Paris anyway, it's probably alright to use them to get cash. But I wouldn't use them to buy the tickets. Otherwise, they'd know where we're going. And we need new phones. We'll get them on the way to the airport."

It was clear to Zach that Sarah had thought this all through while he was down in the lobby. He nodded in agreement. "I guess we have to use the same identities we used before, Robert and Lynn Frederic, because that's what's on our passports, and buy the tickets with cash."

"What choice do we have? Anyway, it's better than using our real names. We'll also need a place to stay in DC where they won't find us."

"Once we have new phones, I can call my receptionist to see if we can stay at her place. I don't think they'd look for us there."

"Okay."

Sarah got up off the bed and sat on a chair, staring out the window.

Zach watched her for a minute, realizing that even though both their lives were in danger, her burden was much worse than his.

CHAPTER 59

ANOTHER MEETING was held at the stately house in Arlington, Virginia. There were no pre-dinner drinks or dinner.

Jack Chauncey, Billy Joe Scranton, Tim Braun, and Theresa Jones were seated in their same positions around the marble table in the small, windowless room. The same fifth man joined them and sat adjacent to Chauncey. The attention and anger of all five was directed squarely at Phoenix, who sat calmly at the end of the table.

"This man you hired to impersonate the President is going to ruin everything," said Jack Chauncey, lips pursed, eyes glaring at Phoenix.

Billy Joe's face was red with anger. Hands balled into fists, he slammed them down on the table. "I thought this whole thing was supposed to go off smooth as silk. What the hell are you doing!"

Tim Braun looked down at his hands on the table. Theresa Jones' make-up was smudged where she was resting her head on her hands, and her smile was now a scowl.

The fifth man spoke. "Never have I seen such incompetence. The man you picked is a menace. He's nuts! What are you going to do about it?"

In addition to anger, their fear was palpable. Phoenix just sat quietly, letting all their concerns be heard. Finally, he spoke, and there was no panic in his voice.

"I admit that my choice of impersonator was not the best, but as I told you all many months ago, we have multiple contingencies. As you know, the idea was to keep the President alive until just the right moment. I understand that the defense bill has now been passed by the House and Senate and is on its way to the President's desk. I will tell Brodsky to get the impersonator to veto it, and then things can proceed.

"The President's daughter will be caught and neutralized, and his double will resign to take custody of Jefferson. The President and Jefferson will then be found dead from a boating accident, the imper-sonator will disappear, and all your troubles will be gone."

Jack Chauncey interrupted. "How do you know the buffoon won't authorize the President to be shot when he wants, as he hired the guards, and they think he's in charge?"

"The guards have been given a code to execute the President that only I know."

"He could still spill the beans later if discovered."

"Maybe I misspoke when I said *disappear*. He will be neutralized as a potential risk."

"And the guards. They could be a risk."

"I know what needs to be done. Also, remember that they think Staples is running the show. We'll be keeping a tighter rein on him, along with a few slight changes, and everything will be fine. Not to worry. The less you know, the safer you are."

With that, he got up from the table and walked out, leaving a table of five unsmiling people, who remained concerned.

"It's easy for him to say that 'the less you know, the safer you are,'" said Billy Joe, his face still red. "If it falls through, we're in deep shit enough already without knowing all his details."

The others around the table nodded in agreement, but the point of no return had long passed.

Phoenix took an Uber back to his hotel suite, where he called Kwan. "Where is my next ten-million-dollar payment?"

"We are not convinced yet you are near completion of the job, and the girl is still alive. We need to show the foul sickness of the imperialistic, capitalist society, that is the United States. Heads of major corporations and members of their own government responsible for killing their president is one thing, but the murdering of his daughter would bring an even stronger emotional response."

"Understood," said Phoenix, grudgingly. "We will take care of the daughter. It will be fine."

"Good. You're being well paid for the job. Don't mess it up."

Mary Ann Temple was distraught. She paced around her small apartment for the thousandth time. Where was June? She didn't return from work and had now been gone for two whole days.

Mary Ann called the Washington Hospital Center and was told June had called in sick and had not been seen for the last few days.

It didn't make sense. June wasn't sick, at least as far as she knew. Mary Ann's next call was to the police, who had her fill out a missing person's form. Now all she could do was wait.

CHAPTER 60

IT HAD BEEN a rough night. Not only had he failed the President, but now Ray had no job to return to. He had been so proud of his position as President Peterman's number one man, and now nothing.

Presently, he was just suspended, but what if he lost his job entirely? How would he pay the rent? Who could he count on? He had given up most of his social life for this job protecting the President, and his live-in girlfriend, Cynthia, had moved out. He envisioned himself alone and on the street.

Most of all, he felt like a failure. The President, his President, had been kidnapped, and he didn't know what to do. There were no leads to follow.

The only potential was that black van by the White House. That's where he had first seen Joey, the man he met at the Lincoln Memorial. Perhaps a surveillance camera might have captured a license plate. But how would he be able to access the tape, as he no longer had clearance?

The whole thing was a mess, and Ray had no answers. Normally someone who never drank more than one or two beers in an evening, he drank four. So, when Ray finally got up late the next morning, it was with a hangover and massive headache.

After a strong cup of coffee, he felt better. He let go of the pessimism he had felt the night before. He had to figure it out. It was imperative that he did. He needed to rescue his president.

First though, he needed clean rooms in which to think. The apartment was a mess, with empty beer bottles sitting by the sofa and dirty plates stacked haphazardly in the kitchen. So, after a shower and a breakfast of scrambled eggs and toast, he spent the next hour cleaning up.

Ray sat down on the sofa and went over everything he knew. Again, he came back to the black van. It would be likely White House surveillance tapes would have recorded the car. How could he look at it? The answer finally came to him.

Frank. Frank Baldwin, his friend. He had covered for Frank more than once, like the time Frank tried to sneak his girlfriend in to see restricted areas of the White House. Ray told Frank's boss at the time that she was a visiting dignitary from Kazakhstan, and he was able to give her a special tour. She just had to nod instead of speak until she was well out of earshot of anyone else. They laughed about it multiple times.

Perhaps he could convince Frank to check the surveillance tapes for a license plate from the van. Frank didn't work weekends, so he wouldn't be in until Monday. He needed to think of a way to convince Frank to do it. To give him the real reason could backfire. He might think Ray had gone nuts.

Director of the Secret Service, James Allen, was starting to feel a little uneasy. Contrary to what he had said in suspending Ray Lincoln, things just didn't seem right. There was the weird press conference, and then squirrel hunting on the White House lawn. Of course, Ray's story was too far-fetched to be believable, but he felt he should investigate further.

Back in his office, Director Allen replayed a tape of the President's press conference. The President's voice seemed a little off, but then again, he had never spent much time directly with President Peterman. His job was more administrative. Still, he couldn't shake the feeling something was wrong.

First thing Monday morning, he went to see Jonathan Brodsky.

"Can I talk to the President?"

"He's not to be disturbed. He's got a cold, and not feeling well."

"I feel I need to speak with him."

Brodsky realized it might be more trouble if he refused.

"Okay, come with me," and he knocked on the President's door.

"Come in," said a bored voice.

On entering, Director Allen saw the President sitting up having breakfast. At least he looked like the real President. Red hair, thinned on top, about six foot and a little round in the middle.

The Director decided to come right out with it.

"Mr. President, I feel I need to tell you there's a rumor going around that you're not the real President of the United States, but an impostor."

Jonathan Brodsky forced a laugh. "How preposterous. Who has been spreading those rumors?"

"A secret service agent who used to work with you, Mr. President, Ray Lincoln."

"Oh yes, I remember him," said Staples. "Good agent, but always coming up with conspiracy theories."

Staples and Brodsky both forced laughs.

"Is there anything else, Director Allen?" asked Brodsky.

"No, sir," said Allen as he left the room.

Director Allen was now even more uneasy. Ray Lincoln could be a pain in the ass, but he couldn't imagine he was into conspiracy theories.

Once the Director had left, Brodsky threw a paper down in front of James Staples.

"Sign it," he said.

"What is it?"

"Not your concern."

"I'm not signing nothin' unless you tell me what it is."

"Okay. It's to veto a bill cutting military spending. You're a military guy, so you wouldn't want that. I've already written out your objections. All you need to do is sign."

"That sounds okay to me. Give me a pen."

CHAPTER 61

SARAH AND ZACH left early to pick up cash and new phones. Once at the airport, Zach called his receptionist.

"Sorry, my boyfriend's visiting, and I only have a one bedroom, so it won't work. But, my sister, Victoria, lives in Adams Morgan, and she's out of town for the next two weeks on vacation. I have the keys, and I'm sure she wouldn't mind if you promise to water the plants. Saves me from having to go over there myself."

"That would be great."

"Her keys are in the lockbox attached to my mailbox. It's the one that's painted pink. The combination is 4,7,3,9."

"Thanks so much."

"No problem."

They boarded the 1:55 flight to Washington, and it left right on time, arriving just after 7 pm in Washington, DC. By the time they picked up keys from Veronica and made their way to her sister's apartment in Adams Morgan, it was already 9 pm, 3 am Paris time. Approaching the White House would have to wait until the following day.

The next morning revealed another dreary January day in Washington, DC. The temperature was in the mid-thirties, and there was a fine mist in the air. It was not enough for an umbrella, but wet enough to feel damp and miserable.

Sarah and Zach took the red line metro near Adams Morgan to Metro Center in DC. From here, they walked towards the White House. Zach stopped abruptly a block away.

"Why are you stopping?" Sarah asked.

"What's our plan?"

"They know I'm allowed entrance. I'm going to demand to see my father. Then I'll know for sure that it's not really him."

"I'm not sure that's a smart idea. If it's an imposter, they're going to try to stop us."

"I'd like to see them stop me," she said, her face set with determination, and her legs moving in longer, faster strides. Zach almost had to run to keep up with her.

They first arrived at a gate outside the White House. Sarah recognized one of the policemen guarding the gate, and he let them in.

Next was the entrance to the White House, where they encountered two marine corp. sentries.

"I'm here to see my father, the President."

"ID's please, ma'am."

"I don't have my real ID, young man. I had to discard it. This one says Lynn Frederic, but I'm really Sarah Peterman. Get any of my dad's secret service agents down here, or you can ask that policeman over there. They'll recognize me. I need to see my father."

The marines looked at her suspiciously, but finally, the sentry who appeared to be senior, placed a call.

"Someone will be right down, ma'am. You two stand over there," he said, pointing just to the right of the door. "We're expecting a number of people here soon."

He was right. Multiple cars arrived, discharging more than thirty guests, including multiple celebrities, who all needed to have their identification verified.

There was quite a crowd by the time the door opened. It wasn't an agent, as Sarah had requested, but instead, a man she didn't recognize, Jonathan Brodsky.

"Yes?" asked Brodsky, smiling.

"I'm Sarah Peterman. This is my friend, Dr. Zach Webster. We're here to see my father."

"ID's?"

"We don't have the correct ones. We have manufactured IDs that say we are Robert and Lynn Frederic."

Brodsky laughed. "Mr. and Mrs. Frederic, you pretend to be the President's daughter and expect to be let in? How stupid do you think we are?"

"Bring down any of my father's agents, and they'll recognize me. I'm not leaving until I see my father," said Sarah, standing rigid, glaring at Brodsky.

"I don't know why you're here, and of course you're not leaving. You're going to be arrested for trying to gain unauthorized entry to the White House."

Brodsky addressed the sentries. "Hold them here. I'll arrange for someone to take them away." He then disappeared behind the door.

The marines nodded. The junior marine, gun in hand, marched Zach and Sarah off to the side of the entrance as other guests were having their IDs checked and being let in by the other sentry. As they didn't seem to be much of a risk, the young marine let his attention wander to the celebrities being let in by his partner.

Zach bent down to tie his shoe, but then stood up quickly, knocking the gun out of the young marine's hand.

"Run," he yelled to Sarah.

The sentry regained his gun. "Stop!"

It was too late. Blocked by the guests trying to gain entrance, the sentry had no clear shot at either Zach or Sarah. Instead, he fired off a warning shot in the air, creating panic and chaos among the crowd. Zach and Sarah moved quickly to the outer gate.

Zach grabbed the nearest Metro cop by the gate and shouted, "There's a crazy man over there shooting off his gun."

The police ran in toward the crowd, searching for the shooter. As they did, Sarah and Zach ran, until they were far from the White House. Neither spoke until they made their way back to the apartment.

"Why did you do that, Zach?" asked Sarah angrily. "I could have gotten someone there to recognize me, like the cop by the gate. He could have told them who I am."

"If what we think is going on really is, I don't think we would've been put in police custody. Much worse, and I don't think we would've been allowed to leave. Ever."

Sarah plunked down on the couch. Zach sat down beside her and took her hand. She pulled it away, the look of determination still on her face. Her hands balled into fists as she spoke.

"I'm going to find my father. I don't know what these bastards are up to. I've got to do something."

"We need to come up with another plan. It's not going to work trying to barge in," said Zach.

"In the meantime, I need to call my son. I need to know he's okay."

Zach handed Sarah the phone. She took a few calming breaths before dialing Jessica, who handed the phone to her son.

"Hi Jefferson. How is everything going? Are you having fun with Aunt Jessica?"

"I'm okay Mom. Are you home? Why can't I come home?"

"I'm sorry, Jefferson, but I'm not home and you can't come home right now either."

"Why not?"

"I can't explain it right now."

"Why? Is it about the guy who had the gun in your office, or the car accident?"

"I'll explain it later. In the meantime, you need to stay with Aunt Jessica."

"It's fun here, but I want to go home. Or how about I stay with Dad?"

Sarah was quiet for a moment. This was now the second time he asked to stay with his father. She didn't want to tell Jefferson that his dad would not have offered, so she lied.

"I think he's out of the country right now on business, so you need to stay there. I'll bring you home as soon as I can. I love you, Jefferson."

"Love you too, Mom."

Hanging up the phone, tears ran down her face. She took Zach's hand and held it tight.

Phoenix picked up the phone on the sixth ring. It was Brodsky again.

"Yeah, Brodsky. What do you want? It better be important."

"It is. The President's daughter and the doctor were here and wanted to see Peterman."

"So, do you have them?"

"They escaped. They know something's up."

Phoenix rubbed his forehead in frustration. He was dealing with idiots. "Of course they know something's up."

"What are you going to do about her? They could ruin everything."

"Not to worry. I already have a plan in motion."

"What are you going to do?"

"From a source in San Diego, I found out where the boy goes to school. That's all you need to know."

Click.

CHAPTER 62

AS FRANK WAS likely at work, Ray texted, and asked him to call when on break. A few minutes later, Frank called back.

"Hey, what's up? I hear you interrupted the Director's Saturday and now you're on vacation."

"That's right. Thought I needed some vacation time. Couldn't stand another minute of working with "'Richy.'"

"I'm with you. Are you doing okay?"

"Sure. Sure. We'll see how it goes. Got lots of other job opportunities just waiting for me if I don't come back," Ray lied.

"That's great. We'll still hang out, right?"

"Of course. Could you take a short walk outside? There's something I need to talk to you about."

"Sure, I'm on a break." Frank walked outside, about 100 yards away from the building. "Okay, go ahead, but make it quick. I'm outside, and I'm freezing my butt off. What's this about?"

"Could you do me a small favor? There was this girl I met, a nurse, outside the White House. She was in a black limousine, parked over by Pennsylvania Avenue. It was on December 19th. She gave me her phone number, but I can't find it. I've looked all over the apartment, and it's nowhere to be seen. I'd like to call her, but I can't. I remember her first name, June, but not her last name, and she's cute."

"So, what do you want me to do about it?" asked Frank.

"Could you see if there is a surveillance video that shows the car, and if so, get it to me?"

"That could get me fired, Ray. You're suspended."

He thought for a minute, then continued in a whisper, "But, if I find it, and it shows the license plate, I could give you the plate number."

"That would be great. Thanks, pal. You're the best."

"I know," said Frank, and he hung up the phone.

After briefly hesitating, Ray picked up the phone again and dialed a number he hadn't called in a very long time. He wasn't even sure it was even still in service.

A man answered. "Hey, who's this?"

"It's Ray, Ray Lincoln. Is this Petey?"

"Ray Lincoln? That you? It's been years. Where you been?"

"Doing this and that."

"Yeah, I know you're a cop now."

"Not anymore. I joined the Secret Service, but now I'm suspended. I need your help."

"Help to do what?"

"I need a piece."

"What for?"

"Protection. What do you think?"

"I don't do that stuff no more. I'm legit now."

"I know that, but I thought you might connect me with someone who could help."

"How do I know I can trust you?"

"You're my cousin. You know I could have had you arrested anytime when I was a cop, but I didn't. You're family."

There was silence for a few moments on the phone. Finally, Petey spoke. "I know a guy who's into that shit. I'll call him."

"Thanks, Petey."

"No problem. Come around some time, okay? My mom would love to see you."

"Sure," said Ray, as he hung up the phone. He knew he wouldn't visit. He had left the old neighborhood and vowed never to return.

CHAPTER 63

IT WASN'T UNTIL later in the day that Frank called back.

"Hey, Frank. What do you have for me?"

"Got you a present."

"Is it what I asked for?"

"Sure is. But there's a catch. I need to have you help me pick out the tux I'm supposed to wear as best man for my brother's wedding. I'm going there after work tomorrow, six o'clock, at *Men's Warehouse* on Connecticut Avenue."

"Okay. I'll be there. Give me a minute, and I'll get paper and pencil to write it down."

"You can put it in your phone, idiot. What era are you from? Hurry up, my balls are freezing outside in the cold."

"First it was your butt freezing off, now your balls. You'll have nothing left."

"You're a real funny guy!"

"Sorry. Go ahead."

"It's at 1024 Connecticut Avenue, NW in the district."

"Not the tux store. I can find that. The license plate."

"Okay. 853-750. DC license plate. Got it?"

"Got it. Thanks so much."

"So be there at six, and after, we go out for beers, on you."

"I'll be there. Anything."

"She must be really hot," Frank laughed, and hung up.

Now that he had the license plate, Ray at least had somewhere to start. He called Janice, an old girlfriend at the DMV in DC. He remembered her as cute, with large breasts which would bounce when she laughed. He wondered if she still dyed her brown hair platinum blond.

"Hey, Janice, remember me? It's Ray Lincoln."

There was silence for a minute. "Ray Lincoln, the guy who ghosted me, the guy who was supposed to call me but never did? Or is it the Ray Lincoln who borrowed $100 from me and never paid me back? Or is it the Ray Lincoln who told me my brother, Nick, was a no-good, worthless parasite?"

"All the above, except that I did pay you back. And I'm sorry for not being there for you, but your brother is a no-good, worthless parasite."

"You're right about Nick," Janice said laughing. "I got him out of the house, and now he's freeloading off someone else. But why are you calling me now? If you're trying to hit me up, it's too late. I've got a new man now, someone who actually cares about me."

"I'm sorry Janice. You're right, I was a jerk. I was a stupid jerk, and I didn't deserve you."

"Okay, okay," said Janice, continuing to laugh. He could picture her breasts bouncing. "What is it you want?"

"Just a license plate lookup. No big deal."

"You should be able to look that up yourself, Mr. Secret Service agent."

"I know, but the computer program that should do it is on the fritz, so could you help?" he lied.

"Okay, what is it?"

"DC plate 853-750."

"Okay. "I'll run it down and let you know."

"Thanks. You're the best."

"You better believe it, Ray, and you missed out," said Janice, and she hung up.

Fortunately, Ray didn't have long to wait.

"The car is registered to a rental agency that loans out limos, called *Limos R Us*, in Crystal City, off Route 1," said Janice.

"You've got to be kidding me, *Limos R Us*. What an original name," he said sarcastically.

"That's the name. Okay, now that I've done something for you, it's your turn."

"I thought you had a new boyfriend."

"It's not that. My other brother, John, is interested in joining the Secret Service. He's been a city cop for about ten years and wants to make a career move. He's put in his application. Could you put in a good word for him?"

"Uh, sure, I'll do what I can," said Ray, immediately feeling guilty for the deception.

"Thanks."

"Thank-you, Janice. I was a fool to leave you."

"Damn right," she said, before hanging up.

CHAPTER 64

JEFF WAS AT SCHOOL, waiting for Aunt Jessica to pick him up. She was running a little late, and there were only a few kids left in the pick-up zone. The teacher assigned to pick-up duty was off talking to one of the parents. A blue van approached, and the man sitting in the passenger seat looked down at a photo on his lap, opened his door and called to Jefferson.

"Hey, Jeff."

Jeff turned toward him but didn't approach. "I'm not supposed to talk to strangers."

"Of course, but we're not strangers. We're friends of your dad."

Jeff's eyes lit up. "Really?"

"Yeah. He told us to come pick you up. He couldn't come get you himself."

"I thought he was out of the country."

"He's back, and he wants to see you."

"Is it okay with my mom?"

"Of course. She said fine. How do you think we knew where you were?"

"Okay. I just need to tell the teacher."

"Fine. Your dad has it all written down here. Let me give it to you, and you can give it to her."

Jeff approached the van with his hand out to receive the paper, but instead, the man grabbed him and threw him into the back of the van.

The teacher saw him being pulled into the van by the corner of her eye.

"Oh my God," she shouted, running over towards the van.

It was too late. The van had already sped off.

CHAPTER 65

SARAH'S PHONE RANG. All Zach could hear was screaming on the other end of the line.

"Oh, my God!" shouted Sarah, as she hung up the phone.

"What's the matter?"

"Jefferson's been kidnapped!"

"What do they want?" asked Zach. "Is there a ransom?"

"I don't know," moaned Sarah.

"Was that the kidnappers?"

"No. It was Jessica. The school called her, and then almost immediately, she got a call from the kidnappers."

"What happened?"

"Jessica said she brought Jefferson to school as usual. At the end of the day, the children were waiting to be picked up, and someone pulled Jefferson into a van. The teacher said another boy told her he thought it was Jeff's father or something like that.

"Jessica was about to call me to get Morgan's number, but before she could, she got a call from someone saying they had Jeff, and they would be in touch about a ransom. They said if anyone called the police, they would kill him immediately, and they wanted my phone number."

"Did she give it to them?"

"Of course."

"Are you sure Morgan didn't pick him up?"

"Unlikely, but I'll call him to find out."

"If not, he should know anyway that his son's been kidnapped."

"Like he'll really care."

"I'm sure he'll care, even if he is a jerk."

"Okay. I'll try him." She picked up her phone with trembling hands and called Morgan, who stated he had not picked Jeff up from school. Zach could hear his anxious voice through the phone.

"Sounds like Morgan cares," said Zach, once Sarah had hung up the phone. "He seems upset."

"Yeah, he is, and of course he blames me. 'You've done something to bring this on. You don't watch him close enough. You're a bad mom.' The shithead."

Zach's eyes followed Sarah around the room as she paced back and forth, crying.

Finally, Sarah's phone rang again.

"Hello."

"We've got your son," said the voice.

"Is he ok? Let me talk to him."

"He's fine, for now. Okay, I'll put him on."

There was silence for a few seconds, and then she heard a voice say, "Mama, I'm scared." Instantly, she knew it was Jefferson.

"Are you alright?"

"Yes, I'm okay."

"Have they hurt you?"

"No, but they won't let me go," he said, and then he was gone.

The caller was back on the phone. "So, now you know he's okay."

"What do you want?"

"We demand $200,000 for his return, and we need you to bring it."

"I'm in Washington, DC."

"We know you are. The kid's in California but the drop-off will be in DC. And, no police, or the kid dies. Got it?"

"Yes," said Sarah, and the call went dead.

Sarah turned to Zach. "They want $200,000, and they want me to bring it, but I don't know when or where yet.

"You know it's a trap. They're not going to kidnap the President of the United States' grandson for $200,000. You'd be walking into their hands."

"What choice do I have? They'll kill Jeff if I don't, and I can't get the police involved."

"I could try Samantha again."

"Can we trust her? She might have set us up in Paris."

"I can't imagine her doing that, but I can't be sure."

Both sat quiet for a minute. Finally, Zach spoke.

"I do know someone in the FBI in DC, if he's still there, Tony Girard. He and his wife were the ones who told me Samantha was having an affair. Tony used to work with missing kids, so maybe he can direct us to the right people. What do you think? This is the kind of thing the FBI does, and I'm sure they'll know how to keep it quiet. We need help."

"I guess. I'm not sure what else to do," said Sarah, tears still running down her face.

Zach moved to sit next to her and put his arms around her. Wiping away the tears, he whispered, "It will be alright."

It took a few phone calls to the FBI in DC to find the right department, but finally he was able to reach Tony.

Sarah listened anxiously as Zach filled Tony in on the details of the kidnapping and ransom request.

All was then quiet in the room, until she heard Zach say, "Thanks, Tony,"

"What did he say?" asked Sarah, quickly, once Zach had hung up the phone.

"Turns out, this is exactly what Tony does at the FBI. He's regional director of missing and kidnapped kids for the entire east coast. He understands the situation and will contact his counterpart in California. They'll keep it as quiet as possible, but they'll need to alert the secret service."

She looked at Zach. "Do you trust him?"

Zach thought for a moment, and then nodded. "He's a good guy. Yeah, I trust him."

"Okay. I don't know what else to do."

"Really there's nothing else to do right now until they contact us again or we hear anything more from Tony. We should just go to bed."

"I can't sleep. You go to bed. I need some time alone here."

Zach nodded. She needed her space. He gave her a hug and headed off to the bedroom by himself. Neither slept well that night.

CHAPTER 66

IT WASN'T UNTIL after 10 am, when Tony finally called Zach's phone. The call was brief, and all Sarah could hear was Zach saying, "Uh huh, uh huh," until the call ended.

"What did he say," demanded Sarah.

"He says they have no information yet, but they're working on it. We're just supposed to wait for instructions from the kidnappers, and then let them know. Not very helpful."

"I can't just sit here while my son is in danger. I need to do something!"

"What can we do? We have no idea where he is. How about if I go out and get us some food? We haven't eaten since breakfast."

"Okay, but I'm going with you. I can't stay here by myself."

"Are you sure? It's awful out there."

"I don't care if I get wet or if I'm cold. I don't care about anything other than getting my son back. And I need to find a Chase Bank and get the ransom money. Chase handles my investments, and I'll need to cash them out."

"Are you sure? Tony didn't say to do that."

"To hell with what Tony says. I'll do anything."

"It's your call. Okay, let's go," said Zach, but before they could leave, Sarah's phone rang.

She answered quickly. "Hello."

"Do you have the $200,000?"

"I just arrived in DC. I'm on the way to the bank to cash out my investments, so I need a little time."

"You've got twenty-four hours."

"I need to talk to him to make sure he's okay."

"He's fine. Get the money," and the phone went dead.

Sarah put down the phone. Her face was ashen. Zach came over to give her a hug, but she motioned for him to stop. She wiped away the tears with her sleeve, and a new look came on her face, one that Zach had never seen. It was one of anger, pure seething rage.

"If they hurt him, I will kill every single one of them. I don't care how long it takes, but I will hunt them down and kill them."

Zach looked at her in surprise, but then he understood. She was Momma Bear, and someone was threatening her cub.

"We need to call Tony back now that we've heard from them," he said quickly.

Sarah nodded in agreement, and Zach placed the call. Tony was not available, but the agent on the phone promised to leave a message for him to call back as soon as possible.

Zach then turned to Sarah, speaking softly. "Time to go. We need to get to the bank before it closes."

"Yes," she agreed, and they left the apartment.

Once at the bank, they met with the manager and explained the situation. Yes, Sarah had enough assets to cover the ransom. He wasn't sure the bank would be able to liquidate her stocks and bonds soon enough, but they would loan her the money which she could repay once her assets were liquidated. She had enough collateral to secure the loan.

On the way back, Tony called.

"We've been trying to track down the phone that had made the calls, but to no avail. We put a trace on Sarah's phone, but unfortunately, the last call was not long enough to locate the source."

Sarah grabbed the phone out of Zach's hands and spoke to Tony directly. "Unless you're able to locate him before I need to pay the ransom, I'm going to do it."

"I need to know the details, when and where, of any dealings you have with them. By no means go by yourself. It could be a trap to lure you in. The ransom amount seems very low to me, considering the risk they're taking. I smell something fishy," replied Tony.

"I will keep you informed, but I will do what I have to do," answered Sarah, as she hung up the phone.

On the way back to the hotel, Zach purchased some crepes from a street vendor. Once in their room, they watched TV without paying much attention. Sarah only ate a third of her meal. It was going to be a long night.

CHAPTER 67

JEFF WAS BEING HELD captive in an apartment, on the third floor of a walk-up on Orange Avenue, the main street in Coronado. It was a modest apartment, with two small bedrooms and a living room that led from the entrance hallway. With the shades pulled down, the apartment was dark. The furnishings were meager and old. Jeff's room was the smallest bedroom, with just enough room for a bed and a television.

Jeff's initial fear had somewhat abated. The two men who had brought him here had not hurt him, but he knew they were bad men.

Phoenix had hired these men sight unseen through a contact in southern California at the last minute. They were not the brightest, but they were available on a moment's notice. One was tall and had a thick beard, and he didn't talk much. The other was his exact opposite, short, bald, and heavy. He seemed to be the guy in charge, the one who gave the orders. They had no idea the boy they kidnapped was the President's grandson.

Jeff had seen *Home Alone* lots of times before, but it was on TV, so it was something to watch. He especially liked seeing the crooks injured by Kevin's tricks in the movie, and he imagined it happening to the guys who kidnapped him.

Baldy, as Jeff liked to call him in his mind, entered his bedroom.

"Hey kid, what do you want to eat?"

"I don't know, but could you please let me go."

"Sorry kid, but I can't."

"My grandpa is President of the United States. He'll get you anything you want."

"And my grandpa is Vladimir Putin," Baldy laughed. "I'll get you a burger and a coke. Stay in your room. My buddy will be watching while I'm out." He closed Jeff's door on his way out.

He returned to Jeff's room about an hour later with a burger and a Coke. Hungry, Jeff finished his meal quickly. He especially enjoyed the Coke, as soda was something his mother never let him drink.

The kidnappers, who found it funny that Jeff drank the soda so quickly, gave him another. They also gave him some cake they bought at the local supermarket. Jeff was on a caffeine and sugar high by the end of the evening.

Even though it was now late at night, Jeff was not remotely sleepy. He moved on to Home Alone 2, and then Home Alone 3. By about 1 am, he was starting to get bored, but still not sleepy. Quietly, he opened the door of his bedroom slightly, and looked out into the living room. The tall guy with the beard had left to sleep in the other bedroom. "Baldy" was watching television in the living room. His eyelids were beginning to droop.

Jeff closed the door and watched the next few minutes of the movie. He then peered out again through the doorway. The living room television was still on, but "Baldy" had not moved. His eyes were now entirely shut.

Slowly, he opened his bedroom door just a little more, enough to get through. Once in the living room, he moved carefully and quietly until he reached the apartment door. It was locked, but a single turn of the doorknob released it.

The click of the lock opening was enough to awaken Baldy. His eyes flew open just in time to see Jeff running out the door.

He yelled for his companion to wake up, and then ran out of the apartment, down the stairs, in pursuit. His companion soon followed, only half-dressed.

Once out of the building, Jefferson didn't know where to go, but he knew to run. He saw what appeared to be stores in the distance with lights on, so he ran toward them. The stores were all closed, and the doors were locked. He could see his pursuers far behind him, but Jeff kept running. Eventually, he spotted a car coming in his direction and waved for it to stop. The driver opened his window and peered down at the boy.

"What's a kid like you doing out at this time of night?" he asked.

"I was taken by some people, and I just escaped. They're chasing me, and they're right behind me."

"Quick, get in."

Jeff jumped into the backseat. The driver locked the doors and drove up Orange to the police station, where they quickly exited the car. Looking back, the captors were nowhere in sight. After knocking on the door, a uniformed policeman finally opened it.

"What do you want?" he said gruffly, having just been awakened from a short nap.

"This boy says he's been kidnapped and just escaped."

"Okay, kid, what's your name, and where do you live?" asked the cop.

"I'm Jeff, and I live with my mom. But she's not here. Some bad men took me, and I just escaped."

"And what's your name?" he asked the driver inquisitively.

"Stan Wilson, but that's not important. I had nothing to do with this. The kid just flagged me down and I brought him here."

The cop turned to Jeff. "Tell me everything that happened."

"Well, I usually live with my mom in San Diego, but I think she's in some kind of trouble, so I've been staying with Aunt Jessica for a couple weeks. She's not really my Auntie, but I call her that cause I know her so well. She's friends with my mom. Some bad men told me they were going to take me to my dad, but then they wouldn't let me go. Oh, and my grandpa's the President."

"The President of what?"

"You know, the President."

"The President of what?"

"You know, the country. President Peterman, but I just call him Grandpa."

Stan Wilson almost fell out of his chair. The cop's eyes widened, and he didn't speak for a while, but when he did, it was, "Holy shit!"

"That's a bad word," said Jeff, looking at him.

"Sorry," the cop responded, and then he picked up his phone. "Chief. Sorry to wake you up, but I have a situation here. I think you should get down here to the station as soon as you can. There's a kid here who says he's the President's grandson, and he's just escaped from being kidnapped."

Jeff could hear a muffled voice on the other end of the phone, and then he heard the cop beside him say, "Yes, that President."

After hanging up the phone, the cop turned to Stan and told him he could leave, after providing his name, address, and phone number.

Stan turned to Jeff. "Are you okay if I go?"

Jeff just nodded, and Stan drove off. It was a story he would tell his children and his grandchildren.

The cop, much friendlier now, made Jefferson some hot chocolate and sat beside him quietly until the police chief arrived. More police arrived, and they went back to search the apartment Jeff described. There was no sign of the kidnappers and nothing else other than some old clothes.

"How do we get in touch with your mom, Jeff?" asked the chief.

"I don't know her new number, but you can call Aunt Jessica."

He recited the phone number he had been asked to memorize, and the chief placed the call. Jessica was awake, too anxious to sleep. She was overcome with relief hearing that Jeff was safe.

Immediately, she called Sarah, who was also awake.

"He's safe. He's okay. He escaped," said Jessica as soon as Sarah had answered.

Sarah poked Zach awake. "He's safe!"

"Thank God," Zach said, waking up quickly. "Where is he?"

"He's at the police station in Coronado. I'm calling them now."

She dialed the station and talked with the police chief, who reassured her that Jefferson was safe and in excellent condition. He then put Jeff on the phone.

"Jefferson, are you okay?"

"I'm good."

"Are you hungry? Did they feed you?"

"Oh yes. I ate a burger and had two sodas and then some cake. Is that okay?" he asked timidly.

"That's fine. I heard how brave you were."

"I just ran out when they were sleeping, and I saw a car, and he brought me to the police station."

"I'm so proud of you."

"What should I do now?" asked Jeff. "Can you come get me?"

"I'm sorry, sweetheart. I'm all the way back east in Washington, DC. Let me talk to the policeman."

"Okay."

While Sarah was talking with the police, Zach called Tony, waking him up, to give him the good news. His instructions were clear. Jeff was to spend the night at the police station, under constant watch, until the FBI arrived the following day. Tony would book a morning flight out of DC, and along with the head of the FBI in California, they would take full responsibility for Jeff's safety. Jeff and Jessica would be moved to an FBI safe house under constant guard.

Zach relayed this information back to Sarah, who then relayed it to the police chief. He was happy to relinquish control to the FBI as soon as they were on the scene.

She then called Morgan to tell him their son was safe, and then slammed her phone down on the table.

"What's the matter?" asked Zach.

"The prick. He still says it's my fault. How could I have let this happen?"

"Of course it's not your fault."

"I don't know about that. I'm going to bed."

CHAPTER 68

DIRECTOR JAMES ALLEN strode down the corridor to the President's quarters. Jonathan Brodsky heard him coming and ushered him into his office.

"I've got important news the President needs to hear."

"The President is not to be disturbed."

"I need to talk to him now," said Allen, raising his voice.

"You can tell me. I'll tell him. It's my job to let him recover from his illness," said Brodsky, matching the volume of the Director.

Hearing the commotion, James Staples left his room and walked into Brodsky's office. "What's going on?" he asked.

Director Allen turned away from the Chief of Staff and addressed the President directly. "Mr. President, your grandson is safe,"

"Why wouldn't he be?" answered Staples.

"I thought you knew. He was kidnapped, but he's okay. He's being safeguarded by the FBI in California as we speak."

"Great news. Thank-you Director Allen." said Staples.

"Yes, thank-you Director. You may leave now," said Brodsky, pointing to the door.

James Allen nodded and left the room. *How is it possible he didn't know his grandson was kidnapped.*

Staples turned to Brodsky. "What's this about kidnapping my grandson?"

"First of all, it's not your grandson, it's Peterman's grandson. Second, it doesn't concern you, so you didn't need to know."

"I don't like it. I don't like kidnapping kids."

"As I said, it's not your concern, so don't get involved. Stay here for a minute. I need to put out something to the press praising the FBI in freeing the President's grandson. Don't do anything stupid before I get back."

Brodsky walked out of his office and down the corridor, leaving James Staples alone in the office.

Things are happening without me knowing, thought Staples. *What else aren't they telling me?*

He looked at Brodsky's desk for any further information but didn't find anything else useful. As he left the Chief of Staff's office, he resolved to keep a closer tab on him.

Brodsky returned and called Jack Chauncey.

"Did you know Peterman's grandson escaped?" asked Brodsky.

"Shit, no. I didn't even know he was kidnapped."

"I don't like it. Things are bad enough babysitting this jackass Phoenix hired to be President."

"Keep your cool. I'm sure Phoenix has things under control," said Chauncey, in a reassuring tone of voice.

"He better."

Jackass, am I? said James Staples to himself, having positioned himself in the hallway outside Brodsky's office to hear the call. Returning to his room, he kept his door partially open. He needed to keep a listen for any more phone calls to his Chief of Staff.

Jack Chauncey was nowhere near as calm as he appeared to Jonathan Brodsky. Sitting at a chair in the room with the marble table, his right foot was tapping faster than a hummingbird's heartbeat on the tile floor, as he called Phoenix.

"What the hell is going on?" demanded Jack.

"A case of bad help. The kid got away," said Phoenix.

"Why are you kidnapping kids? This wasn't part of the plan."

"The plan changed. It was just a way to capture his mom. He was never in any danger. Not now, anyway."

"So did you get the mom?"

"No. Kid escaped before we got her, but we'll get her another way."

"I don't like it. I'm holding up the next payment."

"I don't think so. You've come this far. Remember what I've got in my safe deposit box. I expect the next payment on time. Don't disappoint me."

"Fuck you, Phoenix!"

"Temper, temper," laughed Phoenix, and then he spoke in a conciliatory voice. "Remember, we're partners in this. Everything will be alright."

Jack had no choice. Phoenix had him beat. He'd have to wire the next payment. Why had he started this in the first place?

Phoenix made himself a drink and tried to relax. Taking a few deep breaths, he worked on trying to slow his heartbeat, a technique he had learned years ago. The only way he could make it work would be to remain calm.

CHAPTER 69

RAY DROVE OUT to the limousine rental agency. On his way out, he picked up an old badge that identified him as Secret Service. He knew he could get in real trouble by using it, but he had already committed. *I'm already in deep, might as well keep going*, he said to himself.

It was a short drive to Crystal City, where he found a broken-down sign reading *Limos R Us*. It was hanging at a forty-five-degree angle, as one of the support pillars had fallen. The building didn't look much better, but at least it was standing straight.

Ray got out of his car and went inside. He was met by a man in a grease-streaked jumpsuit, working on a white limousine.

"What can I do for you?" asked the mechanic. "If you're here for a rental, go see Vinny over in the office. He's the boss," and he pointed behind him with his thumb.

"Thanks," said Ray, and headed back to talk to Vinny.

"Are you Vinny?"

"Are you looking to rent a limo?" asked the little man sitting at the desk, smiling through missing teeth.

"No, I'm just here for information."

"I've no time for that. Get lost."

It was time to pull out the old ID. Ray flashed it quickly, making sure to cover up his name.

"I'm from the Secret Service, and the information I need is critical. National security."

"What do you need to know?"

"A few weeks ago, you rented out a black limo to two men and a woman. I think her name was June, but I don't know the names of the others. Do you remember it?"

"Of course. They didn't return it. It was found in West Virginia, abandoned. Fortunately, there was no damage, but I had to pay to get it towed here. What scumbags."

"Did you get their names?"

"I remember they called the woman "June." There was a fat guy and a skinny guy. The fat guy was the one who rented the limo, so I'll have his name in the register."

He pulled out a book and thumbed through it.

"Here it is," he said. "The name's Joey Petrone. I've got a copy of his license here, with his address. Paid me in cash. I should have known something was wrong."

Ray copied it down, but he knew the address wouldn't help. Joey Petrone was already in the ground.

"The girl June, do you remember anything about her, like her last name?" asked Ray.

Vinny scratched his head. "No. Never heard her last name. I do remember she was kind of cute. Not beautiful, but cute. She was a nurse. I asked her what I should do about my swollen leg, and she told me she only worked with hearts."

"Do you know where she works?"

"Actually, I remember, because I have a cousin who works there also. Washington Hospital Center, in DC."

"How about the other guy, not Joey Petrone. Do you remember anything about him?"

"No, can't say I do. He was real quiet and had a mean look on his face. Had some sort of long tattoo on his arm. Didn't want much to do with him."

"Thank-you. You've been really helpful."

"No problem. I'm all for cooperating with the government. By the way, I didn't get your name."

"Tim," said Ray, "Tim Horton."

Ray got in his car and drove off in the direction of The Washington Hospital Center, only stopping for a donut on the way. He arrived at the hospital about twenty minutes later.

Ray hated hospitals. He hated everything about them, the sterility, the smell, the diseases, and most of all, death. He had seen his father die in a hospital after being shot and his mother unresponsive from a stroke. It took him a few minutes to overcome his reluctance, but finally, he walked in.

It was an expansive building, with multiple corridors leading in every direction. Knowing that she *worked with hearts,* he started his hunt by following the signs to the operating room.

"I'm looking for a nurse whose first name is June. She works with hearts." He flashed his badge quickly to the woman at the operating reception desk.

"I don't know of anyone in the cardiac surgery unit named June. Sorry. You can try the cardiac cath lab. It's on the fourth floor."

"Thanks."

It took him more than ten minutes to locate the cardiac catheterization lab, through multiple corridors and two elevators. Again, he struck out, and was directed to try the cardiac care unit on the fifth floor.

After another long journey, again down long sterile corridors, he found the elevator to take him to the cardiac care unit, where again he tried asking for June after flashing his badge.

"We do have a June who works here. I'll page her to come out."

"Thanks so much."

Five minutes later, a nurse poked her head out the door.

"Someone's looking for me? My name is June."

She was silver-haired and looked close to retirement. She was not the June Ray had seen parked on Pennsylvania Avenue.

Initial excitement faded; his shoulders drooped with disappointment. Strike three. *How would he ever find her?*

"Sorry, you're not the June I'm looking for."

Ray turned to walk away, unsure what to do next.

"Maybe you're looking for June Temple. She works on the cardiac floor. That's where patients go after they leave our unit," said June.

Ray turned around immediately. "Where's that?" he asked.

"Straight down the hall, turn left, then turn right at the end and take the elevator to the third floor. Good luck."

"Thanks so much."

Ray walked quickly, trying to remember all the directions. He found the elevator and took it to the third floor. Immediately upon leaving the elevator, he was hit by a familiar smell, the smell he hated. It was the disinfectant, the one he associated with hospitals and death.

He tried to put the smell out of his mind as he approached the receptionist, whose head was down entering information into her computer. Young and pretty, with long dark hair and just a whiff of perfume, she looked up at him and smiled.

"Can I help you?"

"Yes, I'm looking for June Temple. I understand she works here." Again, he flashed his badge.

"Yes, we have a June Temple, but she's not here today. In fact, she didn't show up for her shifts on the weekend, and she never answered her phone. I tried calling her."

"Did anyone go look for her?"

"Not that I know of. Maybe administration checked on her. I don't know. Why do you want to know?"

"Official business. Is there any way you could give me her address?"

"I'll see if I can get it. I'll call my friend Josie in personnel."

After a few minutes on the phone, she hung up and turned back to Ray. "Here it is. 8909 13th Street, Silver Spring, Maryland." She handed him the address.

"Thank you so much for your help," said Ray.

"No problem. I hope she's not in trouble."

Ray turned around to leave.

"My name's Robin by the way. My phone number's on the back of the address I gave you." She smiled as he turned back around.

"I'll be in touch," and he winked at her, returning her smile.

Ray left the hospital, almost running to his car. He couldn't wait to breathe fresh air again, and now he had a real lead. He also had the phone number of a very pretty girl.

By now, it was already starting to get late. He had just enough time to get to *Men's Warehouse* for six to meet Frank. He'd have to go look for June Temple tomorrow.

CHAPTER 70

PHOENIX EXPECTED another call that he wasn't looking forward to, and he didn't have long to wait.

"You told me you were going to kidnap the kid to catch the mother, but you fucked up. We told you that she's crucial to our plans," said Kwan.

"You don't miss much, do you? Don't worry. I've got it covered. It was a case of lousy operatives I had to hire at the last minute, sight unseen in San Diego."

"You were hired and paid to be the best. This is not the best. This is crap. My superiors are getting antsy."

"We know where the girl is now; we're tracking her phone. I've got my best man on it."

"Okay, but you're not getting the next installment of your money until we know she's dead."

"I need to see the money before she dies. It's a major step, and I don't trust you to pay once we do it. After you transfer the remaining money to me, I will have them both killed. Then, I'll give you everything you need to show the world a conspiracy at the highest levels of the US government along with its major corporations. To show my goodwill, I'll still let you hold on to ten percent until you know they are both dead. I give you my word."

"The word of a paid assassin."

"What choice do you have? You've already committed a lot of your government's money. They won't be happy to have lost all that for nothing."

"You have some balls, Phoenix. I will agree to those terms. But first, I need to know the girl is in your custody before I pay, and things need to move quickly. I also need the videos you promised before you get the remaining two million. And things better start going as planned."

"Very well. Agreed. It will happen soon. Have faith."

Phoenix poured himself another martini, this one stronger than the last. He wasn't as confident as he had let on. Finishing the drink in two gulps, he smashed the glass on his coffee table, glass shattering all over the floor.

Never in all his jobs had everything gone so badly. He needed to get things going right again. There was too much money on the line for things to go to shit.

He picked up the phone and called his best man. Marty Green answered.

"Marty, I need you to find Sarah Peterman and pick her up."

"I know where she is. I got the location from her phone."

"Get her. I don't care if you have to do it in broad daylight, but get her."

"Got it, boss."

Phoenix put down the phone. It better go off without a hitch. They couldn't screw up again.

CHAPTER 71

SARAH AWOKE, still feeling guilty. Morgan was right; she hadn't done enough to keep him safe. Her father had been kidnapped, and she hadn't done enough to find him.

Zach stirred, surprised to see Sarah pacing about the room.

"What's the matter, Sarah? Is Jefferson still okay?"

"Yes, he's fine."

"Then what's the problem? I would think you'd be happy."

One look at Sarah, and he knew he said the wrong thing. She looked at him with daggers.

"How am I supposed to feel happy? I risk my son's life, and who knows if he's going to be traumatized by this. And my dad, what's happened to him? I've just been joyriding around with you, when I should be protecting them."

"You know it's not like that. You can't protect anyone if you're the next one attacked. You need to save yourself first before you can save them."

"You don't understand. I need to go for a walk," and she picked up her coat.

"Okay, let me get dressed, and I'll go with you."

"No," said Sarah, definitively. "I need to be alone for a little while."

"Make sure you take your phone with you, in case I hear anything."

Sarah picked up her phone and headed out, and Zach, knowing she needed her space, lay back down on the bed.

Standing behind a tree in the yard, Marty Green was waiting for her. He couldn't believe his luck. She was all alone, with her head down, and not a soul was stirring on the street.

With the collar of his coat pulled up covering part of his face, he walked straight up to her and jammed a chloroform-soaked towel over Sarah's mouth and nose. She fell to the ground, unconscious. Marty looked around again, and no one was anywhere in sight. He lifted her into the trunk of his car, where he proceeded to tie Sarah's hands and feet. With his phone, he took a picture of his captive before closing the trunk.

He then got into the driver's seat and headed off. It was going to be a long drive to West Virginia. Time for a father-daughter reunion.

CHAPTER 72

PHOENIX RECEIVED a text from Marty that all had gone well, along with a photo, and he was now bringing the "package" to the reunion.

Finally, thought Phoenix, *things are proceeding according to plan.*

His first call was to Kwan.

"The girl is in my custody. She will be joining her father later today. See the text I just sent you with a picture of her in the trunk of my associate's car."

"I see it. You will have the money transferred to your account by 5:30 pm today."

"Excellent. If the money is there, they will both be executed at 6 pm."

"It will be. Just keep up your part of the agreement," said Kwan, and the line went dead.

Next, Phoenix dialed Jack Chauncey. He could sense the man's unease just on hearing the word *hello.*

"Things are in motion, which should be completed by the end of the day. The plan has changed, but the results will remain the same.

"The President and his daughter will be executed this evening, and the impostor will commit suicide. There will be a note where he admits to the deception, kidnapping, and deaths of the President and his daughter. The guards at the prison believe it was Staples who gave all the orders. As he is about to be found out, Staples chooses suicide on his own terms rather than certain arrest.

"How are you going to convince your impostor to commit suicide?"

"Did I say he would commit suicide? I should have said it would look like suicide. Not to worry."

"I'm plenty worried," said Jack. "And I'm holding onto the money until we know everything works out the way you say."

"I don't think so. I want my remaining money today. But as I said, I'm a gracious man, and I will let you hold onto the remaining two million until everything is completed. I want the money wired by five pm today.

There was silence on the phone for the next ten seconds.

"I need to discuss this with the others."

"Fine with me, but I need it in my account by 5 pm. If not, the President and his daughter are released, and your video somehow gets leaked to the press.

Again, a brief pause before Chauncey spoke, "The money will be there."

"It's a pleasure doing business with you."

"Fuck you. Just get it done," he said, slamming down the phone.

Phoenix had one last call to make, this time to Brodsky. Through his open door, Staples heard the phone ring.

Brodsky got up and closed his office door. As he did, Staples silently walked into the hallway and put his ear to his Chief of Staff's door. The secret service agents were down at the other end of the hallway, with no view of Brodsky's office.

"How's our guy doing? Keeping him under wraps?"

"Yes," said Brodsky. "I've been watching him and not letting him out in public. I've told everyone that he's got a bad cold."

"It's time. Give him the code to contact the guards in Nuttallburg to finish off the President and his daughter tonight at 6 pm, but not before. She'll be joining him in his cell later today."

"So, you got her, the President's daughter. Why didn't you just kill her instead of bringing her to his cell, and why wait until 6 pm to kill them?"

"I have my own reasons and killing them together just makes it cleaner," said Phoenix. "Give Staples back his phone. He needs to be the one to make the call. The code he needs to give the guards is 236 Charlie. They will know what it means. By delaying the execution until 6 gives us time to terminate Staples prior to their death. The President and his daughter will be found dead by the highway later this evening. Do you have Staples' suicide note I sent you, detailing his plan to take over the presidency, and derailed by you once you realized he was an impostor?"

"I have it, but I didn't realize I'm the person who was supposed to have discovered he was a fake," said Brodsky.

"It must be you. You'll be a hero. Also, I trust that you have put Agent McCoy in the detail guarding him."

"Of course, and I presume McCoy's the one to finish the imposter off."

"Yes. Plant the note, give McCoy the code to give Staples, and then get out of the way."

"Okay. I'll give him the code to give Staples to order the execution for 6 pm tonight. Understood," and Brodsky hung up the phone.

Quickly, James Staples returned to his quarters and silently closed the door. He hadn't heard Phoenix's end of the call, but he had listened to Brodsky's replies and understood he was in danger.

Staples heard his door being opened and jumped back onto his bed. Brodsky smiled at him.

"You've been a good boy. Here's your phone. Don't make any calls until I tell you. Oh, and Phoenix wants you to stay in your office for now. It's going to look suspicious if you continue to stay in your bedroom."

"Okay. I'll do what I'm told," lied James Staples. He would go to his office, but that would be the extent of his cooperation. Doing what he was told was not going to happen.

Brodsky left, closing the door behind him.

CHAPTER 73

IT WAS TIME to follow his first real lead. Ray now knew June's address, and he would take a direct approach, telling her that he knew she was involved in the kidnapping, and that she needed to come clean with what she knew. Unless necessary, Ray would hold off on pretending to still be in the secret service. That's if she hadn't skipped town already.

Ray's phone rang just as he passed the Maryland state line.

"Hello."

"Ray, I'm Zach, Sarah's friend."

"Yeah. I remember. How are you both doing?"

"I'm okay, but Sarah's gone missing."

"What?"

"We got up early and she went for a walk, and she hasn't returned. I tried calling her, but there's no answer. It's been about two hours, and I'm worried. Did she call you?"

"No," said Ray. "Did anything happen before she went out?"

"Yes, her son Jefferson had been kidnapped, but we found out he escaped, and he's safe. She's still very worried about him and her dad."

"Where are you staying?"

Zach gave him their address in DC.

"Are you getting anywhere on your investigation?" asked Zach.

"Well, I've been suspended by the Secret Service, but I'm still on it. I've got a lead I'm working on right now. I'll let you know if I find anything. Let me know if you hear from Sarah."

"Right. Bye."

Zach hung up. There was nothing to do but wait. Hopefully Sarah would call.

Ray's GPS took him to an apartment building at 8909 13th Street, Silver Spring, Maryland, June Temple's address. At the front door was a list of apartments, and next to "3C," was the name "Temple."

Ray rang the buzzer for 3C, and a voice responded, "Yes, can I help you?"

"Are you June Temple?" asked Ray.

"No, I'm Mary Ann, her sister."

"Can I speak with her?"

"She's not here."

Ray frowned. "Can I speak with you?"

"What's this about? Do you have any information about my sister?" she asked nervously.

Ray changed his mind. He would keep up his pretense of still being an active agent.

"I'm Secret Service, ma'am. Can I come in?"

Mary Ann buzzed the door, and Ray walked up to the third floor. He met Mary Ann in the hallway and flashed his badge quickly.

Ray surveyed Mary Ann. She was short and very thin. Wearing what appeared to be an inexpensive, poorly fitting dark wig, she had very pale skin and was dressed in a drab housecoat.

"Do you know where my sister is?" she asked at once.

"No, I don't. I take it you don't either."

"She left for work last week, and never came back. I called the hospital where she works, and they said she called in sick. But she said goodbye to me that morning and claimed she was going to work. I haven't heard from her since. I called the police, but they were no help."

"I'm sorry. Can I come in?"

"Yes, of course. Come in. Where are my manners? Please have a seat," she said, indicating the couch.

Ray sat, and Mary Ann pulled up a chair.

"Do you have any idea where she could be?" he asked.

"No idea. It's not like her to up and disappear, especially with my health."

"Are you okay?"

"Far from it. I've got advanced cancer. The doctors have only given me a couple more months to live."

"I'm sorry."

"I've come to terms with it. June not so much. She kept researching all these experimental remedies."

"Sounds like a caring sister."

"She is," said Mary Ann.

"Did you call the police?"

"Of course. They put out a missing person's report, but nothing so far."

"Did she leave you a note or anything?"

"The police asked the same question. No. I've looked"

"Is there any place she might hide something?"

"I've looked everywhere."

"Did the police search the apartment for any clues?"

"They looked around briefly, but I don't think they found anything."

"Do you mind if I have a look around?" asked Ray.

"Please do. Maybe you can find something that will help the police find her. Go ahead."

Ray looked about. It was a small apartment, consisting of a kitchen/eating area, a living room with a TV, and two bedrooms. He started in the kitchen, opening drawers and cabinets. He pulled out an empty whiskey bottle from the trash.

"Are you or your sister whiskey drinkers?" he asked.

"Good heavens, no. I don't drink any alcohol now and the most June drinks is an occasional glass of white wine."

He returned to the trash and pulled out two vials. One had a label that read *midazolam* and the other *ketamine*.

"Are these medications you take?" he asked.

"No. I have no idea why they're there."

"Curious," said Ray, and then he proceeded to search the living room. Finding nothing useful, he continued to Mary Ann's room. Still nothing useful.

Next was June's room. He dumped the contents of her bedside table onto the bed. This revealed only Chapstick, hand lotion, some cough drops, and a book of crossword puzzles. Nothing but clothes were seen on an inspection of her dresser and closet. If June had made a run for it, she certainly had not taken much with her. There was a small desk in the corner of the room, which also was unrevealing aside from some unpaid bills.

Next, he proceeded to the bathroom, which again provided no clues. June's toothbrush, cosmetics, and hair products were still all present. Considering all the contents left in the apartment, Ray concluded that June most likely had not left of her own free will.

Ray had one other thought.

"Does she have a computer?" he asked.

"Yes, I'll get it. The password is 1234."

Ray entered the password, realizing June could not possibly be a master criminal.

Pulling up google searches, the most recent was titled, *How to make a sleeping potion.*

"Did she make a sleeping potion for you?"

"Of course not," said Mary Ann.

"She must have done it for someone. Any idea who?"

"None at all. Where do you think June could be?"

"I have no idea. Sorry."

He was now certain she was involved somehow, but it still didn't help in locating the President. Disappointed, he thanked Mary Ann, and headed out the door.

Just before walking out of the apartment building, he heard Mary Ann's call.

"Mister, I found something."

CHAPTER 74

RAY TURNED AROUND and shouted back up the stairs, "What is it?"

"It's a letter addressed to me from June."

Ray bounded up the steps two at a time and raced into Mary Ann's apartment. She stood there, nervously twisting the watch band on her wrist.

"Where did you find it?"

"I was straightening up her room after you left, and it was under her pillow."

"Open it."

"Okay, here goes." With trembling hands, she opened the envelope.

My dear Mary Ann. I've made a terrible mistake. I was promised $20,000 to help on a private case. I didn't know what I was getting into until it happened, and by then, it was too late. I had to go through with it, or they would have killed me. It turns out it was to kidnap the President of the United States. I was to make sure the drugs they gave him didn't kill him, and at least I took solace in that.

"Oh my God, what have you done, June?" wailed Mary Ann.

"Is there more?"

Mary Ann continued haltingly.

Afterward, I started feeling a huge amount of guilt and had a hard time keeping it together. I was useless at work, and I know you must have noticed I wasn't myself. I couldn't go to the police. They told me they would find me and kill both of us if I did. Finally, I came up with a plan. I got some drugs to knock out the guards where they were keeping the President, and I'm going to get him out.

If you're reading this note, it means I have failed in my attempt and I am most likely dead. Please don't think bad of me. I wanted the money to help pay for a treatment I heard about in Mexico for your cancer. I'm so sorry.

Mary Ann started crying. Ray went over to her and held her tight. He could feel the tears on his neck.

"Is there anything more?"

Mary Ann nodded and read on.

Enclosed is the card I got from a Secret Service agent outside the White House. He seemed like a good guy. Please find him and give him the card. On the back of it is where we took the President. I hope he's able to do what I was not. Remember, I love you more than I can possibly say. Goodbye, your loving sister, June.

"My name is Ray Lincoln. Is that the name on the card?"

Still sobbing, Mary Ann quietly nodded *yes* and handed the card to Ray. As expected, it was the card he had given June that day by the black limousine. With trepidation, he turned it over and it had only three words written on it: *Nuttallburg Coal Mine.*

Pulling out his phone, he googled the name. It all made sense. The Nuttallburg Coal Mine was a defunct mine in West Virginia.

"I need to go," said Ray. "I'll let you know if I find your sister."

Mary Ann slumped down in a chair, and Ray let himself out. He now knew where he needed to go.

His phone rang shortly after getting on to Georgia Avenue, heading south. The screen on his phone read, "Unknown Caller."

"Hello," said Ray.

"Are you Ray Lincoln?" asked the caller.

"Who's asking?" answered Ray.

"I'm the guy sitting in the Oval Office of the White House."

CHAPTER 75

RAY JAMMED on the brakes in the middle of the road and was almost hit by the car behind him.

"How did you get my number?" asked Ray, as he pulled off to the side of the road.

"I'm the damn President of the United States. I can get anything I want."

"Are you the real Francis Peterman?"

"What do you think? I thought you're the one who figured it out. Look, I don't have much time for questions. They could kill me at any time." said the voice, speaking rapidly.

"Who's 'they'?"

"I told you I don't have time for questions. I need your help, and I need it now. I'll tell you everything if you can get here to help me."

"How do I know I can trust you?"

"You don't," said Staples, "but I swear I'm on the level. I'll tell you more when I see you. They could be listening in right now."

"Where are you right now?"

"I'm in my office. I was told to wait here for further instructions."

"Lock all the doors, and don't let anyone else in. I'll get there as soon as I can. I'm not sure how I'll be allowed into the White House, since I'm no longer in the Secret Service.

"I will leave instructions for them to let you in and bring you to me. Remember, I'm the President, and they'll do what I say."

"Okay. I'll be there as soon as I can."

"Hurry," said Staples, and as he hung up the phone, he locked the door to his office.

Ray made a quick right onto Alaska Avenue. Almost immediately, traffic ground to a halt. A car was stuck, blocking the way, about a hundred yards ahead.

"Shit!" He was tempted to turn his car around and head to West Virginia. After all, he cared much more about the real President Peterman than some fake president. But then again, he could learn more about what he would face at the coal mine by talking to the imposter.

Quickly, he pulled his car to the right of the cars in front of him and sped past them, right tires over the curb onto the sidewalk. Past the car blocking traffic, he drove as fast as he could toward the White House.

The phone in his pocket rang again. This time it was Zach.

"Sarah still hasn't returned. I'm really worried about her," he said, as soon as Ray answered.

"Hang tight, Zach," said Ray. "Hopefully, she shows up soon. I'm finally making progress. I just got a call from a guy who almost straight out admitted that he's impersonating the President. I've also found out where they took Francis Peterman. He's been taken to a coal mine in West Virginia. I'm about to meet with the fake in the White House to find out more. If Sarah's been taken, maybe he can tell us where she might be. I'll let you know if I find out anything more."

Ray hung up before Zach could ask one of the many questions that were on his mind.

CHAPTER 76

RAY LINCOLN arrived at the White House gates and was allowed in after showing his ID. Security had been made aware he was allowed entrance. Upon parking his car, he opened his glove compartment. Cousin Petey's source had delivered, and Ray had his protection, a Glock 19 pistol with attached silencer, tucked neatly inside. Glancing quickly at it, he then closed the compartment. There was no way he'd be allowed to bring it into the White House.

Inside the White House, Jonathan Brodsky was on edge. He was unable to sit at his desk, but instead paced around his office. Despite the temperature reading only sixty-five degrees indoors, his shirt was damp with sweat. A catered lunch was sitting on his desk, but he wasn't the least bit hungry.

Brodsky's first step was to plant the suicide note, supposedly written by James Staples, in the Presidential bedroom. He read it over, for the sixth time.

> *I, James Staples, am about to take my life. Knowing I could do a better job, I came up with a plan to take over as President of the United States, and it worked! I recruited some old friends to help me kidnap and execute the real President.*
>
> *My decision to hire Jonathan Brodsky as my Chief of Staff was a big mistake, as he was the one who discovered that I was an imposter, and he's about to inform the Cabinet.*

I have no desire to go to jail or undergo the humiliation of a court trial. It would probably end with the death penalty anyway.

I have no family. The army was my family, and they kicked me out!

My only regret is that I didn't have time to change the policies of this great nation before I was discovered.

To my friends, I say goodbye.

Jim

Jonathan Brodsky was CIA, but never a field agent. He wanted to stay as far from the action as possible. He would give the code to agent McCoy and then stay out of the way, as directed.

Unlike Brodsky, who preferred others to do the dirty work for him, Walter McCoy lived for action. Finally, he would have his chance.

His job, guarding the corridor leading to the President, usually meant slowly traversing the length of the hallway looking for any signs of trouble. But today, he walked the corridor at record speed, shoes squeaking on the wooden floor.

Using top-level clearance Brodsky had provided him, he had set up a small explosive device in the basement of the White House, under the premise of checking a tip that required inspecting the gas line. A remote trigger sat in his right pants pocket.

McCoy followed Brodsky to the Presidential chambers, where they picked up the shotgun James Staples used to hunt squirrels, and Brodsky placed the suicide note on the bedside table.

Walking back toward the President's office, they encountered Ray's friend, Secret Service Agent Frank Baldwin who looked at them inquisitively.

"What are you doing with that shotgun?" he asked, blocking their way. Frank was a big man, and no one was getting around him without his approval.

"Out of my way. The President wants it by his side," answered Brodsky, whose scowling face would have been close to six inches from Frank Baldwin's, had he not been almost a foot shorter. Instead, Brodsky's narrowed eyes stared at the agent's neck.

"I don't think that's a good idea," said Baldwin.

"It's not for you to decide. What's your name, Agent?" he demanded.

"Baldwin, Frank Baldwin."

"Well, Agent Frank Baldwin. Move aside or I'll have to let Director Allen know of your insolence."

At that, Brodsky pushed his way past, and Agent McCoy followed. Turning around, McCoy glared at Frank, with a look that said *take me on at your peril.*

With a steady gaze and furrowed brows, Baldwin watched their progression down the hallway. Shaking his head slightly, he turned his attention back to the hallway entrance.

Meanwhile, back in his locked office, Staples used the intercom to send word that former Secret Service Agent Ray Lincoln was to be brought to him immediately upon arrival. No one else was to be admitted.

On arriving at the President's office, Jonathan Brodsky made an excuse that he was needed elsewhere, and quickly left. Walter McCoy knocked on the door with his left hand, his right hand in his pocket ready to trigger the diversionary bomb, when appropriate. First, Staples would need to phone the execution code to his friend in West Virginia.

There was no answer to the knocking, so McCoy tried the door. It was locked. He tried knocking again, and still no answer.

Finally, he shouted through the door, "Mr. President, I need to talk to you about something of vital importance."

Still no answer.

Hearing the commotion, Frank turned his attention back to Agent McCoy, but was then distracted by the sudden appearance of his friend, Ray.

"What are you doing here, buddy? I thought you were suspended."

"Hey, Frank. The President wants to see me. Here's my pass. You can read it. It says he wants to see me, and only me, and it's signed by the President."

They walked together to the President's office door.

"What do you want, Agent Baldwin? And who's he?" asked McCoy, pointing at Ray.

"This is Agent Lincoln. He's been instructed to meet with the President alone."

"I don't think he's in," said McCoy, stepping backward.

Ray knocked on the door. "It's Ray Lincoln, Sir."

The door opened, and Ray walked in, quickly closing the door behind him.

"Show me your ID, Agent Lincoln," said the voice behind the desk.

Ray threw an old Secret Service badge with his name onto the desk, and then followed with his driver's license picture ID.

James Staples picked up both and surveyed the man across from him.

"Okay, so you're Ray Lincoln," said Staples, now starting to pace around the room. "Congratulations on finding me out. How did you know?"

"I know President Peterman very well. Too much has happened to make me think he's been the one sitting in that chair. First off, what's your name?"

Staples hesitated, and then, with a sigh, he answered. It was time to come clean if he wanted to survive. "Jim Staples."

"Who hired you, and who's looking to kill you?"

"One and the same. Goes by the name 'Phoenix.' Don't know his real name. Hired me to impersonate Peterman."

"Why?"

Staples stopped his pacing to stare out the window and spoke to Ray in a mellow voice without turning around.

"No idea, but he paid me a lot of money. Now I'm expendable, and they're going to kill me."

"Who's they?"

"Jonathan Brodsky and Agent McCoy, I think.

"Is President Peterman still alive?"

"I think so, for now, but he and his daughter are to be executed at 6 pm this evening, provided I give them a code."

"So, that's where Sarah is. Are you sure?"

"That's what I overheard on the phone."

"What code are you supposed to give them?"

"They haven't told me yet."

"What is it you want?"

"I just want to be protected from the people who are supposed to kill me, and I don't want to go to jail."

For the first time since his arrival in the White House, James Staples was afraid. He turned around to face the agent he hoped would keep him alive with cold sweat on his forehead.

"I can't promise to keep you out of jail, but I can say you saved the President's life by voluntarily admitting the plot, naming names, and ultimately saving his life. And I'll do my best to keep you safe."

Staples took his time answering. Finally, he spoke. "Good enough. Okay, he's in West Virginia. I don't know specifically where, but I think it's in some coal mine."

"Nuttallburg Coal Mine, I've been told. Tell me something I don't know. Has he been moved elsewhere?"

"Not that I know of."

"Are there guards?"

"Yes. I think there are four. One is in the parking lot, one by the entrance to the mine, and two inside. They're all buddies of mine, and Phoenix got me to recruit them."

Back in the hallway, Agent McCoy was becoming anxious, not knowing what was going on inside the office. He realized that he needed to move fast, but he couldn't do it with Frank Baldwin by his side. He put his hand in his right pants pocket and pressed the remote trigger.

CHAPTER 77

AGENT BALDWIN heard the boom resonating from down below, and he ran toward it. There was one other agent by now in the hallway, and he joined Baldwin, running in the direction away from the President's office.

McCoy quickly applied his rubber gloves. He tried the doorknob. Locked. Agent Lincoln had locked it immediately upon entrance to the room.

McCoy was a big man. With no one else in the corridor to worry about, he slammed his shoulder into the door, crashing it open.

Ray Lincoln turned quickly, but not fast enough. Walter McCoy stood there, gun in hand, shotgun cradled in his other arm, and kicked the door closed behind him.

"You," pointing at Ray. "Push that desk against the door so no one comes in. Do it, or I shoot both of you right now."

Ray complied, and with a heave, the door was now blocked by the heavy desk.

"So, you're Ray Lincoln, the agent fired for conspiracy theories and disturbing the Director's weekend," said McCoy with a smirk.

"Suspended. And who are you?" asked Ray, furtively looking around the room for a possible weapon.

"Agent Walter McCoy."

"You're the one who was guarding Sarah Peterman when her car was tampered with."

"You've got a good memory. But enough pleasantries."

He then turned his attention to Staples. "Mr. President, you've got work to do. You need to call your buddies at the mine and give them the code, 236 Charlie at 6 pm. They'll know what to do."

"I don't think so, McCoy. All I need to do is call security, and they'll be here in an instant to take you down," said Staples, suddenly regaining his bravado.

McCoy moved closer to Staples and put the gun against his head.

"I don't think they'd get here soon enough. Time to make the call."

From out in the hallway came the voice of Frank Baldwin. "Mr. President, there was a small bomb placed in the basement, but no serious damage. Is everything okay in there?"

McCoy cocked the trigger of the gun, pressed even more firmly against the imposter's head.

Staples' courage melted as quickly as it had returned. "Yes," he responded. "We're fine. Thank-you."

They could hear Frank Baldwin moving further from the door.

"Okay. Make the call."

James Staples was now sweating profusely again. Picking up the phone, he reluctantly dialed.

"The code is 236 Charlie, at 6 pm." The call finished, he gently put the phone back down on the desk and sat with his head in his hands.

While McCoy's attention was focused on Staples, Ray Lincoln took the opportunity to position himself closer to his adversary.

"Woah, agent boy Lincoln," said McCoy, who noticed the movement. "Keep your distance."

He pointed his gun back at Ray.

"How do you expect to get out of here, McCoy?" asked Ray.

"I've had to improvise. He," pointing at Staples, "was supposed to have committed suicide, but you've made me alter that. Instead, you came in accusing him of being an impostor, grabbed his shotgun, and shot him. Immediately, I rushed in, you pointed the shotgun at me, and I shot you in self-defense. I'll just get rid of the suicide note after I've played the hero."

"You won't get away with it. They'll figure it out. They'll realize that Staples here is a fake," said Ray.

"That doesn't matter. I wouldn't have known he was a fake when I shot you. Plus, your fingerprints will be all over the shotgun, but mine won't," said McCoy, pointing to the gloves on his hands.

With his attention directed at Ray, Jim Staples took his chance. He lunged at McCoy, who was thrown back. They both landed on the floor, and McCoy's gun went off. Ray didn't wait to see if either was hit, as he dove for the shotgun, which had fallen in the struggle.

Staples lay on the floor, writhing in pain. McCoy rose up from the floor and pointed his gun at Ray, but this time, agent McCoy was not quick enough.

The shotgun blast resounded across the room, and McCoy fell to the ground. Blood seeped from both bodies, from Staples' shoulder and McCoy's chest, matching the magenta of the carpet.

The door flew open, desk flying, and in ran Frank Baldwin, staring, eyes bulging, at the scene in front of him. Here was his friend, holding a shotgun with two bodies lying on the floor, one of them the President of the United States.

"Holy shit, Ray. What have you done?" he shouted, gun now pointed at his friend.

"You've got to believe me, Frank. This is not the President. He's being held captive in West Virginia, and I need to get to him. Tell them that by the time you got here, no one else was here. Say the President's been shot and get an ambulance."

Frank looked hard at his friend and lowered his weapon slowly. He then turned to check on the two men lying on the ground. Both were unconscious, but they appeared to be alive.

"I don't know what to believe at this point," said Frank, shaking his head, while trying to bandage the President's shoulder wound.

"You must have had suspicions, with all the weird things going on. I'm not crazy, and I'm not lying. I promise you I'm telling the truth. There's no time to waste. I need to go now, before it's too late."

Ray walked to the door.

"If what you're saying is true, you should report this to Director Allen? That way, he can mobilize the police, the army, whatever."

"I couldn't convince him before, and even if he did eventually believe me, it would be too late. I'm leaving now. If you don't believe me, then shoot me."

Ray stared at his friend, who made no attempt to raise his weapon.

"If I get fired for this, I'll kill you," said Frank.

"I probably won't survive the day, anyway." said Ray.

"You know the back passageways here better than anyone. Now go!"

Ray opened the door, but standing directly behind it was Director James Allen, gun pointed directly at Ray.

Ray dropped the shotgun and raised his hands in the air as Director James Allen strode into the room and surveyed the carnage surrounding him.

"Director, you have to believe me," exclaimed Ray. "This man is not the President. He's not Francis Peterman. And the other guy is Agent McCoy, who was part of the plot. He shot the imposter, wanting to make it look like I was responsible."

Keeping his gun trained on Ray, James Allen checked on the two bodies lying on the floor. He looked closely at the face of the man he had himself wondered about, the man who called himself the President.

"President Peterman has been kidnapped, and if I can't get there fast enough, he won't make it through the night." added Ray. "He's being held prisoner in a coal mine in West Virginia."

Director Allen brought his gaze back to the agent he had suspended, and slowly lowered his weapon.

"Ray, maybe I'm out of my mind, too, but I do believe you. I've been getting more and more suspicious with the strange things he's done. I need to call in a strike force. If we're wrong, we'll probably all get fired, that is if we don't go to jail. We'll get the police and I'll dispatch the Secret Service to assist. I'll…"

Director Allen couldn't finish his sentence, as Agent McCoy sat up, eyes fully open, and put a bullet through his chest.

Responding quickly, Frank Baldwin fired his own weapon. The bullet hit McCoy over his left eye, and this time he went down for good.

Ray stood still, shocked at the devastation in front of him. Frank moved quickly to check Allen, who still had a pulse.

"Go!" shouted Frank, wiping blood off his hands. "I'll tend to them and call for an ambulance. Get going and do what you need to do."

"I'm going. Don't say anything to anyone about him being an imposter until I rescue the President. It could cause them to move up his execution."

"Okay."

Ray didn't wait any longer. He ran down the corridor, through the back hallways, past the kitchen, and then out a side door. No one stopped him. Leaving the White House was easier than getting in.

CHAPTER 78

BY NOW, Francis Peterman had just about given up hope. Why was he still alive? His captors refused to give him any information.

Peterman's appetite had diminished, and he was not even eating much of the meager food of which he was provided. He was losing weight and becoming weaker. Why didn't they just kill him and get it over with? What was happening in the country with him gone, his country? Were his daughter and grandson all right? Did they even know he was missing?

Around three o'clock in the afternoon, Peterman heard a commotion outside his cell.

Looking out, he could see the figure of a young woman, with a burlap bag covering her head. As one of the guards pulled it off, he heard a familiar voice.

"Take your damn hands off me."

He could recognize Sarah's voice anywhere. The next thing he knew, she was thrown into the cell with him.

"Oh my God," said Francis Peterman, with tears in his eyes. "I'm so sorry you've been dragged into this. Are you okay? Did they hurt you?"

"I'm okay. But how are you? You look so thin," she asked, leaning forward to examine her father in more detail.

"I'm alright, but what's going on? Why are you here, and why am I here?"

Sarah sat down on the floor opposite her father. "I really don't know why they brought you here. We've been on the run for the last couple of weeks. I mean me and Zach."

"Who's Zach?" he asked, tilting his head slightly.

"You remember, Zach Webster, the eye doctor. He found out your eye exam, I mean the guy who's pretending to be you, is different from an exam he did on your eyes years ago. He figured out that someone was impersonating you, and they have been after him since."

"There's someone impersonating me? What has he done?"

"Nothing serious so far. They've made two attempts to kill me too, so the two of us have been hiding out while trying to find what happened to you."

"Why did they try to kill you, and who are 'they'?"

"I don't know why, and I don't know who."

"Is Jeff okay? Where is he?" he asked, trying hard to steady his shaking voice.

"I didn't think he was in danger, but they kidnapped him and held him for ransom. I think it was so they could get to me."

"Oh, no," he said quietly, closing his eyes as he rested his head in his hands.

"It's okay, Dad. He escaped. He's fine. He's with the FBI in a safe house."

Francis Peterman opened his eyes, and his face revealed a hint of a smile. "Smart boy."

"Yes, your grandson is very smart and brave, like you."

She stood up and hugged her father again.

"So how did they capture you?" he asked.

"I went out for a walk, and they were waiting."

Very quietly, in Sarah's ear, he finally asked the question he had been waiting to know. "Does anyone know we're here?"

She shook her head. "No, the only ones who know you've been kidnapped besides us are Zach and Ray Lincoln. Ray's been suspended from the Secret Service, but I know he's working on it. I just don't know if he's gotten anywhere."

"Bob Benton must know it's not me, and Rose Goodwin. She'd figure it out."

"Bob Benton was fired, and Rose died in a car fire."

"Rose dead? Bob fired? How could this be?"

"We'll get through this dad, somehow," she said, taking his hands in hers.

He looked at her and tried to find something encouraging to say but found nothing. Instead, he just grasped her hands tightly with his.

CHAPTER 79

RAY PROMISED to call Zach if he found Sarah's location. He dialed him once on the road.

"I just found out where she is. She's been taken to the same location as her father, who's a prisoner in West Virginia. They'll be executed at six tonight, unless I can stop them."

"I shouldn't have let her go out without me," said Zach, miserably.

"I doubt she would have let you stop her. It's not your fault."

"Then take me with you."

"No place for a civilian, Zach."

"I don't care. I need to be there. Don't worry about me. I can handle myself, whatever comes up."

"Okay, you're on the way, and I could use some help. Be there in about ten minutes."

Zach hung up. He was going to be there for Sarah, whatever the cost.

Ray picked him up outside the apartment, and he filled Zach in on what occurred at the White House.

The remainder of the car ride then became quiet as they broke all speeding limits rushing toward Nuttallburg, following routes 66, 81, and 64, until finally turning onto 60 West in West Virginia, about an hour away from their destination.

"Zach, can you handle a gun?" asked Ray, finally breaking the silence.

"I think I could."

"Have you ever shot one before?"

"No," he said, continuing to look straight ahead rather than at his companion.

"Have you ever even picked one up?"

"Don't think I have."

"Have you ever seen the movie, 'Butch Cassidy and the Sundance Kid'?"

"No, why?"

"Well, the final scene is the two of them against the whole damn Mexican army. It could be like what we're facing."

"Are we going to be facing an army?"

"No. I've been told there are four guards. They're probably well trained. Are you up for this? If not, I can let you out now."

Zach looked directly at Ray, speaking in a steady, determined voice. "I need to help. I've been running away from them for the last few weeks. In fact, I've been running my whole life, first for glory, and then from my failures in life. Running from my job in New Hampshire, running from my marriage, running from my kids. I'm done running. It's true, I've never shot a gun in my life. I don't know how much help I'll be, but I'm going to try. I've got to do it."

"Okay then. You're in."

"One question. So, what happens at the end of Butch Cassidy?"

"Butch and Sundance die, of course," answered Ray with a sly smile.

After an initial horrified look, Zach returned the smile. He didn't know why, but somehow the gallows humor made him feel a little more relaxed.

Following their GPS, they followed Route 60, finally stopping at the New River Visitor Center to obtain a map and brochure of the Nuttallburg Coal Mine. From the directions, they eventually made a left onto a narrow and winding road, filled with ice, mud, and potholes.

Zach consulted the map from the visitor center. "This road should lead to a parking lot, next to the New River, near the Nuttallburg coal mine. From the parking lot, we can hike to the mine."

"Okay," Ray nodded."

"I think I've been in this area before," said Zach. "Back when I was in college, some friends of mine and I took a rafting trip down the New River."

"Fun?" asked Ray.

"Not really. The river was a bitch. Really tough rapids. I thought we were going to die. It was the last time I did a rafting trip. Never again."

"I grew up in DC. Never did any rafting trips, but I wouldn't want to. Can't swim."

Ray dodged a pothole, and the car skidded on a patch of ice, causing the front of the car to slam into the frozen bank on the right side of the road. Something fell from the back seat onto the floor. Zach turned around to look. It appeared to be a transistor radio.

"Why did you bring a radio?"

Ray didn't answer; he was busy trying to get the car out of the bank. He put the car in reverse, but to no avail.

It was stuck in the mud and ice, and the more Ray punched the accelerator, the more the wheels just spun uselessly.

Zach climbed out onto the bank and pushed, and with Ray lightly applying his foot to the accelerator, the car slowly pulled itself out, but not before spraying mud onto Zach's pants and shoes. He wiped it off as best as he could before returning to the car. They continued.

"Do you know where the guards are stationed?" asked Zach.

"I was told one in the parking lot, one by the mine, and two inside the mine where they're holding the President, but who knows. There could be more by now."

"What's the plan?"

"We improvise, depending on what we see," Ray answered simply.

"That doesn't give me a lot of hope."

"Don't worry. I'm pretty tough and resourceful. How about you?" he added, with a quick look sideways at Zach.

"I'm tough, too. And what I don't have in muscles I make up for with brains."

"We'll see. Let me know when we're about a half mile away from the parking lot. We'll leave the car on the road and walk in."

"Okay," said Zach, consulting the brochure. "It says that the mine is about a mile hike up from the parking lot. It's steep."

"Can you handle it, Doc?"

"No problem. I run every day. How about you?"

"I'm an Agent, or at least I was, and I stay in shape. So, you don't need to worry about me. Are you nervous, Doc?"

"Of course. I can feel my heart beating in my chest, but I'll be alright. Just tell me what to do, and I'll do it. We're about a half-mile from the parking lot."

Ray stopped the car, pulling it to the side of the road. He grabbed the radio and the gun from the glove compartment, and they headed out on foot, moving cautiously.

The overlying tree branches hung low, covered with ice. A light covering of snow on the ground shimmered in the low rays of the sun. It would have been a beautiful walk, if not for the thought that it might be their last.

CHAPTER 80

PROCEEDING STEALTHILY, Ray and Zach approached the parking lot. Ray spoke to Zach, in a whisper.

"Okay, you want to be useful? You be the distraction. Take the radio and turn it on when I say so. Supposedly there's a guard in the parking lot. When he hears you and the radio, he'll come over and investigate. I'll come from behind and incapacitate him."

"So, it is a transistor radio? I didn't think you could even buy one these days. Why don't you just shoot him?"

"Because it will make a noise, which could bring other unfriendly types."

"Won't the radio make a noise?"

"Not nearly as loud as a gunshot."

"Why am I the distraction?"

"Can you incapacitate the guard with your bare hands?"

"No, I guess not. Okay, I'll do it, but if I die, it's on you."

Ray nodded, indicating that Zach should turn on the radio, and then he left the road for the surrounding woods. Zach clicked it on and walked down to the parking lot, trying to look like a hippy hiker with a 1970's transistor radio by his ear.

At the entrance was a sign that read, *Closed. No trespassing.* Aside from only one car in the parking lot with a smashed-in window, there was no sign of life.

Zach looked about. There was a decrepit, elevated, brown building that reached all the way up the steep hill, held up with wooden stilts. Beneath the stilts was a railroad track, and beyond that ran the raging river.

He came to another sign. This one read, *Nuttallburg Coal Tipple*. It described the building's use as an enclosure for a conveyor belt, which in the mine's heyday, brought coal down the hill to the train tracks below.

Zach had just enough time to read the sign before a man, wearing army fatigues and holding a semi-automatic rifle, came out from behind the car. His gun was pointed straight at him.

"What are you doing here?" he shouted.

"Hey, buddy. Put that thing down. I'm just here to check out the sights. I heard there's a cool abandoned coal mine here."

"Read the sign. No trespassing."

"Hey, it's a free country. Can't I just have a little look around?" asked Zach, trying to stall for time.

"Leave now, and turn off that damn..."

There was a muffled thud, as Ray, sneaking up behind, struck the guard with a rock in the back of his head.

He turned the unconscious guard over, and a trickle of blood fell from his head where the rock had done the damage. Ray hit him again.

"What did you do that for?" asked Zach. "He's already out."

"Want to make sure he doesn't wake up any time soon. Let's go."

They proceeded up the path adjacent to the fallen guard, to the top of the hill, guided by the coal tipple winding its way up to the mine.

As they approached the mine, Ray pushed Zach down on his belly and then lay down himself. A guard was sitting in front of the entrance. There was no vegetation to hide in before getting to the clearing, and no way to approach without being seen.

"Same plan with the guard here?"

"Yes and no," said Ray. "Same thing with the radio. Just duck when I say so."

"Got it." Zach stood up, took a deep breath, turned on the radio, and walked toward the guard.

Hearing the sound, the guard immediately jumped up, rifle raised, as he strode over to the intruder.

"Hey man, what's all the anger about?" asked Zach.

The guard approached Zach with the countenance of a man who would rather shoot than talk. When just feet away, Zach heard the command "Duck," and immediately hit the ground, eyes closed. This was followed by a gunshot and the sound of the guard falling.

Ray rushed over, gun still smoking in his hand, and turned the guard over. Part of his head was gone, and blood was running through a channel in the dirt. Zach opened his eyes, took one look at the crimson stream of blood and brain remnants, and promptly threw up. Medical school had not prepared him for this.

"If you can't handle this, you don't need to go any further," said Ray. "No shame in stopping now. I can take it from here by myself."

"No. I've come this far, and I'm seeing it through." Zach got up from his knees. "What's next?"

"We go on, but carefully. I had to use the gun, and the other guards might have heard the sound, even with the silencer. There's supposed to be two more inside. I'll use this." said Ray, pointing at the fallen man's automatic rifle, spattered with blood and bits of hair. He wiped it clean on his pants and handed his own gun to Zach.

"Now, stay low," Ray added.

As quietly and cautiously as possible, they made their way to the mouth of the mine. Turning a corner, down a long tunnel, they could see another guard, sitting by an elevator, reading some sort of magazine. Quietly hugging the walls of the tunnel, they approached him without making a sound. He only looked up in time to see a rifle butt strike him between his eyes. Knocked out cold, he fell off his chair onto the ground.

The elevator was an old-fashioned type, with a metal scissor gate in front of the door. Ray pushed the summoning button, which rose to their floor with loud, clunking sounds. He motioned for Zach to stand to the side while he stood directly in front of the elevator door, rifle tip through the openings in the metal scissor gate.

Zach held his breath, expecting a firefight. He had never shot a gun before, but if needed, he would. Extending his arm, he put the gun in position to fire.

The elevator opened, and it was empty. Zach released his breath and lowered the gun. The creaking of the metal gate made him wince as they entered through the open door.

With only one level below, they knew which button to push. The descent of the elevator made the same loud clunking sounds, but this time it was combined with an ear-piercing squeal, reminding Zach of chalk against a blackboard.

Again, Ray steadied his weapon, in case they met resistance once the door to the elevator opened. There was none.

They walked down a short tunnel and immediately came to a cell, enclosed with thick metal bars. Standing, holding on to the bars, his middle much thinner than before, and with a thick gray beard, was the man they were looking for, President Francis Peterman.

Instead of greeting their arrival with excitement, Peterman said nothing. He shook his head faintly as they advanced. Ray saw the slight motion, but Zach did not.

"Mr. President, we're here to rescue you. I'm Zach Webster. Don't know if you remember me."

From an outpouching of the tunnel adjacent to the cell, Barty Strang appeared. He too was holding a gun, but it wasn't pointed at them. Instead, with one hand holding Sarah up by the hair, his other hand pointed the weapon at her head.

"Put down your weapons and kick them over here," he shouted.

Zach and Ray put down their guns, kicked them over, and raised their hands in the air.

"You're in for a treat. You'll get to see the President die. I got the code to execute him and his daughter at 6 pm. Rather, my buddy upstairs by the entrance did, and he gave it to me on the walkie-talkie. Can't get reception down here," said Strang, showing his phone, "but the walkie-talkie can be mighty useful. That's how I heard you coming. It was on when you got past my buddy upstairs."

Pointing his gun, he motioned for them to join Peterman in the cell.

CHAPTER 81

ATTENTION MOMENTARILY distracted as Barty Strang opened the cell door, Sarah grabbed the shovel leaning against the wall nearby and hit him to the side of his head. He staggered backwards, but then quickly recovered, raising his gun in Sarah's direction. Ray grabbed his own gun lying on the floor, and in one quick motion, fired a shot, falling Barty to the floor.

Zach ran over to Sarah, wrapping her in a hug. She returned the embrace, but then broke away to check on her father.

"Mr. President, we need to go now," said Ray quietly. "We don't know if there's anyone else here. We've got to move."

As they turned, Strang's eyes, which had been closed, opened. He grabbed his weapon, still by his side, and fired. Ray, whose back was turned, felt the sting of a bullet as it hit the back of his leg. Barty then turned his weapon towards Sarah, but before he could pull the trigger again, he fell backward, a bullet hole over his left eye. Red blood trickled down his forehead into his open mouth.

Sarah and Ray looked over at Zach, surprised. Zach's arm was still raised, gun pointing at the dead man.

"You can put the gun down now, Zach. He's gone," said Ray.

Zach, stunned by his own quick response, slowly lowered his weapon. "I've never shot a gun before. It was a lucky shot."

"Thank God you're lucky," exclaimed Ray, falling to the floor, clutching his wounded leg.

Sarah examined the leg. It was bleeding profusely, and his face was pale. He looked like he was using all his energy to not pass out. She looked over at Zach and shook her head, lips pursed.

"Can you walk, Ray?" asked Zach.

"No way. Get them out of here before someone else comes. Leave me."

"We're not leaving you."

"You need to get the President to safety. Go!"

At that moment, they heard the elevator door opening on the floor above.

"Go," said Sarah. "Get my dad out of here, now. We'll be okay. I need to stay with Ray, or he'll bleed to death. They want my dad."

"I'm not leaving you."

"Go now. They want him!" said Sarah, pointing to her father.

"Whoever it is, I'll lead them out," said Zach, picking up Barty's semi-automatic. "Mr. President, we have to go now."

"But Sarah and Ray," protested Francis Peterman, speaking for the first time.

"We'll be okay, Sir," said Ray, who was now sitting up on the floor, propped against the wall, gun in his hands. Sarah had ripped off his pant leg and was now making a tourniquet.

"Go Dad, now!" shouted Sarah.

"Sarah, as soon as we draw them out, make your way to the entrance and call for help on Ray's phone," said Zach.

Sarah nodded. "We'll be okay. Get going!"

Zach placed the President's arm over his shoulder, his own arm around his waist, and guided him out of the cell.

"I can walk by myself, Zach," said Francis Peterman, regaining some of his own strength, but still moving slowly.

"We need to hurry, Sir. At any moment, the elevator door could open and whoever is taking it down is unlikely to be a friend. There are stairs over here. They don't look great, but we don't have much choice. Can you do it?"

"Of course I can," said the President, who still looked like a stiff wind could knock him over. He ascended the stairs quicker than Zach expected.

Halfway up, the elevator door opened, and out came Marty Green.

Recognizing him, Zach took aim with the rifle, but this time, his accuracy failed. The bullet landed nowhere near Marty, who jumped back into the elevator unharmed. The elevator door closed, and they could hear him hit the up button.

Zach guided the President up the few remaining stairs. Seeing a large coal cart, he quickly wedged it against the metal scissor gate outside the elevator.

"That should hold him a bit longer, Sir, but we need to move fast."

They exited the mine, but the President's poor conditioning from two weeks of confinement affected their pace. They stopped at the top of the path.

"I don't think we can get down it fast enough before he catches up," said Zach. "And shit! I just realized. I don't have the keys to the car. They're in Ray's pocket!"

Quickly regaining his composure, Zach looked around, surveying the mountain top for other alternatives. He spotted the coal tipple, the housing covering the old conveyor belt leading down the hill. Perhaps their assailant would think they were taking the path down and not follow them through the tipple.

"Mr. President. We should take that old tipple down. They won't expect that."

Peterman nodded in agreement, and they made their way over to it. The President stumbled, and Zach helped him up. They reached the tipple and stopped. Many of the floorboards were missing or rotten. A false move on a rotten board would pitch them out of the tipple to the bottom of the hill far below, a fall for which they would not survive.

Zach looked over at the mine. Marty had run out and was now headed to the top of the path looking down.

"Mr. President. We don't have a choice. He'll figure it out soon enough. We must make our way through the tipple to the bottom."

"Okay, Zach, let's go."

Resigned to the danger, they headed down the coal tipple on hands and knees. It was rough going, but they moved forward, one floorboard at a time. The President was slow-moving but determined.

Suddenly, a loose board fell with a crash onto the ground below. Marty Green, who was still at the top of the path, gazed upward and spotted them. He ran to station himself under the tipple, where he could see his quarries moving above him. Firing his gun, he missed both targets by a wide margin. He then ran back up the hill, to the entrance of the tipple, where he continued his pursuit.

Crawling faster than Zach and the President, Zach could hear the scraping of Marty's legs across the boards getting closer and closer.

Now it was Zach's turn to return the gunfire, none of which came anywhere near his pursuer. Zach could feel bullets flying over his head as Marty had momentarily stopped to fire his own weapon.

"Forget about firing that thing. You're not even close to hitting him. We need to keep going. He's gaining on us," shouted the President.

"Shit!" exclaimed Zach. His rifle had just fallen through the opening in the floorboards, and he could feel his heart beating as fast as a hummingbird's.

"Don't worry about that now." Energized by the sound of bullets flying near him, Peterman began to move faster. Zach followed, amazed at how quickly the President was able to crawl, considering his weakened state.

Advancing on a rotten board, President Peterman felt the floor give way, and his legs fell through. He was now dangling high over the hill below, hanging on with just his arms, hands gripping old ropes on the sides of the tipple. His sweat-laden palms and fingers were starting to lose their grip. A fall at this height would mean certain death.

"Help, Zach," exclaimed Peterman. "I can't hold on much longer."

Zach raced forward on his hands and knees as quickly as he could, grabbed Peterman under the arms, and was able to pull him back up. There was no time to rest, as more bullets flew in their direction.

They continued moving down the tipple as fast as they could, but this time with Zach in the lead. The floorboards at this end seemed sturdier.

Reaching the end, they reached a set of rickety stairs leading down to the ground, which they traversed carefully. Once down on ground-level, they could hear Marty still moving down the tipple, just above them.

Zach looked over at the President, who now appeared exhausted, barely able to stand up. He placed Peterman's arm over his neck and supported him with his other arm. The President didn't object.

"What now, Zach?"

He was forced with a decision, and he had to make it quickly.

If their assailant thought they were headed to the parking lot, perhaps they could go in the opposite direction and follow the riverbank downstream.

"Hide behind this bush, Mr. President," and Zach helped Peterman to sit behind a holly shrub, hidden from view of the tipple.

Zach grabbed a rock and joined the President. He waited a few seconds until he could tell their pursuer was about to emerge from the stairs, and then threw the rock as far as he could in the direction of the parking lot. Marty, hearing the noise, ran off in that direction, gun raised.

"Let's go now, Sir. Do you think you can walk?"

President Peterman, gathering his strength, nodded. He followed Zach along the riverbank, but his pace began to slow. Zach had to support him again as they walked.

Marty, after first running towards the parking lot, now heard footsteps in the opposite direction and stopped. *Damn*! Phoenix did not tolerate excuses. Turning around, he ran as fast as he could towards the river.

CHAPTER 82

ZACH COULD HEAR him catching up but had no choice other than to continue as fast as they could. The President's wheezes were becoming louder, and it didn't look to Zach that he had much more strength in him.

Zach spotted an old canoe sitting on the bank of the river, with a lone paddle tucked inside. Some of the wooden boards on the side of the boat looked rotten, but at least it looked minimally seaworthy. Zach helped the President into the front of the canoe, pushed it into the river, and settled himself in back, clutching the paddle. He heard a splash, looked behind, and saw Marty directly behind the boat. His hand grabbed the stern, rocking it, in an effort to capsize the little canoe.

Using his paddle, Zach knocked Marty's hand off the canoe, and they began to float with the current down the river. His attention now was directed at the river itself, as they were hitting the first of some fast-moving rapids.

Hearing a noise behind him, Zach turned. The hand had now reappeared, followed by Marty Green's face and torso, as he started heaving his way up onto the boat.

Using the paddle again, Zach struck, knocking Marty backward. At that moment, the little boat hit a rapid in the river, turning it ninety degrees sideways, and Marty slipped off. A minute later, they heard a scream, looked back, and saw his head hit a large rock in the river. He dropped beneath the water and did not reappear.

The next rapids were faster and deeper. Zach used the paddle to avoid the major rocks as the current pushed them forward, sideways, back, and forward again. They found themselves in chutes between large rocks, speeding through them at a downward angle, following the rapid moving current. President Peterman held on tight to the sides of the canoe. Zach paddled quickly, doing his best to keep the canoe from capsizing.

The little boat then hit a huge, sharp rock at high speed. They could hear crunching, and then the feel of freezing water. The canoe was gone, and in its place were multiple broken-off sections of the wood hull. Zach could see the President just a few feet away. Reaching out, he grabbed him.

"Mr. President, hold onto this board and let it take you down the river. Are you okay?"

President Peterman didn't speak but nodded, indicating to Zach that he was still conscious.

Zach pushed a board toward him and took one himself. Holding on to the President with one hand, he clutched his board and let the current take him downriver. The water was excruciatingly cold, and he knew they would not survive more than a few minutes before hypothermia took over. In the distance was a large chute that ended in a waterfall. Up above them was a tall bridge, crossing the river.

Looking around anxiously, Zach saw a shallow bank up ahead, just before the chute. If they could make the bank, it might be possible to exit the river. Grabbing the President by his collar, kicking frantically, he headed for the shore.

Only ten feet from the riverbank, he felt something cold and firm knock into him, and then float away. It was the pale white, waterlogged corpse of his former pursuer, on its way to the waterfall downstream.

Dismayed by the collision with a dead body, Zach momentarily lost his grip on the President, who was starting to head further downstream.

Zach tossed away the wooden remnant of his boat and swam towards the President, reaching him about twenty feet from the waterfall. Peterman grabbed hold of Zach's shirt-tail, and Zach, swimming with all his might against the current, delivered them to the riverbank just five feet before the falls.

Minutes in the freezing water had felt like hours, and they left the river shivering with cold. Fortunately, there was still a little daylight left, and the sun was out.

Both lay on the shore, panting.

"Mr. President, are you alright?" asked Zach.

A weary voice responded, "I'm okay. Cold as hell, but okay."

"Me too."

Almost immediately, they heard footsteps, and a man in overalls ran out to them.

"What the hell were you two doing out in the water in this temperature? You could have died," he said reproachfully.

"We weren't there by choice," answered Zach, still shivering. "Do you have anything warm we could put on?"

"Hold on a minute. I've got just the thing in the cabin."

He came back with two wetsuits and blankets and directed them to remove their wet clothes before donning the suits. Zach helped the President remove his sopping wet clothes and apply the wetsuit, and then he did the same. The stranger then placed blankets over them. The

President, who was white from exhaustion and exposure, started to regain his color, but he was still weak.

"Lucky for you I was working on our camp here. We run rafting trips in the summer, and this is the place where we get access to the river. I was just doing some maintenance when I saw you two coming out."

"Yes, and we're grateful. How do we get out of here?" asked Zach.

"The visitor center for the New River Gorge National Park is right over there, over the bridge. I think it's open. I can drive you over there. What are your names, by the way?"

"My name's Zach, and this is..."

President Peterman, now looking slightly more like his old self, cut him off before he could say anything more. The forceful tone of his voice caught Zach by surprise.

"My name is Frank. We'd be ever so thankful if you could take us there as soon as you can."

Zach looked at the President quizzically but said nothing.

"Sure. Get in the car. I'll grab the keys and drive you right over."

"Give us your name and address, and we'll send you back these wet-suits," said the President.

"No need. They're in rough shape and we have new ones coming in, so keep them."

"Thank-you."

After he had walked away, Francis Peterman turned to his companion and spoke quietly. "Zach, I don't want anyone to know who I am until I know everything that's been happening."

Zach nodded as the man returned with his keys, and they drove over the bridge to the visitor center. Fortunately, it was still open.

They walked slowly into the visitor center, with President Peterman resting his hand lightly on Zach's shoulder for support. Whispering into his ear, he reminded him, "Remember not to use my name. I'm concerned they might recognize me."

"I don't think so, Sir. You don't look much like yourself right now, with your beard and all," said Zach, "and your voice is a bit hoarse."

"That's nicely put, Zach. I'm sure I look like hell, probably a lot thinner, dressed in a wetsuit, and waterlogged. And you say my voice is a bit off?"

Zach nodded.

"That's good," said the President.

The park rangers brought them over to the roaring fire in the central fireplace, where they cinched the blankets tight over them.

"I'll call an ambulance for you," said one of the rangers.

"No need," said the President. "Could you just drop us in town, so we could get some new clothes? Also, can I borrow your phone for a call?"

Zach interrupted. "I still have my phone, if it works. It was in my pants pocket, and I took it and my wallet out when we put on the wetsuits. Let me see. Yes, it's wet, but I think it's okay. Here," and he handed the phone to the President.

"I just need to finish tidying things up," said the ranger. "We're about to close for the evening, and then I can drive you into town. Be done in about twenty minutes," and he was off.

Peterman dialed Sarah's old number, but of course, there was no answer.

"Mr. President," Zach said quietly, "she doesn't have that phone anymore, and she may not have had her new phone with her when she was kidnapped."

"Makes sense, but I need to reach her."

"We can try Ray's phone."

President Peterman knew Ray's number well and dialed. It was Sarah who answered. Zach could hear Peterman's side of the conversation.

"Thank God you're okay Sarah. Ray's okay too? Great. You're out of the mine and the ambulance just arrived? Great. Yeah, we're okay too. Now, this is important. Don't say anything about me or the kidnapping. You can say you were hiking, and a crazy man shot Ray. We'll work out details later. Love you. Bye."

"Okay, Zach. Tell me everything that's been going on. I need to know it all."

Zach gave a detailed description of everything he could remember, and what he had learned from Ray about the confrontation in the White House. The President was silent the whole time, soaking up all the details.

"Unbelievable," said Peterman. After a minute of silence, he phoned Sarah again.

"Sarah, I need to speak to Ray."

Sarah handed the phone to Ray, who was now being brought into the ambulance on a stretcher.

"Call Director Allen. Find out what happened to the guy who impersonated me and the guy who shot him. I need to figure out how to resolve this without spooking the whole country. Tell the Director to keep quiet about everything for now. Oh, and Zach tells me there was another agent there too, so tell him to also keep his mouth shut."

"Sir, the Director was shot. I've heard he's in surgery right now.

"Sorry to hear that."

"The rogue agent is dead, but your double was just shot in the arm so he should be alright."

"Okay. Find out what you can from that other agent and call me back at this number."

"Will do."

CHAPTER 83

THE PARK RANGER drove them into Fayetteville, where he dropped them off at a used clothing store. The President was still weak, but he was moving better now and no longer needed to hold onto Zach.

The store had a minimal selection, and neither man ended up with well-fitting or appropriate apparel. Zach pulled out his water-soaked wallet and paid with a wet credit card.

Across the street from the clothing store was a Bob Evans Restaurant. Hungry, they made their way over, and the hostess escorted them to a booth. The server came over to take their order.

"I'll have the burger and fries, please," said the President.

"Sarah said you didn't eat red meat or fried food," said Zach.

"Look, I almost died. I've hardly eaten in the last few weeks, and I'm going to eat anything I feel like," said President Peterman. The server looked at him with a surprised look on her face.

"Me too, I guess," said Zach. "Burger and fries for both of us, and how about a chocolate shake."

"Shake for me, too," said Peterman. "But make it vanilla."

The server walked away, looking confused by the conversation of the two oddly dressed men. While waiting for the return phone call, Zach mentioned, without going into details, that he and Sarah had grown quite fond of each other in a very short time.

President Peterman smiled. "I hope to see a lot more of you in the future."

Zach was about to say more, but he was interrupted by Ray's return call.

"Uh huh, that's good news," Zach heard Peterman say.

The President put down the phone and spoke. "The impostor's doing okay. Shoulder wound, and he's at Walter Reed Medical Center. Ray's doing okay too. Just lost a lot of blood."

He then dialed his former Chief of Staff and spoke softly into the speaker, with his hand over his mouth to deaden the sound to anyone overhearing. "Bob, I need your help. Yes, it's me. I know my voice is a bit off. I'll prove it to you. Last month we sat in my office and drank a bottle of Chateau Montelena Chardonnay watching the Washington Commanders get smoked by the Dallas Cowboys. Yeah, they suck."

Zach then heard a condensed, one minute version of the situation, and even though he was a few feet away from the phone, he could hear shouts of surprise on the other end.

"Bob, this is what I need you to do. Contact Tim Danner, my doctor at Walter Reed. The impostor is to be put in isolation other than for the doctors and nurses who need to tend to him, and Tim is to stay in there the whole time and not breathe a word. No one is to know anything. Get us a chopper to bring us to Walter Reed. There's a clearing just to the side of the Bob Evans Restaurant in Fayetteville, West Virginia, where they can land. I need a chopper pilot who's dependable and not one to go blabbing, and I need it now. The pilot's not to say anything to anyone when he arrives here. Thanks, Bob."

Francis Peterman smiled at Zach, who watched him devour his burger and fries with gusto. Zach had no idea what the plan was, but he could tell President Peterman was returning to his old self.

It was dark by the time the helicopter landed outside the restaurant in Fayetteville. The bright lights, along with the noise of its landing, created quite a spectacle for the other patrons dining at the restaurant.

After paying the bill, the two poorly dressed men got up from their seats to head to the chopper. On the way, one of the other diners looked up at them and spoke to Peterman.

"You know, you look a little like the President, except he's a lot taller and younger."

Peterman responded with a smile. "I get that a lot. I guess we look like we could be related."

"You don't look that similar," said the man's wife, shaking her head.

"Have a good evening," said the President, laughing aloud, and they left the restaurant for the helicopter.

The President got in and held the door open, but Zach froze about three feet from the door.

"What's the matter?" asked Peterman.

"I can't do this."

"Why not?"

"I have a fear of heights."

"Just don't look down," shouted the chopper pilot.

"It's not that easy," said Zach.

"Zach, you need to get in here now. The fate of the country hinges on me getting back immediately, so unless you want to figure out a way to get yourself back and miss all the fun, you'll get your ass in the chopper now."

Reluctantly, he did what he was told.

"It will only take about two hours," said the pilot, as he took off. For Zach, flying in a helicopter for two hours would be an eternity.

Back at the Bob Evans Restaurant, the woman looked at her husband and said quietly, "I wonder who those two guys were in those baggy work clothes. Must be important if there was a helicopter for them."

"Maybe they're spies, or CIA or something, trying to hide out here. Maybe they think they can fit in here by wearing those awful clothes," said her husband. "Probably think we're all hicks here."

"I guess we'll never know, she said. "Let's order dessert," and with that, they turned their attention to more important matters, the menu.

CHAPTER 84

TWO HOURS LATER, they touched down at Walter Reed Medical Center in Bethesda, Maryland. Zach immediately exited the moment the chopper landed. His complexion was a pale green, and his legs felt like rubber. This time, it was Francis Peterman who supported him. Within a minute or two of fresh air, Zach began to regain his strength.

The President was met at the helicopter pad by his Chief of Staff, Bob Benton, and his personal physician, Tim Danner. After introducing Zach, the President asked him to stay to one side, while he and the other two took part in a lengthy discussion. Once that concluded, they headed off to a room in the hospital, and the President motioned for Zach to join them.

Once inside the room, Peterman turned to Zach and said, "This is the plan."

Bob Benton interrupted, "Mr. President, do you think it wise to give this young man all these details?"

"Zach helped save my life. He knows everything anyway. We can trust him," said Peterman. He then turned to his personal physician.

"Tim, get what you need."

"It's good to have you back, Sir. I knew something must have been up when they used some hack to give you a physical instead of me," said Danner.

"It's good to be back, Tim." With that, Dr. Danner left the room.

President Peterman continued, "Zach, it is imperative that the country does not know what has transpired. It could create panic. We're going to do a little switch here, and nobody will be the wiser."

Zach looked at him with a confused expression.

"You'll see," said Peterman who smiled, despite his exhaustion and the stomach ache he now felt due to his most recent meal.

"The impostor is in a room down the hall with a bullet wound in his shoulder. The world thinks I have been shot, and it has been reported that the President is going to make a full recovery. I'm going to switch places with him, and no one, except for a few people, will know."

"How are you going to do that, without everyone here knowing? There must be Secret Service agents outside his room, and how are you going to get past them without making a scene?" asked Zach, still unsure.

At that moment, Tim Danner returned with a gurney. It was an old-fashioned variety, with a metal shelf on top and another shelf approximately two feet beneath. A long, white sheet hung from the top layer, covering the lower shelf on all four sides. On top of the sheet were syringes, medicine vials, bandages, and tape, along with shaving cream and a razor.

Dr. Danner helped the President climb up onto the lower shelf, allowing the sheet from above to cover him up.

"Zach, if all goes according to plan, you should meet my doppelganger in just a few minutes. Stay here," said Peterman, as his physician rolled the gurney, with him on it, out into the hallway.

"What are they going to do with those medicine vials and syringes?" asked Zach to Bob Benton.

"Those are just for show. The bandages and razor are what's really needed."

Dr. Danner arrived at the impostor's room. He was well known and liked by the Secret Service agents guarding the man thought to be the President. There was no issue bringing the gurney into the room.

Danner spoke to the two agents in the room. "Please leave for a few minutes. I need to examine the President in private. Reluctantly, they left, waiting outside.

Once they were gone, President Peterman came out from under the sheet covering the gurney and gazed at his double, stunned at his resemblance.

Seeing the President emerge from the gurney, Jim Staples was even more shocked, and was about to cry out. Tim Danner quickly placed his hand over his mouth and shook his head. The President came up beside Staples and talked softly to him.

"This is how it's going to go. I'm going in your bathroom here for a shave. Dr. Danner is then going to bandage me up, so my shoulder looks the same as yours. You're going to get on that gurney and go back to my room and do what you're told by the people in that room."

"And if I don't?" asked Staples.

"Then you will, how shall we say, disappear forever. Your choice." There was a steely look in Francis Peterman's eyes that said he was not bluffing.

"Okay. I'm getting tired of trying to be you, anyway. Can't stand your diet."

President Peterman grinned slightly at the comment, and then went into the bathroom to shave off his beard. Dr. Danner then bandaged his shoulder. Staples took the President's place on the gurney and was wheeled back to the other room by the physician.

Tim Danner returned to see the President having taken his place on the bed.

"Now, let me examine you, to make sure you're in good condition," said Dr. Danner. "You've been through quite an ordeal."

"I'm alright. Tired, and a bit of a stomach ache."

Following the exam, Sarah, who had finally arrived at the hospital, was ushered into the room.

"How is he, Doc?" she asked, looking concerned.

"He's okay. Blood pressure is up a bit, but then again, he's been without his medicine for three weeks. He's lost some weight, but that's probably for the better."

Peterman interrupted. "Not exactly the way I'd choose to lose it, but I'll take it."

Sarah went over to her father's bed and gave him a big hug.

"Ouch," he cried.

"What's the matter, Dad?"

"Remember, my shoulder," he responded with a slight wink.

Sarah couldn't quite keep a straight face, but responded, "Sorry, Dad."

"Watch out for his shoulder, ma'am. Remember he got shot in it," said one of the Secret Service agents.

"I will," she said, and she returned the wink to her father.

"And is Jeff okay?" he asked.

"Yes, he's fine. I just spoke with him on the ambulance ride. He's with the FBI and they're feeding him all the things I don't allow, and he's enjoying all the attention."

"Great. Tell him I'm proud of him, and when he sees me next, he'll get a huge candy bar."

Sarah just shook her head.

Over in the other hospital room, Jim Staples was helped off the gurney and into the bed. His hair was cut very short, and black dye was applied to what remained. He was given a pair of horned-rim glasses and a pair of worker's overalls to wear. Bob Benton stood over the impostor and spoke.

"This is what's happening. In a few minutes, two FBI agents will be arriving to take you to an FBI safe house, where you will be questioned over the next few days for any information you have regarding the events that have taken place. If you cooperate fully, no harm will come to you, and you will be put in the witness protection program. You will be given a new identity and a new place to live. If you do not cooperate or leak any information in the future, it will not go well for you. I don't think I need to dwell on the consequences. Do you understand?"

Jim Staples said nothing but nodded in agreement.

The FBI agents arrived, and escorted Staples out in a wheelchair.

"Wow," said Zach, who had been standing in the corner. "I think you really got to him."

"You don't get to be Chief of Staff by playing softball," said Benton, as they walked over to the President's room. The Secret Service agents in the room were again asked to leave. Sarah left her father's side to rush over to Zach, where she gave him a hug and kiss.

"That's for saving my dad," she said.

"And this is for me," she added, throwing her arms around him, and giving him an even bigger kiss. "Sorry I don't have any champagne and caviar."

Zach's face turned red, catching Francis Peterman's gaze. He felt like he was back in high school, picking up his prom date in front of her parents.

The President looked a bit confused by her latest remark, but then he smiled back at the two of them.

"I'd kiss you myself, Zach, but I think Sarah would be jealous," he said with a laugh.

President Peterman looked over at his doctor and Bob Benton. "When can I get out of here?"

"We think it would be best for appearances to have you spend the night here and leave in the morning, if all goes well," said Benton. "We'll send out a fresh statement to the press that you're recovering fully from the bullet wound shot by a deranged, rogue agent.

Danner nodded and said, "I agree, but I think you should spend the next few days here. You've been through a terrible ordeal, and I think a few quiet days would do you some good."

"Okay. I'll spend the night, but if I feel okay tomorrow morning, I'm leaving," said the President.

Reluctantly, Dr. Danner agreed.

After telling his physician how much better he felt following a good night's rest, Francis Peterman left the hospital early in the morning by wheelchair. He was escorted out by his daughter and the Chief of Staff, to the cheers of the hospital staff. A throng of reporters were waiting outside, held back by multiple Secret Service agents.

President Peterman, the ultimate politician, was not going to waste the moment. Gingerly, he got up from his wheelchair and addressed the crowd of reporters.

"Ladies and gentlemen, I am so pleased you all are here to welcome me back from the hospital. As you can see, I am doing quite well. Thank-you to all the doctors, nurses, and other hospital staff who have nursed me back to health. Time for me to go back to work."

With that, he gave a wave and a smile, and allowed Sarah to wheel him over to the waiting limousine. He was more tired than he let on, but he had never been this excited to head back to work.

CHAPTER 85

ZACH FINALLY made his way back to his apartment. He knew the nightmare was over, but he still bolted the door and attached the inner chain on entering. It would take some time before he felt everything was back to normal.

It was great to be back, but it wasn't the same without Ripley. He'd take care of that soon.

There was still something he had to know, and it kept eating at him. Was Samantha somehow involved? She was the only one who knew that he and Sarah were going to Paris. Could she have set him up? It was time to find out.

With his heart racing, he dialed Samantha's phone. She answered right away.

"Zach, is everything okay? I heard from my parents you left Paris. Where are you? I've been so worried."

Zach didn't waste any time. "I need to know. Did you set me up in Paris?"

"What do you mean?"

"You sent us an email and said to go to the Eiffel Tower where we would get help. Instead, they were waiting for us there. It was a trap."

"I never sent any email. Believe me, I would never do that. I could never do that to the father of my children."

"So, who else would have known we'd be in France?"

Samantha was quiet for a moment, thinking, and then she answered. "Jonathan Brodsky. I called him to help me get everything set up for you."

"You called your boss, the one you had the affair with? I thought that was over," said Zach, anger rising in his voice.

"It's been over for ages. No, I was calling him for you. Plus, he's not my boss anymore. He's President Peterman's Chief of Staff."

Now it was Zach's turn for silence. It all made sense.

"Zach, are you there?"

"Yes, I'm here. Everything's alright. I'll call you in a few days to arrange to see the kids."

"Sure. I'm sorry if I messed things up for you. Look, in some way, I still care about you. I'm glad you're sober now, and that you're safe. I do want the best for you."

"I know. It will all be okay. I shouldn't have doubted you. Sorry."

"That's alright. Maybe we can eventually forgive each other."

"I'd like that," he said, before hanging up the phone and placing his next call.

He called the private number he had been given by Francis Peterman, and the President himself answered.

"Mr. President, Jonathan Brodsky, your new Chief of Staff, the one who took over from Bob Benton, is most definitely involved in the plot. I'm sure he's the one who set Sarah and I up in Paris at the Eiffel Tower.

"Thanks, Zach. I'll take care of it.

CHAPTER 86

OTHER THAN for a few people who were sworn to secrecy, no one else knew that the real President of the United States had switched places with the impostor and was back.

Now in his office, President Peterman picked up the phone to call his administrative assistant, Rose Goodwin, and with a shudder, he remembered that she was forever gone. He made a mental note to call Rose's daughter to express his condolences. The bastards who did this were going to pay.

He instead spoke to Judy Mairston. "Judy, could you please ask Jonathan Brodsky to come to my office. Thank-you."

"Yes, Sir."

Jonathan Brodsky sat in his office, awaiting further instructions from Phoenix. Brodsky correctly believed that Staples had been shot by Walter McCoy, which unfortunately had not been fatal. He had developed a loathing for the impostor, and occasionally had fantasies of seeing him dying in all different, horrible ways. But now, he believed Jim Staples was back, sitting in the Oval Office.

When summoned by the President, Jonathan Brodsky marched in with a scowl on his face.

"What do you want?" asked angrily.

"That's no way to address the President of the United States, Mr. Brodsky," said Peterman. "Yes, it's me, and I'm back."

Bob Benton, who was standing in the corner of the room, moved over to stand behind the President.

Jonathan Brodsky, mouth agape, now understood the situation. He didn't know what to say. What the hell was going on?

Finally, Brodsky spoke. "Mr. President, you're looking well. How's your shoulder?"

"Cut the crap, Brodsky. I know what's going on, and I know that you're in the middle of it."

"I don't know what you're talking about."

"I don't have time to listen to your lies. This is how it's going to be. You have two choices. The first choice is that I have you disappear, perhaps to Guantanamo. No one, including your family, hears from you ever again.

"The second choice is to spill the beans on who's involved. Then you retire in dishonor. We'll find something on you, and if we don't, we'll make it up. Then you go on and live your miserable life wherever, and we never hear from you again."

"Is there a third choice?" asked Brodsky, slumping into a chair.

"No," said Peterman forcefully. "And I need the answer now."

Brodsky looked down at his feet before finally answering. "I don't know all the people involved, but the guy in charge is called 'Phoenix,' and of course, the agent Walter McCoy, who was shot when your double injured his shoulder."

"Who else?"

"I don't know."

"More names, or you're on the next flight for Guantanamo."

"Okay. There's only one other I know for sure, and that's Jack Chauncey, CEO of Decorp. There's others, but I don't know their names."

"Anyone else?"

"That's all that I know, I swear."

Francis Peterman studied him for a few moments and then said, "You may go. Go home, and never say a word about any of this. If you do, no one will hear from you ever again."

Jonathan Brodsky quickly rose, grabbed his coat from his office, and made one quick phone call before leaving the White House. He drove home slowly, trying to come up with a story to tell his wife.

Back in the Oval Office, the President and his Chief of Staff were discussing how to move forward from the limited information they received.

"Bob, we need to figure out the best way to handle this. We need more evidence before we start accusing major CEOs, but we need to do it quietly," said President Peterman.

Benson nodded. "Okay. But I'm still concerned you could be in danger. We don't know how far this conspiracy goes. We should also alert the Vice President, in case he's at risk also."

"I guess so. Go ahead."

Vice President Arnold Richardson was sitting in the glass enclosed patio of his residence, along with his wife, reading the newspaper and drinking sweet tea, when the call from Bob Benton came in.

"I can't believe it, Bob. It sounds incredible. Is this true?"

"Yes, it's true. We don't know how far this conspiracy goes, but I'm alerting you just in case."

"I'll certainly take precautions. Thank you for letting me know. I still say. . ."

Suddenly, there was the sound of a gunshot and breaking glass, as a bullet flew over the heads of the Vice President and his wife, shattering the glass enclosure. Both Richardson and his wife jumped off their chairs to lay prone on the patio floor, as glass shards fell around them.

Immediately, secret service agents came running and began a sweep of the grounds for intruders.

Bob Benton was still on the phone. "What's going on, Arnold? Are you still there?"

"Yes, I'm still here. Someone tried to shoot me!"

CHAPTER 87

IT HAD NOW been some time since Phoenix had heard from his lieutenant, Marty Green. He sensed something must have gone wrong and was now pacing back and forth around his hotel suite. His call to Brodsky had gone unanswered. As much as he disliked getting involved directly, he knew he had to go to Nuttallburg and see for himself.

Driving much faster than the speed limit, he drove his Mercedes to Nuttallburg in under five hours. A light snowfall made the potholes on the final approach to the tipple invisible, and Phoenix cursed as he hit one pothole after another. There was no sign of any guard in the parking lot. *Where was he?*

Almost running up the hill, he looked in vain for a guard at the entrance to the mine. Again, no one. He could feel his throat tighten and his pulse quicken. *Where the hell are they?*

Scouring the area, he came across the guard's body about a hundred feet to the side of the entrance. Blood-streaked mud stuck to his shoes. Ripping off a piece of the dead man's camouflage shirt, he wiped it off.

He found two more dead guards, one by the elevator and the other by the holding cell. The cell itself was empty. *Shit, what the hell happened, and where's Marty?*

His heart was beating faster, and he started to sweat. *Is this fear?* It was not a sensation he was used to feeling.

Phoenix made his way quickly down the hill to his car, where he checked his phone for messages, hoping for good news from Marty Green. There was one text message and one voice mail. The text message was from Kwan, and the voicemail was from Jack Chauncey. Both had the same question, "Has the plan been carried out?"

Arriving back in DC, he turned on his television to see an impromptu press conference, featuring the President with a sling over his arm, reassuring the country that all was well following the bullet wound. Phoenix couldn't tell much by the President's appearance, but the sight of Bob Benton rather than Jonathan Brodsky by his side told him all he needed to know.

It was time to disappear. He'd already received most of his money. Yes, he was leaving some money on the table, but all in all, it had been an excellent haul. The Arlington conspirators would never find him. The North Koreans had more resources to try to track him down, but he was very good at staying hidden.

Phoenix returned a call to Kwan, who answered immediately.

"I need to know, Phoenix, is everything still going according to plan?"

"We can meet tomorrow, and then you'll know everything. Meet me at 10:00 am by the Jefferson Memorial, where we met before."

"Okay," said Kwan, and he hung up. It was not quite the answer he wanted.

The Arlington conspirators were beyond frightened. They hadn't heard anything from Phoenix in the last few days, and they had been unable to reach Jonathan Brodsky.

Billy Joe Scranton, not being used to being left in the dark, was seething with anger. When Jack Chauncey didn't answer his phone call, he got in his car and drove directly to Chauncey's house, where he slammed his fist on the door to announce his presence.

A startled butler brought him into the front room, and after a minute, Jack Chauncey appeared, two glasses of red wine in his hand.

"What the hell is going on?" growled Billy Joe, face six inches from his host's, color as red as the wine.

"Not here. Come with me."

They walked over to the small room with the marble table, where Chauncey closed and locked the door.

"I don't know any more than you know. I can't reach Phoenix either," he said.

"I don't like it. You're responsible for this mess."

"Calm down. I'm taking care of it."

"By doing what, drinking red wine?"

"If it goes bad, the only thing that really ties us to this is Phoenix's video in the bank."

"Yeah, so what?"

"I've made arrangements to get it."

"How?"

"It so happens that I've found a little information about the bank president at Arlington Savings Bank, who I happen to know. Not only has he taken some money out of the bank for personal use, but he has also used it to support his mistress. I've given him three choices. One, I could report him to the government bank examiners. Two, I could start by informing his wife. Three, he could somehow arrange to open safety deposit box number 307, get the article in question, and bring it to me. He's taken option three, so I expect to receive it any time now."

Chauncey could see Billy Joe's anger dissipate in front of him.

"I will let you know when it has been accomplished. So please, finish your wine, and then leave quietly. I don't want any of my other servants seeing you."

Chauncey turned on his heels and walked out. Billy Joe Scranton chugged his wine and left shortly afterward.

By the next day, Jack Chauncey was in possession of the video, and the four industrial leaders felt much more relieved. They believed the imposter was still at the White House, although they had not heard yet from Phoenix that the President had been terminated. At least now there was nothing tying them to the plot, and Phoenix had nothing to use against them.

They all met back at Jack Chauncey's residence, all wanting to be certain that this was the correct video. The house staff was sent home for the day, and they viewed it in the same windowless room around the marble table.

"Okay, now that we've seen it, what do we do with it?" asked Tim Braun.

"Isn't it obvious?" said Billy Joe Scranton. "We destroy it."

"We should bury it," suggested Theresa Jones.

Jack Chauncey made the final decision. "We destroy it, then bury it."

Out in the backyard, they took turns demolishing the SD card with a hammer. Billy Joe's turn was last, and with a great big swing, he smashed it into little bits that flew in all directions.

Gathering up as many pieces as they could find, they buried them beneath the white azalea bush in the flower garden, before returning to the house for one last celebratory drink.

CHAPTER 88

IT WAS A BRIGHT, sunny day in Washington, DC. Even with temperatures just in the high thirties, the joggers and walkers were out in force on the Tidal Basin. Kwan could see them all from his vantage point at the Jefferson Memorial. Hoping for good news, he had a smile on his face. Scouring the crowd for Phoenix, Kwan was surprised to find him suddenly by his side.

Phoenix indicated for him to walk, and they joined the others walking about the Tidal Basin.

"Okay, talk to me," said the North Korean, walking briskly to keep up with his companion.

"It's a shit show," said Phoenix.

Kwan stopped abruptly and stuck out his arm to halt Phoenix's progress. "What the hell does that mean?"

"The President is back in the White House. I don't know what happened. I don't know where the impostor is. I don't even know where my lieutenant is, or if he's even still alive."

"Give me back all the money we paid you," he said, his voice raised.

"I don't think so. I carried out the plan according to your wishes, and unfortunately, things didn't work out as planned. I could disappear with the money, and you'll never find me. And how are your superiors going to feel about you, and how you wasted your country's money? I doubt they'll be too pleased with your efforts either. You'll be a lot easier to find than me. Doubt you live more than a month."

Kwan stood silent, glaring at his companion.

Phoenix continued, "I have a solution that works for both of us. First, you can hold back the remaining two million dollars we agreed to."

Kwan snorted in anger.

"Let me continue," said Phoenix. "Remember that day back in June, when I had you sign with me as one of the owners of safe deposit box number 122 at the Congressional National Bank? I told you there would be useful information for you there, but I didn't say what. I kept the key, this key.

With my key, you can access the box. It contains the incriminating confessions of the conspirators, documenting the plot to kill the President of the United States by the heads of major corporations and by major players within the government itself. It's the copy they don't know exists. You get that to the media around the world, showing the true nature of the imperialist, capitalist system that is the United States. That way, you still get what you need. Granted, it's not as good as revealing the actual murder of the President and his daughter, but at least it's something you can show to your superiors."

Kwan again stood motionless without speaking, considering Phoenix's words, and contemplating his alternatives, for almost a full minute. Finally, he spoke.

"Okay. Give me the key."

"Good decision. You'll never see me again," he said, as he handed over the key and took the long walk back to his hotel suite.

Back at his hotel suite, Phoenix poured himself a celebratory glass of scotch. Even if the end results were not as desired, he was now incredibly rich. Even without the remaining two million dollars from both the Arlington conspirators and the North Koreans, he still made thirty-six million dollars from this job. He could easily sit back on some Caribbean Island and never have to work again. He opened his computer to check his bank account.

"What the fuck?" he exclaimed out loud.

His account showed that the twelve million dollars the North Koreans had paid him recently had now been somehow withdrawn from his account.

Phoenix stared at the screen, not wanting to believe it. He tried refreshing it, but it still showed the same thing. *I've been cheated!*

He sat still for another minute, fingers tapping rhythmically on the desk. Finally, he picked up his phone and made a call. This one was to Zach Webster.

Immediately following, Zach placed a call to the President.

CHAPTER 89

KWAN WALKED quickly through the open doors of the Congressional National Bank. Even though he was successful in removing the twelve million dollars from Phoenix's account, he was still worried. His government had paid six million dollars early on, which he could not get back. For his own hope of survival, the documents needed to be there, and they needed to be incriminating.

After signing for access, he was led to the safe deposit room. Here, he inserted the key and opened the box. Inside was the SD card, which he had been told contained the full confessions. Hopefully, this would be good enough for his superiors. With the card in his pocket, he made his way out of the bank.

Unknown to Kwan, FBI agents had been placed on full surveillance at the Congressional Bank ever since Zach informed the President of Phoenix's call. The bank manager had been instructed to let the FBI know if anyone accessed safe deposit box 122.

Kwan hadn't walked ten feet on the sidewalk before two FBI agents closed in on him from both sides, and there was nowhere for him to run. Slipping a pair of handcuffs over his wrists, they emptied his pockets and removed the SD card.

"You can't do this. I have diplomatic immunity," protested Kwan.

"Can't hear you," said the FBI agent on his right side. "Got a hearing problem."

They shoved the North Korean agent into the waiting, unmarked van, which drove off.

"What do you think is on that?" asked one of the FBI agents to his partner. "We could get a sneak peek by plugging it into my laptop."

"Don't know, don't care."

"Tempted to look?"

"Tempted, yes, but it's not worth our jobs. We're on strict orders to bring it straight to the big man at the White House."

"The big man himself?"

"The big man himself. Still want to get a peek?"

"Okay, so we don't look. Let's get going and be done with it," and they drove off to the White House.

CHAPTER 90

TIM BRAUN from Raymore Industries sat at his desk in the corner office on the 28th floor, pouring over the financials from the prior month. Things looked bad, with red ink everywhere. Fortunately now, due to the veto of the new defense bill, his missile defense system would likely be purchased, and his company should survive.

He was interrupted by a call from the receptionist on the first floor. Two men with badges reading *FBI* asked to see him on a matter they deemed urgent.

"Send them up."

Five minutes later, the men arrived at his office.

"What can I do for you gentlemen?"

"The President would like to see you. He would like to talk with you about how you can assist the country."

Braun sat stone-faced. Thoughts ran through his head. *Does the imposter know I'm one of the conspirators? Is he going to try to blackmail me?*

"Of course. When does he want to see me?"

"Right away. We have orders to bring you to see him presently."

"Alright. Let me just put my computer away, and I'll be right with you."

Within a few minutes, Tim Braun sat in the back of the FBI car on his way to the White House.

Theresa Jones was at her stable, bawling out the trainer for the poor race time of her new colt. He was supposed to be her prize winner, and he was five seconds off the time he needed to finish.

Two men approached and flashed their FBI badges.

"What do you want?" she asked, impatiently.

"We need you to come with us. The President needs to see you."

"You tell him I'm busy right now."

"I'm sorry, ma'am, but he needs you now."

"Okay."

She tried to hide her anger behind her forced smile, but as soon as she sat in the car behind the agents, the smile disappeared. *How dare that imposter demand my appearance.*

Billy Joe Scranton was at home when the FBI agents showed up. He was in an especially good mood as the football team he had bet on won, and he was up five thousand dollars.

"Mr. Scranton, we have been tasked with taking you to the White House to meet with the President."

"Why?" Billy Joe demanded, glaring at the agents.

"We don't know. We were just told to tell you it's for the good of the country."

"I'm a busy man. If the President wants to meet with me, he needs to make an appointment," he said, walking away.

"I'm sorry, Sir. We were told not to take 'no' for an answer. It's supposed to be very important."

"Very well, then. I need to find my coat and hat. Be back in a minute."

Billy Joe Scranton stomped away, slamming a door as he went to retrieve his garments. Five minutes later, he too was in the back of an FBI car.

Jack Chauncey was the last of the conspirators to be picked up. Again, two FBI agents rang the door to Chauncey's mansion.

"Are you Jack Chauncey?" asked one of the agents, once they met in the front hall.

"Of course, and who are you?" he asked angrily, in his best upper-crust accent.

"I'm Agent Rundlett, and this is Agent Halloran. We're from the FBI. The President of the United States would like to see you immediately. It's a matter of vital importance."

"For what reason?"

"I'm not at liberty to say. But please come with us at once."

"Yes, of course."

Within a span of ten minutes, all four of the Arlington conspirators were in FBI cars on the way to the White House.

Once arrived, each was led into a separate room. They were told the President needed to speak with them about an important matter.

Jack Chauncey was the first to be brought into the President's office. Francis Peterman was sitting behind his desk, leaning back in his chair with a slight smile on his face.

"Mr. Chauncey, so good of you to come. Please have a seat," said the President.

"What can I do for you, Mr. President?" asked Chauncey, disappointed to see what he assumed to be the imposter looking relatively healthy.

He suddenly noticed Bob Benton standing in the corner. *What's he doing here?*

He stared again at the man sitting behind the desk. *Could this be the real Francis Peterman?*

His questions were answered immediately.

"Oh no, it's what I can do for you, Mr. Chauncey. As you can probably tell, I'm the real Francis Peterman, and I've got a present for you, a one-way ticket. It's to a beautiful little place called Guantanamo. No one will know you're there. You've simply disappeared. There will be a manhunt for you, but unfortunately, you will never be found."

"I don't understand. Why?"

"I know that you were the leader of the plot to have me assassinated, and my daughter too."

"That's a lie. Anyone who told you that was lying. I don't even know what you're talking about, Mr. President."

"I think you do. Check out this video on my computer. It's most illuminating."

President Peterman turned his computer around for Jack Chauncey to see. As clear as could be, it showed Chauncey at the table speaking.

"We agree with your terms. We will wire the six million deposit by tonight, twelve million according to timelines we've worked out, and the remaining two million upon the confirmation of the death of the President."

"That's a forgery," shouted Chauncey.

"I don't think so, and Jonathan Brodsky has already named you as the conspirator in charge. Game, set, and match."

Jack Chauncey's whole countenance changed. He was accustomed to being in control for most of his adult life, always the one to give orders and ultimatums. Now diminished, a shadow of his former self, he fell back into his chair, crying softly.

Finally, in a quiet voice, he asked, "Are there any other options for me?"

"Sure," said the President. "You can admit your actions and be tried for treason, but you know the punishment for treason."

"I'll do anything," pleaded the CEO of Decorp.

"Okay, here's a third option. We lay a bribery charge on you, which you admit to. Then, you go to jail, maybe for seven to ten years. You donate ninety-five percent of your net worth to charity, and you never speak of this meeting or anything related to the kidnapping plan again. You know what happens if you do. Oh, and the remaining five percent goes in a trust to Rose Goodwin's heirs."

"That leaves me nothing."

"That's correct. Ninety-five and five equals one hundred percent. Would you prefer one of the first two options?"

Jack Chauncey had no choice. He took option three and was led from the President's office by secret service agent Frank Baldwin.

Next up was Theresa Jones. President Peterman didn't waste any time, as the video was playing as she walked in.

Theresa sat quietly and didn't speak. She sat rigid, biting her lower lip.

The video ended, and no one spoke for the next minute. Finally, Francis Peterman broke the silence.

"As you are probably now aware, I am the real President, and you have committed treason. You could be charged with treason and likely executed, or I could send you on an all-expense paid lifetime vacation at

Guantanamo. But if you want the easy way out, you can plead guilty to embezzlement, get probably five or so years in jail, and give away all your net worth to charity, with five percent going to Rose Goodwin's heirs. Oh, just so you know, that includes your racehorses."

Theresa Jones still sat silently, now closing her eyes.

"Do I take it you'd like the third option?" asked the President.

She opened her eyes and nodded slightly.

"Now go."

Frank Baldwin was summoned, and she was escorted out.

Tim Braun was next, and he sat through the video tapping his foot rapidly on the floor. Once it was over, he bowed his head and cried, tears running down his face onto the collar of his well-pressed, Armani shirt.

Last up was Billy Joe Scranton. After seeing the video, he stormed over to the President's desk, pounding it with his fist.

Peterman pressed a buzzer, and Frank Baldwin walked in.

"Do you have something you'd like to say, Mr. Scranton?"

"It's all a pack of lies," bellowed Billy Joe. "I'll see you in court."

"You've been named by all the others, plus the video. I don't think you'll have much of a chance in your trial for treason, and I'm sure you know what the penalty for that is."

Scranton sat back down on his chair, resting his big head on his hands.

"Sounds like you'd like to be tried for treason, then," said Peterman.

"No," said Billy Joe softly. "Do I have any other choices?"

"The same ones I gave to your buddies. Treason, Guantanamo, or the easy way out."

Scranton raised his head quickly, a ray of hope in his eyes.

"What's the easy way?"

"You give away all your money, your possessions, every damn thing you own. I'll let you keep the clothes on your back. You serve five to ten years in jail for some trumped up charge we make up. That's if we don't find something else illegal you've already done."

Defeated, Billy Joe nodded, and then returned his head to his hands.

CHAPTER 91

"JUDY," said President Peterman to his administrative assistant, "could you please see if Majority Leader Randal Gray could spare a few minutes to meet with me this afternoon?"

"Certainly, Sir. You have some free time at 3 pm. I'll see if he can come then."

"Sounds good. Thanks."

Randal Gray showed up right on time at 3 pm. He was not pleased. He was the Majority Leader, after all, and didn't appreciate being summoned.

"Thank-you for coming, Randal," said Peterman. "There's something I need to talk about with you, something that upsets me a great deal."

"What is it, Mr. President?"

"I've heard you've been trying to hold up my health care bill in the appropriations committee, and that you've told Senator Macomber if he votes for it, certain negative family information may come to light."

"Whoever said that is a liar!"

"I'll take you at your word for it, Majority Leader, but if any of his family secrets are leaked, I'll know where it came from."

"How dare you!" said Randal Gray, as he stomped out of the room.

"Judy, could you please ask the Vice President to join me?" asked Peterman over his intercom. "Thank-you."

Within a few minutes, Vice President Richardson knocked on the President's door, and was admitted.

"Yes, Mr. President. What can I do for you?"

"Just had an unpleasant conversation with the Majority Leader. He was trying to blackmail one of the senators who was supporting my health care bill."

"That's terrible. I hope you threatened to expose him."

"I think he got the picture, but really, I wanted to see how you were doing. I heard you had a very scary situation this morning."

"Yes, my wife and I were very frightened, but we're fine."

"That's good. Did the secret service find any intruders?"

"No, they must have gotten away."

"I don't think they did, Arnold. You see, I sent some additional agents to your house to interview your house staff. Your butler was only too happy to tell us, with only the slightest amount of pressure, that you demanded he take your hunting rifle and shoot over your head. You need to treat your staff better, Arnold."

"Why would I do that?"

"To try to take the heat off yourself. I know you were one of the con-spirators who had me kidnapped and almost killed."

"I don't know what you're talking about."

"You had it all figured out, didn't you. I assume that fake Secret Service agent was supposed to kill my double, and then you'd be President."

"No. No. I would never. You've got to believe me."

"Arnold, you're a liar, and you've always been a liar, and a bad one, too. I let my advisers push me into taking you on the ticket, even though I had misgivings, but that's water under the bridge.

"Let me show you something, Arnold. I've got a video for you to see."

Peterman started the video, but Richardson could not bear to watch. He just looked down at the floor, but he did hear himself agreeing to the mission.

"I had to do it," he cried. "If I didn't do it, they would have gotten rid of me too and put someone else in. I was just a pawn. It was Jack Chauncey of Decorp Technologies, Tim Brawn of Stillwater Aerospace, and Billy Joe Scranton of Raymore Industries. Then there was also Theresa Jones of Healthcare America. They recruited this guy Phoenix to run it. Your initiatives were going to ruin their companies. You see, I had to go along. I had no choice."

Peterman sighed. "I don't believe you for a second, Arnold. You would have sold your own mother to be sitting in my chair, so cut the crap, and tell me everything now."

"There's nothing left to tell," said Richardson. "You know everything I know."

"You know what the punishment is for treason, don't you Arnold?"

Arnold Richardson nodded.

"And you realize I could use all my political capital to see it carried out?" Peterman continued.

Richardson looked down at his feet and said nothing.

"As much as I'd like to do it, for the good of the country, that's not going to happen. I do have one question, though, Arnold. Why didn't your people just kill me in the beginning rather than kidnapping me and keeping me in that awful coal mine?"

Richardson looked up and answered in almost a whisper. "That defense bill needed to be vetoed, and if I had taken over immediately, I would have to be the one to do it, and that would have been a real problem for me. It was that damn sweetener you had put in the bill for me, the big money for the tech company in my district. I couldn't veto a bill for my biggest donor."

"Ahh," said the President, nodding his head, understanding. He continued. "Arnold, you will never talk of this again outside of this room. Now go home. If I find you have spoken to anyone about what you have told me, you will pay the ultimate price. I do not need to say more. Now go."

A few days later, Vice President Richardson resigned following a story in the *New York Times* documenting a bribe he received from the Russian government. The next day, another story came out revealing his affair with the wife of House Majority Leader Randal Gray. Arnold Richardson's wife filed for divorce by the following week. Randal Gray and his wife separated shortly afterward.

EPILOGUE

A few weeks later...

"HI DAD, you remember Sarah," said Zach.

"Come on in. Don't stand there on the doorway. Remember, this is your house, too, Zach. Great to see you, Sarah. I remember you when you were just a teen. Come in."

Before taking more than a step inside, Zach was almost bowled over by Ripley, who came bounding and took a flying leap at his owner.

"Hey big guy, how are you doing? Looks like you've put on a few pounds since I left," said Zach, rubbing Ripley's belly.

"We've been eating dinner together," admitted Robert Webster. "I'm not feeding him that dog-food crap you left for him."

"I don't know if I'll ever be able to feed him dog food again, Dad. Thanks," said Zach, sarcastically. "But really, thank-you for taking care of him."

"No problem, Zach, anytime. And Sarah, make yourself at home here."

"Nice to see you too, Mr. Webster," she said.

"You don't need to call me Mr. Webster anymore. You're not a kid. Call me Robert, or I'll have to call you Dr. Peterman."

Sarah smiled back. "Okay, Robert. It's great to see you and be back in the old neighborhood. And this wild beast must be Ripley."

"Sure is. Calm down now Ripley," said Zach, holding him back from jumping on Sarah.

"Come and sit down, both of you, and tell me everything," said Robert Webster.

"Sorry, we can't Dad, but I can tell you that it's all good now, and we're safe."

Robert Webster looked at Zach and realized he was not going to get any more information, at least not now.

He turned his attention back to Sarah and spoke. "You know, when you were teenagers, I thought you and Zach would have made a great couple. I kept telling Zach to ask you out, but he was too shy."

Sarah laughed as Zach blushed.

"Dad, we were just friends then."

"Still just friends?" asked Robert, but he didn't get a reply.

After an awkward silence, he continued. "Zach tells me you have a son. I thought he might be with you."

"He's back in DC with his grandfather, eating chocolate sundaes in the White House, and having a great time."

"Are you two hungry? I could cook up some burgers."

"It's late Dad. I think we just need some sleep right now."

"You know where your bedroom is, Zach. And I've made up a bed for you in the study, Sarah."

"That won't be necessary, Dad."

Now it was Sarah's turn to blush. She realized she hadn't blushed probably since her teenage years.

After a few days of long walks through the old neighborhood, it was time to drive back home.

The drive back to DC was mostly silent, punctuated only occasionally by light discussions of the weather and sports teams. Finally, Zach spoke.

"I know you need to return to San Diego. That's where your life is. That's where Jefferson's school is, and that's where your job is. But I wish it wasn't so. I wish you could stay in DC."

Sarah grabbed Zach's free hand and held it tight. "I wish you could move to San Diego, but I know you can't. Your kids are in DC and your medical practice is there."

After a few more minutes, Zach broke the silence. "So where do we go from here?"

"I don't know. We could start by visiting each other on our time off. I like coming to DC to visit Dad, and now I have even more reason to visit. And you could visit me in San Diego."

"Any chance I get. I guess we take it one step at a time."

"Guess so. Only time will tell."

Zach nodded, and both stayed silent until they reached their destination, the White House entrance. Sarah and Jeff would be flying back to the west coast the following morning.

Sarah kissed him on the cheek and walked quickly away. Zach sat still for a few moments, lost in thought, before restarting the car. A knock on the passenger side window suddenly brought him back to reality. Startled, he turned his head to see. It was Sarah, and she had tears in her eyes. He opened his door and immediately came around to her. She threw her arms around him, and he squeezed her tight. They shared a passionate kiss, and held each other close, neither wanting to let go.

Finally, Sarah pulled away, wiping tears off her face. "I've got to go."

"I know."

This time she walked away without looking back.

He made his way back to his apartment and sat down on the sofa. He felt that familiar lump in his throat, and his mouth went dry. Ripley wanted to be petted, but he was not in the mood.

I've already lost Samantha, Liam, and Emma. Am I going to lose Sarah too?

Her words came back to him. *Only time will tell.*

His phone buzzed. It was a text message from Sarah.

"I love you, Zach. We'll make it work."

Quickly, he texted back. "Love you too. You bet!" and added a heart emoji.

The lump in his throat disappeared, and he called out to Ripley.

"Come here boy. You need some attention!"

After petting and feeding Ripley, it was time to contact Samantha again.

"Hi Sam. I'm back. I'd like to set up a time to see the kids. That is, if it's okay with you."

"Of course it is. They can't wait to see you. And I'm sorry about what happened in Paris."

"It's okay. Everything turned out alright."

"When can you come over to see the kids?"

"How about tomorrow at noon?"

"That's fine. And Zach, if you'd like, we can talk about improving your visitation rights."

"Of course I'd like. Thanks. See you tomorrow."

He put down the phone. This was the best call they'd had in years, and it sounded like she wouldn't be opposed to discussing more alone time with his kids. *Maybe, partial custody?*

He looked over at the cabinet that used to hold his liquor bottles. It was an ugly, old cabinet. He didn't need it anymore. It would be on the street tomorrow.

Ripley came over for more attention, and his mind began to wonder. *What ever happened with that guy who called me about the North Korean agent, the one who planned this whole thing? Will he be caught? Is he even still in the country?*

Phoenix, in fact, was lying on a beach chair, a Rum Punch in his hand. In front of him was the beautiful, blue, Caribbean Sea. Light music was playing in the background. It was a hot day, but Phoenix didn't mind. He had already cooled off in the water twice.

No one would ever find him, not the Americans, nor the North Koreans. He was very good at changing identities, having done it multiple times in his life.

He had gotten over his rage of losing part of his fee from the North Korean agent. He still had eighteen million from the Arlington idiots, and six million from the North Koreans. It was enough to retire in style. Life was good, but there was something wrong. He was bored.

Phoenix was not one to lie about and read a book. He was a man of action, and after a few weeks of sunbathing, he was already itching to put some excitement back into his life. Maybe he wouldn't retire after all.

Stan Wilson told the story of rescuing President Peterman's grandson to his wife and children, who didn't believe him at first. However, when the President called him personally to express his thanks, Stan put his phone on "speaker," so they could all hear. They now looked at him with new respect. The signed portrait from the President with the inscription, "Let me know if you need anything in the future," didn't hurt either.

Back at the White House, Ray Lincoln got his old job back, protecting the President, this time with a huge bump in salary.

As for President Francis Peterman, he carried on like nothing had ever happened, working on pushing through his initiatives on health care and military preparedness. One thing had changed. He was now a big proponent of American beer and could be seen at interviews with a glass of beer by his side. However, once the interviews were over, the beers were discarded, replaced by a glass of white wine.

THE END

ACKNOWLEDGMENTS

To Richard Lederer, the author of multiple books on the English language. He not only took the time to steer me in the right direction, but also asked his editor if she would review my first few chapters.

To Caroline McCullagh, who without charge, graciously read those beginning pages and provided invaluable advice. I've never seen so many red marks on one sheet of paper!

To my hired editor for the full works, Shelley Routledge, who helped me sharpen the narrative through her many recommendations.

To my friend, Bob Niegisch, who read over my first draft, providing helpful comments.

And most importantly, to my wife, Jenny, whose encouragement was instrumental in the writing of this novel. She willingly read and re-read my manuscript many times during its development, finding plot weaknesses, and offering suggestions. Her editing skills were invaluable. I am so fortunate to have her by my side, not just for this book, but for my partner in life.

ABOUT THE AUTHOR

DR. PETER WASSERMAN is a board-certified ophthalmologist born in Queens, New York. After graduating from Dartmouth College, he received his MD degree from the University of Rochester, followed by a residency at the Washington National Eye Center in DC. He practiced ophthalmic surgery in Concord, New Hampshire for 35 years.

Now retired, Dr. Wasserman divides his time between Kennebunkport, Maine and Coronado, California, where he lives with his wife, Jenny, and his dog, Ripley. He has three adult children and one grandchild, who live in New Hampshire, Texas, and Brooklyn, New York.

Fun stories, with plenty of action and humor, have always been his passion. He hopes you enjoy his first book.

Made in United States
Troutdale, OR
07/22/2025

33052272R00239